ICELANDIC TEXTS

GENERAL EDITORS
Sigurður Nordal and G. Turville-Petre

*SAGA HEIÐREKS KONUNGS
INS VITRA*

★

*THE SAGA OF KING HEIDREK
THE WISE*

Saga Heiðreks Konungs ins Vitra

The Saga of King Heidrek
the Wise

Translated from the Icelandic
with Introduction, Notes and Appendices
by
Christopher Tolkien
Lecturer in Old English
New College, Oxford

HarperCollins*Publishers*

HarperCollins*Publishers* Ltd
1 London Bridge Street,
London SE1 9GF

HarperCollins*Publishers*
Macken House, 39/40 Mayor Street Upper
Dublin 1, D01 C9W8, Ireland

www.harpercollins.co.uk

Paperback edition published by HarperCollins*Publishers* 2025

3

First published in *Nelson's Icelandic Texts* series
by Thomas Nelson and Sons Ltd 1960

'The Battle of the Goths and the Huns' first published in
Saga-Book Vol. XIV by the Viking Society for Northern Research,
University College London 1953–57

Copyright © Christopher Tolkien 1953, 1960

Christopher Tolkien asserts the moral right
to be identified as the author of this work.

ISBN 978 0 00 876763 1

Printed and bound in the UK using 100%
Renewable Electricity at CPI Group (UK) Ltd

All rights reserved. No part of this publication may be reproduced,
stored in a retrieval system, or transmitted in any form or by any means,
electronic, mechanical, photocopying, recording or otherwise,
without the prior written permission of the publishers.

Without limiting the author's and publisher's exclusive rights, any unauthorised use
of this publication to train generative artificial intelligence (AI) technologies is
expressly prohibited. HarperCollins also exercise their rights under Article 4(3) of
the Digital Single Market Directive 2019/790 and expressly reserve
this publication from the text and data mining exception.

This book contains FSC™ certified paper and other controlled
sources to ensure responsible forest management.

For more information visit: www.harpercollins.co.uk/green

CONTENTS

Introduction		vii
I 1 *Fornaldarsǫgur*		vii
2 The Cursed Sword		ix
3 The Sámsey Poetry		xi
4 The Good Counsels		xiv
5 The Riddles of Gestumblindi		xviii
6 The Battle of the Goths and the Huns		xxi
7 Conclusion		xxviii
II 1 The Manuscripts		xxix
2 The Text of this Edition		xxxi
3 Previous Editions		xxxiii
4 Previous Translations		xxxiv
Bibliography and Abbreviations		xxxvi
Icelandic Text	*verso*	2
English translation	*recto*	2

Appendix A: Supplementary Texts

1	The beginning of the saga according to the *U*-redaction	*verso* and *recto*	66
2	The verses of the dialogue before the Battle on Sámsey as found in *Ǫrvar-Odds Saga*		69
3	Verses of *Hjálmar's Death-Song* found only in *Ǫrvar-Odds Saga*		73
4	Verses of Hervör's dialogue with the Herdsman not found in *R*		76
5	Verses of *The Waking of Angantýr* not found in *R*		78
6	Riddles peculiar to the *H*-text	*verso* and *recto*	80
7	Verses of *The Battle of the Goths and the Huns* not found in *R*		83

Appendix B: Gudmund of Glasisvellir   84

Appendix C: The References to Óðin   87

Appendix D: The Game of *Hnefatafl*   88

Appendix E: The Riddle of the Sow   90

Appendix F: Fródmar   91

Glossary of Technical Terms   93

Index   97

ACKNOWLEDGMENTS

I wish to thank Professor E. O. G. Turville-Petre, who has guided my work on this Saga throughout and who has given me very many hours of help; Professor Jón Helgason, who has generously allowed me to make use of his manuscript readings; and Mr P. G. Foote, who has read through the whole book, saving me from errors and making many valuable suggestions.

C.R.T.

INTRODUCTION

I

1 *Fornaldarsǫgur*

Heiðreks Saga, or *Hervarar Saga* (an equally common name for it) is one of the *fornaldarsǫgur*, the Sagas of Ancient Times. This term is not an ancient one,[1] and it has been variously applied to cover more or less of the very large class of sagas ('mythical,' 'fabulous' or 'romantic') that have little or no historical authenticity; but whereas most of these are 'late medieval' and belong to Icelandic literature in the period of its catastrophic decline, there is evidence nonetheless that fictional tales on the subject of legendary heroes were flourishing as oral entertainment as early as the beginning of the twelfth century—some seventy odd years before the first of the famous Sagas of Icelanders (or Family Sagas) were written.

At a wedding held at Reykjahólar in the north-west of Iceland in 1119 one Hrólf of Skálmarnes told a 'saga,' which he had composed himself, about 'Hröngvid the viking, and Óláf Lidmannakonung, and the rifling of the mound of Thráin the berserk, and Hrómund Gripsson, and many verses along with it.' This was no doubt a very different matter from the existing *fornaldarsaga* of Hrómund Gripsson, and 'probably resembled in form the Helgi lays of the Edda, i.e. it consisted of verses set in a simple narrative framework of prose'[2]; but it is a remarkable witness to the telling of stories at that date which had nothing to do with the historical personages of the Icelandic 'heroic age,' for Hrómund, as a rather doubtfully historical person, lived in the eighth century. The mention of the opening of Thráin's burial-mound is striking, for this is a very common theme in the written *fornaldarsǫgur* that are extant today (compare the poem called *The Waking of Angantýr* in *Heiðreks Saga*).

It is said in the same passage that King Sverrir of Norway, who died in 1202, was entertained with this story of Hrómund Gripsson, saying

---

[1] It derives in fact from the title of C. C. Rafn's collection, *Fornaldar sögur Norðrlanda*, 1829–30.   [2] Ursula Brown, *Þorgils Saga ok Hafliða*, 1952, 75

that such *lygisǫgur* (fictitious works, literally 'lying tales') were the most amusing of all. This term *lygisǫgur* has sometimes been used to describe the romantic and fantastic sagas based on foreign sources, particularly important among these being the French romances of chivalry, which began to be translated (*riddara sǫgur*) at the court of Norway in the time of Sverrir's grandson, King Hákon Hákonarson (1217–63); and with this literature we are not concerned. But 'there was plenty of romantic stuff in the old heroic poetry, without going to the French books,'[1] and it is to the class of *fornaldarsǫgur* that are based to some degree at least on older poetry—by far the most interesting and important of them—that *Heiðreks Saga* belongs.

The author of the best-known of these works, *Vǫlsunga Saga*, paraphrased into prose the poems of the Poetic Edda that he had before him, and the lost poem *Bjarkamál* is paraphrased in *Hrólfs Saga Kraka*, but the composer of *Heiðreks Saga* chose a different method: he inserted the old verses into the framework of his prose narrative. It was a happy choice, for of the poems that have been preserved in this way *The Battle of the Goths and the Huns* which ends the saga proper, though terribly battered, is now recognised to be perhaps the oldest of all the heroic lays preserved in the North; the verses of *The Waking of Angantýr* have been called by W. P. Ker 'the most wonderful of all the Northern poems after the *Vǫluspá*'; and the charming *Riddles of Gestumblindi* are unique in ancient Norse literature.

It is for this reason, principally, that *Heiðreks Saga* has been so much studied during the last hundred years by German and Scandinavian scholars; but large parts of it are not based on poetry, nor do they provide the framework for poems. The story, for instance, of Höfund's advice to his son Heidrek, and of how his son went against every piece of it, is a form of a widespread European tale that has been foisted, not altogether happily, onto the legendary king. The work is, in fact, something of a gallimaufrey, unkempt, ununified, with many inconsistencies; and though unity of a kind is given to it all in the theme of the terrible sword Tyrfing which passes down the generations, the saga-writer would have needed to be far more ruthless with his material than he was to make a satisfactory design.

His prose is sober and undecorated to a degree, untouched by the dreary inflated rhetoric and lifeless fantasy of the worst of the romantic sagas, but his stories are so condensed that the figures in them have no

[1] W. P. Ker, *Epic and Romance*, 1896, ch. 3, sect. 8

time to emerge as personalities. The little episode of the adultery of Heidrek's wife with a kitchen slave, for example, is hardly more than the skeleton of an amusing tale; it adds nothing to the picture of Heidrek, beyond increasing the number of his wives. The author does not succeed in making him more than a collection of different people going under one name.

As in other *fornaldarsǫgur*, there are scattered through the book many references to ancient customs and practices of the pagan age— 'romantic' appurtenances for the saga-writer and his audience, but nonetheless often preserving the matter of ancient tradition that was still alive in their days. Much of the incident in these sagas is the 'joint-stock' of the genre, and indeed the annotation of one can easily become a matter of listing similar things in other works.[1]

2 *The Cursed Sword*

To consider more closely the matter of *Heiðreks Saga*, it is essential to notice that there are two quite distinct versions of it: an older (*R*), which is found only in one, much damaged manuscript, and a later entirely reworked version, differing from *R* not merely in wording but also in names, in the plots of the stories, and in the inclusion of a great deal of new matter. This is found in two manuscripts, *U* (seventeenth-century) and *H* (fourteenth-century), the latter being, however, a shortened and in some ways distorted form of this later and longer version.[2]

These two versions, *R* and *HU*, are at their most divergent at the beginning of the saga, for the latter brings in a mass of mythological, geographical and genealogical information of which there is hardly a word in *R*, and which was certainly not a part of the first written *Heiðreks Saga*. This is given, with a translation, in Appendix A.

There is here, too, a story of how King Svafrlami forced two dwarfs to forge the sword Tyrfing for him, and of how they retaliated by putting on it a threefold curse, that it would be the death of a man each

---

[1] On *fornaldarsaga* motifs in Family Sagas, see Knut Liestøl, *The Origin of the Icelandic Family Sagas*, 1930, 163 ff.

[2] Details about these manuscripts and their relations are given at the end of the Introduction. Throughout this book the symbols *R*, *H* and *U* are used indiscriminately both for the actual manuscripts and for the redaction of the saga that they represent, wherever this causes no ambiguity; and 'the *HU*-version' is used to refer to what is common to both *H* and *U* and must have stood in their ultimate common original.

time it was drawn, that with it would be done three hateful things and
that the king would get his own death by it. The first of these prophe-
cies is found in R as a plain statement of fact about the sword (p. 2);
but in neither version of the saga is this quality always fulfilled. As to
the second, it has often been questioned what three *niðingsverk* are
meant; but it seems fairly clear that they are the three kinslayings,
Heidrek's killing of his brother Angantýr (p. 22) and of his father-in-
law King Harald (p. 26), and Angantýr the Third's killing of his
brother Hlöd (p. 57). But in the first of these the deed is done with
Tyrfing only in H and U—in R, Heidrek threw a stone at him, and
this, as will be seen, is almost certainly the original; in the second,
Tyrfing is nowhere mentioned; and in the third kinslaying, the verses
of the poem do not presuppose that Hlöd met his death from Tyrfing,[1]
though it is a natural deduction from the prose narrative. Lastly, in
the third prophecy, it is only in H and U that the king who first owned
Tyrfing was himself killed by it; in R it is not so, and here again R's
version is the better, since the account in H and U of the way in which
Arngrím took the sword from the king is incompatible with Tyrfing's
quality of always bringing victory to the bearer.

It seems almost certain that the theme of the threefold curse is a
reshaping of the original material of *Heiðreks Saga*, devised by the maker
of the later version out of his head, or (what comes to the same thing)
out of his knowledge of many other tales; and several of the motives
of this story are found elsewhere (for instance, the three hateful deeds,
niðingsverk, one in each lifespan, to be performed by Starkad through
the curse of Thór, *Gautreks Saga* ch. 7).

But the sword *was* cursed; for in the poem called *The Waking of
Angantýr* the dead viking in his burial-mound tells his daughter twice
(verses 32 and 39) that Tyrfing will bring ruin to all her posterity. In
verse 23 the sword is said to have been forged by dwarfs. It is more
than likely that these verses were the starting-point for the curse-story
in the *HU*-version; and, assuming this, one can readily see the reason
for various alterations in the story as it is told in that version. For
instance, having introduced the prophecy that the king would be slain
by the sword, the 'rewriter' was obliged to see that he was, and he
changed the old form of the story, where the acquisition of Tyrfing and
Eyfura was peaceful. Again, in R Heidrek hurled a stone into the

[1] The poem does not in fact presuppose even that Tyrfing was a sword;
see section 6 below.

darkness—simply, as it appears, from the desire to do mischief—and struck and killed his brother Angantýr, for which reason he was banished; his mother gave him Tyrfing before he went. But the writer of the later version had Heidrek banished merely for setting the two men at loggerheads during the feast; Hervör gave him the sword before he went, and *then* he slew his brother, with the sword; thus the first hateful deed of the curse was accomplished.[1]

The view of the relationship between the two versions which I have outlined here follows from and agrees with the conclusions reached by Jón Helgason in his study of the textual history of the saga[2]; but it meets with a difficulty in the fact, already mentioned, that *The Waking of Angantýr* itself tells us that the sword was cursed. To her father's warning that the sword shall prove the ruin of her family, Hervör retorts that she cares little 'how my sons shall strive hereafter' (verse 40); but the strife of her sons, Heidrek and Angantýr, ends (in *R*) with the latter's death from the stone. If that is the original form of the story for the written *Heiðreks Saga*, one may think that *The Waking of Angantýr* refers here to something that has been lost, since it presumably refers to something. It has also been suggested that Hervör's words really applied to the slaying of Hlöd by his brother Angantýr the Third—who, in the saga, are Hervör's grandsons: that the whole Heidrek-history has been intruded between Hervör's obtaining of the sword on Sámsey and the last part of the saga.[3]

3 *The Sámsey Poetry*

The Waking of Angantýr is unquestionably older than the saga; how much older, I cannot say. It is a powerful poem and has long been admired (it was one of the first of the Norse poems to be translated into English), and expresses with extraordinary force the fear and mystery of the grim dead lying lifeless but sometimes wakeful in their burial-

[1] This is the form of the story in *U*. *H* is here hopelessly distorted, through attempting (as also elsewhere) to combine two versions, the earlier and the later; see below, on the manuscripts.

[2] By the earlier editors as much value was attached to the *H*-text as to the *R*; and though this is certainly wrong so far as the first written *Heiðreks Saga* is concerned, it has to be remembered that the author of the later rewritten version had access to material from some source or sources now lost to us.

[3] This was the view of Schück, who proposed a complex, ingenious and unconvincing theory of an underlying relationship between *Heiðreks Saga* and *Ásmundar Saga Kappabana* (ed. F. Detter in *Zwei Fornaldarsögur*, 1891, 79 ff.).

mounds[1]—*heima í millim*, 'set between worlds,' in the words of Hervör with which, in a sudden diminution of intensity, the poem ends. It is more than a little reminiscent of the meeting of Helgi and Sigrún in the burial-mound in the *Second Lay of Helgi Hundingsbana*, a passage of the most moving poetry in the Poetic Edda.[2]

Both *The Waking of Angantýr* and *The Death-Song of Hjálmar* are poems that, not being complete in themselves, presuppose the existence of some sort of narrative frame to the dialogue; in this respect they differ from *The Battle of the Goths and the Huns*. What this narrative frame to the 'Sámsey Poetry' originally contained has long been argued.[3]

Heiðreks Saga is not the only work in which the story of the battle on Sámsey is told. It forms an episode in another *fornaldarsaga*, the very largely fictitious *Saga of Arrow-Odd* (*Ǫrvar-Oddr*), which includes also a good deal of the Sámsey poetry found in *Heiðreks Saga*.[4] There are many divergences between the two accounts—for example, in *Ǫrvar-Odds Saga* the berserks divide into seven and five—but the most remarkable difference between them is the complete absence in the latter saga of any element of rivalry for the hand of a princess. The meeting on the island between Hjálmar and Arrow-Odd and the berserk sons of Arngrím was here entirely accidental. Again the story turns up in the fifth book of the Latin *Gesta Danorum* of Saxo Grammaticus the Dane, who was born about 1150—showing that the story was already current in the twelfth century. In Saxo's story too the twelve sons of Arngrimus and Ofura came upon Hialmerus and Aruaoddus by chance, not by arrangement.[5]

[1] A conception still alive at least until very recent times, as in the 'hogboy' (Old Norse *haug-búi*, 'mound-dweller') of Maeshowe, the huge prehistoric barrow in the Orkneys.

[2] Vigfusson went much further: from subject, style, and 'the ring and flow of the verses' he attributed both *The Waking of Angantýr* and *Hjálmar's Death-Song* quite certainly to the 'Helgi-poet' (whose Lays, he pointed out, he had known by heart for twenty-five years). Some now think that the Helgi Lays go back to originals composed in Denmark in the tenth century or even earlier; but the question is much debated. In *Eddica Minora* both the poems of the saga are attributed to the twelfth century.

[3] Heinzel 444 ff.; Boer (1888) xxxviii ff., in *Arkiv* VIII (1892) 112 ff., and in 'Om Hervarar saga' 28 ff.; Steenstrup in *Arkiv* XIII (1897) 103 ff.; Olrik in *Arkiv* XIV (1898) 47 ff., and in *Kilderne* II 59 ff.; *Edd. Min.* xxxvii ff.; Nerman 130 ff.

[4] See Appendix A (II and III). For editions of *Ǫrvar-Odds Saga* see Bibliography.

[5] Ed. Holder 166, trans. Elton 204. Six of the brothers bear the same names as in *Heiðreks Saga*, including 'Angantir' and 'Hiorthuar.' See Appendix A (II).

But there is another story, in the sixth book of Saxo's history, which is also connected with the Sámsey traditions. In this, Helgo the Norwegian desired to marry Helga, the daughter of King Frotho of Denmark, and she was promised to him. At the same time there grew up on the island of Sialandia (Zealand) the nine sons of a certain prince, of whom the eldest was named Angaterus or Anganturus; he also was a suitor for the hand of Helga, and he challenged Helgo to fight. Helgo, afraid of a contest in which he must take on nine men single-handed, appealed to Starcatherus (Starkad) for help. On the day of the battle Starcatherus left Helgo still sleeping and met the nine alone; he fought them all at once, as he was well able to do,[1] and killed six without receiving any injury; the last three he slew also, but they wounded him horribly in seventeen places.[2] It is quite clear that this story is from the same tradition as the prose narrative in *Heiðreks Saga*, but much altered through the intrusion of another legend.

As I have said, a great deal of time and thought has been spent on trying to answer the question whether the battle on Sámsey in the earliest form of the story was brought about simply by a chance encounter or not; but the question has not been settled. It seems to me very likely that the old story did make rivalry for the princess the cause of the battle. It is probable that Arrow-Odd stepped into the place of that Sóti to whom Hjálmar refers as his companion in his dying poem (verse 11); and thus Hjálmar and his fate were drawn into the cycle of the life-history of Arrow-Odd. In his saga as we have it the Hjálmar legend has been much altered; Ingibjörg is not indeed forgotten, nor Hjálmar's love for her, but the cause of the battle has been—or else purposely omitted by someone who passed on the tale, wishing perhaps to concentrate attention more exclusively on Arrow-Odd: in Saxo's version he has become so exclusively the hero that he is made to slay Angantýr as well as his eleven brothers.

There is another curious variation in this widely-known legend. The *H*-text of *Heiðreks Saga* says that it was Angantýr who made the vow to have Ingibjörg, not Hjörvard. Now all three versions of the saga, *R* and *U* as well as *H*, agree that in the battle it was Angantýr who fought with Hjálmar.[3] It looks as though the writer of *H* deduced from this that Angantýr must have been Hjálmar's rival, and altered

---

[1] See Appendix A (I)   [2] Ed. Holder 194; trans. Elton 238
[3] Angantýr was traditionally, it seems, the most perilous of all the berserk-brothers; cf. Hjálmar's words to Arrow-Odd in the prose passage after verse 3.

the text—thereby only creating fresh difficulties, for no sooner has Angantýr sworn to have no other woman but Ingibjörg than he goes off and marries the daughter of Bjarmar, with no explanation given. Nonetheless, the agreement in this point with the second of Saxo's stories is curious.[1]

4 *The Good Counsels*

Much of the central prose section of the saga is taken up with the story of how Heidrek disregarded all his father's good advice, and with what result. It is curious that in all the redactions of the saga it is stated, very awkwardly and disconnectedly, immediately before the story of Heidrek's doings at the court of Gardar (p. 28), that he had been given a warning against confiding secrets to his mistress. It is notable that the first, second and sixth counsels, together with this advice against confiding secrets, all belong together: they form a connected anecdote, for the results of breaking them are all demonstrated together, at the court of Gardar. Heidrek fosters the son of a mightier man, and so breaks the sixth counsel[2]; he is suspected of having done violence to his foster-son, and is made prisoner. The men whom he ransomed, so breaking the first two counsels, are at hand to bind him, and they alone. Yet these things would not have happened, if he had followed the advice not to tell his mistress secrets, for it was she who betrayed him.[3] Then why did Heidrek conceal his foster-son? If, at every new turn, he knew very well that he had only to say a word to put an end to the whole business, what is the point of the story?

The point lies precisely in the fact that the boy was not dead at all; that Heidrek was testing the validity of his father's advice.[4] Knut Liestøl showed that this story in *Heiðreks Saga* is a version of a very

[1] The legends of Sámsey lived on till long afterwards in ballads of the Faeroes (deriving ultimately from *Heiðreks Saga*). A 'Ballad of Hjálmar and Angantýr' was taken down from oral recitation in 1846 (Hammershaimb II), and a longer 'Ballad of the sons of Arngrím' was published by Hammershaimb in *Antiquarisk Tídsskrift* 1849–51. Grundtvig, *Danmarks Gamle Folkeviser* I, 1853, no. 19, gives versions of the Danish ballad of 'Angelfyr and Helmer.'
[2] In the event, this feature is obscured: the king and queen of Gardar are only persuaded to permit Heidrek to foster their son through fear of his power.
[3] Why this counsel, clearly essential to the story, is not put in till later seems impossible to say.
[4] The *HU*-version of the story is an improvement on *R*'s, in that the reader is left in doubt as to the fate of the foster-son till the very end; but it is not necessarily therefore the older.

widespread tale, or group of tales, which he called 'The Good Counsels of the Father.' The most strikingly similar among the various foreign analogues is that from the fourteenth-century *Book of Geoffrey de la Tour Landry*, which tells how on his death-bed Cato gave his son Catonnet three good counsels: he must not take service with the emperor; he must not save anyone from death who has deserved it; and he must test whether his wife is capable of keeping a secret. Catonnet did take service with the emperor, and became foster-father to his son; he also saved the life of a condemned thief. He told his wife, as a secret on which his life depended, that he had killed his foster-son and given his heart to his parents to eat. Next day his wife betrayed his secret to someone who told it to the emperor; and the emperor gave orders that Catonnet should be hanged. Catonnet then sent for the emperor's son, who was not dead but had been given into the care of a friend, and saw to it that the hangman kept himself hidden. When Catonnet was led forth to be hanged the hangman was nowhere to be found; and the thief whom Catonnet had set free offered to perform the task. In the nick of time the foster-son appeared; Catonnet was released; and the emperor was upbraided by his son for having condemned Catonnet without attempting to find out the truth.

This is 'the same story' as that in the saga, in essentials of plot. In addition, *three* good counsels are the rule in the many variants of the story; and those are precisely the three (actually four in *Heiðreks Saga*, but the first and second are divisons of one) which concern the 'Gardar episode.' The conclusion must be that these three are the only original ones; the tale found its way into the developing saga, was applied to the persons of Höfund, Heidrek, Sifka and Hrollaug,[1] and *then* the theme of neglecting good advice was extended through a good part of the whole work, so as to cover events which had nothing to do with the connected anecdote of 'The Three Good Counsels of the Father.'

The fourth and fifth counsels, against Heidrek's staying out late with his mistress and riding his best horse in a hurry, remain baffling. In *U* there is no mention of Sifka's death, and these counsels are left in the air; while the account in *H* is shortened and obscure. As for *R*, Heidrek's horse did not in the event come to grief because he was hastening, but because of Sifka's weight; there is no mention of haste, nor any suggestion why there should be any. And why was it to

[1] Hrollaug is the name of the king of Gardar in *H* and *U*; in *R* he is nameless.

Heidrek's disadvantage to be out late with his mistress? It seems that the king wished to put an end to her—understandably enough; he did what he intended, and in no way suffered for it. Perhaps the words 'and it was late in the evening' (p. 30) were added by someone who thought that Höfund's fourth counsel referred to this incident, whereas the author of the saga did not so intend it; but in any case the story has been quite spoilt at this point.

There is a striking divergence between the versions in that in the rewritten one Sifka is made into two people, Sváfa of Hunland, mother of Hlöd, and Sifka of Finland, the treacherous mistress. It is quite certain that Hlöd's mother came from a tradition quite distinct from the 'Good Counsels' story; but the clumsy reappearance of Sifka in *R* (p. 28) to play her part of betraying Heidrek in Gardar is nonetheless, I think, due to the author of the saga, who identified the two women. The 'rewriter' then divided them up again. The name Sifka belonged originally to the mother of Hlöd (see below, p. xxviii).

The *H*-text gives a seventh counsel, 'that he be always gracious to a guest newly come,' and an eighth, 'that he never lay Tyrfing at his feet.' The seventh can be taken as a late addition, extracted from Heidrek's attack on his guest, Gestumblindi (Ódin); but there is no mention anywhere of Heidrek's laying the sword at his feet. It has been said that the point is simply that if he had not done so he would not have been able to strike at Ódin; but there is a possibility that in a different tradition about Heidrek's end he died by his own sword.

To support this there is a curious parallel in the prose of the Eddaic poem *Grímnismál*, where Geirröd, who like Heidrek aroused the anger of Ódin, a visitor to his hall, met his death with his own sword:

> King Geirröd sat and had his sword on his knee, and it was half-drawn. But when he heard that it was Ódin who was there he stood up, and made to take Ódin from the fire. The sword slipped from his hand, and fell with the hilts down. The king stumbled and fell forward, and the sword ran him through, and he got his death.

When one finds that another king, also becoming suddenly aware that the unknown man in his house is Ódin himself, had been warned not to lay his sword at his feet, a connection of some sort seems very likely; but what it was is very hard to say.[1]

---

[1] Whatever story may be thought to underlie the eighth counsel in *H*, it cannot have been a part of the first written *Heiðreks Saga*.

More far-reaching connections between this part of *Heiðreks Saga* and the story of *Grímnismál* were made out by Rudolf Much in an essay on that poem, which can only be briefly mentioned here. His theory turns not only on the likeness just seen, but also on the fact that Óðin was the foster-father of Geirröð, who thrust aside his elder brother Agnar. In *Heiðreks Saga* Gizur was the foster-father of Heiðrek, who killed his elder brother Angantýr; and Gizur is an Óðin-name.[1]

Little is told of Gizur in this role; he plays his part later in the saga (pp. 50 ff.), and there he is called Gizur Grýtingaliði. There is nothing very Óðin-like about him—it is indeed he who utters the words 'Óðin is wroth with you!' (verse 99)—and his surname Grýtingaliði is almost certainly a relic of very ancient Gothic history (see below, p. xxiv); however, as the instigator of strife between Hlöd and his brother Angantýr (verse 87) and in virtue of his name, he has been interpreted as the god himself. In fact, several scholars[2] have isolated one original element in this palpably very composite saga as the story of 'the evil king, Óðin's favourite, who aroused the anger of the god.' According to Wessén, in Gizur two distinct figures have been blended: the Reiðgothic warrior Gizur Grýtingaliði, and King Heiðrek's foster-father, a manifestation of Óðin, who came by his name 'Gizur' only after the story of Angantýr the Third and the Gotho-Hunnic war had been connected with this quite distinct legend of Óðin and his fosterling Heiðrek, and his murder of his brother Angantýr (the Second). It has been suggested, too, that originally it was not Höfund, the wise and just, who instigated the treacherous slaying of King Harald of Reiðgotaland (p. 25), but Óðin.[3]

All this has some plausibility, but of course an abundance of contradictory theories of reduplication, blending and so on have been proposed for every Germanic legend; they can rarely be proved or disproved, and often, as in this case, the possibilities are almost inexhaustible. 'Blendings' and 'reduplications' undoubtedly took place! But 'legends' of the past can only exist for us in written works of art that come from the minds of men who felt themselves quite at liberty to change the

---

[1] It appears, as also does Gestumblindi, in the verse name-lists, the *þulur*; *Skj* A I 681, 682.   [2] Especially Wessén and Boer ('Om Hervarar saga')

[3] Wessén held that the Óðin-names Gizur and Gestumblindi owe their presence in the *þulur* precisely to their occurrence in *Heiðreks Saga*. — It may be noted that a figure called Gestiblindus, king of the Goths, appears in Saxo (ed. Holder 160 ff.), but his connection with these traditions is very hard to unravel (see Wessén).

stories they inherited, to identify this personage with that, and in the course of time to produce such a nexus as no-one can hope to unpick. Most of these questions now yield many possible answers.

5 *The Riddles of Gestumblindi*

A contest of intellect between the disguised Óðin and another is the subject of the Eddaic poem *Vafþrúðnismál*. But whereas in that poem the questions asked by Óðin and the giant Vafthrúdnir are questions of knowledge, in *Heiðreks Saga* the god propounds riddles.

In this episode the *H*-version differs strikingly from *R* and *U* in that it includes seven extra riddles, and there is a great deal more talk between the opponents as the contest proceeds.[1] As regards the order of the riddle-verses, all three versions begin with the same four and end with the same two, but for the rest they are as different in arrangement as they well could be. *H* arranges them on the principle that verses with the same or similar beginnings are placed together (which calls forth a complaint from the king, after Gestumblindi has produced a string of nine all beginning *Hvat er þat undra*). *U* (and perhaps to some extent *R* also) seems to arrange the riddles according to their subjects, but the principle, if it is one, peters out half-way through.

Finnur Jónsson made an elaborate study of the riddles, in which he was concerned to separate the 'genuine' stock from interlopers of a later date. He rejected firstly all verses in the *fornyrðislag* metre,[2] secondly the extra riddles in *H*, and thirdly some of those which have the same subject as another one in the collection. But this is very arbitrary. His third category ignores the distinction between identity of subject and identity of treatment—obviously, two riddles may be on precisely the same subject but rely on quite different qualities in the thing described.[3] As regards the rejection of the *fornyrðislag* verses, Jónsson was assuming that the 'genuine' riddles of Gestumblindi were

[1] An idea of this can be got from the solutions to these extra riddles in *H*, which are printed in Appendix A (VI).
[2] About a third are in *fornyrðislag*, the rest in the more irregular *ljóðaháttr*, in which the third and sixth lines contain more syllables than the other four, and alliterate only within the line. (In both metres the half-strophe is metrically complete in itself.)
[3] The four 'wave'-riddles (verses 62–4 and 67) are clearly closely connected in origin. The three texts vary in the most complex fashion: the 'ingredients' are more or less the same, but their distribution is different—the rewritten version appears to have reversed the second halves of 62 and 63.

all composed by one man; but it is not by any means necessary to think this, and the dissimilarity of the metres is perfectly compatible with the idea of a collector or arranger of riddle-verses that were current in his day.[1] The fact that the solutions are entirely in prose also suggests this. If the writer of the saga had composed a riddle-series of his own he might indeed be expected to have made verse-solutions also; but as it is it looks much more as if he used riddles in verse that were already circulating singly, to which of course the solver would not be expected to improvise verses in answer, or know ready-made solutions.[2]

As has been said earlier, Gestumblindi's riddles are unique, in more senses than one. They are unique in that there are no others in ancient Norse; and even more surprisingly, there is no record in the poetry or in the sagas of a riddle ever having been asked. They are unique also in that there are no parallels to them in the riddle-literature of any other country,[3] apart from the ancient 'Cow-riddle' (verse 70), which is known from all over Europe, and the very curious riddle of the 'Sow with Unborn Litter' (verse 69), discussed in Appendix E.

Riddle-contests which show some striking similarities to that in the saga are, however, known from other literatures. Stories in which a forfeit is paid by the loser form a very large and widespread class, of which the oldest is perhaps the riddle of Samson. There is an interesting parallel in a widespread tale, of which the English Ballad of King John and the Bishop of Canterbury may be taken as typical.[4] In this, the Bishop, with whom the King is displeased on account of the luxury of his life, must die unless he can answer three riddles which the King sets him. He is given a period of grace in which to find out the answers to the questions: What is the King worth? How long will it take him to go round the world? What is the King thinking? The Bishop, dismayed, goes to his half-brother (or brother), a shepherd, who is almost indistinguishable in appearance; and the shepherd subsequently answers the questions before the King, turning them

---

[1] cf. note to verse 54, which is known from a thirteenth-century work on rhetoric. [2] Heusler, *Rätsel* 131 ff.
[3] Echoes of Gestumblindi's riddles are found in Jón Árnason's huge collection of modern Icelandic riddles (*Íslenzkar Gátur*, 1887), but these are pretty clearly literary borrowings from *Heiðreks Saga*. The story of the riddle-match between Heidrek and Gestumblindi (Gestur) has come down in a ballad from the Faeroes, *Gátu Ríma* (Hammershaimb II 26 ff.).
[4] F. J. Child, *The English and Scottish Popular Ballads* I, 1882, 403 ff.

with dexterity: the King is worth twenty-nine pence, for that is one less than Our Lord was worth; he can go round the world in twenty-four hours if he can keep up with the sun; and to the last question, 'What am I thinking?' he answers, 'You are thinking I am the Bishop!'

Characteristic of many variants on this theme is the rank and power of the poser of the riddles, and the substitution of another person cleverer than himself. In the saga, on the other hand, it is the king who answers the questions. It has been pointed out that the contest in the saga shows affinity to a motif well known in fairy-tale literature, in which a prisoner gains his freedom by posing a problem which is of its nature insoluble.[1] Certain of Gestumblindi's enigmas are of this type, insoluble to any but the legendary king, in which the subject of the riddle is a not particularly likely event, described in dark language (verses 54, 65, 69); and it seems quite possible that the riddle-match in the saga was founded on a motif of this kind, with the theme interwoven of the struggle between Ódin, the wise god, and a mortal man.[2]

It was mentioned earlier that the questions of *Vafþrúðnismál* are tests of knowledge pure and simple, and the same is true of other question-poems of the Edda (*Alvíssmál, Fjǫlsvinnsmál*); but the last question asked by Ódin in *Vafþrúðnismál*, which wins him the contest, is the same as his last question to Heidrek: What said Ódin in the ear of Balder? This demanded knowledge of Vafthrúdnir that could only be possessed by Ódin himself; and it is plain that it is the proper conclusion of that poem. But it is equally plain that it is inapposite as the last question of a riddle-match, since it is not a riddle; and it might be thought that it was brought in here as the dramatic conclusion because it had become *the* traditional unanswerable question—not, however, lifted straight from the other poem, for the wording is there quite different.

It is curious that in the Eddaic poem *Vegtamskviða* (*Baldrs Draumar*) Ódin ends by asking the *vǫlva* or wise woman the obscure question: 'What women are they who weep their hearts out, and toss to the sky the corners of the sails (*halsa skautum*)?' This question, very similar to Gestumblindi's wave-riddles (and in the first line, *Hverjar eru þær meyjar*, identical to verse 63/1), immediately reveals to the seer that it is Ódin who is addressing her, though it is difficult to see why it should.

[1] Heusler, *Rätsel* 124; de Vries, 'Heiðreksgaadene' 37
[2] A point of contact between the two might have lain in some form of the tale in which a substitution took place (as in the ballad): Ódin, so often appearing in disguise, became the substitute.

She does not, indeed, give any answer; according to Bugge,[1] the women of these lines must be the wave-maidens lamenting round the burning funeral-ship of the dead god Balder, but even if they are the question does not demand knowledge that must be peculiar to Óðin.

The great majority of the subjects of the riddles are chosen from the natural world, very few of them from the works of men; and nothing comes from outside Scandinavia, nor even perhaps from beyond the confines of Iceland. There is no reference to the Bible; none to the worship of the Church; nothing connected with the business of writing; and very little of the arts and artefacts of daily life and domestic economy. In all this there is the greatest contrast to riddle-collections from other lands.[2] We cannot know how far this situation is accidental and due to the taste of the author, for there is no standard to compare with. Jónsson ascribed them to learned or scholarly activity, but there is nothing specifically 'learned' in them. It is impossible, no doubt, to make a sharp distinction between 'learned' and 'popular'; for this sort of pastime, allied to poetry and poetic perception of the world, delighting in ingenuity and gymnastic feats of language, continued in simpler and often fresher forms to be popular after it had long become a 'learned' thing, the diversion of scholars whose knowledge contained things seen in books and nowhere else—but who might well take an unpretentious theme and treat it so well that it became well known and 'popular' after them.

6 The Battle of the Goths and the Huns

The saga proper ends in a different world from the courts and viking voyages of the seafaring princes of its earlier chapters. It is based on one of the most interesting, and one of the oldest, poems preserved in the North, and it has been an academic battlefield for more than a century—particularly on the question of whether it had a basis in recorded history; the literature of the subject, scattered among periodicals in many languages, would fill a shelf.[3]

---

[1] *Studier* 252. Bugge thought that the *Vegtamskviða* verse was simply an unsuccessful imitation of the end of *Vafþrúðnismál*.

[2] For instance, to the Old English collection (F. Tupper, *The Riddles of the Exeter Book*, 1910), where there are such subjects as coat-of-mail, weathercock, inkpot, churn, chalice, Bible-codex, quill-pen, and so on.

[3] I have sketched the course of the controversy over the historical basis of the poem in the *Saga-Book of the Viking Society* XIV (1955-6) 141 ff. The more important essays on the subject will be found in the Bibliography

Unhappily, it is also a poem that has suffered greatly. We are left with fragments of a poem, comprising some twenty-nine strophes or bits of strophes, of which twenty-six lines are narrative, not speech. The extremely corrupt seventeenth-century manuscripts, which are all we have to go on after verse 83, cut out all the narrative parts (a rejection, characteristic of *fornaldarsaga* method, that may well go back to the author of the rewritten version), and if the end of the saga had not been lost from *R* we should almost certainly have more of the poem. The narrative prose links show in places unmistakable signs of verse-form not far below the surface, echoes of poetry that has crumbled away (e.g. before verses 81, 90, 94, and after 101); but the dividing-line cannot be drawn exactly, and editors have varied in the way they print decayed verses (e.g. 92), where the word-order at least is not that of prose. It is thus extremely probable that there was once a continuous narrative-and-dialogue poem on the Gotho-Hunnic war, independent of its present context—needing no 'saga' to explain it. Part of this poem was perhaps 'dissolved' into prose before it came to the author of the saga we have, in days when forms of it were related by mouth; and contradictions seem to have arisen between the verses that were left and the prose links (e.g. after verse 87).

The true end of the poem may well be preserved in verse 104, but the beginning is pretty clearly lost. Verse 75, containing a list of kings three of whom do not otherwise appear in the legend at all, while one of them (Gizur) is differently represented and may indeed not be the same person, is unquestionably in origin either a bit of a separate poem or else an isolated 'catalogue-strophe.'[1] It is extraordinarily similar in air and structure to parts of the Old English poem *Widsith*.[2]

Most critics have felt certain that there is more than one layer of age in *The Battle of the Goths and the Huns*. Some of the verses (such as 76, 81–6) are notable for their heavily-filled lines, comparable with the technique of *Hamðismál* and *Atlakviða*, probably the oldest of the Eddaic lays, while others are more meagre in verse-content and with less vivid expression. If this is correctly judged, one may think that new verses were composed—again, before the time of the author of the saga—to fill the place of ones that had been lost from the old poem.

---

under: Heinzel; Much, 'Askibourgion'; Schütte; Neckel; Boer, 'Om Hervarar saga'; Schück; von Friesen; and Johansson.

[1] cf. the use of the verse giving the names of the sons of Arngrím, Appendix A (II), verse 1.

[2] Especially *Widsith* lines 18 ff., *Ætla weold Hunum, Eormanric Gotum*, etc.

Since the poem contains things that go back to very remote times and the Gothic kingdoms in the south-east of Europe, the question, When was it composed? cannot in the last analysis be answered; for even if we say, for the sake of argument, that it arose in Norway in the ninth century, or the tenth, yet even so the poet of that age who celebrated the tragedy of Hlöd and Angantýr in his verses must surely himself have known and used poetry, or a particular poem, on the subject that went back far beyond his time.[1] Not only the names, but also the motives of such a verse as 86, for instance, are evidence of great antiquity.

The most remarkable of the place-names of this part of the saga is perhaps *Harvaða-fjǫll*, which occurs in a half-strophe (74) that must be among the strangest fossils in the whole range of Norse. The river *Grafá* (*Gripá*, *Gropá*) which is also found here is totally unknown, but the view is not challenged, I think, that *Harvaða-* is the same name in origin as 'Carpathians.'[2] Since this name in its Germanic form is found nowhere else at all, and must be a relic of extremely ancient tradition, one can hardly conclude otherwise than that these four lines are a fragment of a lost poem (presumably on the subject of Heidrek's death and Angantýr's revenge for him) that preserved names at least going back to poetry sung in the halls of Germanic peoples in central or south-eastern Europe. But what form this poem had, or what relationship it bore to the *Battle of the Goths and the Huns*, is impossible to say.

Another name that points clearly to regions far removed from Scandinavia is *Danparstaðir*, in which lay *Árheimar*, where Angantýr held the funeral-feast for his father.[3] The latter name has never been explained, but *Danparstaðir* seems certainly to contain the Gothic name of the Russian river Dnieper, which is called *Danaper* by the sixth-century Gothic historian Jordanes. The name reappears in the fifth verse of *Atlakviða*, which is suspected of imitating in this *The Battle of the Goths and the Huns*; and there is a shadowy character called *Danpr* who appears in various Norse monuments, but who casts no

---

[1] 'Dass jemals die dichterische Fortpflanzung in prosaischer versiegt und aus dieser wieder ein Lied ganz neu gezeugt worden wäre, hat alle Wahrscheinlichkeit gegen sich,' *Eddica Minora*, p. xiii.

[2] The stem *karpat-* was regularly transformed into *χarfaþ-* by the operation of the Germanic Consonant shift (Grimm's Law). The form *hávaða* found in *U* (manuscript *hanada*) clearly depends on a 'popular etymology' (association with Norse *há-vaði* 'tumult').

[3] The *U*-text reverses this, making *Danparstaðir* a place in *Árheimar*.

light on the original meaning of *Danparstaðir*: indeed, I think he owed his existence precisely to the occurrence of the place-name in the present poem.[1]

None of the other place-names is perfectly clear, though identifications have been proposed for some with greater or lesser plausibility. Much's identification of the *Jassar-fjǫll* with the mountain-chain in Silesia called the Gesenke—the continuation of the line of the Carpathians to the west—has been accepted by several later writers; *Dúnheiðr* has been associated both with the Danube (*Dúna*) and the Russian river Dvina; and *Dylgja* or (*Dyngja*) is perhaps not a place-name at all, but the noun *dylgja* 'enmity'—an interpretation hesitantly adopted in the present text and translation.

When in the third century A.D. the Goths settled in the plains to the north of the Black Sea, after their long migration south-east from the Baltic coasts and the Vistula valley, they were split into two great branches, the Ostrogoths to the east of the Dnieper and the Visigoths to the west of it. In the works of Roman writers two names make their appearance very early in connection with the Goths, *Tervingi* and *Greutungi*, and these have been almost universally equated with the Visigoths and the Ostrogoths respectively[2]; it has often been said too that Gizur Grýtingalidi in *Heiðreks Saga* was originally Gizur of the *Greutungi*, and that the sword Tyrfing derives from the name *Tervingi*.[3] If this latter identification is right, then no doubt the meaning of 'the Tyrfing' (i.e. Visigoths) was forgotten quite early on, for Tyrfing is a sword in *The Waking of Angantýr*; but just how early one cannot say, for the name only occurs once in the actual verse of *The Battle of the Goths and the Huns*, and there, indeed, it is not easy to understand what Angantýr means by his refusal to 'sunder Tyrfing in twain' (verse 83). Any idea that the sword is given a symbolic significance as representative of the Gothic kingdom seems to me very improbable; I think rather that the name of the people had been

---

[1] i.e. *Danpar-* was interpreted as genitive singular of a personal name *Danpr*. On Danpr see *Rígsþula* 49; *Ynglinga Saga* ch. 17; and Arngrímur Jónsson's reproduction of the lost *Skjǫldunga Saga* (*Bibliotheca Arnamagnæana* IX (1950) 336).

[2] *Tervingi* is said to be derived from a Germanic name meaning 'dwellers in the wooded regions' (cf. Gothic *triu* 'tree'), *Greutungi* to have meant 'dwellers in the steppes' (cf. Norse *grjót* 'pebbles, stones,' English *grit*).

[3] More dubious is the idea that Humli, the Hun-king, contains the name of the ancient Ostrogothic royal house of the Amalungs, and that Hlöd, who is called *Humlungr* in verse 83, is also the reflection of an Amal prince.

transformed, as the legend travelled northwards, into the name of a region, and that verse 83 retains that sense: Angantýr will not divide the land (of the Tyrfing) into two parts. The name may, however, have been generally understood as a sword-name already long before the writing of *Heiðreks Saga*; Neckel even suggested that not merely the strange change in the meaning of the name but the whole conception of *The Waking of Angantýr* arose from a false etymology, as if *Tyrfingr* meant 'the weapon hidden under the turf, in a burial-mound' (Norse *torf*).

On the other hand, another school of thought has taken the name Tyrfing to have belonged *primarily* to the Sámsey poetry—with the same etymology, but in this case regarded as the genuine one![1]

Though no real agreement has ever been reached on the matter, I believe that the cumulative evidence of these names points to the later fourth or early fifth centuries, in the years after the Huns made their appearance in history and fell on the Gothic kingdoms north of the Black Sea,[2] as the ultimate source in time of this tradition. I do not think that any of the proposed identifications of the battle in the Norse poem with wars recorded by historians of the Empire has any plausibility at all. However old the voice may be that we hear in these lines, they contain a legend, not 'history' as we understand it. But the matter of legend has roots, however much transformed by poets, and though no actual corresponding event has been found in the meagrely recorded history of those times, and surely never will be, in such things as the 'grave' and the 'stone' on the banks of the Dnieper one is probably being taken back a thousand years even beyond *Heiðreks Saga* to the burial-place of Gothic kings in south-eastern Europe and the high stone in their chief place, on which the king stepped to have homage done to him in the sight of all the people.[3]

But *The Battle of the Goths and the Huns* is known, nevertheless, from outside Scandinavia; for in line 116 of the Old English poem *Widsith*

[1] On this question see especially Neckel; Boer, 'Om Hervarar saga'; de Boor; and Schneider (II.2, 100ff.). Schneider ingeniously accepted the essentials of both views, holding that the sword Tyrfing, primarily the invention of the poet of *The Waking of Angantýr*, made its way into the much older poem through the similarity of its name to that of the *people* Tyrfing—this latter being by then, as a relic from a remote period of Gothic history, quite incomprehensible.

[2] About the year 375 the great Ostrogothic king, Ermanaric, took his own life in fear of the onslaught of the Huns, and he became famous in the North as Jörmunrekk, who appears in several poems of the Poetic Edda.

[3] This was certainly an ancient custom (Bugge (*NS*) 362; Olrik, *Heltedigtning* II 238).

the poet speaks in one breath, without further comment, of *Heaþoric, Sifeca, Hliþe* and *Incgenþeow*. Although the phonetic correspondence is certainly not exact, the similarity of these names, all mentioned together, to *Heiðrekr, Sifka, Hlǫðr* and *Angantýr* is very striking; and when two lines later in *Widsith* we find:

> Wulfhere I sought and Wyrmhere; seldom was warfare stilled, when the host of the Hrædas about the Vistula forest had to defend with their hard swords their ancient dwelling-place from the people of Attila

—with the further exact correspondence of *Wyrmhere* and *Ormarr*— any suggestion of mere coincidence may well seem quite out of the question, though not everyone has thought so.

The word *Hrædas* in *Widsith* means 'Goths,' and is in origin the same name-element as appears in Norse as *Reið-* (earlier *Hreið-*) in *Reiðgotar* and *Reiðgotaland*, the land and people over whom King Heidrek came to rule in the saga. The evidence suggests to me that this name was a poetic, honorific designation of the Goths, of general scope, and not the name of a particular branch or community. In later times Icelandic geographers seem to have conceived Reidgotaland very vaguely, as meaning little more than that if a man travelled eastwards he would cross the borders of Poland and enter Reidgotaland. A Gothic dwelling *á stǫðum Danpar*, on the banks of the Dnieper, is at least not in complete contradiction to such an idea.[1]

It is curious that the Reidgoths themselves do not appear in the saga at all, the people of the land being called *Gotar* throughout; even the name of the land is not mentioned in *The Battle of the Goths and the Huns*. From that poem we learn that the land of the Huns lay south (verse 91) and east (verse 77, but U has 'south' in its corresponding prose-passage) of the land of the Goths, and from the prose that the forest of *Myrkviðr* lay between them. This occurs often in the poems of the Edda as the name of a dark boundary-forest,[2] but the eleventh-

---

[1] *Austr frá Polena er Reiðgotaland, Hauksbók* 155. Snorri Sturluson (*SnE* 186) identified it with Jutland, which depends on a false etymology (connection with *reið*, 'carriage' or 'riding'), so that *Reiðgotaland* was opposed to *Eygotaland*, the mainland and the islands. The same identification is made in the H-text of the saga. — All the versions of the saga place Reidgotaland to the west of Gardaríki, i.e. Russia (p. 28).

[2] e.g. *Lokasenna* 42, where *Myrkviðr* is the boundary of Múspell, the land of fire. In ancient times the settled lands of a people were naturally often separated from their neighbours by the primeval forest, and in Norse the word *mǫrk* (originally 'boundary,' cf. Modern English *march*) means 'forest' (cf. verse 76).

century chronicler Thietmar of Merseburg applies the name *Miriquidui*[1] to the Erzgebirge, the mountains on the north-western borders of Bohemia. This is not necessarily its original application, however, and it is possible that an older signification of the name (in so far as it applied to any definite region of the world) was the whole of the vast mountain-system that extends from the Erzgebirge to the Transylvanian Alps, the wooded mountain-barrier *par excellence*.[2]

Now in *Widsith* it is said that the host of the Goths fought the Huns *ymb Wistlawudu*, 'about the Vistula forest.' It is this more than anything else that has divided opinion on the original *mis-en-scène* of *The Battle of the Goths and the Huns*, and has led several writers to look away from the Black Sea and towards regions much further to the north-west.[3] Into this discussion I cannot go here, and will only say that if the Norse and English poems reflect the same legendary-historical events, as I assume they do, then it looks as if the setting of them has been shifted in *Widsith*. But real certainty is out of the question.

Saxo Grammaticus also knew *The Battle of the Goths and the Huns*, but he blended it with another legendary war and produced the most confused, 'doubled' account, with both a land-war and a sea-war going on together.[4] Angantýr the Goth has disappeared, and been replaced by Frotho, king of the Danes,[5] and the names and relationship of the Hunnish leaders have been forgotten: Saxo remembered only that there were two, and he made them into brothers, naming them both *Hun*. There are, however, one or two points where the similarity is very close, most especially in the numbers of the fleet of Olimarus, king of the *Orientales* (Russians), who was allied with the Huns. According to verse 102 of the Norse poem there were six *fylki*, in each *fylki* six 'thousands,' and in each 'thousand' thirteen 'hundreds'; in Saxo's account Ericus the spy (whose part is similar to that of Gizur Grýtingalidi) reported that he had seen six kings each with his fleet, each fleet containing five thousand ships, and each ship holding three hundred rowers.

[1] i.e. *Mirkuuidu. Monumenta Germaniae Historica* V 807.
[2] The application of the word *hrís* (normally 'scrub, brushwood') to *Myrkviðr* in verse 82 is surprising, but an extension of meaning to 'forest' does not seem incredible. In verse 91 it is called *heiðr* ('heathland').
[3] The most important essays are those of Much, Schütte, von Friesen, and Johansson.
[4] Saxo Book V; ed. Holder 154 ff.; trans. Elton 190 ff.
[5] No doubt the identification of Reidgotaland with Jutland helped in this.

The battle on Dúnheiðr in *Heiðreks Saga* bears, as pointed out by Hollander, a strong resemblance to the account of the battle of *Vínheiðr* (Brunanburh) in *Egils Saga* ch. 52, not only in motifs but even in quite marked verbal resemblances in the prose.

7 Conclusion

The concluding section of the saga as it now stands is concerned with the history of Sweden down to the early twelfth century, and has every appearance of being a quite separate work. It is only found, of course, in the seventeenth-century copies, and it cannot be said therefore when it was added on.[1]

It remains to ask whether there are any indications of the manner in which the many different ingredients of *Heiðreks Saga*, differing so widely in their age and atmosphere, came to be threaded together. The key to the maze of conflicting possibilities lies perhaps in the three appearances of a figure called Angantýr. There seems no need to think that any one of them is a deduction from another; more likely, it was precisely the existence of separate legends treating of different persons with the same or similar names that attracted these legends together.

The lines of *Widsith* seem to show that Heidrek (Heathoric) was first a king of the Goths, with his sons Hlöd (Hlithe) and Angantýr (Ingentheow), and (perhaps) a mistress called Sifka.[2] No doubt he had acquired a considerable 'history' in the North before the more or less organised body of tradition that we have in *Heiðreks Saga* had been formed. At some stage, one might guess, this developing Heidrek-legend made contact with the story of Angantýr the berserk and his death on the island of Sámsey, through the agreement, or similarity, of his name with that of Heidrek's son, the Gothic prince. One of the two Hervörs probably owes her existence to the other; and the connection of Hervör the Second with Ormar (*Widsith*'s Wyrmhere, and thus an ancient figure) may suggest that a new Hervör, on the model of the warrior-woman in *The Battle of the Goths and the Huns*, was born to

---

[1] See p. 59, note 1, where a short bibliography is given.

[2] If Sifeca in *Widsith* is a woman, she has no company. It is possible that Sifeca was misunderstood to be a woman in Scandinavia (in Norse feminine weak nouns end in -*a*, which is the Old English ending of the masculines), or else that the writer of the Old English line was mistaken in thinking Sifeca to be a man.

make a connecting-link between the generations, and that it was by this route that 'Tyrfing' came to be buried in the great grave-mound of the berserks on Sámsey.

II

1 *The Manuscripts*

There are a great many manuscripts of this saga, but the vast majority are copies of ones still existing and thus of no value for the establishment of the text.[1]

The only significant manuscript of the *R*-version is the vellum Gl.kgl.sml.2845 4to, of the Royal Library in Copenhagen, probably written late in the fourteenth or early in the fifteenth century. There is a large lacuna in the text, where one page is missing in the ninth gathering, and the conclusion of the saga, from the end of the ninth verse of *The Battle of the Goths and the Huns*, has also disappeared.

The manuscript of the *H*-version is A.M. 544 4to, *Hauksbók*, where the saga was written out by Haukr Erlendsson, who died in 1334. Here its end is again missing, for there is a gap in the manuscript between the 76th and 77th pages[2]; but there are two seventeenth-century paper manuscripts, A.M. 281 4to and A.M. 597b 4to, which contain a number of selections from *Hauksbók*, among which is the riddle-match from *Heiðreks Saga*. Both these manuscripts go back independently, through a copy, to *Hauksbók* in a less damaged state than it is in now, and thus we have the text of the *H*-version as far as the end of the riddles. How far the saga extended beyond this point in *Hauksbók* before the missing leaves were lost it is impossible to say. The two late copies end abruptly with the words, 'And Óðin was angered against him because he struck at him, and that night the king was slain.'

The *U*-version is found in a little paper manuscript (R: 715 of the University Library in Uppsala) of the mid-seventeenth century, written by one Páll Hallsson in Eyjafjörður. It is extremely corrupt (the verses in places make no sense at all), and is full of marginal entries and corrections to the text, these corrections being mostly either guesses or variants from other sources, *Ǫrvar-Odds Saga* or the

---

[1] A description of them all, and their interrelations, is given by Helgason.
[2] 76 verso ends in the middle of Heidrek's answer to Gestumblindi's second riddle; 77 recto begins inside *Fóstbrœðra Saga*.

Hervarar Rímur of Ásmundur Sæmundsson, a re-working of *Heiðreks Saga* into verse, related textually to the *U*-version.

Lastly, there is A.M. 203 fol. of the University Library in Copenhagen. This is a collection of 'Heroic Sagas,' written throughout by Jón Erlendsson, priest of Villingaholt in the south-west of Iceland, who died in 1672. Erlendsson had a manuscript of the *R*-version before him, and this he copied virtually completely. But at verse 81/3, just before his exemplar broke off (at the point where all copies of *R* break off) he went over to another manuscript, now lost, descending from the same original as *U*, and from this point *203* has independent value. He also included from this second manuscript the fuller *U*-version of the beginning of the saga, and here again *203* has textual value.

A trace of the *U*-version, carrying its history back before 1600, has been found in a Latin work by Arngrímur Jónsson, written in Iceland in the winter of 1596–7 on the basis of sagas gathered from 'at least twenty-six parchements.' This work contains a short abstract of *Heiðreks Saga* which certainly belongs to the *U*-redaction, and it is possible that the text Jónsson used was the original of *U*.[1]

The more important divergences between the redactions have been referred to already. It is unquestioned that *H* and *U* both descend from a version of the saga which cannot have been composed much after 1300, and which had been completely rewritten, in part on the basis of inferences drawn from the saga itself and in some cases apparently by purely arbitrary alteration, and in part on the basis of a written or oral tradition that cannot now be defined.

U (its manifold textual errors apart) seems to represent this retelling of the saga (*X*) fairly well, whereas *H* is a drastic and by no means careful abridgement of *X*, with the added complication that Haukr (if, as seems likely enough, he was responsible for this version and not merely its scribe) had available another source over and above *X*. What this was is not perfectly clear, but in passages where its use is certain it seems to have a close affinity to *R*.[2]

R is undoubtedly far nearer to the original saga (though certainly not free from errors and minor alterations) and the loss of it after only a few verses of *The Battle of the Goths and the Huns* is a great mis-

---

[1] Jón Helgason, 'Et tapt Håndskrift af Heiðreks Saga,' in *Festskrift til H. Falk*, 1927, 215 ff.
[2] The attempt to combine two incompatible accounts causes great confusion in *H*. For particularly clear examples see Helgason lxvi, lxxiii–lxxiv.

fortune; but it is equally certain that all manuscripts of the saga go back ultimately to the same written original (*A*). Between *A* and *R* there is one copy at least, as is shown in Appendix A (IV); and the common base-manuscript itself seems to have contained errors.[1]

The situation can be shown in a very condensed fashion thus:

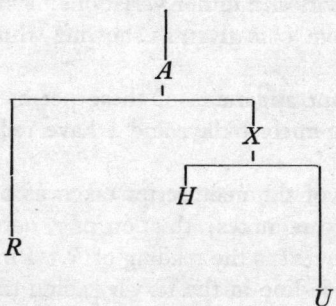

and it would follow that agreement between *RH* or *RU* would establish the text, at least of *A*, whatever the third text says. But the doubtful nature of *H*'s second source makes this uncertain: if it came between *A* and *R* in the above scheme it would invalidate the principle in respect of *RH* agreements against *U*. On the other hand, there are several cases where *H* seems to offer a much better reading in the verses than do *R* and *U* in agreement (e.g. verse 19/5).

2 The Text of this Edition

Thus in presenting a single text of *Heiðreks Saga* one could either follow *U* throughout its length or else, as has been done in this book, make a compilation: *R*, filled up in the lacuna from *U* and at the end from *U/203*. I have also given as an Appendix the beginning of the saga, where the divergence between the redactions is most extreme, in the form it has in *U/203*.

In the verses of the first part of the saga I have followed *R* pretty strictly, and noted all significant deviations made from it in the printed text; and where the text is dependent on the seventeenth-century manuscripts I have made *203* the basis and noted all deviations from it, rather than *U*, since *203* makes on the whole fewer errors.

---

[1] e.g. *R* and *U* agree (p. 5) in the erroneous *Una-* for *Munar-vágr*; *R* and *H* agree (verse 66/4) in *hǫlðum*; etc.

Where *H* and *U* agree against *R* in the poetry the variants cited are virtually complete; where *H* disagrees with *RU* the variants are fairly full, especially where a reading from *H* has been adopted by the editors of *Eddica Minora* and *Skjaldedigtning*.[1] But where *U* disagrees with *RH* the variants given are relatively few, since this manuscript is so full of errors and minor variations; sometimes a manifestly erroneous reading from *U* is given as showing which of the other texts it supports.

A complete variant apparatus of these poems conventionally presented would be extremely bulky, and I have reduced it therefore in these ways:

(i) The reading of the manuscript taken as basis is as a rule not given again in the textual notes; thus on p. 7, note *b*, 'nema *Qrv.*, *U*' means that *eða* in the text is the reading of *R*.[2] I indicate that a variant refers to a whole verse-line in the text by using the word 'thus.'

(ii) In fairly minor errors of the manuscript taken as basis the emended text is also not cited again in the textual notes; thus on p. 4, note *a*, '*þó R*' means that '*þá*' in the text is emended.

(iii) In the portion of the text after the end of *R*, a reading cited from *203* by itself means that the reading adopted in the text is actually found in *U*.

(iv) Lastly, only the first maker of an emendation is given, and this only in a very limited number of cases.

The text is normalised throughout, as also are the textual notes except in a few cases; in details like the form of negative constructions I have retained the manuscript usage. The section-numbering of the text is not that of the original.

Apart from trivial corrections, few emendations have been made, and those are largely substitutions of the reading of another manuscript; to restore alliteration or complete the sense in some extremely corrupt passages I have adopted the emendations of certain manuscripts that are not independent witnesses to the text. In *The Battle of the Goths and the Huns* there have been a great many conjectural restorations published, many of them highly arbitrary, and of these I have cited hardly any; there is an extensive variant apparatus in *Eddica Minora* (1903).

[1] These editions were made before the interrelations of *R*, *H* and *U* had been worked out.
[2] The symbols used for manuscripts of *Qrvar-Odds Saga* are explained in Appendix A (II). The variants cited from this saga are full but not complete, and only the readings of the vellum manuscripts have been cited.

In all this there is a good deal that is a matter of personal choice, and it is inevitable that some of the decisions will seem arbitrary.

3 Previous Editions

The following list includes only the most important editions. Further details can be found in *Islandica* V and XXVI, by Halldór Hermannsson, Ithaca, N.Y., 1912 and 1937.

Hervarar saga på Gammal Götska med Olai Verelii uttolkning ock notis, Uppsala 1672. (Based on *U*; with Swedish translation.)

Hervarar saga ok Heiðreks kongs, ed. Stefán Björnsson, Copenhagen 1785. (Based on A.M. 345, a manuscript of the *R* tradition; with Latin translation.)

In *Fornaldur sögur Nordrlanda*, ed. C. C. Rafn, I, Copenhagen 1829, 409 ff. (text from A.M. 345) and 513 ff. (text from *H*).

Hervarar saga ok Heiðreks konungs, ed. N. M. Petersen, Copenhagen 1847 (*Nordiske Oldskrifter* III). (*H* supplemented by *R*; with Danish translation.)

In *Antiquités Russes* I, Copenhagen 1850, 115 ff. (*H* and A.M. 345; with Latin translation.)

In *Norröne Skrifter af sagnhistorisk Indhold*, ed. Sophus Bugge, Christiania 1873. (*H* and *R*. A great advance on all previous editions, and the standard for many years. The manuscript of the Introduction was lost and never published.)

Heiðreks Saga (*Hervarar Saga ok Heiðreks Konungs*), ed. Jón Helgason, Copenhagen 1924 (*S.T.U.A.G.N.L.* XLVIII). (Diplomatic text of *R* and *U*, normalised text of *H*. The standard text, with definitive introduction on the manuscript relations.)

There is a diplomatic print of the *H*-text in the edition of *Hauksbók* (see Bibliography); and a Russian edition by I. Scharovolski, Kiev 1906, which I have not seen; details are given in *Islandica* V.

Editions of Poems Only

In *Corpus Poeticum Boreale*, ed. G. Vigfusson and F. York Powell, I, Oxford 1883 (with English translations).

In *Eddica Minora*, ed. A. Heusler and W. Ranisch, Dortmund 1903. (The most useful edition.)

In *Den Norsk-Islandske Skjaldedigtning*, ed. Finnur Jónsson, Copenhagen 1912-15. (A, Text according to the manuscripts; B, emended Text.)

In *Den Norsk-Isländska Skaldediktningen*, revised by E. A. Kock, Lund 1946–9.

4 Previous Translations

The appearance of a prose translation of *The Waking of Angantýr* by Dr George Hickes in his *Linguarum vett. septentrionalium Thesaurus* I, 1705 gave this poem an extraordinary vogue in the eighteenth century. It reappeared in Dryden's *Miscellany Poems* VI, 1716, 387 ff., and in *Five Pieces of Runic Poetry translated from the Islandic Language*, 1763 (Hickes' translation, emended by Thomas Percy, but published anonymously), and then there was a spate of Gothic Odes and Runic Odes based on *The Waking of Angantýr* by poets who were quite unconstrained by any understanding of the original. In T. J. Mathias' *Runic Odes ... in the manner of Mr. Gray* verse 37 becomes:

> Rash Virgin, to thy pray'r I yield:
> Lo! Trifingus stands reveal'd!
> Blazing like the noon-day sun, etc.

There were further attempts by W. Williams (*Gentleman's Magazine* LX, 2 (1790), 844), and by an anonymous poet in *Poems chiefly by Gentlemen of Devonshire and Cornwall* I, 1792, 114 ff. ('Virgin of intrepid brow, Surely more than woman thou'); Anna Seward (*Llangollen Vale, with Other Poems*, 1796), objecting to the expressions in Dr Hickes' translation that they had 'a vulgar familiarity,' and making changes in the names 'for their better accommodation to the verse' (Hjálmar becomes 'blooming Hiaralmo'), produced a version that she herself described, inadequately, as a 'bold Paraphrase.' In 1801 M. G. Lewis (*Tales of Wonder* I 34 ff.) added a 'catastrophe' of his own invention, in which Hervör goes up in flame and out of her mind as soon as she touches the sword, while 'flames amid her ringlets play.'

A century later, it was translated by Beatrice Barmby (in *Gísli Súrsson: a Drama*, 1900, 176 ff.) into rhymed verse fairly close to the original, and again by E. M. Smith-Dampier (*The Norse King's Bridal*, 1912), of which the lines 'Men called me a mortal, till thus I yode, To seek thee out in thine abode' give an impression of the style.

Hjálmar's Death-Song was translated from Verelius' text by the

Hon. W. Herbert (*Select Icelandic Poetry*, Pt. I, 1806, 71 ff.); a free version ('Proud domains and palaces Five I ruled with puissant hand'), but recognisable.

The verse of the saga was translated in *C.P.B.* (1883; see Previous Editions) into simple and rather impressive prose; and Miss Kershaw translated *The Battle of the Goths and the Huns*, together with text and commentary, in *Anglo-Saxon and Norse Poems* (1922). In 1936 L. M. Hollander (*Old Norse Poems*) translated the major poems of the saga into an inventive if rather bizarre alliterative verse.

The whole saga has only once before been translated into English, by Miss Kershaw (*Stories and Ballads of the Far Past*, 1921), who followed the *H*-text; the poems are translated into modern riming stanzas. This book also contains translations, with informative introductions, of the Faeroese ballads derived from *Heiðreks Saga*.

In the present edition (risking the epithet 'bizarre') I have striven for a close line-by-line translation of the poetry within the limits of an imitation of the metres and alliterative schemes of the originals. Inevitably one gets far more rising rhythms (ending on a stressed monosyllable) in Modern English than in Old Norse, and equally inevitably the demands of alliteration and accuracy together have meant pressing into service a few words that some may think should now be allowed to die in peace, even in translating heroic poetry.

BIBLIOGRAPHY AND ABBREVIATIONS

Acta Phil. Scand.	*Acta Philologica Scandinavica*, 1926–
Andrews	A. L. Andrews, 'Studies in Fornaldarsögur Norðrlanda. II. The Hervarar Saga,' in *Modern Philology* XI (1914) 77 ff., XVIII (1920) 29 ff., XXI (1923) 187 ff.
Ant. Russes	*Antiquités Russes*. See list of previous editions
Arkiv	*Arkiv för nordisk filologi*, 1883–
Björn.	See list of previous editions (Björnsson)
Boer (1888)	See *Qrvar-Odds Saga*
Boer, 'Om Hervarar saga'	R. C. Boer, 'Om Hervarar saga,' in *Aarbøger for nordisk Oldkyndighed og Historie* (1911) 1 ff.
de Boor	H. de Boor, 'Die nordische und die deutsche Hildebrandsage. 3. Ásmundar saga und Hervarar saga,' in *Zeitschrift für deutsche Philologie* L (1924) 175 ff.
Bugge (*NS*)	*Norröne Skrifter*. See list of previous editions
Bugge, *Studier*	S. Bugge, *Studier över de Nordiske Gude- og Heltesagns Oprindelse*, 1881–9
C.P.B.	*Corpus Poeticum Boreale*. See list of previous editions
Edda, Poetic	Refs. to *Edda*, ed. G. Neckel, 1927
Edd. Min.	*Eddica Minora*. See list of previous editions
Egils Saga	ed. S. Nordal (*Íslenzk Fornrit* II, 1933)
Elton	*The First Nine Books of ... Saxo Grammaticus*, translated by Oliver Elton, 1894 (*Folk-Lore Society* XXXIII)
Ettmüller	L. Ettmüller, *Altnordisches Lesebuch*, 1861
Eyrbyggja Saga	ed. E. Ó. Sveinsson (*Íslenzk Fornrit* IV, 1935)
Falk, *Altnord. Waffen.*	H. Falk, *Altnordische Waffenkunde*, 1914
F.A.S.	*Fornaldar sögur Nordrlanda* I–III, ed. C. C. Rafn, 1829–30
Flateyjarbók	I–III, Christiania 1860–8
Fornmanna Sǫgur	I–XII, Copenhagen 1825–37
von Friesen	O. von Friesen, *Rökstenen*, 1920, section 'Om folknamnet hreiðgotar,' 109 ff.
Fritzner, *Ordbog*	J. Fritzner, *Ordbog over det gamle norsk Sprog*, 1883–96
Gautreks Saga	*Die Gautrekssaga*, ed. W. Ranisch (*Palaestra* XI, 1900)

Grundtvig	Suggestions by Svend Grundtvig mentioned in Bugge, *NS*
Hákonar Saga Góða	In *Heimskringla* I
Hammershaimb	V. U. Hammershaimb, *Færöiske Kvæder* II, 1855
Haralds Saga Hárfagra	In *Heimskringla* I
Hauksbók	ed. Finnur Jónsson and Eiríkur Jónsson, Copenhagen 1892–6
Heimskringla	I–III, ed. Bjarni Aðalbjarnarson (*Íslenzk Fornrit* XXVI–XXVIII, 1941–51)
Heinzel	R. Heinzel, 'Über die Hervararsaga,' in *Sitzungsberichte der Kaiserlichen Akademie der Wissenschaften zu Wien* (*Phil.-Hist. Classe*), CXIV (1887) 417 ff.
Helg. Hund.	*Helgakviða Hundingsbana* I and II (see Edda)
Herrmann	P. Herrmann, *Erläuterungen zu den ersten neun Büchern der dänischen Geschichte des Saxo Grammaticus*. Pt II, *Die Heldensagen des Saxo Grammaticus*, 1922
Heusler, *Rätsel*	A. Heusler, 'Die Altnordischen Rätsel,' in *Zeitschrift des Vereins für Volkskunde* XI (1901) 117 ff.
Holder	*Saxonis Grammatici Gesta Danorum*, ed. A. Holder, 1886
Hollander	L. M. Hollander, 'The battle on the Vin-heath and the battle of the Huns,' in *Journal of English and Germanic Philology* XXXII (1933) 33 ff.
Hoops	*Reallexikon der germanischen Altertumskunde*, ed. J. Hoops, I–IV, 1911–19
Hrólfs Saga Kraka	ed. F. Jónsson (*S.T.U.A.G.N.L.* XXXII, 1904)
Johansson	A. Johansson, 'Þiaurikr miR Hraiþkutum,' in *Acta Phil. Scand.* VII (1932) 97 ff.
Jónsson	Finnur Jónsson, 'Um þulur og gátur,' in *Germanistische Abhandlungen zum LXX Geburtstag K. von Maurers*, 1893, 489 ff.
Kock, *FF*	E. A. Kock, *Fornjermansk Forskning*, 1922
Kock, *NN*	E. A. Kock, *Notationes Norrœnæ* (*Lunds Universitets Årsskrift* 1923–44)
Lex. Poet.	*Lexicon Poeticum Antiquæ Linguæ Septentrionalis*, ed. Finnur Jónsson, 1931
Liestøl	K. Liestøl, 'Die Guten Ratschläge in der Hervararsaga', in *Festschrift für Eugen Mogk*, 1924, 84 ff.
Lokasenna	See *Edda*

Much	R. Much, 'Der Sagenstoff der Grímnismál,' in *Z.f.d. Alt.* XLVI (1902) 312 ff.
Much, 'Askibourgion'	R. Much, 'Askibourgion Oros,' in *Z.f.d.Alt.* XXXIII (1889) 1 ff.
Neckel	G. Neckel, *Beiträge zur Eddaforschung*, 1908
Nerman	B. Nerman, *Studier i Svärges hedna litteratur*, 1913
Óláfs Saga Helga	In *Heimskringla* II
Óláfs Saga Tryggvasonar	In *Heimskringla* I
Olrik, *Heltedigtning*	Axel Olrik, *Danmarks Heltedigtning* II: *Starkad den gamle og den yngre Skjoldungrække*, 1910
Olrik, *Kilderne*	Axel Olrik, *Kilderne til Sakses Oldhistorie* II: *Norröne Sagaer og Danske Sagn*, 1894
Petersen	See list of previous editions
Rigsþula	See *Edda*
Saxo	See Holder, Elton
Schneider	H. Schneider, *Germanische Heldensage* I–III (*Grundriss der germanischen Philologie* X, 1928–34)
Schück	H. Schück, *Studier i Hervararsagan* (*Uppsala Universitäts Årsskrift* 1918)
Schütte	G. Schütte, 'Anganty-Kvadets Geografi,' in *Arkiv* XXI (1905) 30 ff.
Skj.	*Skjaldedigtning.* See list of previous editions
SnE.	*Edda Snorra Sturlusonar*, ed. Finnur Jónsson, 1931
S.T.U.A.G.N.L.	*Samfund til udgivelse af gammel nordisk litteratur*
Verelius	See list of previous editions
de Vries, *Altgerm. Religion.*	J. de Vries, *Altgermanische Religionsgeschichte* (*Grundriss der germanischen Philologie* XII, 1935–7)
de Vries, 'Heiðreksgaadene'	J. de Vries, 'Om Eddaens Visdomsdigtning. 8. Heiðreksgaadene,' in *Arkiv* L (1934) 36 ff.
Vǫlsunga Saga	ed. M. Ólsen (*S.T.U.A.G.N.L.* XXXVI, 1906–8)
Wessén	E. Wessén, 'Gestumblindi,' in *Festskrift tillägnad Hugo Pipping*, 1924, 537 ff.
Ynglinga Saga	In *Heimskringla* I
Z.f.d.Alt.	*Zeitschrift für deutsches Altertum*, 1841–
Qrv.	*Qrvar-Odds Saga* (see below)
Qrvar-Odds Saga	ed. R. C. Boer, Leiden 1888; ed. R. C. Boer, Halle 1892 (*Altnordische Saga-Bibliothek* 2)

ICELANDIC TEXT
AND
ENGLISH TRANSLATION

HÉR HEFR UPP SǪGU HEIÐREKS KONUNGS INS VITRA[a]

I

Sigrlami hét konungr, er réð fyrir Garðaríki[1]; hans dóttir var Eyfura,[2] er allra meyja var fríðust. Þessi konungr hafði eignazk sverð þat af dvergum,[3] er Tyrfingr[4] hét ok allra var bitrast, ok hvert sinn, er því var brugðit, þá lýsti af svá sem af sólargeisla. Aldri mátti hann svá hafa beran, at eigi yrði hann manns bani, ok með vǫrmu blóði skyldi hann jafnan slíðra. En ekki var þat kvikt, hvárki menn né kvikvendi, er lifa mætti til annars dags, ef sár fekk af honum, hvárt sem var meira eða minna. Aldri hafði hann brugðizk í hǫggi eða staðar numit, fyrr en hann kom í jǫrð, ok sá maðr, er hann bar í orrostu, mundi sigr fá, ef honum var vegit.[5] Þetta sverð er frægt í ǫllum fornsǫgum.

[a] *Title from H, no title in R*

[1] Gardaríki or Gardar was the name of the Swedish realm in Russia, extending south from Lake Ladoga into the lands of the Dnieper.

[2] In *H*, *U* and *Ǫrvar-Odds Saga* ch. 29 Eyfura ('island fir') is the daughter of Svafrlami, who (in *HU*) is the son of Sigrlami, the son of Óðin. See Appendix A (I).

[3] The dwarfs (*dvergar*) had an important place in the ancient mythology. They were dwellers underground or in rocks, the owners of treasure, and above all renowned for their skill, especially in metals. Dwarfs made the sword Dáinsleif, Óðin's spear Gungnir, Mjǫllnir the hammer of Thór, hair of gold for Thór's wife Sif, and Skídbladnir the ship of the gods (*SnE.*, *passim*).

HERE BEGINS THE SAGA OF KING HEIDREK THE WISE

I

Sigrlami was the name of a king who ruled over Gardaríki[1]; his daughter was Eyfura,[2] most beautiful of all women. This king had obtained from dwarfs[3] the sword called Tyrfing,[4] the keenest of all blades; every time it was drawn a light shone from it like a ray of the sun. It could never be held unsheathed without being the death of a man, and it had always to be sheathed with blood still warm upon it. There was no living thing, neither man nor beast, that could live to see another day if it were wounded by Tyrfing, whether the wound were big or little; never had it failed in a stroke or been stayed before it plunged into the earth, and the man who bore it in battle would always be victorious, if blows were struck with it.[5] This sword is renowned in all the ancient tales.

---

[4] On the origin of the name Tyrfing see Introduction, p. xxiv. As the name of a sword it occurs in a verse of the eleventh-century poet Arnór Thórdarson (Jarlaskáld), *Skj*. A I 349.

[5] With this description of Tyrfing's qualities cf. *SnE*. 154: 'Now I have drawn Dáinsleif which the dwarfs made, which must cause a man's death every time it is bared, and which never fails in its stroke; and the wound never heals, if one is scratched with it.'

2

Maðr hét Arngrímr[1]; hann var víkingr ágætr. Hann sótti austr í Garðaríki ok dvalðisk um hríð með Sigrlama konungi ok gerðisk forstjóri fyrir liði hans, bæði lands at gæta ok þegna, því at konungr var nú gamall.

Arngrímr[a] gerðisk nú svá mikill hǫfðingi, at konungr gipti honum dóttur sína ok setti hann mestan mann í ríki sínu; hann gaf honum þá sverðit Tyrfing. Konungr settisk þá um kyrrt, ok er ekki frá honum sagt fleira.

Arngrímr fór með konu sína Eyfuru norðr til ættleifða sinna ok nam staðar í ey þeiri, er Bólm[b2] hét. Þau áttu tólf sunu; inn elzti ok inn ágætasti hét Angantýr, annarr Hjǫrvarðr, þriði Hervarðr, fjórði Hrani, ok Haddingjar tveir; eigi eru nefndir fleiri.[3] Allir váru þeir berserkir,[4] svá sterkir ok miklir kappar, at aldri vildu þeir fleiri fara í hernað en tólf, ok kómu þeir aldri svá til orrostu, at eigi hefði þeir sigr; af þessu urðu þeir ágætir um ǫll lǫnd, ok engi konungr var sá, er eigi gæfi þeim þat, er þeir vildu hafa.

Þat var tíðenda eitthvert sinn jólaaptan, at menn skyldu heit strengja[5] at bragarfulli,[6] sem siðr er til; þá strengðu heit Arngríms synir. Hjǫrvarðr strengði þess heit,[7] at hann skyldi eiga dóttur Ingjalds Svíakonungs,[8] þa mey, er fræg var um ǫll lǫnd at fegrð ok atgǫrvi, eða enga konu ella.

Þat sama vár gera þeir brœðr ferð sína tólf ok koma til Uppsala ok ganga fyrir konungs borð, ok þar sat dóttir hans hjá honum. Þá segir Hjǫrvarðr ørendi sitt konungi ok heitstrenging, en allir hlýddu, þeir er inni váru. Hjǫrvarðr biðr konung segja skjótt, hvert ørendi

---

[a] Angrímr R
[b] Bólm H, Bólmr U, Hólmr R

[1] A history of Arngrím's forebears is given in the HU-version; see Appendix A (I).

[2] H (and 203, here probably influenced by H) says that Bólm was in Hálogaland in the north of Norway, but more probably it is to be identified with the island Bolmsö in Lake Bolmen in southern Sweden; cf. *í Bólm austr* in Appendix A (II), verse 1.

[3] But the remaining six are named in other sources; see Appendix A (II). Berserks frequently number twelve in the sagas.

[4] See Glossary s.v. *berserkr*

[5] To 'make fast a vow' (*heit strengja*) meant to make a vow so solemn that it could not under any circumstances be broken. *Heitstrenging* (and very often

2

There was a man named Arngrím,[1] who was a great viking. He journeyed east to Gardaríki, and dwelt a while with Sigrlami the king; he became the captain of his host, for the protection of both land and liegemen, since the king was now old.

Arngrím became then so great a lord that the king gave him his daughter in marriage, and established him as the greatest man in his realm; the sword Tyrfing he gave him also. Afterwards the king took to his rest, and nothing more is told of him.

Arngrím went north, together with his wife Eyfura, to the land of his inheritance, and settled in the island called Bólm.[2] They had twelve sons; the eldest and most renowned was named Angantýr, the second Hjörvard, the third Hervard, the fourth Hrani, and then the two Haddings; no more are named.[3] They were all berserks,[4] champions so great and strong that on their forays they were never more than twelve, and they never went into battle without gaining the victory; for this they were famed in every land, and there was no king who would not grant them what they demanded.

Now it happened one Yule-eve that men were to make solemn vows[5] at the Bragarfull,[6] as the custom is; and the sons of Arngrím made their vows. Hjörvard made the vow[7] that he would marry the daughter of Ingjald, king of the Swedes,[8] a woman famed through every land for her beauty and accomplishment, or no woman else.

That same spring the twelve brothers set out, and coming to Uppsala they went before the king's table, where his daughter sat beside him. Then Hjörvard declared before the king his mission and his vow, while all within the hall listened; and he told the king to say quickly

---

this particular one) becomes a constantly recurring theme in the late sagas, and is frequently associated with the great mid-winter feast, Yule.

[6] The first element of *bragar-* or *braga-full* is related to such words as O. E. *brego* 'lord.' In view of the description in *Ynglinga Saga* ch. 36, the 'lord's cup' has been taken to be a toast drunk at inheritance-feasts in memory of the dead king; by others *braga(r)-full* has been connected with the god Thór, who is called *Ásabragr*; cf. especially *Hákonar Saga Góða* ch. 14.

[7] In *H* it is Angantýr who makes the vow; see Introduction p. xiii.

[8] The Swedish king is called Yngvi in *HU*. His daughter's name was Ingibjörg (see verse 10).

hann skal þangat eiga. Konungr hugsar þetta mál ok veit, hversu miklir þeir brœðr váru fyrir sér ok af ágætu kyni komnir. Í því bili stígr fram yfir konungs borðit sá maðr, er hét Hjálmarr inn hugumstóri, ok mælti til konungs, 'Herra konungr, minnizk þér nú, hvé mikinn sóma ek hefi yðr veitt, síðan er ek kom í þetta land, ok hversu margar orrostur ek átta at vinna ríki undir yðr, ok hefi ek yðr látit heimila mína þjónustu. Nú bið ek yðr, at þér veitið mér til sœmðar ok gefið mér dóttur yðra, er minn hugr hefir jafnan á leikit; ok er þat makligra, at þér veitið mér þessa bœn heldr en berserkjunum, þeim er illt eitt hafa gǫrt bæði í yðru ríki ok margra annarra konunga.'

Nú hugsar konungr hálfu meir ok þykkir nú þetta mikit vandamál, er þessir tveir hǫfðingjar keppask svá mjǫk um dóttur hans. Konungr segir á þessa leið, hvárrtveggi sjá er svá mikill maðr ok vel ættborinn, at hvárigum vill hann synja mægða, ok biðr hana kjósa, hvárn hon vill eiga. Hon segir svá, at þat er jafnt, ef faðir hennar vill gipta hana, þá [a] vill hon þann eiga, er henni er kunnr at góðu, en eigi hinn, er hon hefir sǫgur einar frá ok allar illar, sem frá Arngríms sonum. Hjǫrvarðr býðr Hjálmari á hólm[1] suðr í Sámsey[2] ok biðr hann verða hvers manns níðing, ef hann gengr fyrr at eiga frúna en þetta einvígi er reynt. Hjálmarr kveðr sik ekki skulu dvelja.

Fara nú Arngríms synir heim ok segja feðr sínum sitt ørendi, en Arngrímr kvezk aldri fyrr hafa óttazk um ferð þeira. Þessu næst fara þeir brœðr til Bjarmars [b] jarls,[3] ok gerir hann í móti þeim veizlu mikla; ok nú vill Angantýr fá dóttur jarls, er Sváfa hét, ok var nú drukkit brúðlaup þeira.

Ok nú segir Angantýr jarli draum sinn: honum þótti þeir brœðr staddir í Sámsey, ok fundu þar fugla marga ok drápu alla; þá sneru þeir annan veg á eyna, ok flugu í móti þeim ernir tveir, ok þóttisk hann ganga í móti ǫðrum, ok áttu þeir hart viðskipti, ok settusk niðr báðir, áðr létti. En annarr ǫrninn átti [c] við brœðr hans ellifu, ok þótti honum ǫrninn efri verða. Jarl segir, at þann draum þurfti ekki at ráða, ok þar væri honum sýnt fall ríkra manna.

[a] þó R   [b] Bjartmarr *HU throughout*   [c] átt R

[1] See Glossary s.v. *hólmganga*. But the *hólmganga* on Sámsey in this saga means no more than 'battle on an island,' with of course prearrangement, and has little in common with the precisely-conducted duels described elsewhere.

[2] Sámsey is now called Samsö, an island lying to the north of Fyn, between Jutland and Zealand.

[3] In *U* Jarl Bjarmar (see Glossary s.v. *Jarl*) is said to have ruled over Aldeigjuborg, the Swedish colony on Lake Ladoga.

what the issue of his errand there should be. The king pondered these words, remembering how powerful the brothers were, descendants of a glorious line; but at that moment the man called Hjálmar the Greathearted stepped forward over the king's table. 'Lord king!' he said, 'call to mind now what great honour I have brought you since I came to this land, and how many battles I have fought to win kingdoms under your authority; all my service I have bestowed on you. I ask you now to grant my request, for the increase of my honour, and give me your daughter, on whom my heart has always been set; and it is more fitting that you should grant this request to me rather than to these berserks, who have done nothing but evil, both in your realm and in those of many other kings.'

Now the king pondered more deeply still, and very difficult he thought it, that there should be such contention over his daughter between these two chieftains. At last he spoke thus. He said they were both such great men and so nobly born that he would not refuse to be allied with either, and he told his daughter to choose whom she would have. She answered that that was fair, and that if her father would give her in marriage she would rather have a man that she knew good of than one of whom she knew tales only, and those all evil, as of the sons of Arngrím. Then Hjörvard challenged Hjálmar to a duel[1] south on Sámsey,[2] and cursed him as an outcast, to be loathed and despised by every man, if he married the lady before the issue of this single combat; and Hjálmar said that nothing would keep him back.

Now the sons of Arngrím departed home and told their father of the result of their quest; and Arngrím said that never before had he feared for them on their travels. After that the brothers journeyed to the jarl Bjarmar,[3] and he made a great feast for them. Now Angantýr desired to marry Sváfa, the jarl's daughter; and so their wedding-feast was held.

Then Angantýr told the jarl of a dream that he had had: he said that he had dreamed that the brothers were on Sámsey, and that there they came upon many birds, and slew them all. Then they took another path upon the island, and two eagles flew against them; Angantýr dreamed that he attacked one of them, and they had a bitter struggle, but they both sank down before all was over. The second eagle fought with his eleven brothers, and it seemed to him that the eagle had the upper hand. The jarl said that this dream needed no interpreting, and that the downfall of mighty men had been revealed to him.

3

En er þeir brœðr koma heim, búask þeir til hólmstefnu, ok leiðir faðir þeira þá til skips ok gaf þá sverðit Tyrfing Angantý; 'hygg ek,' segir hann, 'at nú muni þǫrf vera góðra vápna.' Hann biðr þá nú vel fara; eptir þat skiljask þeir.

Ok er þeir brœðr koma í Sámsey, sjá þeir, hvar tvau skip liggja í hǫfn þeiri, er Munarvágr[a] hét; þau skip hétu askar.[1] Þeir þóttusk vita, at Hjálmarr mundi þessi skip eiga ok Oddr inn víðfǫrli, er kallaðr var Ǫrvar-Oddr. Þá brugðu Arngríms synir sverðum ok bitu í skjaldarrendr, ok kom á þá berserksgangr; þeir gengu þá sex út á hvárn askinn. En þar váru svá góðir drengir innanborðs, at allir tóku sín vápn, ok engi flýði ór sínu rúmi, ok engi mælti æðruorð; en berserkirnir gengu með ǫðru borði fram, en ǫðru aptr ok drápu þá alla. Síðan gengu þeir á land upp grenjandi.

Hjálmarr ok Oddr hǫfðu gengit upp á eyna at vita, ef berserkirnir væri komnir. Ok er þeir gengu ór skóginum til skipa sinna, þá gengu berserkir út af skipum þeira með blóðgum vápnum ok brugðnum sverðum, ok var þá genginn af þeim berserksgangrinn; en þá verða þeir máttminni en þess á milli sem eptir nǫkkurs kyns sóttir. Þá kvað Oddr[2]:

(1) Þá var mér ótti
einu sinni,
er þeir grenjandi
gengu af ǫskum
ok emjandi
í ey stigu,[b]
tírarlausir,
váru tólf saman.

Þá mælti Hjálmarr til Odds, 'Sér þú nú, at fallnir eru menn okkrir

---

[a] Munarvágr *em. after H and Ǫrv.*, Unavágr *R (cf. Helg. Hund. I, 31);* *elsewhere* Mun- *R*, Unavágar *or* Unnarvágr *U throughout except verse 25*
[b] ok . . . stigu *Ǫrv., om. RU*

[1] The use of the word 'ash' in the sense 'ship,' rare in Norse, was probably originally the name for Scandinavian war-vessels current in England and Germany during the Viking period; cf. O.E. *æsc*, frequent in this sense. (H. Falk, 'Altnordisches Seewesen,' *Wörter und Sachen* IV (1912) 87.)

3

When the brothers came home they made themselves ready for the encounter; and their father accompanied them to the ship, and gave Angantýr the sword Tyrfing, saying, 'I think that good weapons will be needed now.' Then he said farewell, and after that they parted.

When the brothers came to Sámsey they saw that two ships were lying in the anchorage called Munarvág, ships of the kind called 'ashes'.[1] They thought that these would be the ships of Hjálmar and Odd the Far-traveller, who was called Arrow-Odd. Then the sons of Arngrím drew their swords and gnawed the rims of their shields, and the berserk-frenzy came upon them; they went out onto the two ships, six on each. But the men on board were so stout-hearted, that all seized their weapons, and none left his place or uttered any word of fear. The berserks went up one side and down the other, and slew them all; and then they went howling up on shore.

Hjálmar and Odd had gone up onto the island to see if the berserks had arrived; and as they were returning from the forest to their ships the berserks left the vessels with their weapons bloody and their swords drawn; but the berserk-fury had now left them, and berserks become weaker then than at other times, as after certain kinds of sickness. Then Odd spoke[2]:

> (1) Fear beset me
> for a single moment,
> as they left the longships
> loudly bellowing,
> crying terribly
> climbed the island,
> twelve together,
> inglorious men.

Then Hjálmar said to Odd, 'Do you see that all our men are slain?

---

[2] A fuller form of the verse dialogue that follows is found in *Qrvar-Odds Saga*, and is given in Appendix A (II).

allir, ok sýnisk mér nú líkast, at vér munum allir Óðin gista í kveld í Valhǫllu.'¹ Ok þat eitt segja menn, at Hjálmarr hafi mælt æðruorð.

Oddr svarar, 'Þat mundi mitt ráð vera, at vit flýðim undan á skóg, ok munum vit ekki mega tveir berjask við þá tólf, er drepit hafa tólf ina frœknustu menn er váru í Svíaríki.'

Þá mælti Hjálmarr, 'Flýjum vit aldri undan óvinum okkrum ok þolum heldr vápn þeira; fara vil ek at berjask við berserki.'

Oddr svaraði,ᵃ 'En ek nenni eigi at gista Óðin í kveld, ok skulu þessir allir dauðir berserkir, áðr kveld sé, en vit tveir lifa.'

Þetta viðrmæli þeira sanna þessar vísur, er Hjálmarr kvað:

(2) Fara halir hraustir
af herskipum,
tólf menn saman
tírarlausir;
vit munum í aptan
Óðin gista
tveir fóstbrœðr,ᵇ
en þeir tólf lifa.

Oddr segir:

(3) Því mun orði
andsvǫr veita:
þeir munu í aptan
Óðin gista
tólf berserkir,
en vit tveir lifa.

Þeir Hjálmarr sá, at Angantýr hafði Tyrfing í hendi, því at lýsti af sem sólargeisla.

Hjálmarr mælti, 'Hvárt viltu eiga við Angantý eða við brœðr hans ellifu?'

Oddr segir, 'Ek vil berjask við Angantý; hann mun gefa stór hǫgg með Tyrfingi, en ek trúi betr skyrtu minni en brynju þinni til hlífðar.'

Hjálmarr mælti, 'Hvar kómum vit þess til orrostu, at þú gengir fram fyrir mik? Því viltu berjask við Angantý, atᶜ þér þykkir þat

ᵃ Oddr svaraði om. R
ᵇ fóstbrœðr Qrv., berserkir R, fullhugar U
ᶜ at om. R

[1] See Appendix C

I think it is most likely that we shall all be Óðin's guests in Valhöll tonight.'[1] And it is said that these were the only words of fear that Hjálmar ever uttered.

'My advice,' Odd answered, 'would be that we should escape into the forest, for the two of us will not be able to contend with these twelve, who have slain twelve of the stoutest men in the kingdom of the Swedes.'

But Hjálmar said, 'Let us never flee away from our enemies, but rather endure their weapons; I shall go out to fight with the berserks.'

'I have no mind to spend tonight with Óðin,' Odd answered; 'all these berserks shall be dead men before nightfall, but we two shall live.'

These words of theirs are vouched for by these verses which they uttered:

(2) Strong are the warriors
the warships leaving,
twelve together,
inglorious men;
we shall be this evening
under Óðin's roof,
two sworn-brothers,
but the twelve shall live.

Odd spoke:

(3) To that speech of yours
I say in answer:
They shall be this evening
under Óðin's roof,
the twelve berserks;
we two shall live!

Now Hjálmar and his companion saw that Angantýr had Tyrfing in his hand, for a light shone from it like a ray of the sun.

'Will you take on Angantýr alone,' said Hjálmar, 'or his eleven brothers?'

'I will fight with Angantýr,' said Odd; 'he will give great blows with Tyrfing, and I put more trust in my shirt for protection than in your corslet.'

'Where have you ever taken precedence over me in battle?' said Hjálmar. 'You wish to fight with Angantýr because you think it the meira þrekvirki. Nú em ek hǫfuðsmaðr þessar hólmgǫngu; hét ek ǫðru konungsdóttur í Svíþjóðu en láta þik eða annan ganga í þetta einvígi fyrir mik, ok skal ek berjask við Angantý,'—ok brá þá sverðinu ok gekk fram í móti Angantý, ok vísaði hvárr ǫðrum til Valhallar.[1] Snúask þeir í móti Hjálmarr ok Angantýr ok láta skammt stórra hǫggva á milli.

Oddr kallar á berserki ok kvað:

(4) Einn skal við einn
    eiga, nema sé deigr,[a]
    hvatra drengja,
    eða[b] hugr bili.

Þá gekk fram Hjǫrvarðr, ok áttusk þeir Oddr við hart vápnaskipti; en silkiskyrta[2] Odds var svá traust, at ekki vápn festi á, en hann hafði sverð svá gott, at svá beit brynju sem klæði; ok fá hǫgg hafði hann veitt Hjǫrvarði, áðr hann fell dauðr. Þá gekk til Hervarðr ok fór sǫmu leið, þá Hrani, þá hverr at ǫðrum, en Oddr veitti þeim svá harða atsókn, at alla felldi hann þá ellifu brœðr. En frá leik þeira Hjálmars er þat at segja, at Hjálmarr fekk sextán sár, en Angantýr fell dauðr.

Oddr gekk þar til, er Hjálmarr var, ok kvað[3]:

(5) Hvat er þér, Hjálmarr?
    Hefir þú lit brugðit;
    þik kveð ek mœða
    margar[c] undir;
    hjálmr er þinn hǫggvinn,
    en á hlið brynja,[d]
    nú kveð ek fjǫrvi
    of[e] farit þínu.

---

[a] *thus* R, eiga orrostu Ǫrv. (M), orrostu heyja Ǫrv. (AB), U
[b] nema Ǫrv., U
[c] miklar Ǫrv., U
[d] *thus* Ǫrv., U, ok in síða brynja R (*without alliteration*)
[e] ok R

[1] See Appendix C

sterner test. But I am the principal in this combat; and it was not this that I promised the princess in Sweden—to let you or anyone else enter this duel on my behalf. It is I who shall fight with Angantýr'— and he drew his sword and went forward to meet him. Each showed the other the way to Valhöll[1]; and now Hjálmar and Angantýr turned on each other, and wasted little time between the great strokes they gave.

Odd called out to the berserks, saying:

> (4) Singly shall they fight,
> the strong heroes,
> unless they be soft,
> or their spirit fail them!

Then Hjörvard stepped forward, and had with Odd a stern exchange; but Odd's silken shirt[2] was so sure a protection that no weapon could bite on it, and he had a sword so good that it cut into armour like cloth, and he gave Hjörvard few blows before he fell dead. Then Hervard stepped forward, and things went the same way with him; then Hrani; and so one after another, and Odd attacked them so fiercely that he felled all the eleven brothers. But of the grim game between Hjálmar and his foe there is this to tell, that Hjálmar got sixteen wounds, but Angantýr fell dead.

Odd went up to Hjálmar, and said[3]:

> (5) Hjálmar, what ails you?
> Your hue is altered;
> many the wounds are
> that waste your strength;
> cleft is your helmet
> and the coat on your side:
> I say you have seen
> the sum of your days.

---

[2] Arrow-Odd got his 'silken shirt' from a fairy woman in Ireland; the story is told in *Qrvar-Odds Saga* chs. 22, 24, and the *U*-version also mentions that it came from Ireland. This idea of a *skyrta* against which all weapons are powerless is extremely common in the late sagas; cf. Åke Lagerholm, *Drei Lygisögur* (*Altnordische Saga-Bibliothek* 17, 1927, 69).

[3] *Qrvar-Odds Saga* has four additional verses of this poem, which are given in Appendix A (III).

Hjálmarr kvað:

(6) Sár hefi ek sextán,
slitna brynju,
svart er mér fyrir sjónum,
séka ek^a ganga;
hneit mér við hjarta
hjǫrr Angantýs,
hvass blóðrefill
herðr í eitri.[1]

Ok enn kvað hann:

(7) Áttak at fullu^b
fimm tún^c saman,
en ek því aldri
unða ráði^d;
nu[2] verð ek liggja
lífs andvani,^e
sverði undaðr,^f
í Sámseyju.^g

(8) Drekka í hǫllu
húskarlar mjǫð
menjum gǫfgir
at míns fǫður^h[3];
mœðir marga
mungát fira,^j
en mik eggja spor
í eyju^k þjá.

(9) Hvarf ek frá hvítri
hlaðs beðgunni^l[4]

---

^a séka sé ek *R*   ^b *thus R* (aktag *MS*), áttak á foldu *Ǫrv.*, *U*
^c tún *RU*, bú *Ǫrv.* (*M*), ból *Ǫrv.* (*AB*)
^d en ek ... ráði (láði *U*) *RU*, en ek unða því eigi láði *Ǫrv.* (*AB*) *and similarly Ǫrv.* (*M*)   ^e *thus RU*, lítt megandi *Ǫrv.*
^f sundaðr *R*   ^g *thus R*, Sámseyju í *Ǫrv.*, Sáms í eyju *U*
^h Drekka ... fǫður *R, and similarly U* (*later corr. to text of Ǫrv.*); Drekkr með jǫfri / jarla mengi / ǫl glaðliga / at Uppsǫlum *Ǫrv.*
^j fira *Ǫrv.*, *U*, fenja *R*   ^k ey *R*
^l Hvarf ... beðgunni (bedgungi *MS*) *R*, Leiddi mik en hvíta / hilmis dóttir *Ǫrv. and similarly U*

Hjálmar spoke:
> (6) Wounds have I sixteen,
> slit is my corslet,
> sight is darkened,
> I see not my way;
> to my heart pierced me,
> poison-hardened,[1]
> Angantýr's blade —
> bitter the point was.

More he said:
> (7) Farms I owned there
> five together,
> my lot in that land
> yet loved I never;
> now[2] must I lie here
> of life bereft,
> here on Sámsey
> by the sword wounded.

> (8) Mead they are drinking,
> adorned with gems,
> the throng of his folk
> in my father's hall[3];
> ale overmasters
> many a warrior,
> but the marks of the blade
> torment me here.

> (9) I went away
> from that white maiden[4]

---

[1] cf. verse 41/6. This is a widespread conception, not only in Norse (cf. *Beowulf* 1459, of the sword Hrunting); Falk, *Altnord. Waffen.* 3 ff.

[2] Lines 5–7 of verse 7, with very slight variation from the form they have in *RU*, are found also in *Hildibrand's Death-Song (Edd. Min.* 54).

[3] On the remarkable divergence between the two saga-texts here (that of *Ǫrvar-Odds Saga* meaning: 'Now the crowd of his court / with the king are drinking / their ale gladly / at Uppsala') see Appendix A (III).

[4] The Valkyrie name *Gunnr* ('battle') is common in kennings for women, and thus either *hlaðs-gunnr* (*hlað* 'lace, embroidery') or *beð-gunnr* (*beðr* 'bed') would form a complete kenning. Perhaps *hlaðs beðr* ('bed of embroidery') should be taken to mean 'cloak,' and *hlaðs beð-gunnr* 'lady of the cloak.'

á Agnafit[1]
útanverðri[a];
saga mun sannask
sú er hon sagði mér,
at aptr koma
eigi mundak.

(10) Drag þú mér af hendi
hring inn rauða,
færðu inni ungu
Ingibjǫrgu;
sá mun henni
hugfastr tregi,
er ek eigi køm
til Uppsala.[b]

(11)[2] Hvarf ek frá fǫgrum
fljóða sǫngvi
ótrauðr gamans
austr við[c] Sóta[3];
fǫr skundaða ek
ok fórk í lið
hinzta[d] sinni
frá hollvinum.

(12) Hrafn flýgr austan[e]
af hám meiði,
flýgr honum eptir
ǫrn í sinni;
þeim gef ek erni
efstum bráðir,
sá mun á blóði
bergja[f] mínu.

[a] útanverða Qrv., U
[b] er ek ... Uppsala R; Qrv. and U as in Appendix A (III), verse ii
[c] austr við RU, út með Qrv.
[d] hinzta Qrv. (B), innsta RU
[e] austan RU, sunnan Qrv. (AB)
[f] berigia R

on the outer shore
of Agnafit[1];
her fore-telling
true will prove now:
I shall return not
ever again.

(10) The red-gold ring —
from my wrist take it,
to Ingibjörg
I ask you, bear it;
it will give her
grief long-lasting
when I come not ever
to Uppsala.

(11)[2] I went from delight
of women's singing,
for joy eager
east with Sóti,[3]
sped my journey
to join the host,
left for the last time
loyal companions.

(12) From the high treetop
hurries the raven,
from the east flying,
the eagle his escort;
food for the eagle
I find for the last time:
he shall make his meal
on my blood now.

---

[1] Agnafit: the low-lying coastal stretch along the outflow of Lake Mälaren, where present-day Stockholm lies.
[2] Verse 11 should probably follow verse 9, as it does in *U*; see Appendix A (III).
[3] It is possible that Sóti was Hjálmar's original companion; see Introduction p. xiii.

Eptir þat deyr Hjálmarr. Oddr segir þessi tíðendi heim í Svíþjóð, en konungsdóttir má eigi lifa eptir hann ok ræðr sér sjálf bana.[1] Angantýr ok brœðr hans váru lagðir í haug í Sámsey með ǫllum vápnum sínum.

Dóttir Bjarmars var með barni; þat var mær einkar fǫgr. Sú var vatni ausin[2] ok nafn gefit ok kǫlluð Hervǫr. Hon fœddisk upp með jarli ok var sterk sem karlar, ok þegar hon mátti sér nǫkkut, tamðisk hon meir við skot ok skjǫld ok sverð en við sauma eða borða. Hon gerði ok optar illt en gott, ok er henni var þat bannat, hljóp hon á skóga ok drap menn til fjár[a] sér. Ok er jarl spyrr til þessa stigamanns, fór hann þangat með liði sínu ok tók Hervǫru ok hafði heim með sér, ok dvalðisk hon þá heima um stund.

Þat var eitt sinn, er Hervǫr var úti stǫdd því nær, er þrælar nǫkkurir váru, ok gerði hon þeim illt sem ǫðrum. Þá mælti í þrælinn, 'Þú, Hervǫr, vilt illt eitt gera, ok ills er at þér ván, ok því bannar jarl ǫllum mǫnnum at segja þér þitt faðerni, at honum þykkir skǫmm, at þú vitir þat, því at inn versti þræll[b] lagðisk með dóttur hans, ok ertu þeira barn.'

Hervǫr varð við þessi orð æfar reið ok gengr þegar fyrir jarl ok kvað:

> (13) Áka[c] ek várri
> vegsemð hrósa,
> þótt hon[d] Fróðmars
> fengi[e] hylli[3];
> fǫður hugðumk ek
> frœknan eiga,
> nú er sagðr fyrir mér[f]
> svína hirðir.

---

[a] fjarr R [b] þræll er R [c] Ætla U [d] hefði U
[e] fengi *em. Petersen*, fengit RU [f] nú er mér hann sagðr U

[1] In *Ǫrvar-Odds Saga* (ch. 15) Ingibjörg did not kill herself, but fell back dead in her chair when she saw Hjálmar's ring; and Odd burst out laughing, with the words 'They shall enjoy now in death what they could not have in life.' — The suicide of a woman, rather than survive her husband or her betrothed, is found several times in Norse legends, and seems to reflect an ancient custom of suttee—of which the most vivid evidence is found in the famous account of the ship-burial on the Volga by the Arab Ahmed ibn Foszlan, who saw it (for translation, see Waddy, *Antiquity*, VIII, 1934, 58).

After that Hjálmar died. Back in Sweden Odd told these tidings; but the king's daughter could not live on after Hjálmar, and she took her own life.[1] Angantýr and his brothers were laid in a mound on Sámsey with all their weapons.

Bjarmar's daughter was with child; and it was a girl of great beauty. She was sprinkled with water,[2] and given a name, and called Hervör. She was brought up in the house of the jarl, and she was as strong as a man; as soon as she could do anything for herself she trained herself more with bow and shield and sword than with needlework and embroidery. She did more often harm than good, and when it was forbidden her she ran away to the woods and killed men for her gain. When the jarl heard of this highwayman he went to the place with his men and seized Hervör and brought her home with him; after that she dwelt at his house for a while.

One day Hervör chanced to be standing near some slaves, and she treated them ill, as she did everyone else. Then one of them said to her, 'Your only wish is to do evil, Hervör, and evil is to be expected from you; the jarl forbids everyone to speak to you of your parentage, because he is ashamed that you should know of it—for the basest serf lay with his daughter, and you are their child.'

Hervör was enraged at these words, and she went at once to the jarl, and said:

(13) Little can I glory
in our lofty name,
though Fródmar's favour
was found by my mother[3];
I thought that I had
a hero for father,
but now I am told
he tended the swine!

---

[2] This custom undoubtedly prevailed in Iceland, Norway and the Orkneys during the heathen age without any connection with Christian baptism; but its ultimate origin may nonetheless lie in contact with the Christian peoples of the British Isles, for there is no record of it from Swedish or South Germanic territory. (K. Maurer, *Die Wasserweihe des german. heidentums*, 1880.)

[3] On these puzzling lines see Appendix F

Jarl kvað:

(14) Logit er mart at þér
of lítil efni,[a]
frœkn[b] með fyrðum
var[c] faðir þinn taliðr;
stendr Angantýs[d]
ausinn moldu
salr í Sámsey
sunnanverðri.

Hon kvað:

(15) Nú fýsir mik,
fóstri, at vitja
framgenginna
frænda minna;
auð mundu þeir
eiga nógan,
þann skal ek ǫðlask,
nema ek áðr fǫrumk.

(16) Skal skjótliga
um skǫr búa
blæju[e] líni,[1]
áðr braut fari;
mikit býr í því,
er á morgin skal
skera bæði mér
skyrtu ok ólpu.[f]

Síðan mælti Hervǫr við móður sína ok kvað:

(17) Bú þú mik at ǫllu
sem þú bráðast[g] kunnir,

---

[a] *thus em. on basis of corr. in U;* lítil of frétt *R,* ef litil er *U, later corr. to* ef lítit er efni   [b] frœkn *U, om. R*   [c] var *om. R, added later in U*
[d] Angantýr *R*   [e] bleiku *U*
[f] *thus U,* ólpu ok skyrtu *R (with bad alliteration)*
[g] bráðast *A.M. 345 (Helgason þ. xliv),* hraðast *U,* hvatast *R (without alliteration)*

The jarl answered:
> (14) A lie has been told you
> with little substance:
> high among heroes
> men held your father;
> Angantýr's hall
> with earth sprinkled
> stands on Sámsey's
> southern border.

Hervör spoke:
> (15) Foster-father,
> I am filled with longing
> to seek them out,
> my slain kinsmen,
> for store of wealth
> they surely own;
> to me shall it pass
> if I perish not!
>
> (16) I will wrap swiftly
> around my hair
> a linen headgear[1]
> ere I hasten away;
> much rests on it,
> that when morning comes
> cloak and kirtle
> be cut for me.

Afterwards Hervör spoke to her mother, and said:

> (17) As quick as you can
> equip me in all ways,

---

[1] Unless these lines imply 'I will bind up my hair so that I may be taken for a man,' one must follow *Skj.* in emending *um* to *af*, and translate: 'the linen cloth shall be taken from my hair,' i.e. Hervör will cast away her woman's attire.

sannfróð[a] kona,
sem þú son mundir;
satt[b] eitt mun mér
í svefn bera,
fæ ek ekki hér
ynði it næsta.

Síðan bjósk hon í brott ein saman ok tók sér karlmanns gørvi ok vápn ok sótti þar til, er víkingar nǫkkurir váru, ok fór með þeim um hríð ok nefndisk Hervarðr. Litlu síðar tók þessi Hervarðr forræði liðsins,[c] ok er þeir kómu til Sámseyjar, þá beiddisk Hervarðr at fara upp á eyna ok sagði, at þar mundi vera féván í haugi; en allir liðsmenn mæla í móti ok segja, at svá miklar meinvættir gangi þar ǫll dœgr, at þar er verra um daga en víða um nætr annars staðar. Þat fæsk um síðir, at kastat var akkerum, en Hervarðr sté í bát ok reri til lands ok lendi í Munarvági í þann tíma, er sól settisk, ok hitti þar mann þann er hjǫrð helt.

Hann kvað[1]:

(18) Hverr er ýta[d]
í ey kominn?
Gakk þú sýsliga[e]
gistingar til!

Hon kvað[f]:

(19) Munka ek ganga
gistinga til,[g]
því ek engi kann
eyjarskeggja[2];
segðu elligar[h]
áðr vit skiljum[j]:
hvar eru Hjǫrvarðs[k]
haugar kenndir?

[a] sannfróð *em. Ettmüller*, sannfund *R*, -find *U*, -reynd *Bugge*
[b] satt *U*, fátt *R*   [c] liðins *R*
[d] *thus R*, hverr einn saman *H*, þú ert einn með oss *U*
[e] greiðliga *H*, skiælega *U*   [f] Hon kvað *om. R*
[g] lines 1–2 *so placed in HU*, in *R after* skiljum *line 6*
[h] elligar *RU*, hraðliga *H*   [j] *thus RU*, áðr heðan líðir *H*
[k] Hjǫrvarði (Her- *U*) *HU*

> wisest of women,
> as you would your son!
> In dreams is told me
> the truth only;
> no contentment
> shall I taste here now.

After that she made ready to depart alone, and taking the gear and weapons of a man she made her way to a place where there were some vikings, and for a time she went roving with them and called herself Hervard. A short while after, this Hervard became captain of the band, and when they came to Sámsey she demanded to be allowed to go up on the island, saying that there would be promise of treasure in the burial-mound; but all the men of the company spoke against it, saying that such creatures of evil walked there both by day and by night that it was worse there in daylight than in many other places in the dark. But at last she had her way, and the anchor was dropped; Hervard got into a boat, and rowing to the shore landed in Munarvág at the hour of sunset, and there came upon a man who tended a flock. He spoke[1]:

> (18) Who among mortals
> moves on the island?
> Now flee you fast
> to find shelter!

She answered:

> (19) Flee I will not
> to find shelter,
> none do I know
> of the native people[2];
> rather tell me
> ere we turn away:
> where do the cairns lie
> called after Hjörvard?

---

[1] The *HU*-version has more verses here than *R* has; see Appendix A (IV).
[2] *eyjar-skeggjar*, lit. 'island-bearded,' a name (found also elsewhere) supposed to have arisen simply from the unkempt hair and wild appearance of the dwellers on remote islands.

Hann kvað:
> (20) Spyrjattu at því,
> spakr ertu eigi,[a]
> vinr víkinga,
> ertu vanfarinn;
> fǫrum fráliga,
> sem okkr fœtr toga;
> allt er úti
> ámátt[b] firum.

Hon kvað:
> (21) Hirðum ei at fælask
> við fnǫsun[c] slíka,
> þótt um alla ey
> eldar brenni;
> látum okkr eigi
> lítit hræða
> rekka slíka,
> rœðumk fleira við![d]

Hann kvað:
> (22) Heimskr þykki mér
> sá er heðan[e] ferr,
> maðr einn saman
> myrkvar grímur;
> hyrr er á sveimun,
> haugar opnask,
> brenn fold ok fen,
> fǫrum harðara!

Enda tók hann þá hlaup heim til bœjar, ok skildi þar með þeim. Nú sér hon því næst út á eyna, hvar haugaeldrinn[1] brenn, ok gengr hon þangat til ok hræðisk ekki, þótt allir haugir væri á gǫtu hennar. Hon óð fram í þessa elda sem í myrkva, þar til er hon kom at haugi berserkjanna.

[a] eingi R
[b] úti ámátt H, víti á nátt (?) R; hverfum heim báðir U line 8
[c] fnǫsun H, þrǫsun R, line om. U
[d] látum . . . við R and similarly U; látum eigi okkr / rekka liðna (*read* liðna rekka) / skjótla skelfa, / skulum við talask H
[e] heðra H, til hauga U

Then the herdsman said:

> (20) Do not ask me —
> you are not wise!
> Friend of vikings,
> you are far astray;
> fare we as fast as
> feet can bear us —
> out in the open
> all is evil for men.

She answered:

> (21) We'll not faint nor fear
> at such fire's crackling,
> though all the land
> be alight with flame;
> men such as these
> are matter too small
> to make us tremble —
> let us talk further!

He spoke:

> (22) Fool I call him
> who fares onward,
> a man all alone
> in the murky night;
> fires are moving,
> mounds are opening,
> burns field and fen —
> let us faster run!

And he ran off home to the farm, and thus they parted. Now Hervör saw where out upon the island burned the fire of the barrows,[1] and she went towards it without fear, though all the mounds were on her path. She made her way into these fires as if they were no more than mist, until she came to the barrow of the berserks.

---

[1] *hauga-eldrinn*: the fire that burns over treasure hidden in burial-mounds, called also *málmlogi* or *vaflogi*, 'metal-fire,' 'hovering fire,' a widespread belief for many ages; many examples from a later period are given by Jón Árnason, *Íslenzkar þjóðsögur og Æfintýri* I, 1862, 276 ff.

Þá kvað hon:

(23) Vaki þú, Angantýr,
vekr þik Hervǫr,
eingadóttir
ykkr Sváfu *a* 1;
selðu *b* ór haugi
hvassan mæki,
þann er Sigrlama *c*
slógu dvergar.

(24) Hervarðr, Hjǫrvarðr,
Hrani, Angantýr!
Vek ek yðr alla
undir viðar rótum,
hjálmi 2 ok með brynju,
hvǫssu *d* sverði,
rǫnd ok með reiði, *e*
roðnum geiri.

(25) Mjǫk eru orðnir
Arngríms synir,
megir meingjarnir, *f*
at moldarauka, 3
er engi gerir *g*
sona Eyfuru
við mik mæla
í Munarvági. *h*

(26) Hervarðr, Hjǫrvarðr,
Hrani, Angantýr!
Svá sé yðr ǫllum
innan rifja
sem þer í maura

a Sváfu *RU*, Tófu *H*   *b* selðu mér *HU*   *c* Svafrlama *HU*
d hvǫssu *HU*, hǫssu *R*   *e* reiði *HU*, om. *R*
f thus *U*, megin meingjarnar *R*, megir at meinsamir *H*
g gerir *RU*, skal *H*
h Munarvági *RH*, Munarheimi *U* (*elsewhere always* Un-)

1 Tófa, Hervör's mother in the *H*-version, is not otherwise mentioned in the saga; in *H*'s prose she is left unnamed.

Then she spoke:

(23) Wake, Angantýr,
wakes you Hervör,
Sváfa's[1] offspring,
your only daughter;
the keen-edged blade
from the barrow give me,
the sword dwarf-smithied
for Sigrlami.

(24) Hervard, Hjörvard,
Hrani, Angantýr!
From the roots of the tree
I arouse you all,
with[2] helm and corslet,
keen-edged weapon,
gear and buckler
and graven spear.

(25) All but to dust
have Arngrím's children,
men of evil,
in the mound been turned,[3]
if of Eyfura's sons
no single one
to me will speak
in Munarvág.

(26) Hervard, Hjörvard,
Hrani, Angantýr!
May it seem to you all
within your ribs
as if in mound of maggots

---

[2] The second half of this verse may refer to Hervör (cf. verse ii in Appendix A (V)), or to the dead berserks, who were 'laid in a mound on Sámsey with all their weapons.'

[3] Lit. 'Arngrím's sons have as good as become increase of mould' (*moldarauki*), i.e. they have nearly turned to dust in the barrow.

                    mornið haugi,
                    nema sverð selið
                    þat er sló Dvalinn¹;
                    samir ei draugum
                    dýrt^a vápn bera.^b

Þá kvað Angantýr:
        (27)   Hervǫr dóttir,
                    hvat^c kallar svá?
                    Full feiknstafa
                    ferr þú þér at illu;
                    œr ertu orðin
                    ok ørviti,²
                    villhyggjandi,
                    vekr upp dauða menn.^d

        (28)³   Gróf ei mik faðir^e
                    né frændr aðrir;
                    þeir hǫfðu Tyrfing
                    tveir, er lifðu,⁴
                    varð þó eigandi
                    einn um síðir.^f

Hon kvað:
        (29)⁵   Segir þú eigi satt,^g
                    svá láti áss þik
                    heilan í haugi,^h
                    sem þú hafir eigi
                    Tyrfing með þérⁱ;
                    trauðr ertu^k
                    arf at veita^l
                    eingabarni.^m

---

^a dýrt *RU*, dýr *H*   ^b fela *HU*   ^c hví *HU*
^d dauða menn *RU*, *reversed H*   ^e faðir niðr *HU*
^f varð ... síðir *HU*, urðu eigandi / enn um síðir *R*
^g eigi (einn *H*) satt mér *HU*   ^h haugi *HU*, haugi sitja *R*
ⁱ með þér *HU*, om. *R*   ^k *thus R*, trautt er þér at veita *HU*
^l *thus R*, arfa þínum *H*, arf, Angantýr *U*   ^m *thus RU*, einar bœnir *H*

¹ Dvalin seems to have been one of the most renowned of all the dwarfs, and often appears in the Eddaic poetry (especially *Vǫluspá* 14, *Fáfnismál* 13, *Hávamál* 143).

>   you mouldered away,
>   if you fetch not the sword
>   forged by Dvalin[1];
>   it becomes not ghosts
>   costly arms to bear.

Then Angantýr answered her:

> (27) Why do you hail me,
>   Hervör, daughter?
>   To your doom you are faring
>   filled with evil!
>   Mad you are now,
>   your mind darkened,[2]
>   when with wits wandering
>   you wake the dead.
>
> (28)[3] No father or kinsman
>   in cairn laid me;
>   they kept Tyrfing,
>   the two survivors[4] —
>   one alone did
>   wield it after.

Hervör answered:

> (29)[5] You give me a lie!
>   May the god let you
>   rest whole in your howe
>   if you're holding not
>   Tyrfing with you;
>   unwilling you are
>   to give the heirloom
>   to your only child.

---

[2] These two lines are found in three poems of the Edda (*Lex. Poet.* s.v. *œrr*).

[3] Two lines are clearly missing from this verse, probably after line 2; Bugge suggested 'It was our slayers who laid us in the mound' (implying 'And so I did not receive my sword in burial').

[4] i.e. the two who were still alive when Angantýr died, Hjálmar and Arrow-Odd.

[5] This verse is obviously badly corrupted. No doubt originally there was a stop at the end of the fourth line: 'if you have it not!'

Þá opnaðisk haugrinn, ok var sem eldr ok logi væri allr haugrinn.
Þá kvað Angantýr:

(30) Hnigin er helgrind,
haugar opnask,
allr[a] er í eldi
eybarmr at sjá[b];
atalt er úti
um at lítask,
skyntu, mær, ef þú mátt,
til skipa þinna.

Hon svarar:

(31) Brennið eigi svá
bál á nóttum,
at ek við elda
yðra hræðumk[c];
skelfr eigi meyju
muntún[1] hugar,
þótt hon draug sjái
fyrir[d] durum standa.

Þá kvað Angantýr:

(32) Segi ek þér, Hervǫr,
hlýð þú til enn,[e]
vísa dóttir,
þat er verða mun:
sjá mun Tyrfingr,
ef þú trúa mættir,
ætt þinni, mær,
allri spilla.[2]

(33) Muntu[3] son geta
þann er síðan mun
Tyrfing hafa[f]
ok trúa magni[g];

[a] allr H, allt R, verse om. U [b] thus H, eygrims sjá R
[c] fælumk H, verse om. U [d] í H
[e] thus R, hlýttu til meðan H, om. U [f] hafa RU, bera H
[g] magni RU, afli H

[1] *mun-tún* is not known elsewhere, but there are many other kennings of similar type; lit. 'the house, enclosed place (*tún*) of the mind,' i.e. the breast.

Then the barrow opened, and it was as if the whole mound were fire and flame. Angantýr spoke again:

> (30) Hel's gate is lifted,
> howes are opening,
> the isle's border
> ablaze before you;
> grim outside now
> to gaze around you —
> to your ships, if you can,
> quick now, maiden!

She answered:

> (31) No blaze can you light,
> burning in darkness,
> that your funeral fires
> should with fear daunt me;
> unmoved shall remain
> the maiden's spirit,[1]
> though she gaze on a ghost
> in the grave-door standing.

Then Angantýr said:

> (32) I tell you, Hervör —
> hear my words out! —
> what shall come to pass,
> prince's daughter:
> trust what I tell you,
> Tyrfing, daughter,
> shall be ruin and end
> of all your family.[2]
>
> (33) You[3] shall bear offspring
> who in after days
> shall wield Tyrfing
> and trust in his strength;

---

[2] On the significance of this prophecy see Introduction pp. x-xi.

[3] It is strange that Angantýr, who is not yet persuaded to yield up the sword, should here tell Hervör that she will have a son who will, in fact, wield it. The verse must be displaced from a point later in the poem.

þann munu^a Heiðrek
heita lýðar,
sá mun ríkastr alinn
undir rǫðuls tjaldi.¹

Þá kvað Hervǫr:

(34) Maðr þóttumk ek
mennskr til^b þessa,
áðr ek sali yðra
sœkja réðak^c;
sel þú mér ór haugi
þann er hatar brynjur,
hlífum hættan,
Hjálmars bana.^d

Þá kvað Angantýr:

(35) Liggr mér undir herðum
Hjálmars bani,
allr er hann útan
eldi sveipinn^e;
mey veit ek enga
fyrir mold ofan^f
at hjǫr þann^g þori
í hǫnd bera.^h

Hervǫr kvað:

(36) Ek mun hirða
ok í hǫnd^j nema
hvassan mæki,
ef ek hafa mættak;
uggi ek eigi
eld brennanda;
þegar loga lægir
er ek lít yfir.^k

---

^a munu *H*, mun *RU*   ^b til *HU*, om. *R*
^c thus *H*, sœkja hafðak *R*, tók kanna *U*
^d hlífum ... bana *R*; see *Appendix A (V)*
^e sveipinn *HU*, svifinn (*with* e *over first* i) *R*
^f thus *R*, moldar hvergi *HU*   ^g þann hjǫr *HU*
^h nema *HU*   ^j í hǫnd *RU*, í hendr *H*
^k þegar ... yfir *RH*, þann er framliðnum / fyrðum leikr um sjónir *U*

> by the name Heidrek
> known to his people,
> born the strongest
> beneath the sun's curtain.[1]

Then Hervör said:

> (34) A human indeed
> I was held to be
> ere I came hither
> your hall seeking;
> hater of mailcoats
> from the mound give me,
> peril to bucklers,
> bane of Hjálmar!

Angantýr answered:

> (35) Beneath my back is laid
> the bane of Hjálmar,
> all around it
> enwrapped with fire;
> in the world walking
> no woman know I
> who would dare in her hand
> to hold this sword.

Then Hervör said:

> (36) I will guard it
> and grasp it in hand,
> the keen-edged sword,
> can I but obtain it;
> no fear have I
> of the fire burning;
> the flame grows less
> as I look towards it.

---

[1] *rǫðuls tjald*: *tjald* means a tent, curtaining, or wall-hangings; it is common in kennings for the sky, as here. — After this verse there is an omission of two in *R*, which are given in Appendix A (V).

Þá kvað Angantýr:

(37) Heimsk^a ertu, Hervǫr,
hugar eigandi,
er þú at augum
í eld hrapar;
heldr vil ek selja þér
sverð^b ór haugi,
mær in unga,
má ek þér ei synja.

Hervǫr kvað^c:

(38) Vel gerðir þú,
víkinga niðr,
er þú seldir mér
sverð ór haugi;
betr þykkjumk nú,
bragningr,^d hafa,
en ek Nóregi
næðak ǫllum.

Angantýr kvað:

(39) Veizt eigi þú,
vesǫl ertu máls,^e
fullfeikn^f kona,
hví þu fagna skalt;
sjá mun Tyrfingr,
ef þú trúa mættir,
ætt^g þinni, mær,
allri spilla.^h

Hon segir:

(40) Ek mun ganga
til gjálfrmara,[1]
nú er hilmis mær
í hugaⁱ góðum;

---

^a heimsk *RHU*, heimsks *Skj*.
^b heldr . . . sverð *RH* (ek vil heldr *H*), selja *and* sverð *reversed U*
^c Hervǫr kvað *om. R*   ^d buðlungr *HU*
^e mála *HU*   ^f fláráð *HU*   ^g ætt *U, om. R* (*cf. verse 32*)
^h sjá mun . . . spilla *RU, om. H*   ⁱ hugum *H*, hug *U*

Angantýr answered:

> (37) Fool you are, Hervör,
> in your heart's daring,
> with eyes open
> to enter the fire!
> The blade from the barrow
> I will bring, rather;
> O young maiden,
> I may not refuse you.

Hervör answered:

> (38) Son of warriors,
> you do well in this,
> the blade to me
> from the barrow yielding;
> king, to keep it
> I count it dearer
> than were all Norway
> beneath my hand.

Angantýr spoke:

> (39) You see it not —
> you're in speech accursed,
> woman of evil! —
> why you're rejoicing;
> trust what I tell you,
> Tyrfing, daughter,
> shall be ruin and end
> of all your family.

Hervör spoke:

> (40) I will go my way
> to the wave-horses,[1]
> chieftain's daughter
> cheerful-hearted;

---

[1] *gjálfr-marr* 'sea-horse,' i.e. ship

lítt rœki ek þat,[a]
lofðunga vinr,[b]
hvat[c] synir[d] mínir
síðan deila.[e]

Hann kvað:

(41) Þú skalt eiga
ok una lengi,
hafðu á hulðu
Hjálmars bana;
takattu á eggjum,
eitr er í báðum;
sá er manns mjǫtuðr
meini verri.

(42) Far vel, dóttir,
fljótt gæfa ek þér
tólf manna fjǫr,
ef þú trúa mættir,
afl ok eljun,
allt it góða,
þat er synir Arngríms
at sik[f] leifðu.

Hon kvað:

(43) Búi þér allir,
brott fýsir mik,
heilir í haugi,
heðan vil ek skjótla[g];
helzt þóttumk nú
heima í millim,
er mik umhverfis
eldar brunnu.

[a] *thus RU*, lítt hræðumk þat *H*
[b] vinr *RU*, niðr *H*
[c] hvat *RU*, hvé *H*
[d] *after* synir *the lacuna begins in R*
[e] deila *H*, telja *U*
[f] at sik *H*, eptir *U*
[g] brott ... skjótla *H*, fysir mik *and* vil (mun *U*) ek skjótla *reversed U*

> I care not at all
> O kings' companion,
> how my sons shall
> strive hereafter.

Angantýr spoke:

> (41) You shall keep Tyrfing
> with contentment long;
> the bane of Hjálmar
> in hiding keep;
> touch not the edges —
> in each is poison;
> worse than deadly,
> doom-bringer to men.
>
> (42) Fare well, daughter!
> fain would I give you
> twelve heroes' lives —
> trust what I tell you! —
> the goodly strength
> and strong endurance
> that Arngrím's sons
> left after them.

And now Hervör said:

> (43) May you all lie unharmed
> in the howe resting —
> to hasten hence
> my heart urges;
> I seemed to myself
> to be set between worlds,
> when all about me
> burnt the cairn-fires.

4

Hervǫr[a] fór nú ofan til strandar, ok er dagaði, sá hon at skip váru burt, ok hǫfðu víkingar hrazk, er þeir heyrðu dunur ok sá elda á eynni.

Hervǫr dvalðisk nú í Sámsey, þar til hon fekk sér far í burt; er nú eigi sagt frá ferðum hennar, fyrr en hon kom til Guðmundar[1] konungs af Glasisvǫllum[b]; hon nefndisk þá enn Hervarðr ok lét sem væri ein kempa. Þessi Hervarðr var þar einkanliga vel tekinn. Hafði Guðmundr konungr mikinn mannfjǫlða; hann var þá[c] svá gamall, at þat er sǫgn manna, at hann skorti eigi á hundrað[d] vetra, ok var þó hraustr maðr. Hǫfundr sonr hans var þá fullroskinn; var hann þá at ǫllum stórmálum kallaðr.

Þat bar þar til eitt sinn, at Guðmundr konungr lék at tafli ok var á hann tafli mjǫk leikit. Þá spurði konungr, ef nǫkkurr maðr væri sá þar, er honum kynni ráð til tafls at leggja. Þá stóð upp Hervarðr ok gekk til taflsins, ok hafði hann litla hríð ráðit taflinu, áðr en konungi gekk betr. En á meðan Hervarðr[e] var at taflinu, hafði einn hirðmaðr konungs tekit upp sverðit Tyrfing ok brugðit ok mælti, at hann sá aldri betra sverð; ok sem Hervarðr heyrði þat ok sér beran Tyrfing, er lýsti af um hǫllina sem sólargeisla, þá snýr Hervarðr þangat ok þrífr til sverðsins ok hjó af þeim hǫfuðit, sem brugðit hafði. Eptir þat snýr Hervarðr þegar út. Menn konungs eggjuðusk at fara eptir honum, at hefna lagsmanns síns. Konungr svarar ok bað þá vera kyrra,—'mun yðr þykkja í manni þessum minni hefnd, en þér ætlið, því kvennmann ætla ek hann vera[f]; hygg ek þó við þat vápn, er hon hefir, at hverjum yðar yrði dýrkeypt, at taka hana af lífi.'

Hervǫr kom sér til víkinga ok var í hernaði um hríð; en er henni leiddisk svá vera, fór hon til Bjarmars[g] jarls ok settisk til hannyrðanáms. Fór nú mikil fregn af fríðleik hennar.

Hǫfundr sonr Guðmundar konungs beiddi fǫður sinn, at honum skyldi ráðs leita, ok vill hann kvángask. Guðmundr konungr tók því vel ok segir, at Hervǫr dóttir Angantýs var þá heima hjá Bjarmari jarli fóstra sínum, segir, at sá kostr þótti beztr ok allgǫfgastr þeira er

---

[a] U followed from this point [b] blæis- U (for Glæsis-)
[c] þó U [d] um hundruð U [e] Hjǫrvarðr U
[f] ætla ek hann vera om. U [g] Bjartmars U (with -t- throughout)

[1] On Gudmund of Glasisvellir see Appendix B

4

Now Hervör went down to the shore, and when the dawn came she saw that the ships were gone, and that the vikings had taken fright when they heard the thunders and saw the fires on the island.

Hervör tarried then on Sámsey until she got a passage away, and of her travels nothing more is told until she came to King Gudmund[1] of Glasisvellir; she still called herself Hervard, and behaved like any warrior. This Hervard was received extremely well. King Gudmund had a great following; and he was then so old that his years were not short of a hundred, so men say, yet he was still an active man. His son Höfund was at that time a grown man, and he was summoned to counsel in all matters of great moment.

It happened one day that King Gudmund was playing at chess, and was getting very much the worst of the game; the king asked whether there was anyone who could give him advice on his play. Then Hervard stood up and went to the board, and did not long have a hand in the game before the king's fortune turned. But while Hervard was at chess one of the king's courtiers had taken up the sword Tyrfing and drawn it, saying that he had never seen a better blade; and when Hervard heard this, and saw Tyrfing unsheathed, as it flashed like a sunbeam through the hall, she swung round and snatched the sword and struck off the head of the man who had drawn it. After that Hervard at once went out. The king's men egged one another on to pursue Hervard and take revenge for their companion; but the king spoke and told them to be still—'for your vengeance on this man,' he said, 'will seem smaller than you now think, because it is my guess that he is a woman; but I think that with that weapon which she wields her slaying will be dearly bought by every man of you.'

Hervör went off to join vikings, and was out raiding for a time; and when she grew weary of that she went to Bjarmar the jarl, and settled down to fine work with her hands. Many tales were then told of her beauty.

Höfund, the son of King Gudmund, asked his father to make a match for him, for he wished to marry. King Gudmund received this well, and said that Hervör the daughter of Angantýr was then at the house of the jarl Bjarmar, her foster-father; this match, he said, was thought the best and the most illustrious of any that he knew of. Then

hann vissi. Váru þá menn sendir til Bjarmars jarls með þessari mála-
leitan. Jarl tók því vel, en Hervǫr veitti eigi afsvǫr ok bað jarl sjá fyrir
sínum kosti. Var þetta þá at ráði gǫrt, at Hervǫr var gipt Hǫfundi.
Þau áttu tvá sonu; hét inn eldri Angantýr, en inn yngri Heiðrekr.
Hvárrtveggi þeira var inn fríðasti at sjá, meiri ok sterkari en aðrir
menn; báðir váru þeir spakir at viti ok inir mestu atgørvismenn.
Angantýr var líkr fǫður sínum at skaplyndi ok vildi hverjum manni
gott; faðir hans unni honum mikit, ok við alla alþýðu var hann vinsæll.
En svá mart gott sem hann gerði, þá gerði Heiðrekr engum manni
færa þat illt var; Hervǫr unni honum meira. Hǫfundr sendi Heiðrek
þá í burt til fóstrs þeim manni, er Gizurr[1] hét; hann var manna
vitrastr; ok fœddisk Heiðrekr þar upp.

Þat var einn tíma, at Hǫfundr lét gera veizlu mikla á Grund, ok
bauð til sín ǫllum stórmenni um ríki sitt, nema Heiðreki ok Gizuri.
En er veizlan var sett ok menn sátu við drykk, þá kom þar Heiðrekr
konungssonr inn gangandi; því urðu menn ófegnir. Angantýr bauð
honum til sætis hjá sér; þat þektisk hann.

Hann[a] var ekki kátr ok sat lengi við drykkju um kveldit; en er
Angantýr bróðir hans gekk út, þá talaði Heiðrekr við þá menn er honum
váru næstir, ok kom hann svá sinni rœðu, at þeir urðu rangsáttir,
ok mælti hvárr illt við annan. Þá kom Angantýr aptr ok bað þá
þegja. Ok enn í annat sinn, er Angantýr var út genginn, þá minnti
Heiðrekr þá á, hvat þeir hǫfðu við mælzk, ok kom þá svá, at annarr
sló annan með hnefa. Þá kom Angantýr til ok bað þá sátta vera til
morgins. Enn þriðja sinn,[b] er Angantýr gekk í brott, þá spurði Heiðrekr þann, er hǫggit hafði fengit, hvárt hann þyrði eigi at hefna sín;
svá kom hann þá sinni fortǫlu, at inn lostni hljóp upp ok drap sessunaut
sinn; ok þá kom Angantýr at. En er Hǫfundr varð þessa varr, bað
hann Heiðrek burt ganga ok gera eigi fleira illt í þat sinn. Síðan gekk
Heiðrekr út ok Angantýr bróðir hans ok í garðinn ok skilðusk þar.

Þá er Heiðrekr hafði litla hríð gengit frá bœnum, þá hugsaði hann,
at hann hafði þar of lítit illt gǫrt, snýr þá aptr til hallarinnar ok tók upp
stein einn mikinn ok kastaði þangat, sem hann heyrði menn nǫkkura
talask við í myrkrinu. Hann fann, at steininn mundi eigi mannin

---

[a] R resumes with ... sér. Hann var ekki kátr, etc.
[b] sinn om. R

[1] On Gizur see Introduction p. xvii.

men were sent to jarl Bjarmar to negotiate, and the jarl received it well; Hervör did not refuse, and told the jarl to act on her behalf. And so it was resolved, and Hervör was married to Höfund.

They had two sons; the elder was called Angantýr, and the younger Heidrek. Both of them were beautiful in face, and bigger and stronger than other men; both were wise in understanding and men of the greatest accomplishment. Angantýr was like his father in nature, and wished everybody well; his father loved him deeply, and he was much liked by the whole people. But as much good as Angantýr did, so much more mischief than any other man did Heidrek do; and it was him that Hervör loved the more. Höfund sent Heidrek away to be fostered by Gizur,[1] wisest of men, and with him Heidrek was brought up.

One day Höfund had a great feast made at Grund, and he invited to it all the men of rank in his kingdom, except Heidrek and Gizur. And when the feast was prepared and men sat drinking, in walked Heidrek the king's son; no-one there was glad to see him. Angantýr offered him a seat beside him, and that Heidrek accepted.

He was gloomy, and sat drinking far into the evening; but when his brother Angantýr went out Heidrek began to talk to the men who were next to him, and such a turn did he give to his words that they fell out, and each abused the other; but then Angantýr came back and told them to be still. Again a second time, when Angantýr had gone out, Heidrek reminded them of what they had said; and it ended with one of them striking the other with his fist. Then Angantýr came up and told them to be at peace till morning. But when Angantýr went away for the third time Heidrek asked the man who had been given the blow whether he had not the courage to avenge himself; and he so worked on him with his persuasions that the one who had been struck leapt up and slew his bench-fellow. Then Angantýr came in. But when Höfund heard of this he told Heidrek to go away and make no more mischief at that time; and afterwards Heidrek went out with his brother Angantýr into the courtyard, and there they parted.

When Heidrek had walked from the buildings for a short time, it came into his heart that he had not yet done enough harm, and turning back towards the hall he took up a great stone and hurled it in the direction from which he heard men talking together in the darkness. He

misst hafa, ok gekk til ok fann mann dauðan ok kenndi Angantý bróður sinn.

Heiðrekr gekk þá í hǫllina fyrir fǫður sinn ok segir honum þetta. Hǫfundr kveðr hann skulu verða í brottu ok koma aldri honum í augsýn ok kvað hitt makligra, at hann væri drepinn eða hengdr.[a] Þá mælti Hervǫr drottning ok segir, at Heiðrekr hefir illa til gǫrt, enda er mikil hefndin, ef hann skal aldri koma í ríki fǫður síns ok fara svá eignalauss í brott. En orð Hǫfundar stóðusk svá mikils, at þat gekk fram, sem hann dœmði, ok engi var svá djarfr, at móti þyrði at mæla eða Heiðreki friðar at biðja. Drottning bað þá Hǫfund ráða honum nǫkkur heilræði[1] at skilnaði þeira.

Hǫfundr kvezk fá ráð mundu honum kenna ok kvezk hyggja, at honum mundi illa í hald[b] koma, 'en þó, er þú biðr þessa, drottning, þat ræð ek honum it fyrsta ráð, at hann hjálpi aldri þeim manni, er drepit hefir lánardrottin sinn. Þat ræð ek honum annat, at hann gefi þeim manni aldri fríun, er myrðan hefir félaga sinn; þat it þriðja, at hann láti eigi opt konu sína vitja frænda sinna, þótt hon beiði þess; þat it fjórða, at hann sé eigi síð úti staddr hjá frillu sinni; þat it fimmta, at hann ríði eigi inum bezta hesti sínum, ef hann þarf mjǫk at skynda; þat it sétta, at hann fóstri aldri gǫfugra manns barn en hann er sjálfr.[2] En meiri ván þykkir mér, at þú munir þetta eigi hafa.'

Heiðrekr sagði at hann hefði við illan hug ráðit, ok kvað sér mundu óskylt at hafa. Gengr þá Heiðrekr út ór hǫllinni. Móðir hans stendr þá upp ok gengr út með honum ok fylgir honum ór garðinum ok mælti, 'Nú hefir þú svá fyrir þér búit, sonr minn, at þú munt ekki aptr ætla; þá hefi ek litil fǫng á at hjálpa þér. Mǫrk[3] gulls er hér ok eitt sverð, er ek vil gefa þér; en þat heitir Tyrfingr, ok hefir átt Angantýr berserkr, móðurfaðir þinn; engi[c] maðr er svá ófróðr at eigi hafi heyrt hans getit; ok ef þú kømr þar er menn skiptask hǫggum, láttu þér hugkvæmt vera, hversu Tyrfingr hefir oft sigrsæll verit.' Nú biðr hon hann vel fara, ok skiljask síðan.

---

[a] hengt *R*   [b] haldi *R*   [c] eing *R*

[1] Höfund's good advice, and the story of Heidreks treatment of it, is discussed in the Introduction, pp. xiv ff.

[2] 'People say that he who fosters another's child is himself of less distinction,' *Haralds Saga Hárfagra* ch. 40.

[3] See Glossary s.v. *mǫrk*

heard that the stone did not miss its mark, and he went there and found a man lying dead; and he recognised his brother Angantýr.

Then Heidrek went into the hall and stood before his father, and told him what had come to pass. Höfund said that Heidrek must go, and never come into his sight again; he said that he deserved rather to be struck down or hanged. Then Hervör the queen spoke and said that Heidrek's act indeed deserved ill, but that the vengeance would be heavy if he were never again to enter the realm of his father and to journey thus empty-handed away. But the word of Höfund carried such weight that things went as he had given judgment, and no-one was bold enough to dare gainsay it, or sue for peace for Heidrek. Then the queen asked Höfund to give him some good advice[1] at their parting.

Höfund said that in few matters would he give him counsel, and that he thought it would be of little use to him—'but since you ask this, queen, this counsel I give him first, that he give no help to a man who has slain his lord; and I counsel him second, never to deliver a man who has murdered his fellow; third, not to allow his wife to be often visiting her kinsfolk, even though she entreat him; fourth, not to be late abroad with his mistress; fifth, not to ride his best horse when he is in a great hurry; and sixth, never to foster the son of a man more powerful than he is himself.[2] But I think it more than likely that you will make no use of this.'

Heidrek said that Höfund had given this advice with evil intent, and that he was not obliged to observe it. Then he went out of the hall. His mother rose and went out with him; she accompanied him out of the courtyard, and said, 'My son, you have now so done for yourself that you will not be thinking of coming back, and I can do little to help you. But here is a mark[3] of gold and a sword, which I will give you; the sword is called Tyrfing, which your mother's father, Angantýr the berserk, owned—there is no-one so ignorant that he has not heard tell of him; and if you find yourself where blows are being given, never let it leave your mind how often Tyrfing has gained the victory.' She wished him farewell; and then they parted.

5

En er Heiðrekr hefir skamma hríð farit, þá hittir hann menn nǫkkura ok einn bundinn; spyrjask þeir tíðenda, ok spyrr Heiðrekr, hvat þessi maðr hefði gǫrt, er svá var við búit. Þeir segja, at hann hefir svikit lánardrottin sinn. Heiðrekr spyrr, ef þeir vili taka fé fyrir hann, en þeir játa því; hann fær þeim hálfa mǫrk gulls, en þeir láta hann lausan. Sá býðr Heiðreki sína þjónustu; en hann segir, 'Hví muntu mér heldr trúr, ókunnum manni, en þú sveikt lánardrottin þinn, ok far þú brott frá mér.'

Litlu síðar hittir Heiðrekr enn nǫkkura menn ok einn bundinn. Hann spyrr, hvat sá hefir rangt gǫrt; þeir segja hann hafa myrðan félaga sinn. Hann spyrr, ef þeir vildi fé fyrir hann; þeir játa því; hann gaf þeim aðra hálfa mǫrk gulls. Sá býðr Heiðreki sína þjónustu, en hann neitar.

Síðan ferr Heiðrekr langar leiðar ok kømr þar, er hét Reiðgotaland.[1] Þar réð fyrir konungr sá, er Haraldr hét, gamall mjǫk, ok hafði átt mikit ríki til forráða; hann átti engan son. En með því minnkaðisk hans ríki, at jarlar nǫkkurir fóru á hendr honum með her, en hann hafði barizk við þá ok fengit jafnan ósigr; en nú hǫfðu þeir sæzk með því móti, at konungr galt þeim skatt á hverjum tólf mánuðum. Heiðrekr nam þar staðar ok dvalðisk með konungi um vetrinn.

Svá bar at eitt sinn, at til konungs kom mikit lausafé; þá spyrr Heiðrekr, hvárt þat væri skattar konungs.

Konungr segir, at þat veit annan veg við; 'skal ek þetta fé gjalda í skatt.'

Heiðrekr segir, at þat væri ósœmiligt, at konungr sá, er svá hefði haft mikit ríki, gyldi skatt vándum jǫrlum; væri meira snjallræði at halda orrostu í mót þeim. Konungr segir, at hann hefði þess freistat ok farit ósigr.

Heiðrekr mælti, 'Svá munda ek yðr mega helzt launa gott yfirlæti at vera hǫfuðsmaðr þessar farar, ok þat hugða ek, ef ek hefða liðskost, at mér mundi ekki mikit þykkja at berjask einn[2] við tignari menn en þessir eru.'

---

[1] On Reidgotaland see Introduction p. xxvi
[2] *berjask einn* 'to fight alone' does not square with *ef ek hefða liðskost*; perhaps *einn* is an error for *enn* 'yet, still.'

5

Now when Heidrek had journeyed for a little while he fell in with some men, and one of them was bound; they asked each other for news, and Heidrek asked what the man had done, who was treated in this way. They answered that he had betrayed his lord. Then Heidrek asked if they would accept a ransom for him, and when they said that they would he gave them half a mark of gold, and they let the man go free. He offered Heidrek his service, but he answered, 'Why should you, who have betrayed your own lord, be any more faithful to me, a stranger? Get away from me!'

Not long after Heidrek again met some men, and one of them bound. He asked what crime he had committed, and they told him that he had murdered his comrade. He asked if they would take a ransom for him; they said that they would, and he gave them the other half mark of gold. This man also offered Heidrek his service, but again he refused it.

Long were the roads that Heidrek travelled after that, until he came to the country called Reidgotaland.[1] There ruled a king whose name was Harald, very aged, and he had held a great realm under his hand; he had no son. But his authority was diminished, for there were certain jarls, who made war upon him with their army; he had fought with them, but always been worsted; and now they had made peace on the condition that every twelve months the king should pay them tribute. In this land Heidrek rested, and dwelt with the king over winter.

Now it happened one time that a great quantity of goods and money was brought to the king, and Heidrek asked whether this was tribute to him; but the king replied that the case was very different — 'I must pay this money out in tribute myself.' Heidrek said that it was a shameful thing that a king who had held dominion over so wide a realm should pay tribute to these evil jarls, and that it would be a better course to make war upon them; but the king answered that he had attempted that, and been worsted.

'I would best be able to repay you for your good favour,' said Heidrek then, 'by becoming the leader of this enterprise; and it has come into my mind that if I had the men it would not seem to me a great matter to fight[2] with men of higher estate than these are.'

Konungr segir, 'Ek mun fá þér liðskost, ef þú vilt berjask við jarla, ok mun þat vera þín gæfufǫr, ef þú ferr góða fǫr; mest ván ok, at þú finnir sjálfan þik fyrir, ef þú mælir þér dul.'

Eptir þat lætr konungr safna her miklum, ok var þat lið búit til herferðar. Þar var Heiðrekr hǫfðingi fyrir liðinu; fóru síðan á hendr jǫrlum þessum, herja þegar ok ræna, er þeir koma í ríki þeira. En er jarlar spyrja þetta, þá fóru þeir í mót þeim með mikinn her, ok er þeir finnask, þá varð orrosta mikil; var Heiðrekr þá í ǫndverðri fylking ok hafði Tyrfing í hœgri hendi, en við því sverði stóð ekki, hvárki hjálmr né brynja, ok drap hann þá alla, er honum váru næstir, ok þá hljóp hann fram ór fylkingu ok hjó til beggja handa, ok svá fór hann langt í herinn, at hann drap báða jarla, ok síðan flýði sumt lið, en mestr hluti var drepinn. Heiðrekr fór þá yfir ríkit ok skattaði allt landit undir Harald konung, sem fyrr hafði verit; ferr heim við svá búit með ógrynni fjár ok mikinn sigr. Haraldr konungr lætr þá ganga í mót honum með mikilli sœmð ok býðr honum með sér at vera ok hafa svá mikit ríki, sem hann beiðisk sjálfr.

Þá bað Heiðrekr dóttur Haralds konungs, er Helga hét, ok hon var honum gipt. Tók þá Heiðrekr til forráða hálft ríki Haralds konungs. Heiðrekr gat son við konu sinni; sá hét Angantýr. Haraldr gat son í elli sinni, ok er sá ekki nefndr.[1]

---

[1] According to H and U he was called Hálfdan.

'I will give you a force of men,' answered the king, 'if you will fight with the jarls, and this expedition will make your fortune, if you suceed in it; but if you deceive yourself, it is more than likely that it is you that will pay dearly for the error.'

After that the king had a great host gathered, and the force was made ready for the campaign; Heidrek was captain of the host. They went then against these jarls, and when they came into their realm they began at once to rob and to ravage. When the jarls heard of it they went out against them with a great army, and at their meeting there arose a mighty battle. Heidrek was in the forefront, and he held Tyrfing in his right hand; nothing withstood that sword, neither helm nor corslet, but he slew all before him, and then he rushed forward from the rank and hewed on both sides, and made his way so far into the opposing host that he slew both the jarls. Then some of their army turned to flight, but the most part were slain. Heidrek passed over that land, laying it under tribute to King Harald, as it had been before; and with matters thus he returned home with great triumph and uncounted wealth. King Harald had him met with great honour, and invited him to stay with him, and possess as great a domain as he should ask for.

Then Heidrek asked for the daughter of King Harald, whose name was Helga, and she was married to him; and Heidrek took over the rule of half the realm of King Harald. Heidrek had a son by his wife, and he was called Angantýr; King Harald also had a son in his old age, but his name is not told.[1]

6

Í þann tíma kom hallæri mikit á Reiðgotaland, svá at til landauðnar þótti horfa. Þá váru gǫrvir hlutir af vísendamǫnnum ok felldr[1] blótspánn[2] til, en svá gekk frétt,*a* at aldri mundi ár koma*b* fyrr á Reiðgotaland en þeim sveini væri blótat, er œztr væri á landinu. Haraldr konungr segir, at sonr Heiðreks væri œztr, en Heiðrekr segir, at sonr Haralds konungs væri œztr; en ór þessu mátti engi leysa fyrr en þangat væri farit, er allar órlausnir váru trúar, til Hǫfundar konungs. Heiðrekr er inn fyrsti maðr til þessar ferðar tekinn ok margir aðrir ágætir menn. Sem Heiðrekr kom á fund fǫður síns, þá var honum vel fagnat; hann sagði ǫll ørendi sín fǫður sínum ok beiðir dóms af honum. En Hǫfundr segir svá, at Heiðreks sonr var ágætastr á því landi.

Heiðrekr segir, 'Svá lízk mér sem þú dœmir minn son til dráps, eða hvat dœmir þú mér þá fyrir sonarskaða minn?'

Þá mælti Hǫfundr konungr, 'Þá skalt beiðask, at inn fjórði hverr maðr[3] sé á þínu valdi, sá er við blótit er staddr, ella muntu son þinn eigi láta til blóts; mun þá eigi þurfa at kenna þér ráð síðan, hvat þú skalt at hafask.'

a freckt *R* *b* kom *R*

[1] The casting of chips or twigs in divination is often mentioned in Norse literature and several times by Roman authors; cf. especially Tacitus, *Germania* ch. 10, who describes how the pieces of wood were marked with certain signs and cast onto a cloth, after which the soothsayer would pick them up and make prediction from them.

[2] *blótspánn*, 'sacrificial (divining) chip': there was an intimate connection

6

At that time there came so great a famine upon Reidgotaland that it seemed likely to lay waste the land. Then lots were cast by soothsayers, the sacrificial chip[2] cast[1] and augury made, and the answer came that there would never be plenty in Reidgotaland until the highest-born youth in the land was sacrificed. King Harald declared that Heidrek's son was the noblest-born, but Heidrek held that it was King Harald's; and this deadlock no-one could resolve until recourse was had to King Höfund, whose decisions were always to be trusted. Heidrek was chosen as leader for this journey, and with him many other noble men. When Heidrek met his father he was well received, and he told him all his errand, and asked him for his judgment. Höfund said that it was Heidrek's son who was the most noble in that land.

'It seems to me,' said Heidrek then, 'that you condemn my son to death; and what then do you adjudge me for the loss of him?'

King Höfund answered, 'You must demand that every fourth man[3] who is present at the sacrifice be put under your authority, or else you will not surrender your son to the sacrifice; after that there will be no need to advise you on what you should do.'

---

between sacrifice and divination (*hlaut* 'sacrificial blood' and *hlutr* 'lot' are related words), and it seems likely that the twigs of sortilege were dipped in the blood of the victims. The question is discussed by J. de Vries, *Altgerm. Religion.* I § 211, II § 116.

[3] *H* and *U* say 'every other man'; *R*'s *iiii hverr* is probably an error for *annarr hverr*.

7

Nú er Heiðrekr kom heim í Reiðgotaland, þá var þings kvatt. Heiðrekr tekr svá til orðs, 'Þat var atkvæði Hǫfundar konungs fǫður míns, at minn sonr sé ágætastr á þessu landi, ok er hann til blóts kosinn; en þar í mót vil ek eiga forráð á inum fjórða hverjum manni, er kominn er til þings þessa, ok vil ek, at[a] þér lofið mér þetta.'

Nú var svá gǫrt; síðan heimtask þeir í lið hans. Eptir þat lét hann blása saman liðinu ok setr upp merki, veitir nú atgǫngu Haraldi konungi, ok verðr þar mikill bardagi, ok fellr þar Haraldr konungr ok mart lið hans. Heiðrekr leggr nú undir sik allt ríki þat, er átt hafði Haraldr konungr, ok gerðisk þar konungr yfir. Heiðrekr kvezk nú gjalda fyrir son sinn þetta lið allt, er drepit var, ok gaf hann nú þenna val Óðni.[1] Kona hans var svá reið eptir fall fǫður síns, at hon hengði sik sjálf í dísarsal.[2]

Þat var eitt sumar, at Heiðrekr konungr fór með her sinn suðr í Húnaland[b] ok barðisk við konung þann, er Humli hét, ok fekk sigr ok tók þar dóttur hans, er Sifka hét, ok hafði heim með sér. En at ǫðru sumri sendi hann hana heim, ok var hon þá með barni, ok var sá sveinn kallaðr Hlǫðr ok var allra manna fríðastr sýnum, ok fóstraði hann Humli móðurfaðir hans.

Á einu sumri fór Heiðrekr konungr með her sinn til Saxlands.[3] En er Saxakonungr spyrr þat, þá býðr hann honum til veizlu ok biðr hann taka af lǫndum sínum slíkt er hann vill, ok þat þiggr Heiðrekr konungr. Þar sá hann dóttur hans, fríða ok fagra at áliti, ok þessar meyjar biðr Heiðrekr, ok hon var honum gipt; var þá aukin veizlan, ok síðan fór hann heim með konu sína ok tók með henni ógrynni fjár.

Heiðrekr konungr gerðisk nú hermaðr mikill ok eykr á marga vega mjǫk sitt ríki. Kona hans beiðisk opt at fara til fǫður síns, ok þat lét hann eptir henni, ok fór með henni Angantýr stjúpsonr hennar.

---

[a] at *om.* R   [b] Hundland R

[1] See Appendix C

[2] The *dísir* may be defined as female guardian spirits, associated with a man from his birth, and appearing especially before a battle or at the time of death; the conception is not clearly distinct from that of the *fylgju-konur* (see Glossary s.v. *fylgja*). On the worship of the *dísir* see Appendix A (I), p. 67, *n.* 5. R, U and H all agree here in the singular *dísar*, which is remarkable, though not

7

Now when Heidrek came home to Reidgotaland a council was called; and Heidrek began thus: 'This was the decree of King Höfund my father, that it is my son who is the highest-born in this country, and he is chosen for the sacrifice; but in exchange I will have authority over every fourth man who has come to this council; and it is my wish that you grant this to me.'

And so it was done, and the men joined his following. Then Heidrek had his host mustered with a trumpet-blast, and he set up a standard, and attacked King Harald; a great battle arose, and there fell the king and a great part of his host. Heidrek laid under him all the realm that had been King Harald's, and became king over it. He said that he would deliver up instead of his son all the host that had been killed, and he gave the slain to Óðin.[1] His wife was so wrathful at the death of her father that she hanged herself in the hall of the Dís.[2]

One summer King Heidrek went south with his army into the land of the Huns and fought with the king, who was named Humli, and defeated him; there he captured his daughter, Sifka, and brought her home with him. But he sent her back the summer after, she being then with child; the boy was called Hlöð, in appearance the most beautiful of men, and he was brought up by Humli, his mother's father.

One summer King Heidrek went with his army to Saxland.[3] When the king of the Saxons heard of this he invited Heidrek to a feast, and told him to take such of his dominions as he wished; this offer Heidrek accepted. There he saw the king's daughter, fair and beautiful in face; he asked for her, and she was married to him. So the feast was made a double one, and afterwards Heidrek went home with his wife and took with her uncounted treasure.

King Heidrek became now a great warrior, and greatly extended his kingdom in many ways. His wife often asked to visit her father, and he indulged her in that; her stepson Angantýr went with her.

---

unique; it is conceivable that the temple of a goddess is meant (cf. *Vanadís* as a name of Freyja, *SnE.* 38).

[3] Saxland: (Northern) Germany

Eitt sumar, er Heiðrekr konungr var í hernaði, þá kømr hann til Saxlands í ríki mágs síns. Hann leggr skipum sínum í leynivág nǫkkurn ok gengr á land ok einn maðr með honum, ok koma um nótt á konungs- bœinn ok venda at skemmu þeiri, er kona hans var vǫn at sofa í, ok urðu varðhaldsmenn ekki varir við kvámu þeira. Hann gengr í skem- muna ok sér, at maðr hvíldi hjá henni ok hafði hár fagrt á hǫfði. Sá maðr, er með konungi var, segir, at hann var hefnisamr um minni sakir. Hann svarar, 'Eigi mun ek þat gera nú.'

Konungr tók sveininn[a] Angantý, er lá í annarri sæng, ok hann skar lepp mikinn ór hári þess manns, er hvíldi í faðmi konu hans, ok hafði hvárttveggja með sér, hárleppinn ok sveininn; gekk síðan til skipa sinna.

Um morguninn leggr konungr í lægit, ok gengr í móti honum allt fólkit, ok var þar veizla búin. Heiðrekr lætr þá þings kveðja, ok þá váru honum sǫgð mikil tíðendi, at Angantýr sonr hans var bráðdauðr orðinn. Heiðrekr konungr mælti, 'Sýni mér líkit!'

Drottning segir þat auka mundu harm hans; honum var þó þangat fylgt. Þar var dúkr vafðr saman ok hundr innan í.

Heiðrekr konungr mælti, 'Illa hefir sonr minn nú skipask, ef hann er orðinn at hundi.'

Síðan lét konungr leiða sveininn á þingit ok sagði, at hann hefði reynt mikil svik at drottningu, ok tjáði allan atburð; biðr þangat stefna ǫllum mǫnnum, er sœkja mætti þingit, ok er mjǫk var alþýða komin, þá mælti konungr, 'Eigi er enn gullkárinn kominn.' Þá var enn leitat, ok fannsk maðr í steikara húsi ok band um hǫfuð. Margir undruðusk, hví hann skyldi til þings, þræll einn vándr. En er hann kom til þings, þá mælti Heiðrekr konungr, 'Hér megu þér nú þann sjá, er konungs- dóttir vill eiga heldr en mik.'

Hann tók nú leppinn ok bar við hárit, ok átti þat saman at fara. 'En þú, konungr,' segir Heiðrekr, 'hefir oss gott gǫrt jafnan, ok skal af því ríki þitt standa í friði fyrir oss, en dóttur þína vil ek eigi lengr eiga.'

Heiðrekr fór nú heim í ríki sitt ok sonr hans.

[a] svein *R*

One summer, when Heidrek was out on a foray, he came to Saxland, the realm of his wife's father; he laid his ships into a hidden creek and went ashore with one other man. They came at night to the king's dwelling and went to the chamber where his wife used to sleep, and the watchmen were not aware of their coming. Heidrek went into the chamber and saw that a man slept beside her, a man with fair hair on his head. The man who was with the king said that Heidrek was one to be vengeful over lesser things than that, but the king answered, 'I shall not do it now.'

He took the boy Angantýr, who lay in another bed, and he cut a great lock of hair from the head of the man who slept in his wife's arms, and taking both the boy and the lock of hair away with him he went back to his ships.

Next morning he put into the anchorage, and all the people came out to meet him, and a feast was prepared. Heidrek had a meeting called, and there great news was told to him, that his son Angantýr had died a sudden death. 'Show me the corpse!' said the king.

The queen said that that would only add to his grief; but nonetheless he was brought to the place, and there was a cloth folded up, and inside it a dog.

'My son has had a change for the worse,' said King Heidrek, 'if he has turned into a dog.'

Then he had the boy brought to the meeting, and saying that he had discovered great treachery in the queen he made plain the whole affair. He commanded that every man who could come to that meeting should be summoned to it, and when almost all the people had come he said, 'He of the golden curls is still not here.' A further search was made, and the man was found in the kitchen, with a band about his head. Many there wondered why a base slave should be wanted at the meeting; but when the man came there King Heidrek said, 'Here now may you see the one whom the king's daughter prefers to me.'

Then he took up the lock and tried it against the man's hair, and there was no question of its not matching. 'But you, king,' said Heidrek, 'have always dealt well with us, and therefore your kingdom shall have peace from us; but your daughter I will keep no longer.'

Then Heidrek went home into his own kingdom, together with his son.

Á einu sumri sendir Heiðrekr konungr menn í Garðaríki þess ørendis at bjóða syni Garðakonungs[1] heim til[a] fóstrs ok vill nú reyna at brjóta ǫll heilræði fǫður síns. Sendimenn koma á fund Garðakonungs ok segja honum ørendit ok vináttumál. Garðakonungr kvað þess enga ván, at hann fengi þeim manni í hendr son sinn, er kenndr er mǫrgum illum hlutum.

Þá mælti drottning, 'Mæl þú eigi svá, herra; heyrt hafi þér, hvé mikill maðr hann er ok sigrsæll, ok er meiri vizka[b] at taka vel hans sóma, ella stendr eigi þitt ríki í friði.'

Konungr mælti, 'Þú munt mikit á þessu vinna.'

Nú er sveinninn seldr í hendr sendimǫnnum, ok fara þeir heim. Heiðrekr konungr tekr vel við sveininum ok veitir honum góða uppfœzlu ok ann mikit. Sifka Humladóttir var þá í annat sinn með konungi,[2] en honum var þat ráðit, at hann skyldi engan hlut henni segja, þann er leyna skyldi.

Eitt sumar sendir Garðakonungr Heiðreki orð, at hann kœmi austr þangat at þiggja veizlu ok vináttuboð at honum. Heiðrekr býsk nú með miklu fjǫlmenni ok konungssonr[c] með honum ok Sifka. Heiðrekr kom nú austr í Garðaríki ok tók þar ágæta veizlu.

Einn dag þessarar veizlu fóru konungar á skóg ok mart lið með þeim at beita hundum ok haukum; en er þeir hǫfðu lausum slegit hundunum, fara sérhverir um skóginn; þá urðu þeir tveir saman fóstrar. Þá mælti Heiðrekr við konungsson, 'Hlýð þú boði mínu, fóstri. Hér er bœr skammt í frá; farðu þangat ok fel þik ok þigg til hring þenna; vertu þá heim búinn, er ek læt sœkja þik.'

Sveinninn kvezk ófúss þessarar ferðar, en gerði þó sem konungr beiddi. Heiðrekr kom heim um kveldit ok var ókátr ok sat skamma stund við drykkju. En er hann kom í sæng, mælti Sifka, 'Hví eru þér ókátir, herra? Hvat er yðr? Eru þér sjúkir? Segið mér!'

Konungr segir, 'Vandi er mér at segja þetta, því at þar liggr við líf mitt, ef eigi er leynt.'

Hon kvezk leyna mundu ok gerisk blíð við hann ok fór eptir ást-

---

[a] til *om. R*   [b] vizk *R*   [c] konungs- *em.*, hans *R*

[1] In the *HU*-version this king is called Hrollaug, his son Herlaug, his daughter Hergerd, and his queen Herborg (the last only in *U*). The story of the events in Gardaríki is different in this version; see Introduction, §4.

[2] In the rewritten version of the saga Heidrek's mistress at the time of his visit to Gardar is a distinct person from the Hun king's daughter; see Introduction p. xvi.

One summer King Heidrek sent men into Gardaríki with the errand of inviting the son of the king of Gardar[1] to be fostered in his house; for Heidrek meant now to try breaking all his father's good counsels. The messengers came into the presence of the king of Gardar and told him their errand and message of friendship; but the king said that it was not likely he would hand over his son to a man who was known for his many evil qualities.

Then the queen said, 'Do not say that, lord! You have heard how great a conqueror he is, and it would be greater wisdom to accept the honour he offers you, or else your kingdom will not remain at peace.'

'You will do a great deal to bring this about,' said the king.

Then the boy was delivered over to the messengers, and they departed home. King Heidrek received the boy well and gave him a good upbringing, and loved him dearly. Sifka, Humli's daughter, was then for a second time with the king[2]; and he had been given counsel that he should not tell her anything that must be kept secret.

One summer the king of Gardar sent word to Heidrek to come out east and be his guest at a feast and friendly meeting. Then Heidrek made ready to go with a great company of men, together with the king's son and Sifka. Heidrek came now east into Gardaríki and was entertained there to a noble feast.

One day during this feast the kings went to the woods to hunt with hawks and hounds, and many men with them; and when they had slipped the hounds they went their separate ways in the forest. Foster-father and foster-son found themselves alone together. Then Heidrek said to the prince, 'Do what I tell you, foster-son; there is a farm not far from here: go there and hide yourself, and take this ring for your pains; and be ready to come home when I have you sent for.'

The boy said that he did not like the business, but nonetheless he did as the king said. Heidrek came home in the evening and was downcast; he sat at his drink only a little time. When he came to bed, Sifka said, 'Why are you sad, lord? What troubles you? Are you sick? Tell me!'

'It is a hard thing for me to tell of,' answered the king, 'for my life is at stake if it is not kept secret.'

Sifka said she would not give it away, and was affectionate towards him, pressing for an answer with a show of love. At last he said to her, samliga. Þá segir hann henni, 'Vit konungssonr várum staddir tveir hjá eik einni; þá beiddisk fóstri minn eplis, er ofarliga var á trénu; síðan brá ek Tyrfingi ok hjó ek ofan eplit, ok var þat fyrr gǫrt en ek gætta til, hvat á lá, at manns bani skyldi verða, ef brugðit væri, en vit tveir til. Síðan drap ek sveininn.'

Um daginn eptir við drykkju spyrr drottning Garðakonungs Sifku, hví Heiðrekr væri svá ókátr. Hon segir, 'Œrit er til, hann hefir drepit son konungs ok þinn'; segir síðan allan atburð.

Drottning segir, 'Þat eru mikil tíðendi, ok látum eigi upp komask.' Gekk þá drottning í burt þegar óŕ hǫllinni með harmi miklum. Konungr finnr þetta ok kallar Sifku til sín ok mælti, 'Hvat rœdduzk þit drottning við, er henni fekk svá mikils?'

'Herra,' segir hon, 'mikit er til gǫrt, Heiðrekr hefir drepit son ykkarn, ok meiri ván, at eptir vilja hans fœri, ok er hann dauða verðr.'

Garðakonungr biðr taka Heiðrek ok fjǫtra; 'ok er nú orðit eptir því, er ek gat til.'

En Heiðrekr konungr var þar orðinn svá vinsæll, at þetta vildi engi gera. Þá stóðu upp tveir menn í hǫllinni ok kváðu eigi skyldu þar við nema, ok lǫgðu þeir fjǫtur á hann. En þá menn hafði Heiðrekr leyst frá dauða báða. Þá sendi Heiðrekr menn leyniliga eptir konungssyni. En Garðakonungr lætr þá blása saman fólki sínu ok segir þeim, at hann[a] vill láta Heiðrek festa á gálga; ok í því kømr konungssonr hlaupandi at fǫður sínum ok biðr hann eigi þat níðingsverk fyrir ætlask at drepa inn ágætasta mann ok sinn fóstrfǫður.

[a] hann *om.* R

'The king's son and I were standing together, the two of us, beside a tree, and my foster-son asked for an apple that grew high up on the tree. Then I drew Tyrfing and cut down the apple, and it was done before I remembered what spell was laid on the sword, that it should prove the death of a man if it were drawn; but we two were alone. Then I killed the boy.'

On the next day at the drinking the queen of Gardar asked Sifka why Heidrek was so gloomy. 'There is reason enough for that!' she answered; 'he has slain your son and the king's!' — and then she told the whole story.

'This is terrible news,' said the queen; 'we must not let it get abroad.' Then she went at once out of the hall in great grief. The king, seeing this, called Sifka to him and said, 'What were you speaking of with the queen, that has troubled her so greatly?'

'There is much cause for it, lord,' said Sifka; 'Heidrek has slain your son, and it is like enough that he has done it deliberately; he deserves death!'

The king of Gardar commanded that Heidrek be seized and set in shackles; 'and now,' he said, 'things have fallen out as I surmised.'

But King Heidrek had made himself so well-liked that no-one would do this. Then two men rose up in the hall, and said that there was nothing to stop them, and they laid fetters on the king; but both those men Heidrek had redeemed from death. Then Heidrek sent men out secretly to fetch the prince; but the king of Gardar had his people summoned by the trumpet, and told them that he would have Heidrek hanged. At that moment the king's son came running to his father and begged him not to think of doing that loathsome deed, the slaying of his foster-father and the noblest of men.

8

Heiðrekr er nú leystr, ok nú býsk hann þegar til heimferðar. Þá mælti drottning, 'Herra, lát eigi Heiðrek svá í brott fara, at þit séð ósáttir; eigi gegnir ríki þínu þat. Bjóð honum heldr gull eða silfr.'

Konungr gerir svá, lætr bera fé mikit til Heiðreks konungs ok kvezk vilja gefa honum ok eiga enn við hann vingan.

Heiðrekr segir, 'Ekki skortir mik fé.'

Garðakonungr segir drottningu. Hon mælti, 'Bjóð honum þá ríki ok eigur stórar ok fjǫlmenni.'

Konungr gerir svá. Heiðrekr konungr segir, 'Œrnar á ek eigur ok fjǫlmenni.'

Garðakonungr segir enn drottningu. Hon mælti, 'Bjóð honum þat þá, sem hann mun þiggja, en þat er dóttir þín.'

Konungr segir, 'Þat hugða ek, at mik mundi eigi þat henda, en þó skaltu ráða.'

Þá fór Garðakonungr á fund Heiðreks konungs ok mælti, 'Heldr en vit skiljum ósáttir, vil ek, at þú fáir dóttur minnar með svá miklum sóma sem þú kýss sjálfr.' Heiðrekr þiggr nú þetta blíðliga, ok fór nú dóttir Garðakonungs heim með honum.

Nú er Heiðrekr konungr heim kominn ok vill nú flytja Sifku í brott ok lætr taka hest sinn inn bezta, ok var þat síð um kveld. Nú koma þau at á einni; þá þyngisk hon fyrir honum, svá at hestrinn sprakk, en konungr gekk af fram. Þá skyldi hann bera hana yfir ána; þá gerask engi fǫng[a] á ǫðru en hann steypir henni af ǫxl sér ok brýtr í sundr hrygg hennar ok skilr svá við hana, at hana rekr dauða eptir ánni.

Heiðrekr konungr lætr þá efna til veizlu mikillar ok gengr at eiga dóttur Garðakonungs. Dóttir þeira hét Hervǫr; hon var skjaldmær ok fœddisk upp í Englandi með Fróðmari jarli.[1]

Heiðrekr konungr sezk nú um kyrrt ok gerisk hǫfðingi mikill ok spekingr at viti. Heiðrekr konungr lét ala gǫlt mikinn; hann var svá

---

[a] faug R (for faung)

[1] Later in the saga the foster-father of Hervör the younger is called Ormar, which is the reading of H and U in the present passage.

8

Heidrek was now released, and at once he prepared to set out on his journey home. 'Lord,' said the queen then, 'do not let Heidrek depart thus, without your being reconciled; that will be of no profit to your kingdom. Offer him rather gold and silver.'

The king did this, and had a great quantity of money borne to King Heidrek, saying that he wished to give it to him, and to have his friendship once more.

But Heidrek answered, 'I have no lack of money.'

The king told the queen of this, and she said, 'Offer him then a dominion, great possessions and many liegemen.'

The king did so, but Heidrek said, 'I have abundance of possessions and a multitude of followers.'

The king of Gardar told this also to the queen, and she said, 'Then offer him what he will accept: your daughter.'

'I did not think that I should ever come to that,' said the king; 'but you shall have your way.'

Then the king of Gardar went to meet King Heidrek and said, 'Rather than that we part unreconciled, I would have you take my daughter, with as great honour as you yourself shall choose.' And now this offer Heidrek accepted gladly, and the daughter of the king of Gardar went home with him.

King Heidrek was now at home, and he wished to rid himself of Sifka; he took his best horse, and it was late in the evening. They came to a river, and she grew too heavy for the horse, so that it collapsed from exhaustion; but the king left it and walked on. He then had to carry her over the river; there was nothing else for it, but to cast her down from his shoulders and break her backbone, and so he left her drifting away dead down the stream.

Then King Heidrek had a great feast prepared, and he married the daughter of the king of Gardar. Their daughter was named Hervör; she was a warrior woman, and she was brought up in England with Fródmar the jarl.[1]

King Heidrek now settled down in his kingdom, and he became a great lord, and very wise. He had a great boar reared, which was as

mikill sem ǫldungar þeir, er stœrstir váru, ok svá fagr, at hvert hár þótti ór gulli vera.[1] Konungrinn leggr hǫnd sína á hǫfuð geltinum, en aðra á burst ok sverr þess, at aldri hefir maðr svá mikit af gǫrt við hann, at eigi skuli hann hafa réttan dóm spekinga hans, en þeir tólf skulu gæta galtarins, eða ella skal hann bera upp gátur þær, er hann gæti eigi ráðit. Heiðrekr konungr gerisk ok nú inn vinsælasti.

[1] The *HU*-version says here that King Heidrek worshipped Frey, and gave him the largest boar of his herd, called the *sonargǫltr*; it was sacrificed at the *sonarblót* at the beginning of February, 'for a good season' (*U*). Here as elsewhere the sacred *sonargǫltr* is associated with the making of vows (*heitstrengingar*) on the eve of Yule. The connection of the boar with the cult of Frey is often seen, e.g. in the boar Gullinbursti which drew Frey's chariot, in the name Sýr ('Sow') given to his sister Freyja, etc. (*SnE.* 38, 66).

huge as the strongest fully-grown bulls, and so fair of coat that every hair seemed to be of gold.[1] The king laid one hand on the head of the boar and the other on its bristles, and swore that no man had ever done him so great a wrong that he should not have just judgment from his counsellors, those twelve who had to tend the boar; or else he should propound riddles which the king could not solve. King Heidrek now became a man of many friends.

9

Maðr hét Gestumblindi,[1] ríkr ok mikill óvinr Heiðreks konungs. Konungr sendi honum orð, at hann kœmi á fund hans at sættask við hann, ef hann vil halda lífinu. Gestumblindi var ekki spekingr mikill, ok fyrir þá sǫk, at hann veit sik vanfœran til at skipta orðum við konunginn, hann veit ok, at þungt mun vera at hlíta dómi spekinganna, því at sakir eru nógar, þat ráð tekr Gestumblindi, at hann blótar[a] Óðin til fulltings sér ok biðr hann líta á sitt mál ok heitr honum miklum gœðum.

Eitt kveld er þar drepit á dyrr síðla, ok gengr Gestumblindi til hurðar ok sér mann kominn; hann spyrr þann at nafni, en hann nefndisk Gestumblindi ok mælti, at þeir skyldu klæðum skipta, ok svá gera þeir. Bóndi ferr nú í brott ok felr sik, en komandinn gengr inn, ok þykkjask allir þar kenna Gestumblinda, ok líðr af nóttin.

Um daginn eptir gerir sjá Gestumblindi fǫr sína á fund konungs, ok hann kvaddi vel konunginn. Konungr þagði.

'Herra,' segir hann, 'því kom ek hingat, at ek vil við yðr sættask.'

Þá svarar konungr, 'Viltu þola dóm spekinga minna?'

Hann segir, 'Er ekki fleiri undanlausnir?'

Konungr mælti, 'Vera skulu fleiri, ef þú þykkisk til fœrr at bera upp gátur.'

Gestumblindi segir, 'Lítt mun ek til þess fœrr, enda mun harðr á annat borð þykkja.'

'Viltu,' segir konungr, 'heldr þola dóm spekinga minna?'

'Þat kýs ek,' segir hann, 'at bera fyrr upp gáturnar.'

'Þat er rétt ok vel fallit,' segir konungr.

Þá mælti Gestumblindi:

> (44) Hafa vildak[b]
> þat er hafða í gær,[c]
> vittu,[d] hvat þat var:

[a] boltar R
[b] thus R, hafa vil ek dag U, hafa ek þat vilda H (perhaps originally í dag 'today,' Andrews)
[c] thus H (þat er em., er ek H), þat í gær hafða(k) RU
[d] vittu RU, konungr, gettu H

[1] This name no doubt derives from *Gestr inn blindi* (in U it is once actually written thus), 'the blind stranger,' Óðin as the wandering disguised old man, with one eye and a hat drawn down over his face. He bore the name *Gestr* when he appeared to St Óláf (*Flateyjarbók* II 134 f.).

9

There was a man called Gestumblindi,[1] a powerful man and a great enemy of King Heidrek. The king sent him word to come and be reconciled, if he cared for his life. Now Gestumblindi was no great sage, and because he knew that he was incapable of vying with the king in words, and knew too that it would go heavy with him if he had to abide by the judgment of the wise men, for his crimes were many, he decided on this plan: to sacrifice to Óðin for help, to ask him to look after his case, and to promise him many gifts.

Late one evening there came a knock upon the door, and when Gestumblindi went to it he saw that there was a man there. He asked him what his name was, and the stranger called himself Gestumblindi, and said that they were to change clothes. This they did, and then Gestumblindi went away and concealed himself; but the stranger went into the house, and everyone thought that they recognised Gestumblindi; and the night passed away.

On the next day this Gestumblindi made his way to see the king, and gave him a respectful greeting. The king sat silent.

'Lord,' said Gestumblindi, 'I have come here because I wish to be reconciled with you.'

'Will you submit to the judgment of my wise men?' answered the king.

'Are there no other ways of redeeming myself?' asked Gestumblindi.

'There are others,' said the king, 'if you think yourself able to propound riddles.'

'I have no great skill in that,' Gestumblindi replied, 'but the other way seems hard.'

'Then will you rather submit to the judgment of my counsellors?' asked the king.

'I choose rather to propound riddles,' said Gestumblindi.

'That is right and fitting,' said the king.

Then said Gestumblindi:

> (44) Would that I had now
> what I had yesterday,
> find out what that was;

lýða lemill,
orða^a tefill,^b
ok orða upphefill.
Heiðrekr konungr,
hyggðu at gátu!

Konungr segir, 'Góð er gáta þín, Gestumblindi, getit er þessar.¹ Fœri honum mungát! Þat lemr margra vit, ok margir eru þá margmálgari, er mungát ferr á, en sumum vefsk tungan, svá at ekki verðr at orði.'

Þá mælti Gestumblindi:

(45) Heiman ek fór,^c
heiman ek fǫr gerða,²
sá ek á veg vega;
var þeim vegr undir^d
ok vegr yfir
ok vegr á alla vega.
Heiðrekr konungr,
hyggðu at gátu!^e

'Góð er gáta þín, Gestumblindi, getit er þessar; þar fórtu yfir árbrú, ok var árvegr undir þér, en fuglar flugu yfir hǫfði þér ok hjá þér tveim megin, ok var þat þeira vegr.'³

Þá mælti Gestumblindi:

(46) Hvat er þat drykki,^f
er ek drakk í gær,
var þat ei vín né vatn
mjǫðr né mungát^g
né matar ekki,
ok gekk ek þorstalauss þaðan?
Heiðrekr konungr,
hyggðu at gátu!

^a ok orða *HU*
^b lýða . . . tefill *RHU* (*without alliteration*), ýta lemill *Bugge*, óða lemill *Kock NN* § 792
^c fór *HU*, om. *R*
^d thus *RU* (þar for þeim *U*), vegr var undir *H*
^e gatum *R*
^f drykki *R*, drykkja *H* (*from this point* '*H*' *signifies agreement of 281 and 597*)
^g thus *H*, né mungat *U*, né in heldr mungát *R*

> mankind it mars,
> speech it hinders,
> yet speech it will inspire.
> This riddle ponder,
> O prince Heidrek!

'Your riddle is good, Gestumblindi,' said the king; 'I have guessed it.[1] Bring him some ale! — that mars the wits of many a man, and many are the more talkative when ale gets the upper hand; but with some the tongue gets all entangled, so that no word comes out.'

Then said Gestumblindi:

> (45) From home I journeyed
> and from home faring[2]
> I looked on a way of ways;
> a way there was under
> and a way over,
> and on all sides ways there were.
> This riddle ponder,
> O prince Heidrek!

'Your riddle is good, Gestumblindi,' said the king; 'I have guessed it. You went across a bridge over a river, and the way of the river was beneath you, but birds flew over your head and on either side of you, and that was their way.'[3]

Then said Gestumblindi:

> (46) What drink was it
> I drank yesterday;
> it was not wine nor water,
> nor mead, nor ale,
> nor aught of food,
> yet thirstless thence I fared?
> This riddle ponder,
> O prince Heidrek!

---

[1] The phrase *Góð er gáta þín, getit er þessar* is a regular long line, and was perhaps a formula of introduction to riddle-solutions (Heusler, *Rätsel* 137).

[2] This curious repetition is paralleled in the Eddaic poem *Fjǫlsvinnsmál* 46: *Hvaðan þú fórt, hvaðan þú fǫr gerðir?*

[3] The sixth line of the verse probably refers in fact to the 'Earth-way' (*fold-vegr*), the earth simply, for lines 4–6 seem to refer to three different 'ways,' River, Sky, Earth. But none of the texts report the king as solving the riddle in this way.

'Góð er gáta þín, Gestumblindi, getit er þessar; þar lagðisk þú í forsœlu, er dǫgg var fallin á grasi, ok kœldir svá varir þínar ok stǫðvaðir svá þorsta þinn.'

Þá mælti Gestumblindi:

(47) Hverr er sá inn hvelli,
er gengr harðar gǫtur
ok hefir hann fyrrum*a* um farit;
mjǫk fast kyssir
sá er hefir munna tvá
ok á gulli einu gengr?
Heiðrekr konungr,
hyggðu at gátu!

'Góð er gáta þín, Gestumblindi, getit er þessar; þat er hamarr sá, er hafðr er at gullsmíð; hann kveðr hátt við, er hann kømr á harðan steðja, ok þat er hans gata.'

Þá mælti Gestumblindi:

(48) Hvat er þat undra,
er ek úti sá
fyrir Dellings*b* durum[1];
ókvikvir*c* tveir
andalausir
sáralauk[2] suðu?
Heiðrekr konungr,
hyggðu at gátu!

'Góð er gáta þín, Gestumblindi, getit er þessar; þat eru smiðbelgir; þeir hafa engan vind, nema þeim sé blásit, ok eru þeir dauðir sem annat smíði, en fyrir þeim má líkt smíða sverð sem annat.'

Þá mælti Gestumblindi:

a fyrrum *RU*, þær fyrr *H*
b Dellings *RU*, dǫglings *H throughout*
c ókyrrir *HU*

[1] What this phrase meant to the maker of these riddles is impossible to say. In *Hávamál* 160 it is said that the dwarf Thjódrørir sang before Delling's doors, which (in view of the fact that Delling is the father of Dag (Day) in *Vafþrúðnismál* 25) may mean that he gave warning to his people that the sun was coming up, and they must return into their dark houses; the phrase would then virtually mean 'at sunrise.' As regards dǫglings for Dellings in *H*, the Dǫglingar were the descendants of *Dagr* (according to *SnE.* 183).

'Your riddle is good, Gestumblindi,' said the king; 'I have guessed it. You lay in the shade, and dew had fallen on the grass, and thus you cooled your lips and quenched your thirst.'

Then said Gestumblindi:

> (47) Who is that shrill one
> on hard ways walking,
> paths he has passed before;
> many are his kisses
> for of mouths he has two,
> and on gold alone he goes?
> This riddle ponder,
> O prince Heidrek!

'Your riddle is good, Gestumblindi,' said the king; 'I have guessed it. That is the hammer, which is used in the goldsmith's art; it screams shrilly when it beats on the hard anvil, and the anvil is its "path".'

Then said Gestumblindi:

> (48) What strange marvel
> did I see without,
> in front of Delling's door[1];
> two things lifeless,
> twain unbreathing,
> were seething a stalk of wounds?[2]
> This riddle ponder,
> O prince Heidrek!

'Your riddle is good, Gestumblindi,' said the king; 'I have guessed it. Those are smith's bellows; they have no wind unless they are blown, and they are as lifeless as any other work of smith's craft, but with them one can as well forge a sword as anything else.'

Then said Gestumblindi:

---

[2] 'They boiled a wound-leek,' i.e. they forged a sword. The characteristic periphrasis *sára-laukr* (it is found elsewhere) thus moves out of the sphere of poetic device (kenning) into that of riddle simply by virtue of its context; similarly at verse 65/6, etc.

(49) Hvat er þat undra,
     er ek úti sá
     fyrir Dellings durum;
     fœtr hefir átta,
     en fjǫgur augu
     ok berr[a] ofar kné en kvið?
     Heiðrekr konungr,
     hyggðu at gátu!
'Þat er kǫngurváfur.'
Þá mælti Gestumblindi:

(50) Hvat er þat undra,
     er ek úti sá
     fyrir Dellings durum;
     hǫfði sínu vísar
     á helvega,[b]
     en fótum til sólar snýr?
     Heiðrekr konungr,
     hyggðu at gátu!

'Góð er gáta þín, Gestumblindi, getit er þessar; þat er laukr; hǫfuð hans er fast í jǫrðu, en hann kvíslar, er hann vex upp.'
Þá mælti Gestumblindi:

(51) Hvat er þat undra,
     er ek úti sá
     fyrir Dellings durum;
     horni harðara,
     hrafni svartara,
     skildi[c] hvítara,[1]
     skapti réttara?[d]
     Heiðrekr konungr,
     hyggðu at gátu!

Heiðrekr mælti, 'Smækkask nú gáturnar, Gestumblindi; hvat

[a] ok *om. HU*, berr þat *H*
[b] á helvega *RU*, helju til *H* (*read* heljar)
[c] skjalli *HU*
[d] *H reverses lines 6–7, U as R*

[1] The reading of *HU*, 'whiter than the white of egg,' is probably the

(49) What strange marvel
did I see without,
in front of Delling's door;
eight are its feet
and four its eyes,
and knees above belly it bears?
This riddle ponder,
O prince Heidrek!

'Spiders,' said the king.
Then said Gestumblindi:

(50) What strange marvel
did I see without,
in front of Delling's door;
its head turning
to Hel downward,
but its feet ever seek the sun?
This riddle ponder,
O prince Heidrek!

'Your riddle is good, Gestumblindi,' said the king; 'I have guessed it. It is the leek; its head is fast in the ground, but it forks as it grows up.'

Then said Gestumblindi:

(51) What strange marvel
did I see without,
in front of Delling's door;
harder than ram's horn,
than raven blacker,
more straight than shaft,
than shield whiter?[1]
This riddle ponder,
O prince Heidrek!

'Your riddles become trifling, Gestumblindi,' said Heidrek; 'what

---

original; in *SnE*. 24 it is said that a thing washed in the well of Urd becomes 'whiter than what is called *skjall*, which lies within the egg-shell.'

þarf lengr yfir þessu at sitja? Þat er hrafntinna, ok skein á hana sólargeisli.'

Þá mælti Gestumblindi:

>(52) Báru brúðir
> bleikhaddaðar
> ambáttir tvær
> ǫlker^a til skemmu;
> ei var þat hǫndum horfit
> né hamri at^b klappat,[1]
> þó var^c fyrir eyjar útan
> ǫrðigr sá er^d gerði.
> Heiðrekr konungr,
> hyggðu at gátu!

'Góð er gáta þín, Gestumblindi, getit er þessar; þar fara svanbrúðir[2] til hreiðrs síns ok verpa eggjum; skurm á eggi er eigi hǫndum gǫrt né hamri klappat, en svanr er fyrir eyjar útan ǫrðigr, sá er þær gátu eggin við.'

Þá mælti Gestumblindi:

>(53) Hverjar eru þær rýgjar
> á reginfjalli,
> elr við kván kona,
> mær við meyju^e
> mǫg^f um getr,
> ok eigut þær varðir vera?
> Heiðrekr konungr,
> hyggðu at gátu!

'Góð er gáta þín, Gestumblindi, getit er þessar; þat eru hvannir tvær ok hvannarkálfr[3] á milli þeira.'

Þá mælti Gestumblindi:

^a ǫlker *em. Edd. Min.*, ǫl *RH*, áðr *U*
^b hmri at *R*, hamri *HU*
^c þá er *HU*
^d sá er ker (konungr *U*) gerði *HU*
^e mær við meyju *H, om. R*
^f *R adds* þar til er *before* mǫg, *U corrupt*

[1] In *R* the last four lines are absurdly referred to ǫl 'ale,' but of course what is not made with hand or hammer is not the 'ale' but the 'cask.' *H* offers a better but not really satisfactory text.

need is there to spend more time at this? — That is the obsidian, with a sunbeam shining on it.'

Then said Gestumblindi:

> (52) Pale-haired bondmaids,
> two brides together,
> carried to the storehouse
> a cask of ale;
> no hand turned it,
> no hammer forged it,[1]
> yet outside the islands
> upright sat its maker.
> This riddle ponder,
> O prince Heidrek!

'Your riddle is good, Gestumblindi,' said the king; 'I have guessed it. Female swans[2] go to their nests and lay their eggs; the egg-shell is not made by hand nor is it forged by hammer; and the swan by whom they engendered the eggs bears himself erect, outside the islands.'

Then said Gestumblindi:

> (53) What women are they
> on the wild mountain;
> woman by woman begets,
> a girl by a girl
> begets a son —
> yet no men do these maidens know?
> This riddle ponder,
> O prince Heidrek!

'Your riddle is good, Gestumblindi,' said the king; 'I have guessed it. These are two angelicas, and a young angelica[3] between them.'

Then said Gestumblindi:

---

[2] *H* says 'Eider-ducks,' but the agreement of *R* and *U*, and also perhaps the adjectives *bleikhaddaðar* and *ǫrðigr*, show that 'Swans' is the original solution.

[3] i.e. a young angelica-shoot growing up from the same root as the other full-grown stalks. A species of angelica (*hvǫnn*) is common in the far north of Europe and was much used for flavouring; in *Óláfs Saga Tryggvasonar* (ch. 92) it is mentioned as being sold in the market at Nidarós.

(54)[1] Fara ek sák[a]
foldar moldbúa,
á sat nár [b2] á nái;
blindr reið blindum
brimreiðar[3] til,
jór [c] var andar vanr.
Heiðrekr konungr,
hyggðu at gátu!

'Góð er gáta þín, Gestumblindi, getit er þessar; þar fanntu hest dauðan á ísjaka ok orm[d] dauðan á hestinum, ok rak þat allt saman eptir ánni.'[4]

Þá mælti Gestumblindi:

(55) Hverir eru þeir þegnar,
er ríða þingi at
sáttir[5] allir saman [e];
lýða sína
senda þeir lǫnd yfir
at byggja bólstaði? [f]
Heiðrekr konungr,
hyggðu at gátu!

'Góð er gáta þín, Gestumblindi, getit er þessar; þat er Ítrekr ok Andaðr,[6] er þeir sitja at tafli sínu.'

Þá mælti Gestumblindi:

(56) Hverjar eru þær snótir [g]
er um [h] sinn drottin

[a] søg R, sá (ek) HU
[b] nár A.M. 748, naðr Cod. Worm, RHU (or corruptions of naðr)
[c] þá jór R
[d] orm H, ǫrn R
[e] thus RU (allsáttir U), ok eru sextán saman H
[f] thus RH, at sigra menn sérhverja U
[g] snótir em. Edd. Min., brúðir RH (without alliteration), drósir U
[h] um HU, om. R

[1] The first three lines of this verse are quoted in the grammatical treatise of Óláf Hvítaskáld (died 1259) as an example of a riddle, but it is not said where they come from. (B. M. Ólsen, Den tredje og fjærde grammatiske Afhandling, 1884, 31, 114, 232). The MSS are A.M. 748 I 4to (c. 1300), and A.M. 242 fol. (Codex Wormianus) from the end of the fourteenth century.
[2] All three versions here agree in the undoubted error naðr 'snake,' anti-

(54)[1] A dweller in the soil
I saw passing,
a corpse[2] on a corpse there sat;
blind upon blind one
to the billows[3] riding,
on a steed without breath it was borne.
This riddle ponder,
O prince Heidrek!

'Your riddle is good, Gestumblindi,' said the king; 'I have guessed it. You came upon a dead horse on an icefloe, and on the horse a dead snake, and they all floated together down the river.'[4]

Then said Gestumblindi:

(55) What thanes are they
to the thing riding,
all at one[5] together;
across the lands
their liegemen sending
seeking a place to settle?
This riddle ponder,
O prince Heidrek!

'Your riddle is good, Gestumblindi,' said the king; 'I have guessed it. These are Ítrek and Andad,[6] sitting at their chequerboard.'

Then said Gestumblindi:

(56) What women are they
warring together

---

cipating the solution, a corruption which no doubt crept in before ever the verse was incorporated into *Heiðreks Saga*.

[3] *brimreið*: Norse *reið* meant 'riding' or 'vehicle,' but *brimreið* (once recorded elsewhere) seems to mean 'sea,' as does the cognate O.E. *brim-rad*; it is not impossible that the Norse word was influenced by the English.

[4] The correct solution is probably simply 'dead snake on an icefloe' (Bugge, *NS* 358), *blindr* and *nár* designating the dead snake, *blindum* and *nái* the icefloe, for in riddling language all inanimate objects may be called 'dead' and 'blind' (cf. verse 48). The horse (*jór*) is simply the icefloe.

[5] If the 'thanes' who ride to the 'thing' (meeting) are the kings in chess, one would not expect them to be called either *sáttir* or *sextán* (sixteen); but in fact it is not clear what the game is (*tafl* may mean any sort of board-game).

[6] *Ítrekr* may have been a name for Óðin, and *Anduðr* or *Ǫnduðr* is found in a list of giant-names, so that it is just conceivable that the pieces in this game were thought of as representing a conflict between the gods and the giants. The solution in *H* is: *þat er tafl Ítreks konungs*.

vápnlausan^a vega¹;
inar jarpari^b hlífa
um alla daga,
en inar fegri fara?
Heiðrekr konungr,
hyggðu at gátu!

'Góð er gáta þín, Gestumblindi, getit er þessar; þat er hnettafl; inar døkkri verja hnefann, en hvítar sœkja.'²

Þá mælti Gestumblindi:

(57) Hverr er sá inn eini,
er sefr í ǫsgrúa^c³
ok af grjóti einu gǫrr;
fǫður né móður
á sá inn fagrgjarni,^d⁴
þar mun hann sinn aldr ala?
Heiðrekr konungr,
hyggðu at gátu!

'Þat er eldr fólginn á arni, ok tekr ór tinnu.'

Þá mælti Gestumblindi:

(58) Hverr er sá inn mikli,
er líðr^e mold yfir,
svelgr hann vǫtn ok við;
glygg hann óask,
en gumna^f eigi
ok yrkir á sól til saka?
Heiðrekr konungr,
hyggðu at gátu!

'Góð er gáta þín, Gestumblindi, getit er þessar; þat er myrkvi;

---

^a -lausar *HU*
^b jǫrpsku *H* (*read* jǫrpu), *line om. U*
^c ǫsgrúa *RU*, ǫskugrúa *H*
^d fjárgjarni *H*, fár- *U*
^e líðr *RU*, ferr *H*
^f gumna *RU*, guma 597

¹ The reading of *R* means that the women kill their weaponless lord; that of *HU*, that the women themselves are weaponless.

> before their defenceless king[1];
> day after day
> the dark guard him,
> but the fair go forth to attack?
> This riddle ponder,
> O prince Heidrek!

'Your riddle is good, Gestumblindi,' said the king; 'I have guessed it. This is the game of *hnefatafl*; the darker ones defend the *hnefi*, but the white ones attack.'[2]

Then said Gestumblindi:

> (57) Who is it lonely
> in the hearth-pit[3] sleeping,
> solely from stone he's made;
> for brightness eager[4]
> he's without parents,
> and there will he live out his life?
> This riddle ponder,
> O prince Heidrek!

'That is fire hidden in the hearth,' said the king; 'it is struck out of flint.'

Then said Gestumblindi:

> (58) Who is that great one
> over ground passing,
> swallowing water and wood;
> the wind fearing,
> but fleeing no man,
> and waging war on the sun?
> This riddle ponder,
> O prince Heidrek!

'Your riddle is good, Gestumblindi,' said the king; 'I have guessed

---

[2] On the game of *hnefatafl* see Appendix D
[3] The word *ǫsgrúi* (i.e. *ǫsk-grúi*), not otherwise recorded, seems to mean the ash-pit, or hollow in the hearth, where the fire was kept alight overnight.
[4] *fagr-gjarn* is not recorded elsewhere. U's *fár-gjarn* means 'eager for damage.'

hann líðr yfir jǫrðina, svá at ekki sér fyrir honum ok eigi sól, en hann er af, þegar vind gerir á.'

Þá mælti Gestumblindi:

(59) Hvat er þat dýra,
er drepr fé manna
ok er járni kringt^a útan;
horn hefir átta,
en hǫfuð ekki,
ok fylgja því margir mjǫk?^b
Heiðrekr konungr,
hyggðu at gátu!

'Þat er húnn í hnettafli.'[1]

Þá mælti Gestumblindi:

(60) Hvat er þat dýra,
er Dǫnum[2] hlífir,
berr blóðugt bak,
en bergr firum,
geirum mœtir,
gefr líf sumum,^c
leggr við lófa
lík sitt gumi?^d[3]
Heiðrekr konungr,
hyggðu at gátu!

'Þat er skjǫldr; hann verðr opt blóðugr í bardǫgum ok hlífir vel þeim mǫnnum, er skjaldfimir eru.'

Þá mælti Gestumblindi:

(61) Hverjar eru þær leikur,
er líða lǫnd yfir
at forvitni fǫður^e[4];

^a kringr R
^b thus R, ok fylgir margr U, ok rennr sem hann má H (ok rennr er renna má Bugge)
^c sumum HU, firum R (firum RHU in line 4)
^d gumi RH, guma U   ^e thus H, line om. RU

[1] H's solution adds: 'It has the same name as a bear; it runs as soon as it is thrown.' The riddle is a play on two homonyms, *húnn* 'bear's cub,' and another word *húnn* (usually meaning 'masthead') here evidently meaning a 'die.' There is a further play on the two meanings of *horn*, 'horn' and 'corner,

it. That is fog; it passes over the earth, so that one cannot see because of it, not even the sun; but it is gone, so soon as the wind gets up.'

Then said Gestumblindi:

> (59) What is that creature
> that kills men's flocks —
> with iron all about it is bound;
> eight its horns are
> but head it has none:
> there are many that move at its side?
> This riddle ponder,
> O prince Heidrek!

'That is the *húnn* in *hnefatafl*,'[1] said the king.

Then said Gestumblindi:

> (60) What is that creature,
> a cover to the Danes,[2]
> with back gory,
> yet guardian of men;
> spears it encounters,
> to some gives life,
> in its hollow hand
> a man holds his body?[3]
> This riddle ponder,
> O prince Heidrek!

'That is the shield,' said the king. 'In battles it often becomes bloody, and it is a good protection for those who are nimble with it.'

Then said Gestumblindi:

> (61) Who are those playmates
> that pass over the lands,
> by their father unceasing sought[4];

---

angle.' Though called *hnefatafl* in the solutions in both *R* and *H*, this is not the same game as that described in Appendix D.

[2] *Danir* 'Danes,' i.e. 'men' or 'warriors' in general

[3] *R*'s text means that the inner side of the shield is called its *lófi* (palm); *U*'s (reading *guma*) means: 'It (the creature) lays its body against a man's palm.'

[4] *forvitni* means 'curiosity, desire for knowledge,' but the significance of the recurrent formula *at forvitni fǫður* has never been explained.

hvítan skjǫld
þær um vetr bera,*a*
en svartan um sumar?
Heiðrekr konungr,
hyggðu at gátu!*b*1

'Þat eru rjúpur; þær eru hvítar um vetr, en svartar um sumar.'
Þá mælti Gestumblindi:

(62)² Hverjar eru þær snótir,
er ganga *c* syrgjandi
at forvitni fǫður;
mǫrgum mǫnnum
hafa þær at meini orðit,*d*
við þat munu þær sinn aldr ala?
Heiðrekr konungr,
hyggðu at gátu!

'Þat eru Hlés *e* brúðir,³ er svá heita.'
Þá mælti Gestumblindi *f*:

(63) Hverjar eru þær meyjar,
er ganga margar saman
at forvitni fǫður;
hadda bleika
hafa þær inar hvítfǫldnu,*g*
ok eigut *h* þær þar varðir vera?
Heiðrekr konungr,
hyggðu at gátu! *j*

'Þat eru bylgjur, er svá heita.'
Þá mælti Gestumblindi:

---

a thus RU (haust *for* vetr U), þær á vetrum við síðu bera H; *alliteration lacking*; hávetr A.M. *738 (Helgason p. xv)*, Skj.
b Heiðrekr . . . gátu! *om.* R
c ganga HU, ganga margar R
d mǫrgum . . . orðit R, mǫrgum hafa manni / þær at meini komit HU
e Hlés *em.*, edles (eðlis) R
f þá . . . Gestumblindi *om.* R
g hvítfǫldnu H, -fǫlduðu R
h eigu R, eiga H, eigur U
j Heiðrekr . . . gátu! *om.* R

> in time of winter
> white their shields are,
> but black they bear in summer?
> This riddle ponder,
> O prince Heidrek![1]

'Those are ptarmigans,' said the king. 'They are white in winter, but black in summer.'

Then said Gestumblindi:

> (62)[2] What women are they
> wandering mournful,
> by their father unceasing sought;
> to men uncounted
> they have caused evil,
> and thus they will live out their lives?
> This riddle ponder,
> O prince Heidrek!

'Those are the maids of Hlér[3] who are thus named,' said the king.
Then said Gestumblindi;

> (63) Who are those maidens
> going many together,
> by their father unceasing sought;
> pale their hair is
> and their hoods are white,
> yet these maidens know no man?
> This riddle ponder,
> O prince Heidrek!

'Those are the waves that are thus named,' said the king.
Then said Gestumblindi:

---

[1] In this and in several subsequent verses I have restored the address to the king; *H* only misses the lines out once (in a verse where *R* has them). *U* only puts them in a few times, at the beginning of the contest.

[2] On this and the two following riddles, and also verse 67, of which the solution is in every case 'Waves,' see Introduction pp. xviii and xx-xxi.

[3] 'maids of Hlér,' i.e. waves; Hlér (who appears in the solution in *U*) is the sea-god Ægir under another name; his daughters were nine in number, but little is known of him (*SnE*. 78, 116, 175).

(64) Hverjar eru þær ekkjur,
    er ganga allar saman
    at forvitni fǫður;
    sjaldan blíðar ᵃ
    eru þær við seggja lið
    ok eigu þær ᵇ í vindi vaka?
    Heiðrekr konungr,
    hyggðu at gátu!

'Þat eru Ægis ekkjur, svá heita ǫldur.'
Þá mælti Gestumblindi:

(65) Mjǫk ᶜ var forðum¹
    nǫsgás vaxin,
    barngjǫrn sú er bar
    bútimbr saman;
    hlífðu henni
    hálms bitskálmir,
    þó lá drykkjar
    drynhraun² yfir.
    Heiðrekr konungr,
    hyggðu at gátu! ᵈ

'Þar hafði ǫnd búit hreiðr sitt í milli nautskjálka, ok lá haussinn ofan yfir.'
Þá mælti Gestumblindi:

(66) Hverr er sá inn mikli,
    er mǫrgu ræðr
    ok horfir til heljar hálfr;
    ǫldum ᵉ bergr
    ok við ᶠ jǫrð sakask,
    ef hann hefir sér vel traustan vin?

ᵃ blíðir R   ᵇ þær om. HU
ᶜ mjǫk RH (alliteration lacking), nær U, næsta Skj., cf. Kock NN § 2360
ᵈ Heiðrekr . . . gátu! om. R
ᵉ ǫldum em. Bugge (for alliteration), hǫlðum RH, Kock NN § 2361 (reading hjarl for jǫrð), ýtum U
ᶠ við HU, om. R

¹ This line is corrupt; the editors of C.P.B. noted 'We are unable to mend

> (64) What women are they
> wandering together,
> by their father unceasing sought;
> kind they are but rarely
> to the race of men,
> and they must awake in the wind?
> This riddle ponder,
> O prince Heidrek!

'Those are the women of Ægir,' said the king; 'that is what the waves are called.'

Then said Gestumblindi:

> (65) A goose grew large,[1]
> longed for offspring,
> to build her abode
> she brought timber;
> straw-biting swords
> in safety kept her,
> lay there above her
> the booming drink-rock.[2]
> This riddle ponder,
> O prince Heidrek!

'A duck had built its nest between the jaw-bones of an ox,' said the king, 'and the skull roofed it over.'

Then said Gestumblindi:

> (66) What is that great one
> that governs much,
> and half of it Helward turns;
> with the earth striving,
> saviour of mortals,
> if his friend be firm and sure?

---

this' (adding, testily, 'What duck is meant?') and no-one else has been more successful.

[2] *drykkjar drynhraun*: *hraun* meant a stony waste, in Iceland used especially of cold lava-fields. The upper part of the skull is described, apparently, as a scree, with the bones of the head as stones; what the beast drinks is the river which runs down into the depths of the mountain.

Heiðrekr konungr,
hyggðu at gátu!'

'Góð er gáta þín, Gestumblindi, getit er þessar; þat er akkeri með góðum streng; ef fleinn hans er í grunni, þá bergr þat.'
Þá mælti Gestumblindi:

(67) Hverjar eru þær brúðir,
er ganga í brimskerjum ^a
ok eigu ^b eptir firði fǫr;
harðan beð hafa þær
inar hvítfǫldnu ^c konur ^d
ok leika í logni fátt?
Heiðrekr konungr,
hyggðu at gátu! ^e

'Þat eru bárur, en beðir þeira eru sker ok urðir, en þær verða lítt sénar í logni.'
Þá mælti Gestumblindi:

(68) Sá ek á sumri
sólbjǫrgum ^{f 1} á ^g
verðung vaka ^h
vilgi ² teita ^j;
drukku jarlar
ǫl þegjandi
en œpanda
ǫlker stóð. ^k
Heiðrekr konungr,
hyggðu at gátu!

'Þar drukku grísir gylti, en hon hrein við.'
Þá mælti Gestumblindi ^l:

---

^a -skerjum *R*, -serkjum *HU* (*but* -skerjum *U prose*); brimserkjum í *H*
^b eigu *U*, eiga *RH* (*late form*)
^c hvítfǫldnu *H*, -fǫlduðu *R*
^d konur *RU*, *om. H*
^e Heiðrekr . . . gátu! *om. R*
^f sólbjǫrgum *HU* (sel- *U*), sólbjǫrg of *R*
^g á *RU*, í *H*
^h *thus HU* (vuka *U*), bað ek vel lifa *R*
^j teita *H*, teiti *R*, *U corrupt*

> This riddle ponder,
> O prince Heidrek!

'Your riddle is good, Gestumblindi,' said the king; 'I have guessed it. That is an anchor with a good rope; if its fluke is in the ground it will keep one safe.'

Then said Gestumblindi:

> (67) What women are they
> walking in the skerries —
> along the firth they fare;
> white their hoods are
> and hard their bed,
> unstirring when still is the weather?
> This riddle ponder,
> O prince Heidrek!

'Those are the waves,' said the king. 'Their beds are skerries and shingle, and they are not much seen in calm weather.'

Then said Gestumblindi:

> (68) In season of summer
> at sundown[1] I looked
> on a household astir —
> happy they were not[2];
> ale men drank there
> without speaking,
> screaming loudly
> stood the ale-butt.
> This riddle ponder,
> O prince Heidrek!

'Piglets were sucking a sow,' said the king, 'and she was squealing.'
Then said Gestumblindi:

---

^k en ... stóð R, en œpandi ǫlker stóðu H and corruptly U
^l þá ... Gestumblindi om. R

[1] *sólbjargir*, lit. 'sun-saving,' sunset; known in various forms from Scandinavian dialects, but not otherwise from the old literature.
[2] *vilgi* can mean 'very much' or 'not at all.' If the latter, as assumed here, the writer is no doubt emphasising the mirthless silence of these particular 'jarls' (see Glossary, s.v.) over their drink.

(69) Hvat er þat undra,
er ek úti sá
fyrir Dellings durum;
tíu hefir tungur,
tuttugu augu,
fjóra tigu fóta,
fram líðr^a sú vættr?
Heiðrekr konungr,
hyggðu at gátu!

Konungr mælti þá, 'Ef þú ert sá Gestumblindi, sem ek hugða, þá ertu vitrari^b en ek ætlaða; en frá gyltinni segir þú nú úti í garðinum.'
Þá lét konungr drepa gyltina, ok hafði hon níu grísi, sem Gestumblindi sagði.[1] Nú grunar konung, hverr maðrinn mun vera.

Þá mælti Gestumblindi:

(70) Fjórir hanga,
fjórir ganga,^c[2]
tveir veg vísa,
tveir hundum varða,
einn eptir drallar
ok jafnan heldr saurugr.^d
Heiðrekr konungr,
hyggðu at gátu!

'Góð er gáta þín, Gestumblindi, getit er þessar; þat er kýr.'
Þá mælti Gestumblindi:

(71)[3] Sat ek á segli,[4]
sá ek dauða menn[5]
blóðshol^e bera[6]

---

^a ferr hart H, fram gengr U
^b vittari R
^c hanga and ganga reversed H, verse om. U
^d thus R, ok optast óhreinn H
^e blóðshol em. Ant. Russes; blóþ hold R with stroke through þ, = blóðs Bugge, blóðugt Skj.; blóðshold H; verse om. U

[1] On the history of this riddle see Appendix E
[2] Many of the foreign parallels to this riddle place the 'hanging' before the 'ganging.'
[3] In this riddle, based on a complex word-play, there is firstly substitution

(69) What strange marvel
did I see without,
in front of Delling's door;
ten its tongues are
and twenty its eyes,
with forty feet
fares that creature?
This riddle ponder,
O prince Heidrek!

'If you are the Gestumblindi I took you for,' said the king then, 'you are cleverer than I thought. You are speaking now of the sow out in the yard.'

Then the king had the sow killed, and it had nine piglets inside it, as Gestumblindi had said.[1] The king now began to suspect who this man must be.

Then said Gestumblindi:

(70) Four are hanging,
four are walking,[2]
two point the way out,
two ward the dogs off,
one ever dirty
dangles behind it.
This riddle ponder,
O prince Heidrek!

'Your riddle is good, Gestumblindi,' said the king; 'I have guessed it. That is the cow.'

Then said Gestumblindi:

(71)[3] On a sail I sat[4]
and saw dead men[5]
bearing a blood-vein[6]

---

of homonyms and then replacement of the homonym by a synonym. This kind of thing was called *oflióst*, and is described in *SnE*. 193.

[4] Here the substitution is: *veggr* = a wall, but *veggr* also = a sail (*segl*).

[5] Here the substitution is: *valr* = a falcon, but *valr* also = the slain (*dauðir menn*).

[6] The equation here seems to be: *æðr* = an eider-duck, but *æðr* also = a vein (*blóðs-hol*, 'blood-cavity, blood-hollow,' not elsewhere recorded). This seems satisfactory, but has not been accepted by recent editors.

í bǫrk*a* viðar.*b*1
Heiðrekr konungr,
hyggðu at gátu!*c*

'Þar saztu á vegg*d* ok sátt val bera æði í hamra.'
Þá mælti Gestumblindi:

(72) Hverir eru þeir tveir,
er tíu hafa fœtr,
augu þrjú
ok einn hala?
Heiðrekr konungr,
hyggðu at gátu!

'Þat er þá, er Óðinn ríðr Sleipni.'²
Þá mælti Gestumblindi, 'Segðu þat þá hinzt,*e* ef þú ert hverjum konungi vitrari':

(73) Hvat mælti Óðinn
í eyra Baldri,
áðr hann væri á bál hafðr?³

Heiðrekr konungr segir, 'Þat veiztu einn, rǫg vættr!'—ok þá bregðr Heiðrekr Tyrfingi ok hǫggr til hans, en Óðinn brásk í valslíki ok fló á brott; en konungr hjó eptir ok af honum vélifiðrit aptan, ok því er valr svá vélistuttr ávallt síðan.

Óðinn mælti þá, 'Fyrir þat, Heiðrekr konungr, er þú rétt til mín ok vildir drepa mik saklausan, skulu þér inir verstu þrælar at bana verða.' Eptir þat skilr með þeim.⁴

a bǫrk R, 597, bjǫrk 281
b viðar H, virðar R
c Heiðrekr . . . gátu! om. R
d vegg H, veg R
e hinzt em. Bugge, fyrst R

[1] The last equation has not been found. For *í hamra* in R's solution H has *í klóm sér* (in its claws); and in C.P.B. it was proposed to read *í bjǫrk kviðar* 'in the belly's birch' = 'in his talons,' but this fails to provide a homonym. (Further discussion by Kock, NN § 2363.)

to the bark of a tree.¹
This riddle ponder,
O prince Heidrek!

'In this,' said the king, 'you sat on a wall and saw a falcon bearing an eider-duck to the crags.'
Then said Gestumblindi:

(72) Who are those twain
that on ten feet run,
three their eyes are
but only one tail?
This riddle ponder,
O prince Heidrek!

'Thus it is,' said the king, 'when Ódin rides upon Sleipnir.'[2]
Then said Gestumblindi, 'Tell me this then last of all, if you are wiser than any other king':

(73) What said Ódin
in the ear of Balder,
before he was borne to the fire?[3]

'You alone know that, vile creature!' cried King Heidrek, and he drew Tyrfing and slashed at Ódin, but he changed himself into the shape of a hawk and flew away; yet the king, striking after him, took off his tailfeathers, and that is why the hawk has been so short-tailed ever since.

Then Ódin said, 'For this, King Heidrek, that you have attacked me, and would slay me without offence, the basest slaves shall be the death of you.' And after that they parted.[4]

---

[2] Ódin's horse Sleipnir had eight legs, and Ódin only one eye.
[3] On the implications of this last question see Introduction p. xx. Gestumblindi's words before the verse are no doubt themselves founded on verse, but attempts to resurrect it (e.g. Bugge, Kock in *NN* § 3177) are pure guesswork.
[4] Text, translation and commentary for the seven riddles found only in *H* are given in Appendix A (VI).

10

Þat er sagt, at Heiðrekr konungr ætti þræla nǫkkura, þá er hann hafði tekit í vestrvíking; þeir váru níu saman. Þeir váru af stórum ættum ok kunnu illa ófrelsi sínu. Þat var á einni nótt, þá er Heiðrekr konungr lá í svefnstofu sinni ok fátt manna hjá honum, þá tóku þrælarnir sér vápn ok gengu fyrir konungs herbergi ok drápu fyrst útvǫrðuna; því næst gengu þeir at ok brutu*ᵃ* upp konungs herbergit ok drápu þar Heiðrek konung ok alla þá, er inni váru. Þeir tóku sverðit Tyrfing ok allt fé þat, er inni var, ok hǫfðu á brott með sér; ok engi vissi fyrst, hverir þetta hǫfðu gǫrt eða hvert hefnda skyldi leita.

Þá lét Angantýr, sonr Heiðreks konungs, kveðja þings, ok á því þingi var hann til konungs tekinn yfir ǫll þau ríki, er Heiðrekr konungr hafði átt. Á þessu þingi strengði hann heit, at aldri skyldi hann fyrr setjask í hásæti fǫður síns en hann hefði hefnt hans.

Litlu eptir þingit hverfr Angantýr á brott einn saman ok ferr víða at leita þessa manna. Eitt kveld gengr hann ofan til sjávar með á þeiri, er Grafá*ᵇ* hét; þar sá hann þrjá menn á fiskibát, ok því næst sá hann, at maðr dró fisk ok kallar, at annarr skyldi fá honum agnsaxit at hǫfða fiskinn; en sá kvezk eigi laust mega láta.

Hinn mælti, 'Taktu sverðit undan hǫfðafjǫlinni ok fá mér,' en sá tók ok brá ok sneið hǫfuð af fiskinum, ok þá kvað hann vísu:

(74) Þess galt *ᶜ* hon gedda
    fyrir Grafár *ᵈ* ósi,
    er Heiðrekr var veginn
    undir Harvaða *ᵉ* fjǫllum.[1]

Angantýr kenndi þegar Tyrfing. Gekk hann þá brott í skóg ok dvalðisk þar, till þess er myrkt var. En þessir fiskimenn reru at landi ok fara til tjalds þess, er þeir áttu, ok lǫgðusk til svefns. En nær miðri nótt kom Angantýr þar ok felldi á þá tjaldit ok drap þá alla níu þræla,

---

ᵃ brottu *R*
ᵇ Gripá *U*; Greipá *203* (here following *R* but prob. influenced by *U*-text)
ᶜ galt *U*, allt *R*
ᵈ Gropár *U*, Greipár *203*
ᵉ Harvaða with æ written over first a *R*, Hanaða *U* (for Hávaða)

[1] This name, and the other place-names occurring in this part of the saga, are discussed in the Introduction, pp. xxiii f.

10

It is told that King Heidrek had certain slaves whom he had captured on a viking foray into the west. They were nine in all, of noble families, and they little liked their captivity. One night, when King Heidrek lay in his sleeping-chamber with few men near him, the slaves got themselves weapons and went up to the king's lodging. First they slew the watchmen, and then they advanced on the king's quarters and broke into them; there they slew Heidrek the king and all who were within. They took the sword Tyrfing and all the treasure that was in the house, and carried it off with them; and no-one knew at first who had done this, or where to seek vengeance.

Then Angantýr, the son of King Heidrek, had an assembly summoned, and there he was taken for king over all the realms which King Heidrek had held. At this assembly he made a solemn vow never to sit upon the high seat of his father until he had avenged him.

A little while after the assembly Angantýr departed alone, and wandered far and wide searching for these men. One evening he was walking down to the sea beside the river called Grafá, and there he saw three men in a fishing-boat; presently he saw one of the men catch a fish, and heard him call out to one of his companions to pass him the bait-knife to cut off the fish's head; but the other man said that he could not spare it.

Then the first one said, 'Take the sword from under the head-board, and pass it to me,' and taking it he drew it, and cut off the fish's head; then he spoke a verse:

> (74) The pike has paid
> by the pools of Grafá
> for Heidrek's slaying
> under Harvad-fells.[1]

Then Angantýr knew at once that it was Tyrfing. He went away into the forest and stayed there till it was dark; but these fishermen rowed to land and went to the tent which they had, and laid themselves down to sleep. But towards midnight Angantýr came up and pulled en tók sverðit Tyrfing, ok var þat þá til marks, at hann hafði hefnt fǫður síns.

Ferr Angantýr nú heim. Því næst lætr Angantýr gera veizlu mikla á Danparstǫðum[a] á þeim bœ, er Árheimar heita, at erfa fǫður sinn. Þá[1] réðu þessir konungar lǫndum, sem hér segir:

(75) Ár kváðu Humla
Húnum[b] ráða,
Gizur Gautum,[2]
Gotum Angantý,
Valdar Dǫnum,[3]
en Vǫlum Kjár,[4]
Alrekr inn frœkni[c][5]
enskri þjóðu.

Hlǫðr, sonr Heiðreks konungs, fœddisk upp með Humla konungi, móðurfǫður sínum, ok var allra manna fríðastr sýnum ok drengiligastr. En þat var fornt mál þann tíma, at maðr væri borinn með vápnum eða hestum; en þat var til þess haft, at þat var mælt um þau vápn, er þá váru gǫr þann tíma, er maðrinn var fœddr, svá ok fé, kykvendi, yxn eða hestar, ef þat var þá fœtt; ok var þat allt fœrt saman til virðingar tignum mǫnnum, sem hér segir um Hlǫð Heiðreksson:

(76) Hlǫðr var þar borinn
í Húnalandi
saxi ok með sverði,
síðri brynju,
hjálmi hringreifðum,[6]

---

[a] Dap- and Dam- U (Damp- 203); cf. verse 82/6
[b] Húnum papp. fol. 120 (Helgason p. xxxviii), fyrir her R
[c] Alrek inn frœkna Bugge

[1] From this point to the end of verse 76 there is nothing corresponding in the U-text, which omits all the narrative parts of the poem (see textual notes).

[2] On this verse see Introduction p. xxii. The *Gautar* were the inhabitants of southern Sweden, the *Geatas* of Beowulf. It cannot be said what relationship, if any, this Gizur bore to Gizur Grýtingalidi the Goth of the next section of the saga. The names *Gautar* and *Gotar* (Goths) are ultimately related to each other.

[3] A king of the Danes called Valdar appears at the end of this saga, and a *Valdarr inn mildi* in a genealogy in *Flateyjarbók* (I 26-7), but nothing is known of either. The meaningless line *Valdarr Dǫnum* in *Guðrúnarkviða* II (19) is doubtless taken from this verse.

[4] *Valir* is the Norse form of the general North and West Germanic name

the tent down on top of the slaves, and killed all nine of them; and he took the sword Tyrfing, as a sign that he had avenged his father.

And now Angantýr returned home, and immediately afterwards he had a great funeral feast held at the place called Árheimar, on the banks of the Dnieper, to honour the memory of his father.

These[1] were the kings who ruled over the lands in those days, as it is told here:

> (75) Of old they said Humli
> of Huns was ruler,
> Gizur of the Gautar,[2]
> of Goths Angantýr,
> Valdar the Danes ruled,[3]
> and the Valir Kjár,[4]
> Alrek the valiant[5]
> the English people.

Hlöd, the son of King Heidrek, had been brought up in the halls of King Humli, his mother's father, and he was the most valiant of all men, and the most beautiful in appearance. There was an old saying at that time, that a man was born with weapons or horses; and the explanation of this is that it was said of those weapons which were being made at the time when the man was born, and so likewise with beasts, sheep, oxen, or horses, which were born at the same time: all this was gathered together in honour of men of noble birth, as is told here concerning Hlöd, the son of Heidrek:

> (76) In the Hun-kingdom
> was Hlöd's birthplace,
> with sword and cutlass
> and corslet hanging,
> ring-adorned helmet[6]

---

for the Celtic peoples; the English cognate still survives in the name Wales. It was also applied to the Romans (O.E. *Rum-walas*); and since *Kjárr* is very probably the Norse transformation of Latin *Caesar*, it is likely that the reference here is to the Eastern Roman Emperor. Cf. *Widsith* (ed. R. W. Chambers, 1912), lines 20, 76–8, and notes.

[5] This king appears in a genealogy in *Flateyjarbók* (I 25), but he is unknown in any English tradition. The change from accusative to nominative here is odd (see textual note).

[6] See Falk, *Altnord. Waffen.* 163

hvǫssum^a mæki,¹
mari vel tǫmum
á mǫrk² inni helgu.³

Nú spyrr Hlǫðr fráfall fǫður síns ok þat með, at Angantýr bróðir hans var til konungs tekinn yfir allt þat ríki, sem faðir þeira hafði átt. Nú vilja þeir Humli konungr ok Hlǫðr, at hann fari at krefja arfs Angantý bróður sinn, fyrst með góðum orðum, sem hér segir:

(77) Hlǫðr reið austan,^b
Heiðreks arfi,
kom hann at garði,
þar er Gotar byggja,^c
á Árheima
arfs at kveðja,
þar drakk Angantýr
erfi Heiðreks.^d

Nú kom Hlǫðr í Árheima með miklu liði, sem hér segir:

(78) Segg fann hann úti
fyrir sal hávum
ok síðfǫrlan^{e 4}
síðan kvaddi:
Inn gakktu, seggr,
í sal hávan,
bið mér Angantý
andspjǫll bera!^f

Sá gekk inn fyrir konungsborð ok kvaddi Angantý konung vel ok mælti síðan:

^a hǫssum *R*
^b sunnan *U prose, verse om. U*
^c bygdia *R*, byggðu *Skj.*
^d Heiðreks konungs *R*
^e síðfǫrlan *R*, síðfǫrull hann *Kock FF § 16*
^f verse 78/1–4 om. *U*; lines 5–8 = *U 1–4*, after which *U* continues andspjǫll lia, / orða tveggja, / tveggja eðr þriggja, / ef hann til vill

¹ The distinction here implied between *mækir* and *sverð* is found elsewhere (Fritzner, *Ordbog*, s.v. *mækir*). The former was in origin probably a long two-edged sword, but the words became interchangeable (cf. verses 36–7, of Tyrfing); and *sax* and *sverð* are not always distinguished. (Cf. Falk, *Altnord. Waffen.* 9 ff.)

² The existence of sacred groves and tree-sanctuaries among Germanic peoples, and the worship of the divinities who dwelt in them, is widely attested in many ancient sources (esp. Tacitus, *Germania* chs. 9, 39, 40, 43). Most

and harsh-edged sword,[1]
horse well-broken
in the holy forest.[2,3]

Now Hlöd learnt of the death of his father, and learnt too that Angantýr his brother had been made king over all the realm which their father had held. Then Humli the king and Hlöd resolved that Hlöd should go and demand his inheritance from Angantýr his brother, using fair words at first, as is thus told:

(77) Hlöd rode from the east,
heir of Heidrek,
he came to the court
claiming his birthright,
to Árheimar,
the homes of the Goths;
there drank Angantýr
arval for Heidrek.

And so Hlöd came to Árheimar with a great following, as is told in this verse:

(78) A man he found lingering
late in the open[4]
by the high dwelling,
and hailed him thereafter:
Friend, now hasten
to the high dwelling,
demand of Angantýr
that with me he speak!

The man went in, up to the king's table, and hailed Angantýr with fair words; and then he said:

---

famous in the North was the grove at Uppsala where the bodies of the victims were hung. See J. de Vries, *Altgerm. Religion.* I 289 ff.; H. M. Chadwick, *The Cult of Othin*, 1899.

[3] This verse was perhaps originally meant literally, as an expression of that precocity among gods and heroes which is found elsewhere, the preceding prose being an attempt to rationalise it.

[4] *síðfǫrull* 'late abroad,' emphasising that the man was not in the hall drinking with the king. Kock's emendation applies the word to Hlöd; he translates it as 'far-travelling' (= *víðfǫrull*), comparing O.E. *side and wide* 'far and wide.'

(79) Hér er Hlǫðr kominn,
Heiðreks arfþegi,[a]
bróðir þinn
inn bǫðskái[b];
mikill er sá maðr ungr[c]
á mars baki,
vill nú, þjóðann,[d][1]
við þik tala.[e]

En er konungr heyrði þetta, þá varpaði hann knífinum á borðit, en sté undan borðinu ok steypti yfir sik brynju ok hvítan skjǫld í hǫnd, en sverðit Tyrfing í aðra hǫnd. Þá gerðisk gnýr mikill í hǫllinni, sem hér segir:

(80)[f] Rymr var í ranni,[2]
risu með góðum,
vildi hverr heyra
hvat Hlǫðr mælti
ok þat[g] er Angantýr
andsvǫr veitti.

Þa mælti Angantýr, 'Vel þú kominn, Hlǫðr bróðir, gakk inn með oss til drykkju, ok drekkum mjǫð eptir fǫður okkarn fyrst til sama ok ǫllum oss til vegs með ǫllum várum sóma.'

Hlǫðr segir, 'Til annars fórum vér hingat en at kýla vǫmb vára.' Þá kvað Hlǫðr:

(81) Hafa vil ek hálft allt
þat er Heiðrekr átti,[h]
kú ok af kálfi,
kvern þjótandi,
al ok af oddi,
einum[3] skatti,[j][4]

---

[a] arfi U [b] bǫðskai U (bandskai MS for baud-), beðskammi R
[c] maðr ungr R, mǫgr U [d] nú þjóðann R, sá þundr U
[e] mæla U [f] verse om. U [g] þau Bugge
[h] from this point 203 follows the U-redaction
[j] lines 5–6 before 3–4 U, 203 and most edd.

[1] It is possible to take þjóðann as the subject of vill, i.e. Hlöd.
[2] Very similar lines are Hamðismál 23, Styrr varð í ranni, and Bragi's Ragnarsdrápa 3, rósta varð í ranni, both referring to the tumult in the hall of Ermanaric, king of the Goths, when he was attacked.

(79) Hlöd is come here,
Heidrek's offspring,
your own brother,
for battle eager;
mighty this youth is
mounted on horseback;
king![1] he claims now
converse with you.

When the king heard that, he cast down his knife upon the board and rose from the table; he put on his coat of mail, and took his white shield in one hand and the sword Tyrfing in the other. Then there arose a great din within the hall, as is thus told:

(80) Clamour woke in the court,[2]
with the king rising
each would hearken
to Hlöd's greeting
and learn what answer
Angantýr gave.

'You are welcome, Hlöd, my brother!' said Angantýr then. 'Come in and drink with us; and first let us drink mead in memory of our father, for concord between us, and for the honour of us all, with all the dignity we have!'

But Hlöd answered, 'We have come here for something other than the filling of our bellies.' Then he said:

(81) Half will I have
of Heidrek's riches,
of cow and of calf,
of creaking handmill,
tools and weapons,
treasure[4] undivided,[3]

---

[3] The translation 'undivided' is not certain. Bugge took *einn* here as 'unique, remarkable,' comparing *Beowulf* 1458 ('that was one of ancient treasures,' i.e. it was unique among them).

[4] *skatti* has been adduced as a survival of non-Norse language in the poem; for Norse *skattr* always means 'tax, tribute,' whereas here it means 'treasure,' as do the cognate words in O.E., O.H.G., and Gothic. The only other exception is the phrase *Niflunga skattr* (of the Nibelung hoard).

þý ok af þræli
ok þeira barni[a];

(82) hrís þat it[b] mæra,[c]
    er Myrkviðr heitir,[d]
    grǫf[1] þá ina helgu,[e]
    er stendr á Gotþjóðu,[f]
    stein[1] þann inn fagra,[g]
    er stendr á stǫðum Danpar,[h]
    hálfar herváðir,[j2]
    þær er Heiðrekr átti,
    lǫnd ok lýða[k]
    ok ljósa bauga.

Þá segir Angantýr, 'Eigi ertu til lands þessa kominn með lǫgum, ok rangt viltu bjóða.' Þá kvað Angantýr:

(83) Bresta mun fyrr,[l] bróðir,
    in blikhvíta lind[m]
    ok kaldr geirr
    koma við annan[n3]
    ok margr gumi
    í gras hníga
    áðr en Tyrfing
    í tvau deilak
    eða þér, Humlungr,
    hálfan arf gefa![o]

Ok enn kvað Angantýr:

---

[a] bǫrnum 203 and corruptly U
[b] hrísi því inu U, 203
[c] mæra Atlakviða 5, meira R, mæta U, 203 (later corr. to mæra in 203)
[d] thus U, er Myrkviðir heita R, 203
[e] ina helgu U, 203, ennu góðu R
[f] á Goðþjóðu U (with Goð- for Got- throughout), gotþjóða 203 (elsewhere goð-), á gǫtu þjóðar R
[g] fagra U, 203, meira R (for mæra)
[h] Danpar U, Dampar R, Dampnar 203
[j] herborgir 203 and corruptly U
[k] ok lýða U, 203, om. R
[l] fyrr em. Björn., for R, áðr U, 203

slave and bondmaid
and their sons and daughters;

(82) the renowned forest
that is named Mirkwood,
the hallowed grave[1]
in Gothland standing,
the fair-wrought stone[1]
beside the Dnieper,
half the armour[2]
owned by Heidrek,
lands and liegemen
and lustrous rings!

Then Angantýr said, 'You have no title to this land, and you are resolved to deal unjustly'; and then he said:

(83) The bright buckler
shall break, kinsman,
the cold lances
clash together,[3]
grim men unnumbered
in the grass sinking,
ere the heritage I share
with Humli's grandson
or ever Tyrfing
in twain sunder!

Yet more Angantýr uttered:

---

^m *thus* U, 203 (iij U, minn 203, *for* in), lindin blikhvíta R (*with bad alliteration*)

ⁿ ok kaldr . . . annan U, 203, *om*. R

^o áðr . . . gefa U, 203 (tuenn ra U, midt 203 *for* tvau). R *reads corruptly* ek mun Humlung / hálfan láta / eða Tyrfing / í tvau deila. *Then follows* Býð ek þér, frændi, til heilla sátta mikit ríki ok œrit fé, tólf hundruð vápna . . . (*sc.* vápnaðra manna?); *here* R *ends*

[1] On the grave and the stone see Introduction p. xxv
[2] *herborgir*, 'fortresses' might be thought the more natural demand.
[3] cf. *Beowulf* 3021–2, 'Many a spear cold in the morning (*gar morgenceald*) shall be grasped in hand.'

(84) Ek mun bjóða þér
bjartar vigrar,[a][1]
fé ok fjǫlð meiðma,
sem þik[b] fremst tíðir;
tólf hundruð[c] manna,
tólf hundruð[c] mara,
tólf hundruð[c] skálka,[2]
þeira er skjǫld bera.

(85) Manni gef ek hverjum
mart at þiggja,
annat œðra
en hann á at ráða[d];
mey gef ek hverjum
manni at þiggja,
meyju spenni ek hverri
men at hálsi.

(86) Mun ek um þik sitjanda
silfri mæla,
en ganganda þik
gulli steypa,
svá á vegu alla
velti baugar[3];
þriðjung[4] Gotþjóðar,
því skaltu einn ráða.

Gizurr Grýtingaliði,[e][5] fóstri Heiðreks konungs, var þá með

[a] bjartar vigrar *em. Skj.*, fagrar veigar (aigar *U*) *U, 203* (*without alliteration*), bauga fagra *Bugge*
[b] þik *em. Bugge*, mik *U, 203*
[c] thus *Edd. Min.*, hundruð gef ek þér *U, 203*
[d] á at ráða *em. Helgason*, aradi *U*, anijdi *203*; *other suggestions in editions and Kock FF § 18*
[e] Gyrtinga- *203*

[1] It is notable that verse 84/1-4 and verse 103/1-4 are almost the same, 103/2 being the difficult expression *basmir óskerðar*. The original may well be altogether perverted here. The prose of *R* where it breaks off is paraphrasing a verse of similar content, and there Angantýr offers Hlöd *mikit ríki* ('great dominion').
[2] *skálkr*, here meaning 'attendant, servant' (as do the cognate words in O.E., O.H.G. and Gothic), invariably means 'rogue' elsewhere in Norse; but

(84) I will give you
gleaming lances,[1]
wealth and cattle
well to content you;
thralls a thousand,
a thousand horses,
a thousand bondmen[2]
bearing armour.

(85) Each shall get of me
gifts in plenty,
nobler than all that
he now possesses;
to every man
shall a maid be given,
the neck of each
by necklace clasped.

(86) I will measure you in silver
as you sit in your chair,
upon you departing
I will pour down gold,
rings shall go rolling
round about you[3];
a third[4] of Gothland
shall you govern over.

Gizur Grýtingalidi,[5] the foster-father of King Heidrek, was at

---

there is evidence that in Scandinavia also the word originally meant 'servant.' The same sense-development took place in the English word 'shalk' (*New English Dictionary*, s.v.).

[3] The conception of these lines was discussed by Grimm (*Rechtsalterthümer*, 1828, 668 ff.), who cited from a Frankish text the story of how Theodoric imposed as a penalty on the Visigoths that the Frankish ambassador should sit on his horse outside the Gothic hall, while the Goths cast *solidos* upon him till he and his horse and the point of his lance were covered.

[4] The 'third of Gothland' offered to Hlöd agrees with the clauses of several ancient Germanic laws restricting the inheritance of the baseborn; among the Langobards a bastard inherited one third (Grimm, op. cit. 476).

[5] *Grýtingaliði*, apparently 'vassal or retainer of the *Grýtingar*' (on whom see Introduction p. xxiv). Neckel, however (*Beiträge* 263), held that *liði* was here a distinct word meaning 'lord,' not otherwise recorded in Norse.

Angantý konungi; hann var þá ofrgamall. Ok er hann heyrði boð Angantýs, þótti honum hann ofmikit bjóða ok mælti:

(87)[1] Þetta er þiggjanda
þýjar barni,
barni þýjar,[a][2]
þótt sé borinn konungi [b];
þá hornungr
á haugi sat,[3]
er ǫðlingr
arfi skipti.

Hlǫðr reiddisk nú mjǫk, er hann var þýbarn ok hornungr kallaðr, ef hann þægi boð bróður síns[4]; sneri hann þá þegar í burt með alla sína menn, til þess er hann kom heim í Húnaland [c] til Humla konungs, móðurfǫður síns, ok sagði honum, at Angantýr bróðir hans hefði eigi unnt [d] honum helmingaskiptis.

Humli konungr spurði allt tal þeira; varð hann þá reiðr mjǫk, ef Hlǫðr dóttursonr hans skyldi ambáttarsonr heita, ok mælti:

(88) Sitja skulu vér í vetr
ok sælliga lifa,
drekka ok dœma[5]
dýrar veigar;
kenna Húnum
hervápn [e] búa,
þau er frœknliga [f]
skulum fram bera.

[a] þya ok *203*, þia ok *U*
[b] konungi *em. Björn.*, konungr *U, 203*
[c] Húnaland *U throughout,* Huma- *or* Humla- *203*
[d] eigi unnt *em. Bugge,* unnat *U, 203*
[e] hervápn *papp. fol. 120,* vápn at *U, 203 (without alliteration)*
[f] frœknliga *em. Bugge,* djarfliga *U, 203 (without alliteration)*

[1] The proverb-poem *Málsháttakvæði* contains a reference to the quarrel at the court of Angantýr: *Gizur varð at rógi saðr, etja vildi jǫfrum saman, Skj.* A II 135 ('Gizur was justly accused of slander—he wished to set the lords against each other').

[2] There are many examples of such emphatic repetitions in the old poetry, and several where the first phrase is repeated in reverse, as here (e.g. *Sigurðarkviða skamma* 17).

[3] Since herdsmen often sat on mounds, it has been thought that Gizur's

that time at the court of King Angantýr; he was now very aged. When he heard Angantýr's offer it seemed to him that he offered too much, and he said:

> (87)[1] A bountiful offer
> for a bondmaid's child —
> child of a bondmaid,[2]
> though born to a king!
> The bastard son
> did sit on a mound[3]
> while the prince was
> parting the heritage.

Hlöd became greatly enraged at being called a bastard and the son of a slave-girl, if he should accept his brother's offer,[4] and immediately he went away with all his following, and returned home to the land of the Huns, to King Humli his mother's father, and told him that his brother Angantýr had refused him an equal division of the inheritance.

Humli the king asked then concerning all that had passed, and he was very angry that Hlöd, his daughter's son, should be called the son of a bondmaid; and he said:

> (88) In winter unstirring
> let us sit content,
> in converse drinking[5]
> the costly wine;
> let us teach the Huns
> to tend their wargear,
> which bold-hearted
> we shall bear to war.

---

words are tantamount to calling Hlöd an abusive name. But other passages connect the sitting on mounds with kingship; especially noteworthy is that in *Flateyjarbók* II 70, describing how a twelve-year-old prince named Björn, who was being brought up in his uncle's house, protested against his deprivation of the kingdom by sitting on his father's barrow; 'then for the first time he claimed the kingdom.'

[4] This is slightly at variance with what Gizur has said in the preceding verse. The meaning is apparently that the acceptance of a third only would lay Hlöd open to be called such names.

[5] *drekka ok dœma* is an alliterative formula of frequent occurrence, and *drekka dýrar veigar* is found more than once in the Poetic Edda.

(89) Vel skulum þér, Hlǫðr,
herlið búa
ok framliga[a]
hildi heyja[b][1]
með tólf vetra[c] mengi
ok tvævetrum fola,
svá skal Húna
her of[d] safna.

Þenna vetr sátu þeir Humli konungr ok Hlǫðr um kyrrt. Um várit drógu þeir her saman svá mikinn, at aleyða var eptir í Húnalandi vígra manna. Allir menn fóru tólf vetra gamlir ok ellri, þeir er herfœrir váru at vápnum, ok hestar þeira allir fóru tvævetrir[e] ok ellri; varð nú svá mikill fjǫlði manna þeira, at þúsundum mátti telja, en eigi færi[f] en þúsundir, í fylkingar. En hǫfðingi var settr yfir þúsund hverja, en merki yfir hverja fylking, en fimm þúsundir í hverri[g] fylking, þeira er þrettán hundruð váru í hverri, en í hvert hundrað fernir fjórir tigir, en þessar fylkingar váru þrjár ok þrír tigir.[2]

Sem þessi herr kom saman, riðu þeir skóg þann, er Myrkviðr heitir, er skilr Húnaland ok Gotaland. En sem þeir kómu af skóginum, þá váru byggðir stórar ok vellir sléttir, en á vǫllunum stóð borg ein fǫgr; þar réð fyrir Hervǫr, systir Angantýs ok Hlǫðs, ok með henni Ormarr[h] fóstri hennar; váru þau sett þar til landgæzlu fyrir her Húna; hǫfðu þau þar mikit lið.

Þat var einn morgun um sólar upprás, at Hervǫr stóð upp á kastala einum yfir borgarhliði; hon sá jóreyki stóra suðr til skógarins, svá lǫngum fal sólina. Því næst sá hon glóa[j] undir jóreyknum, sem á gull eitt liti, fagra skjǫldu ok gulli lagða, gyllta hjálma ok hvítar brynjur; sá hon þá, at þetta var Húna herr ok mikill mannfjǫlði.

---

[a] fromliga *U*, fránliga *203*
[b] *thus U, 203* (hildir *203*) (*without alliteration*); *suggested emendations in editions and Kock NN § 3185*   [c] vetra gǫmlu *U, 203*   [d] af *203*
[e] hestar ... tvævetrir *em.* Bugge; hestum því at allir fóru tvævetrir *203*, at hestum tuttugu vetra *U*   [f] færi *em.* Verelius, færrum *U*, smærri *203*
[g] hverja *203*   [h] Ormarr *U*, Ormur *203 throughout*   [j] gjǫrla *203*

[1] These two lines are probably wholly corrupt; *hildi heyja* has no doubt replaced a distinct phrase (the rest of the verse is concerned with the *mustering* of the Hun army).

(89) Well shall for you, Hlöd,
the host be armed,
fearless-hearted
shall we fight this war,[1]
with twelve-year-old warriors
and two-winter foals,
so shall we muster
the might of Hunland.

All that winter Humli and Hlöd remained quiet; but in the spring they gathered together an army so vast that afterwards the land of the Huns was utterly despoiled of all its fighting-men. All men went, from twelve years old and upwards, who were able to bear weapons in war, and all their horses went, of two years old or more. So great was the multitude that the men of the phalanxes could be counted by their thousands only, and by nothing less than thousands; a captain was set over every thousand, and a standard over every phalanx. There were five thousands in every phalanx, each thousand containing thirteen hundreds, and in each hundred were four times forty men; these phalanxes were thirty-three in number.[2]

When this host had gathered together they rode through the forest called Mirkwood, which divided the land of the Huns from the land of the Goths; and when they came out of the forest they were in a land of broad populous tracts and level plains. On the plains stood a fair stronghold, over which Hervör, the sister of Hlöd and Angantýr, had command, together with Ormar her foster-father; they were set there to defend the land against the army of the Huns, and they had a strong garrison.

One morning at sunrise Hervör stood on a watchtower above the fortress-gate, and she saw a great cloud of dust from horses' hooves rising southwards towards the forest, which for a long time hid the sun. Presently she saw a glittering beneath the dustcloud, as though she were gazing on a mass of gold, bright shields overlaid with gold, gilded helms and bright corslets; and then she saw that it was the army of the Huns, and a mighty host.

---

[2] Verse 102 has 'six,' not 'thirty-three,' and that is certainly right, for it agrees with Saxo (Introduction p. xxvii); the latter figure must depend on a copyist's error at some stage.

Hervǫr gekk ofan skyndiliga ok kallar lúðrsvein sinn ok bað blása saman lið; ok síðan mælti Hervǫr, 'Takið vápn yður ok búizk til orrostu, en þú, Ormarr, ríð í mót Húnum ok bjóð þeim orrostu[a] fyrir borgarhliði inu syðra.'

Ormarr kvað:

(90) Skal ek víst ríða
ok[b] rǫnd bera,
Gota[c] þjóðum
gunni at heyja.[1]

Þá reið Ormarr af borginni mót Húnum; hann kallaði þá hátt, bað þá ríða til borgarinnar,—'ok úti fyrir borgarhliðinu suðr á vǫllunum þar býð ek yðr til[d] orrostu; bíði[e] þeir þar annarra, er fyrr koma.'

Nú reið Ormarr aptr til borgarinnar, ok var þá Hervǫr albúin ok allr hennar herr. Síðan riðu þau út af borginni með allan herinn móti Húnum; hófsk þar allmikil orrosta. En með því at Húnar hafa lið miklu meira, sneri mannfallinu í lið þeira Hervarar, ok um síðir fell Hervǫr ok mikit lið umhverfis hana. En er Ormarr sá fall hennar, þá flýði hann ok allir þeir, er lítt dugðu.[f] Ormarr reið dag ok nótt, sem mest mátti hann, á fund Angantýs konungs í Árheima; Húnar taka nú at herja um landit víða ok at brenna.

Ok sem Ormarr kom fyrir Angantý konung, þá kvað hann[2]:

(91) Sunnan em ek kominn
at segja spjǫll þessi:
sviðin er ǫll in mæra[g]
Myrkviðar[h] heiðr,[i]
drifin ǫll Gotþjóð
gumna blóði.

Ok enn kvað hann:

(92) Mey veit ek Hervǫru
Heiðreks dóttur,[k]

[a] orð 203   [b] ok í U, í 203   [c] Gauta U, 203   [d] í 203
[e] biðja 203   [f] lítt dugðu U, 203, lífit þágu Bugge and later editions
[g] in mæra added Edd. Min., mǫrk ok papp. fol. 120 (alliteration lacking in U, 203)
[h] Myrkviðar later corr. in 203 from -heiðar, Myrkheiðr U
[i] heiði 203, om. U
[k] Mey ... dóttur em. Scharovolski (cited by Helgason), Mey veit ek Heiðreks U, 203

[1] This verse is corrupt; the prose context suggests strongly that Ormar

Hervör went down swiftly and called her trumpeter, and ordered him to blow a summons to the host; and then she said, 'Take your weapons and make ready for battle; but do you, Ormar, ride to meet the Huns, and challenge them to battle before the south gate of the stronghold.'

Ormar answered:

> (90) Surely shall I ride,
> my shield holding,
> to give battle
> for the Gothic people![1]

Then Ormar rode out of the fortress towards the Huns; he called out in a great voice and told them to ride on to the fortress — 'and outside the stronghold-gate, in the plains to the south, there I offer you battle; and let them await the others, those who first come there.'

Now Ormar rode back to the fortress, and Hervör was ready, and all her army. They rode out of the stronghold with all the garrison to meet the Huns; and there a most mighty battle arose. But since the Huns had by far the larger army the slaughter became heavier in Hervör's host; and at last Hervör fell, and a great company around her. When Ormar saw her fall he fled away, and all the rest, who were fainthearted. Day and night Ormar rode, as fast as he could, to reach King Angantýr in Árheimar; but the Huns began now to ravage and burn far and wide across the land.

When Ormar came before Angantýr the king, he said[2]:

> (91) From the south have I come
> to speak these tidings:
> fire in the marches
> of Mirkwood is raging,
> with the gore of men
> all Gothland's sprinkled!

And more he spoke:

> (92) I know that Hervör
> Heidrek's daughter,

---

said he would *challenge the Huns* (i.e. 'to fight the Goths'), and lines to this effect have doubtless been lost after *bera*.

[2] On the very damaged verses that follow see Introduction, p. xxii

systur þína,
svigna til jarðar;
hafa Húnar
hana fellda
ok marga aðra
yðra þegna.

(93) Léttari^a gerðisk hon at bǫð^{b1}
en við biðil rœða,
eða í bekk at fara
at brúðargangi.^{c2}

Angantýr konungr, þá er^d hann heyrði þetta, brá hann grǫnum ok tók seint til orða ok mælti þetta um síðir: 'Óbróðurliga vartu leikin, in ágæta systir!'³ Ok síðan leit hann yfir hirðina, ok var ekki mart liðs með honum. Hann kvað þá:

(94) Mjǫk várum vér margir,
er vér mjǫð drukkum;
nú erum vér færi,
er vér fleiri skyldum.

(95) Sé ek eigi mann^e
í mínu liði,
þótt ek biðja
ok baugum kaupa,
er muni ríða
ok^f rǫnd bera
ok þeira^g Húna
herlið finna.

Gizurr gamli sagði:

(96) Ek mun þik^h engis
eyris krefja

---

^a léttari *em. Petersen*, littari *203, om. U*
^b at bǫð *em. Edd. Min.*, at baðni *U*, á hauðri *203*
^c eða ... -gangi *203*; ad leik i sarna enn ad lundur geingu *U*, at leiki járna, en und líni ganga *Edd. Min., cf. Kock FF § 19*
^d er *om. 203*
^e mann *em. Bugge*, þann *U, 203*
^f í *U, 203*
^g þeir *U, 203*
^h þar *203*

[1] A word meaning 'battle' is needed here; bǫð (cf. *baðni U*) supplies a

> your own sister,
> has sunk to the earth;
> the Hun foemen
> felled the maiden
> and many more
> of your men by her —

> (93) in war[1] more happy
> than in wooer's converse,
> or at bridal banquet[2]
> on bench to seat her.

When King Angantýr heard this, he drew back his lips, and was slow to speak; at last he said, 'In no brotherly fashion have you been treated, my noble sister.'[3] Then he cast his eye over his following, and no great company was there with him; and he said:

> (94) Full many we were
> at the mead-drinking;
> when more are needed
> the number is smaller.

> (95) I see not the man
> among my lieges,
> not though I begged him
> and bribed him with rings,
> who would surely ride,
> his shield bearing,
> to seek out the host
> of the Hun people.

Then Gizur the old spoke:

> (96) No single ounce
> do I ask from you,

---

b-alliteration, but the MS forms suggest that a disyllabic form underlies them. The line is overfilled and altogether corrupt.

[2] The *brúðargangr* was the procession of the bride and ladies from the *brúðarhús* (bride's chamber) to the *stofa* (see Glossary) for the feast. The divergence between the manuscripts here is remarkable; the ingenious restoration of U in *Eddica Minora* is a virtual repetition of the preceding lines: *járna leikr* a kenning for 'battle,' and *ganga und líni* 'to be wedded.'

[3] Some editors give these words of Angantýr as verse.

né skjallanda[a]
skarfs[1] ór gulli[2];
þó mun ek ríða
ok[b] rǫnd bera,
Húna þjóðum
herstaf[c] bjóða.[3]

Þat váru lǫg Heiðreks konungs, ef herr var í landi, en lands-konungr haslaði[d] vǫll[4] ok lagði orrostustað, þá skyldu víkingar ekki herja, áðr orrostan væri reynd.

Gizurr herklæddisk með góðum hervápnum ok hljóp á hest sinn, sem ungr væri. Þá mælti hann til konungs:

(97) Hvar skal ek Húnum
hervíg kenna?

Angantýr konungr kvað:

(98) Kenndu dylgju[e][5]
á[f] Dúnheiði,
orrostu undir[g][6]
Jassarfjǫllum[h];
þar[j] opt Gotar
gunni[k] háðu
ok fagran sigr
frægir vágu.[l]

Nú reið Gizurr í burt ok þar til er hann kom í her Húna; hann reið eigi nær en svá, at hann mátti tala við þá. Þá kallar hann hári rǫddu ok kvað:

[a] skjallanda em. Bugge, skialldanda U, skulldanda 203   [b] í U, 203
[c] herstaf A.M. 202k, gunni at U, 203 (without alliteration)
[d] haslaði later corr. in 203 from halsaði (U unclear)
[e] at Dilgju U, á Dylgju 203 later corr. to Dyngju   [f] ok á U, 203
[g] ok á þeim ǫllum U, 203, ǫldnum for ǫllum Kock FF § 20
[h] thus U, 203, later corr. in 203 to Jǫsur-   [j] bar U, báru 203
[k] gunni em. Verelius, gū U, ok geir 203, eggleik Edd. Min.   [l] fengu 203

[1] The word *skarfr* only occurs here, though relatives of it are known, and it is cited in a nineteenth-century dictionary with the meaning 'diobolus, 4 skilling' (Haldorsen, *Lexicon Islandico-Latino-Danicum*, 1814).
[2] Bugge understood *skjallandi skarfr ór gulli* to mean 'a piece of gold of sufficient weight to make a ringing noise when thrown into a shield or bowl'; Saxo (ed. Holder 298) has a story of how the Frisians once had to pay a tax by casting coins into a shield, but only those that made a noise loud enough

> no single coin[1]
> of clinking gold[2];
> yet ride I shall,
> my shield bearing,
> and to the Hun army
> offer the war-staff.[3]

Now it was the law of King Heidrek that if an army were invading a land and the king of that country marked out a field with hazel-poles[4] and ordained a place of battle, then the raiders should do no ravaging before the battle's issue was decided.

Gizur now clad himself for war with good weapons, and leapt upon his horse as if he were a youth. Then he said to the king:

> (97) Where shall the Huns be
> to war bidden?

The king answered:

> (98) On the Danube-heath
> below the Hills of Ash
> shall you call them to fight,[5]
> their foes meeting[6];
> there often Goths
> have given battle,
> renown gaining
> in noble victories.

Now Gizur rode away until he came to the host of the Huns; but he rode no nearer than within earshot, and called out in a great voice:

---

to catch the ear of the toll-gatherer, who was sitting twelve rooms away, were reckoned up.

[3] *herstaf* must be accounted a very early, and rather surprising, emendation, for A.M. 202k descends from A.M. 203 and is not an independent witness to the text (Helgason p. xxxviii); *herstafr* is not otherwise known; it might mean 'battle-stave,' 'battle-rune' (cf. *Beowulf* 501, *beado-run*), but it is reminiscent of the phrase 'to send out the war-arrow (*her-ǫr*),' as a token that war threatened.

[4] It is likely that originally only a very small area was 'hazelled,' and that in later use *hasla vǫll* meant no more than 'determine a place of battle.'

[5] On this emendation, made also in verse 100, see Introduction p. xxiv.

[6] This emendation is based on the almost identical first half of verse 100, though the repetition of three lines out of four tells nothing for certain, of course, about the fourth.

(99) Felmtr er yðru fylki,
feigr er yðarr vísir,
gnæfar^a yðr gunnfani,^b
gramr er yðr Óðinn!

Ok enn:

(100) Býð ek yðr dylgju^c
á^d Dúnheiði,
orrostu undir
Jassarfjǫllum^e; . . .[1]
ok láti svá Óðinn flein fljúga
sem ek fyrir mæli![2]

Þá Hlǫðr hafði heyrt orð Gizurar, þá kvað hann:

(101) Taki þér Gizur
Grýtingaliða,^f
mann Angantýs,
kominn af Árheimum!

Humli konungr sagði, 'Eigi skulum árum spilla, þeim er fara einir saman.'[3]

Gizurr mælti, 'Ekki gera^g Húnar oss felmtraða^h né hornbogar[4] yðrir!'[5] Gizurr drap þá hest sinn með sporum ok reið á fund Angantýs konungs ok gekk fyrir hann ok kvaddi hann vel. Konungr spurði, hvárt hann hefði fundit konunga.^j Gizurr mælti, 'Talaða ek við þá ok stefnda ek þeim á vígvǫll á Dúnheiði^k í^l dylgjudǫlum.'^m

Angantýr spyrr, hvat mikit lið Húnar hafa. Gizurr mælti, 'Mikit er þeira mengi':

---

^a gnæfr *203*
^b gunnfari *203*
^c at Dilgju *U*, at Dylgju *203 later corr.* to Dyngju
^d ok á *U, 203*
^e Jassar- *203 (later corr.* to Jǫsur-), Jassa- *U. After this 203 has* hræse yðor at há hverju *and U* hrosi yðor at hái hverjum
^f Grýtingaliða *added Bugge, om. U, 203*
^g gerar *203*
^h vélaða *203*
^j konunginn *U,* konung *203*
^k Dúna heiði *U*
^l á *U, 203*
^m Dingju- *U, 203*

> (99) Daunted are your legions,
> doomed your leader,
> banners rise over you,
> Óðin is wrathful!

And then he said:

> (100) On the Danube-heath
> below the Hills of Ash
> I call you to fight,
> your foes meeting; . . .[1]
> may Óðin let the dart fly
> as I prescribe it![2]

When Hlöð heard the words of Gizur, he cried:

> (101) Seize you Gizur
> Grýtingaliði,
> Angantýr's man
> come from Árheimar!

But Humli the king answered him, 'We must not harm heralds who ride alone.'[3]

Then Gizur said, 'Neither the Huns nor their hornbows[4] make us afraid!'[5] Then he struck spurs to his horse and rode back to King Angantýr, and went before him, and greeted him with fair words. The king asked whether he had met with the kings of the Huns, and Gizur answered, 'I spoke with them, and summoned them to the battlefield on the Danube Heath, in the dales of strife.'

Angantýr asked how great was the host of the Huns, and Gizur replied, 'Huge is their multitude':

---

[1] The words following *Jassarfjǫllum* in the manuscripts are quite incomprehensible, and the passage beyond repair. Neither *há* 'hide' nor *hár* 'rowlock' would give any sense. (Cf. Kock, *FF* § 23, *NN* § 2377.)

[2] Gizur here clearly hurls his javelin over the Huns, and so dedicates them to the god (see Appendix C). The verse is obviously corrupt.

[3] Humli's words, or some of them, are often given as verse.

[4] *hornbogi* is a rare word in Norse, in Scandinavia apparently known only as the name of a foreign weapon, and of somewhat uncertain meaning (but probably 'bow reinforced with horn'). (Falk, *Altnord. Waffen.* 91.)

[5] This odd sentence, with *Húnar gera* in the third person followed by *yðrir* ('your'), is no doubt the confused remnant of a verse.

(102) Sex ein eru
seggja^a fylki,
í fylki hverju
fimm þúsundir,
í^b þúsund hverri^c
þrettán hundruð,^d
í hundraði hverju
halir^e fjórtaldir.[1]

Angantýr spyrr nú til Húna hers[f]; þá sendi hann menn alla vegu frá sér ok stefndi hverjum manni til sín, er honum vildi lið veita ok vápnum mátti valda. Fór hann þá á Dúnheiði með lið sitt, ok var þat allmikill herr; kom þá á móti honum herr Húna, ok hǫfðu lið[g] hálfu meira.

Á ǫðrum degi hófu þeir sína orrostu ok bǫrðusk allan þann dag ok fóru at kveldi í herbúðir sínar. Þeir bǫrðusk svá átta daga, at hǫfðingjarnir váru þá allir heilir, en engi vissi manntal, hvat mart fell. En bæði dag ok nótt dreif lið til Angantýs af ǫllum áttum, ok þá kom svá, at hann hafði ekki færa flokk en í fyrstu. Varð nú orrostan enn ákafari en fyrr; váru Húnar ákafir ok sá þá sinn kost, at sú ein var lífs ván, ef þeir sigruðusk,[h] ok illt mundi Gota griða at biðja. Gotar vǫrðu frelsi sitt ok fóstrjǫrð fyrir Húnum, stóðu því fast, ok eggjaði hverr annan. Þá á leið daginn, gerðu Gotar atgǫngu svá harða, at fylkingar Húna svignuðu[j] fyrir; ok er Angantýr sá þat, gekk hann fram ór skjaldborginni ok í ǫndverða fylking ok hafði í hendi Tyrfing ok hjó þá bæði menn ok hesta; raufsk þá fylking fyrir Húna konungum, ok skiptusk þeir brœðr[k] hǫggum við. Þar fell Hlǫðr ok Humli konungr, ok þá tóku Húnar at flýja, en Gotar drápu þá ok felldu svá mikinn val, at ár stemmdusk ok fellu ór vegum, en dalir váru fullir af dauðum mǫnnum ok hestum.

^a sex ... seggja *U*, v.c. eru í *203*
^b í *om. U, 203*
^c hverri þúsund *203*, hverri *U*
^d hundruð manna *U, 203*
^e hals *203*
^f hers *om. 203*
^g liðu *203*
^h sigruðusk ei *U, 203*
^j svignaði *203*
^k þeir brœðr *om. 203*

(102) Of soldiers have they
six phalanxes,
every phalanx
has five thousands,
every thousand
thirteen hundreds,
and a full hundred
is four times counted.[1]

Angantýr learnt now of the strength of the Hunnish host, and then he sent out messengers to every quarter, summoning to him every man who could bear arms and would give him service. He marched then to the Danube Heath with his army, and it was very great; and the Hunnish host came against him, and it was as great again.

On the next day they began the battle, and all that day they fought, and in the evening they went to their tents. They fought thus for eight days without the captains being wounded, but no-one could number the fallen. But both by day and night men thronged in to Angantýr from every quarter, and thus it was that he had no fewer men than at the beginning of the battle. And now the fighting grew yet more bitter than before; the Huns were ferocious, seeing their case, that only in victory lay hope of life, and that it would be of little avail to ask quarter of the Goths. But the Goths were defending their freedom and the land of their birth against the Huns, and for this they stood firm, and each man urged on his comrade. When the day was far spent the Goths pressed on so hard that the Hunnish legions gave way before them; and seeing this Angantýr strode out from behind the shield-wall and up into the foremost rank, and in his hand he held Tyrfing, and he cut down both men and horses; then the ranks fell apart before the kings of the Huns, and brother struck at brother. There Hlöd fell and Humli the king, and the Huns took to flight; but the Goths slew them, and made such carnage that the rivers were choked and turned from their courses, and the valleys were filled with dead men and horses.

---

[1] *halir fjórtaldir*, lit. 'men four times counted,' i.e. 'quadrupled,' which is obscure. The prose before verse 89 has *fernir fjórir tigir*, 'four times forty.' In neither passage do the words *púsund* and *hundrað* (usually = 120) appear to be used as numbers at all.

Angantýr gekk þá at kanna valinn ok fann Hlǫð[a] bróður sinn; þá kvað hann:

  (103) Bauð ek þér, bróðir,
     basmir [b][1] óskerðar,[c]
     fé ok fjǫlð meiðma,
     sem þik[d] fremst tíddi;
     nú hefir þú hvárki
     hildar at gjǫldum
     ljósa bauga
     né land ekki.

Ok enn kvað hann:

  (104) Bǫlvat er okkr, bróðir,
     bani em ek þinn orðinn;
     þat mun æ[e] uppi,
     illr er dómr norna.[2]

---

[a] Hlǫðr 203
[b] basmir *em. Verelius*, basnir U, *empty space* 203
[c] óskir tvær 203
[d] þik *em. Petersen*, mik U, 203
[e] æ *em. Bugge* (cf. Vǫlospá 16), enn U, 203

[1] The reading *basmir* with a sense 'rings' or 'treasure' has been generally accepted *faute de mieux*, but in fact the word is unknown (suggestions concerning it are made by Bugge, *NS*, and Kock, *NN* § 2378).

[2] The Norns were the embodiment of the conception of fate in the ancient mythology, shading off into that of other supernatural women (*dísir, fylgjur,*

Angantýr went to search among the slain, and finding his brother Hlöd he said:

> (103) Treasures[1] uncounted,
> kinsman, I offered you,
> wealth and cattle
> well to content you;
> but for war's reward
> you have won neither
> realm more spacious
> nor rings glittering.

And then he said:

> (104) We are cursed, kinsman,
> your killer am I!
> It will be never forgotten;
> the Norns'[2] doom is evil.

---

valkyrjur). Usually there are three Norns, sometimes many; some are good, but some evil. In *Vǫlospá* 20 the Norns are named *Urðr*, *Verðandi* and *Skuld* (Past, Present, and Future), but probably only *Urðr* is an ancient name; this is cognate with O.E. *wyrd* (whence come the weird sisters in Macbeth, and Mod. English 'weird'), and is perhaps derived from an Indo-European root meaning 'to weave'—the conception of the weaving of destiny is found in Norse and elsewhere in Germanic. See especially *Fáfnismál* 12–13, *SnE.* 23–4, and *þáttr af Nornagesti* (ed. Bugge, *NS* 77; *Flateyjarbók* I 358).

SAGA HEIÐREKS KONUNGS INS VITRA

11[1]

Angantýr var lengi konungr í Reiðgotalandi[a]; hann var ríkr ok hermaðr[b] mikill, ok eru frá honum komnar konunga ættir. Sonr hans var Heiðrekr úlfhamr,[c][2] er síðan var lengi konungr á Reiðgotalandi[a]; hann átti dóttur, er Hildr hét; hon var móðir Hálfdanar snjalla, fǫður Ívars ins víðfaðma.[d][3] Ívarr inn víðfaðmi kom með her sinn í Svíaveldi, sem segir í konunga sǫgum[4]; en Ingjaldr konungr inn illráði[5] hræddisk her hans ok brenndi sik sjálfr inni með allri hirð sinni á þeim stað er á[e] Ræningi[6] heitir. Ívarr inn víðfaðmi lagði þá undir sik allt Svíaveldi; hann vann ok Danaveldi ok Kúrland,[7] Saxland ok Eistland ok ǫll austrríki allt til Garðaríkis; hann réð ok vestra Saxlandi ok vann hlut Englands; þat er kallat Norðumbraland.[f] Ívarr inn víðfaðmi lagði þá undir sik allt Danaveldi, ok síðan setti hann þar yfir Valdar konung ok gipti honum Álfhildi dóttur sína. Þeira sonr var Haraldr hilditǫnn ok Randvér, er síðan fell á Englandi.[8] En Valdarr andaðisk í Danmǫrk; tok þá Randvér Danaríki ok gerðisk konungr yfir; en Haraldr hilditǫnn lét gefa sér konungsnafn í Gautlandi,[g][9] ok síðan

---

[a] -gauta- *203 later corr. to* -gotha-
[b] hermaðr *A.M. 202k*, aui maðr *U*, aur maðr *203*
[c] úlfshamr *203*, úlfhamp *U*
[d] vydfarn- *U*, wijdfarm- *203*, *throughout*
[e] á *added Bugge, cf. Ynglingatál 27*
[f] Norðimbra- *203*
[g] Gotlandi *U, 203*

[1] The history of Sweden described in this last section of the saga is for the most part extremely obscure, and the following notes are mainly limited to some indications of place and time, and of corroboration or disagreement in other Scandinavian works. The best English translation of Snorri Sturluson's *Heimskringla*, often referred to below, is *The Stories of the Kings of Norway*, trans. Morris and Magnússon (The Saga Library, I–III, 1893–1905). Some modern works bearing on the subject are: H. Schück, *Sveriges förkristna konungalängd*, 1910, and the same author in *Arkiv* XII (1896) 217 ff.; B. Nerman, *Svärges älsta konungalängder*, 1914, and *Det svenska rikets uppkomst*, 1925; G. Turville-Petre, *The Heroic Age of Scandinavia*, 1951.

[2] Arngrímur Jónsson, in his Latin epitome of the lost *Skjǫldunga Saga*, says that this name either means that Heidrek was a shape-shifter, taking the form of a wolf, or else is a figurative indication of his savagery (*Bibliotheca Arnamagnæana*, 1950, 353). Arngrímur gives the same genealogy to Ívar as is found here.

[3] Ívar was one of the most famous of the half-legendary kings of the North, but it is impossible to know how much truth there is in the descriptions of his

THE SAGA OF KING HEIDREK THE WISE

II[1]

Angantýr was long king in Reidgotaland; he was mighty, and a great warrior, and lines of kings are sprung from him. His son was Heidrek Wolfskin,[2] who afterwards was long king in Reidgotaland; he had a daughter who was named Hild, and she was the mother of Hálfdan the Valiant, the father of Ívar the Wide-grasping.[3] Ívar came to Sweden with his army, as is told in the sagas of the kings[4]; but King Ingjald the Wicked[5] feared his host and burned himself and all his retinue with him in his own house, at the place called Ræning.[6] Then Ívar the Wide-grasping made all Sweden subject to himself; he conquered also Denmark and Kúrland,[7] the land of the Saxons and the land of the Esths, and all the eastern realms as far as the confines of Gardaríki; he ruled also the land of the Saxons to the west, and conquered that part of England which is called Northumbria. Ívar the Wide-grasping subjected to himself all the realm of the Danes, and set over it King Valdar, giving to him Álfhild his daughter for his wife. Their sons were Harald War-tooth and Randvér, who was afterwards slain in England.[8] But Valdar died in Denmark, and Randvér succeeded to the Danish realm and became king over it; Harald War-tooth took to himself the name of king in Gautland,[9] and afterwards laid beneath

---

vast realm (a very similar account of his conquests is given in *Ynglinga Saga* ch. 41). His father is said to have been the great-grandson of Hrothgar, king of the Danes in *Beowulf*, and he himself may have reigned in the later seventh century.

[4] i.e. *Heimskringla*

[5] Ingjald, most famous of the Yngling kings of Sweden, was the great-grandson of Adils, the Eadgils of *Beowulf*. The story of how he increased his power by inviting all the petty kings to his inheritance feast at Uppsala and burning the hall down over their heads is told in *Ynglinga Saga* chs. 34 ff., and the story of his own burning in ch. 40.

[6] This name is found also in the verse of the *Ynglingatal* cited by Snorri (op. cit. ch. 40); it was probably a place on Tosterö in Lake Mälaren. The original form of the name is discussed by A. Noreen, *Ynglingatal*, 1925, 243.

[7] Modern Latvia, west of the Gulf of Riga

[8] The sources do not agree in the section of the genealogy between Ívar and Harald War-tooth (cf. *Flateyjarbók* I 26), and the personages involved, Valdar and Randvér, are very obscure. Harald War-tooth is an important figure in Saxo's history (ed. Holder 246 ff., trans. Elton 296 ff.).

[9] i.e. modern Götland, the land of the Geatas in *Beowulf*

lagði hann undir sik ǫll framan nefnd ríki, er Ívarr konungr inn víðfaðmi hafði átt.¹

Randvér konungr fekk Ásu, dóttur Haralds konungs ins granrauða*ª* norðan ór Nóregi²; sonr þeira var Sigurðr hringr.³ Randvér konungr varð bráðdauðr, en Sigurðr hringr tók konungdóm í Danmǫrk. Hann barðisk við Harald konung hilditǫnn á Brávelli í eystra Gautlandi,*ᵇ* ok þar fell Haraldr konungr ok mikill fjǫlði liðs.⁴ Þessarar orrostu hefir helzt verit getit í fornum sǫgum, ok mest mannfall í orðit, ok sú, er Angantýr ok hans bróðir Hlǫðr bǫrðusk á Dúnheiði. Sigurðr konungr hringr réð Danaríki til dauðadags, en eptir hann Ragnarr konungr loðbrók⁵ sonr hans.

Sonr Haralds hilditannar hét Eysteinn inn illráði; hann tók Svíaríki eptir fǫður sinn ok réð því, þar til er synir Ragnars konungs⁶ felldu hann, svá sem segir í hans sǫgu.⁷ Þeir synir Ragnars konungs lǫgðu þá undir sik Svíaveldi, en eptir dauða Ragnars konungs tók Bjǫrn sonr hans járnsíða⁸ Svíaveldi, Sigurðr Danaveldi, Hvítserkr Austrríki, Ívarr inn beinlausi England.⁹ Synir Bjarnar járnsíðu váru þeir Eiríkr ok Refill; hann var herkonungr ok sækonungr, en Eiríkr var *ᶜ* konungr yfir Svíaríki eptir fǫður sinn, ok lifði litla hríð. Þá tók ríkit Eiríkr sonr

---

ª granrauða *em. Ant. Russes,* Garnranda *U,* Gotranda *203*
ᵇ Gotlandi *U, 203*
ᶜ var *om. 203* (réð *for* var yfir *U*)

¹ It is debated to what extent Harald War-tooth actually won back his grandfather Ívar's great kingdom, but it seems likely that he was king of all Denmark and at least a large area in Sweden.

² He was king of Agdir in the south of Norway; but according to *Ynglinga Saga* ch. 48 his daughter Ása married Gudröd, king of Westfold; their son was Harald the Black, father of Harald the Fair-haired.

³ Sigurd Ring is said in most sources, as here, to have been Harald's nephew, but elsewhere he appears as ruler in Sweden (e.g. Saxo, ed. Holder 250); see next note.

⁴ As the text says, this was one of the greatest of all battles in Scandinavian history, and was long celebrated by poets and chroniclers; it took place about the middle of the eighth century, and part of the name almost certainly survives in Bråviken, the narrow gulf in Östergötland at the head of which Norrköping lies, but it is quite uncertain what actually happened there. It is not clear what territories Sigurd Ring ruled over, but it is not unlikely that his hosts at Brávǫll represent the rising of parts of Sweden against the Danish supremacy in the North, and the bringing of that supremacy to an end.

⁵ Ragnar Lodbrók was the pre-eminent viking hero of legend, and a central figure in the body of popular tales that grew up round the coming of the Danish 'Great Army' to England in 865, and the death of St Edmund, king of East Anglia. A viking leader named Ragnar certainly existed, and led a raid

him all the realms aforesaid, over which King Ívar the Wide-grasping had been lord.[1]

King Randvér took as his wife Ása, daughter of King Harald the Red-bearded, from Norway in the north,[2] and their son was Sigurd Ring.[3] The death of King Randvér was sudden, and Sigurd Ring succeeded to the kingdom of the Danes. He fought with King Harald War-tooth at Brávöll in eastern Gautland, and there fell King Harald and a mighty array.[4] This battle, and that which Angantýr and Hlöd his brother fought on the Danube Heath, are the most renowned in the ancient tales, with the greatest count of slain. King Sigurd Ring ruled over Denmark till the day of his death, and his son King Ragnar Hairy-breeches[5] after him.

The son of King Harald War-tooth was named Eystein the Wicked; he succeeded to the Swedish realm after his father, and ruled over it until the sons of King Ragnar[6] slew him, as is told in his saga.[7] The sons of King Ragnar subjected to themselves the realm of the Swedes, but after the death of King Ragnar his son Björn Ironside[8] took the Swedish throne, Sigurd the Danish, Hvítserk the Eastern kingdom, and Ívar the Boneless England.[9] The sons of Björn Ironside were Eirík and Refil; Refil was a war-lord and a sea-king, but King Eirík ruled Sweden after his father, and he lived only a little while. Then Eirík the son of Refil inherited the kingdom; he was a great warrior

---

up the Seine to Paris in 845, while some at least of the numerous legendary progeny of Lodbrók were historical persons, leaders in the viking campaigns in the West after the middle of the ninth century. The tradition that intrudes Lodbrók into the line of the kings of Sweden is quite unhistorical. See A. Mawer, in *Saga-book of the Viking Society* VI (1908) 68 ff.; Herrmann, 613 ff.

[6] The sons of Ragnar were many, by different wives, and show many variations in the sources (of which the chief are Saxo, ed. Holder 300 ff., and *Ragnars Saga*, ed. M. Olsen, *S.T.U.A.G.N.L.* XXXVI). The four who appear here are said in *Ragnars Saga* to be the sons of Áslaug, who was herself the daughter of Sigurd Fáfnir's Bane and Brynhild, and thus the Lodbrók legend is linked to the story of the Nibelungs.

[7] *Ragnars Saga*, chs. 9–12

[8] Björn Ironside was one of the leaders of the celebrated viking voyage to the Mediterranean in 859–62.

[9] According to *Ragnars Saga* ch. 7, because Ragnar Lodbrók broke the three nights' abstinence after their wedding that his wife demanded, their eldest son Ívar was born with gristle instead of bones, and could not walk; but he made up for this in cunning. He was the most famous of the original leaders of the Danish attack on England in the reign of Æthelred I, but before the movement into Wessex in 870 he had disappeared from history.

Refils; hann var mikill hermaðr ok allríkr konungr. Eiríks synir Bjarnarsonar[a] váru þeir Qnundr[b] uppsali ok Bjǫrn konungr; þá[c] kom Svíaríki enn í brœðraskipti; þeir tóku[d] ríki eptir Eirík Refilsson.

Bjǫrn konungr eflði þann stað, er at Haugi heitir; hann var kallaðr Bjǫrn at Haugi[1]; með honum var Bragi skáld.[2] Eiríkr hét sonr Qnundar[e] konungs, er ríki tók eptir fǫður sinn at Uppsǫlum; hann var ríkr konungr. Á hans dǫgum hófsk til ríkis í Nóregi Haraldr konungr inn hárfagri, er fyrstr kom einvaldi í Nóreg[f] sinna ættmanna.[3] Bjǫrn hét sonr Eiríks[g] at Uppsǫlum; hann tók ríki eptir fǫður sinn ok réð lengi.[4] Synir Bjarnar váru þeir Eiríkr inn sigrsæli ok Óláfr; þeir tóku ríki eptir fǫður sinn ok konungdóm; Óláfr var faðir Styrbjarnar ins sterka. Á þeira dǫgum andaðisk Haraldr konungr inn hárfagri.[5]

Styrbjǫrn barðisk við Eirík konung fǫðurbróður sinn á Fýrisvǫllum; þar fell Styrbjǫrn.[6] Síðan réð Eiríkr Svíaríki til dauðadags; hann átti Sigríði ina stórráðu.[7] Óláfr hét sonr þeira, er til konungs var tekinn í Svíþjóð eptir Eirík konung; hann var þá barn, ok báru Svíar hann eptir sér; því kǫlluðu þeir hann skautkonung, en síðan Óláf sœnska. Hann var lengi konungr ok ríkr; hann tók fyrst kristni Svíakonunga, ok um hans daga var Svíþjóð kǫlluð kristin.[8]

---

[a] Eiríks synir Bjarnarsonar *em. Munch*; Bjarnar synir *U, 203*
[b] Qnundr *em. Munch*, Eiríkr *U, 203*   [c] þó *203*   [d] taka *203*
[e] Eiríkr ... Qnundar *U*, Qnundr konungr hét sonr Eiríks *203*
[f] Nóregi *203*   [g] Qnundar *203*

[1] In 829 a king of the Swedes called Bernus (Björn) invited the Emperor Louis the Pious to send Christian missionaries into Sweden, an invitation that led to the founding of the church at Birka on Lake Mälaren by St Anskar; and it has been generally supposed that this king was Björn of the Barrow. But see G. Turville-Petre, *Origins of Icelandic Literature*, 1953, 35 f., for reasons against this identification.

[2] Bragi Boddason the Old, if not the founder of scaldic poetry, is the first known scaldic poet. It appears that he lived in Norway, and probably during the latter part of the ninth century. See *C.P.B.* II 2 ff.; L. M. Hollander, *The Skalds*, 1945, 25 ff.; J. de Vries, *Altnordische Literaturgeschichte* I, 1941, 91 ff. Bragi is named as scald of Björn of the Barrow in the *Skáldatal* or List of Scalds (*Edda Snorra Sturlusonar*, ed. G. Jónsson, 1949, 340), and in *Egils Saga* ch. 59 it is said that having fallen foul of King Björn of Sweden Bragi ransomed himself by composing, in one night, a *drápa* of twenty stanzas in his praise.

[3] Harald the Fair-haired is a traditional translation of his name; but 'fair' means 'beautiful' (for explanation of the name see *Haralds Saga Hárfagra* ch. 4). Harald became master of every state in Norway after the battle of Hafrsfjörd, which is now thought to have been fought about 885–90. The Swedish king contemporary with Harald is called Eirík son of Emund, not of

and a very mighty king. The sons of Eirík son of Björn were Önund of Uppsala and King Björn, and in those days Sweden came again to be divided between brothers; they had the kingdom after Eirík the son of Refil.

King Björn built the place called Barrow, and he was called Björn of the Barrow[1]; Bragi the skald dwelt with him.[2] The son of King Önund was named Eirík, who succeeded his father on the throne at Uppsala; he was a mighty king. In his days Harald the Fair-haired raised himself to the throne in Norway, first of his kindred to bring Norway under the rule of one king.[3] The son of King Eirík at Uppsala was named Björn, who possessed the kingdom after his father, and ruled it long.[4] The sons of Björn were Eirík the Victorious and Óláf, who succeeded to the realm and kingly power after their father. Óláf was the father of Styrbjörn the Strong. In their days King Harald the Fair-haired died.[5]

Styrbjörn fought with King Eirík his father's brother at Fýrisvellir, and there Styrbjörn fell.[6] Eirík ruled the realm of Sweden thereafter till the day of his death, and his wife was Sigríd the Ambitious[7]; their son was named Óláf, and he was adopted as king in Sweden after King Eirík. He was then a child, and the Swedes carried him about with them, and therefore they called him Cloak-king, but afterwards Óláf the Swede. He was king for a long time and very mighty. First of the kings of Sweden he received the Christian faith, and Sweden was in name Christian in his days.[8]

Önund, by Snorri, who says also that this Eirík died when Harald had been ten years king of all Norway (op. cit., chs. 13, 28).

[4] Snorri says that this Björn was king of Sweden for fifty years (*Haralds Saga Hárfagra* ch. 29).

[5] It is now thought that Harald died about 940–5.

[6] It was during the battle of Fýrisvellir that Óðin appeared to Eirík, as described in Appendix C. Fýrisvellir is near Uppsala; the battle probably took place about 985, and the death of Eirík about 995. The story of Styrbjörn and the battle of Fýrisvellir is told in *Styrbjarnar þáttr*, *Flateyjarbók* II 70 ff.

[7] Eirík's widow got this name after burning two suitor kings (including Harald Grenski of Westfold, father of St Óláf) in her hall, saying that 'she would make these little kings tired of courting her' (*Óláfs Saga Tryggvasonar* ch. 43).

[8] King Óláf came to the throne of Sweden at the same time as Óláf Tryggvason (995–1000) embarked on the conversion of Norway; and he was baptised in Västergötland by an English bishop about 1008. His extreme unpopularity with the Swedes forced him ultimately to retire to Västergötland, where he built a church at Skara; he died in 1021 or 1022.

Qnundr hét sonr Óláfs konungs sœnska,¹ er konungdóm tók eptir hann ok varð sóttdauðr. Á hans dǫgum fell Óláfr konungr helgi á Stiklastǫðum.² Eymundr*ᵃ*³ hét annarr sonr Óláfs sœnska, er konungdóm tók eptir bróður sinn; um hans daga heldu Svíar illa kristni. Eymundr*ᵃ* var litla hríð konungr.

Steinkell hét ríkr maðr í Svíaríki ok kynstórr; móðir hans hét Ástríðr dóttir Njáls Finnssonar*ᵇ* ins skjálga af Hálogalandi; en faðir hans var Rǫgnvaldr inn gamli. Steinkell var fyrst*ᶜ* jarl í Svíþjóð, en eptir dauða Eymundar*ᵈ* konungs tóku Svíar hann til konungs; þá gekk konungdómrinn ór langfeðgaætt í Svíþjóð inna fornu konunga. Steinkell var mikill hǫfðingi; hann átti dóttur Eymundar*ᵉ* konungs; hann varð sóttdauðr í Svíþjóð nær því er Haraldr konungr fell á Englandi.⁴ Ingi*ᶠ* hét sonr Steinkels, er Svíar tóku til konungs næst eptir Hákon.*ᵍ*⁵ Ingi var þar lengi konungr ok vinsæll ok vel kristinn⁶; hann eyddi blótum í Svíþjóð ok bað fólk allt þar at kristnask; en Svíar hǫfðu ofmikinn átrúnað á heiðnum goðum ok heldu fornum siðum. Ingi konungr gekk at eiga þá konu, er Mær hét; bróðir hennar hét Sveinn. Inga konungi þokknaðisk engi maðr svá vel, ok varð Sveinn því í Svíþjóð inn ríkasti maðr. Svíum þótti Ingi konungr brjóta forn landslǫg á sér, er hann vandaði um þá hluti marga, er Steinkell faðir hans hafði standa látit. Á þingi nǫkkuru, er Svíar áttu við Inga konung, gerðu þeir honum tvá kosti, hvárt hann vildi heldr halda við þá forn lǫg eða láta af konungdómi. Þá mælti Ingi konungr

---

ᵃ Eymundr *em. Verelius,* Eyvindr *U, 203*
ᵇ Njáls Finnssonar *em. Árni Magnússon in A.M. 192,* Niatz sinz son *203,* malzfinz son *U*
ᶜ fyrstr *203*
ᵈ Eyvindar *U, 203*
ᵉ Eyvindar *203, U has corruption of* Qnundar
ᶠ Ingimundr *(elsewhere* Ingi *or abbreviated* Ing*) U*
ᵍ Steinkel *203*

¹ King Óláf was forced by the Swedes to appoint his young son as joint ruler (*Óláfs Saga Helga* ch. 94). This son was born on the eve of the feast of St Jacob (James), and was christened Jacob; but the Swedes objected to this strange name, and called him Önund (ibid., ch. 88).
² St Óláf, expelled by Knút in 1028, was leading a large and various army into Norway in the midsummer of 1030 when he was met by a vast host drawn from northern and western Norway at Stiklastadir, about forty miles from Nidarós (modern Trondheim). There are records of the battle in many sources; Snorri gives a detailed account in *Óláfs Saga Helga,* chs. 209 ff.
³ *Eyvindr* of the manuscripts is an undoubted error for *Eymundr*; the suc-

The son of King Óláf the Swede was named Önund[1]; he inherited the kingdom after him and died of a sickness. In his time King Óláf the Saint fell at Stiklastadir.[2] Eymund[3] was the name of the second son of Óláf the Swede, who inherited the realm from his brother; and in his days the Swedes neglected the Christian faith. Eymund was king for only a little time.

There was a mighty man in Sweden, and of high lineage; his name was Steinkel, and his mother was Ástríd, daughter of Njál the son of Finn the Squinter from Hálogaland; his father was Rögnvald the Old. At first Steinkel was a jarl in Sweden, but after the death of Eymund the Swedes took him for their king; and the Swedish throne passed from the ancestral line of the ancient kings. Steinkel was a mighty prince; his wife was the daughter of King Eymund; and he died of a sickness in Sweden about the time that King Harald fell in England.[4] The son of Steinkel was called Ingi, whom the Swedes took for king next after Hákon.[5] Ingi was king for a long time, well-liked and a good Christian[6]; he put down sacrificing in Sweden and ordered all the people of the land to become Christian; but the Swedes had too strong a belief in the heathen gods and held to their ancient ways. King Ingi's wife was a woman called Mær; her brother's name was Svein. No man was more dear to King Ingi than he, and Svein became thereby the mightiest man in Sweden. But the Swedes thought that King Ingi had infringed their rights under the ancient law of the land, when he found fault with many things that Steinkel his father had let be; and at a certain assembly which the Swedes held with King Ingi they gave him the choice of two things, either to observe the ancient laws or else to give up his throne. Then King Ingi spoke, and

---

cessor of Önund-Jacob is called Emund or Eymund in several sources. With his death about 1060 the ancient line of the Yngling kings came to an end.

[4] This refers to the death of Harald Hardrádi, king of Norway, at Stamford Bridge in 1066. The statement that Steinkel died about the same time is found also in *Magnús Saga Berfœtts* ch. 12 (*Heimskringla* III).

[5] The writer of 203 has no doubt put *Steinkel* instead of *Hákon* here because the latter is not otherwise mentioned in the text; but the succession Steinkel-Hákon-Ingi is found in *Magnús Saga Berfœtts* ch. 12 and elsewhere. Ingi of Sweden was a contemporary of Magnús Barefoot of Norway, and an account of their relations is given loc. cit.

[6] The following account of the religious opposition of the Swedes to King Ingi, the raising up of Svein the Sacrificer, and the burning of his house, agrees with what is told in more condensed fashion in *Flateyjarbók* II 424 f. (cf. also *Magnússona Saga* ch. 24, *Heimskringla* III).

ok kvazk eigi mundu kasta þeiri trú, sem rétt væri; þá œptu Svíar upp ok þrøngðu honum með grjóti ok ráku hann af lǫgþinginu.[1]

Sveinn mágr konungs var eptir á þinginu; hann bauð Svíum at efla blót fyrir þeim, ef þeir gæfi honum konungdóm. Því játa þeir allir við Svein; var hann þá til konungs tekinn yfir alla Svíþjóð. Var þá fram leitt hross[2] eitt á þingit ok hǫggvit í sundr ok skipt til áts, en roðit[a] blóðinu blóttré.[3] Kǫstuðu þá allir Svíar kristni, ok hófusk blót; en þeir ráku Inga konung á burt, ok fór hann í vestra Gautland. Blót-Sveinn var þrjá vetr konungr yfir Svíum.

Ingi konungr fór með hirð sína ok sveit nǫkkura, hafði þó lítinn her; hann reið austr um Smáland[4] ok í eystra Gautland ok[b] svá í Svíþjóð, reið bæði dag ok nótt ok kom óvart Sveini snemma um morgun. Þeir tóku á þeim hús ok slógu í eldi ok brenndu þat lið, er inni var. Þjófr hét lendr maðr, er þar brann inni; hann hafði áðr fylgt Blót-Sveini. Sveinn gekk út ok var drepinn. Ingi tók svá konungdóm at nýju yfir Svíum ok leiðrétti þá enn kristnina ok réð ríkinu til dauðadags ok varð sóttdauðr.[5]

Hallsteinn hét sonr Steinkels konungs, bróðir Inga konungs, er konungr var með Inga konungi bróður sínum. Synir Hallsteins váru þeir Philippus ok Ingi,[6] er konungdóm tóku[c] í Svíþjóð eptir Inga konung gamla. Philippus átti Ingigerði dóttur Haralds konungs Sigurðarsonar[7]; var hann skamma stund konungr.

[a] riodid U, riodudu 203
[b] ok om. 203
[c] tók 203, t° U

[1] In Óláfs Saga Helga ch. 77 Snorri says that it was the old custom in Sweden, in the heathen time, to hold the principal sacrifice at Uppsala in the month of gói (mid-February to mid-March), and that at that time of year the lǫgþing (legislative and judicial courts) were held, with people coming to it from every part of Sweden. To this occasion, no doubt, the present passage refers.

[2] It is probable that the Germanic peoples of the heathen age only ate horse-flesh at sacrifices; but the horse was certainly one of the chief sacrificial animals (horses are mentioned, for instance, in Thietmar of Merseburg's account of the great January sacrifice at Lejre in Zealand).

[3] The 'sacred tree' of Uppsala is described in a scholion (134) to Adam of Bremen's twelfth-century history of the bishops of Hamburg: *prope templum est arbor maxima late ramos extendens, aestate et hyeme semper virens: cuius illa generis sit nemo scit,* and beside it, according to the scholiast, was a well where human sacrifices were drowned. All this bears a close resemblance to

said that he would not leave the true faith; whereat the Swedes cried out, and pelted him with stones, and drove him from the law-assembly.[1]

Svein, the king's kinsman, remained behind at that assembly, and he offered to make sacrifice for the Swedes if they would grant him the kingdom; all agreed to Svein's offer, and he was accepted as king over all the Swedish realm. Then a horse[2] was led forth to the assembly, hewn in pieces, and divided up for eating, and the sacrificial tree[3] was reddened with its blood. Thereafter all the Swedes cast off the Christian faith, and sacrifices were instituted, and they drove King Ingi away; he departed into western Gautland. For three years Svein the Sacrificer was king over the Swedes.

King Ingi went with his own bodyguard and some followers, though it was only a small force; he rode east across Småland[4] and into eastern Gautland, and so into Sweden; he rode by day and night and came upon Svein unawares in the early morning. They seized the house over their heads and set it on fire, and burnt all the company who were inside. There was a landed man called Thjóf who was burnt there; he had been in the following of Svein the Sacrificer. Svein came out and was cut down. And so Ingi took the kingship of the Swedes anew, and restored the Christian faith; he ruled the realm till the day of his death, and died of a sickness.[5]

King Steinkel had a son called Hallstein, and he was king together with King Ingi his brother. The sons of Hallstein were Philip and Ingi,[6] who inherited the throne of Sweden after King Ingi the Old. Philip married Ingigerd, the daughter of King Harald the son of Sigurd[7]; and he was only a short time king.

---

what is said of the 'world-tree,' Yggdrasill, in the Eddaic poems *Vǫluspa* (19) and *Fjǫlsvinnsmál* (19–20). See also p. 47 above, note 2.

[4] The extreme south-east of Sweden, south of Östergötland. Ingi rode through Östergötland and so into *Svíþjóð*, the ancient kingdom of Sweden, as opposed to Götland.

[5] King Ingi died about 1110.

[6] Ingi Hallsteinsson died in 1125; he appears in *Haraldssona Saga* ch. 22 (*Heimskringla* III) as the husband of Brigida, daughter of Harald Gilli, the Irishman who claimed to be a son of Magnús Barefoot and made his way to the throne of Norway in the thirties of the twelfth century.

[7] Harald Hardrádi, son of Sigurd Sýr ('Sow')

APPENDICES

A	Supplementary Texts	*verso* and *recto*	66
B	Gudmund of Glasisvellir		84
C	The References to Ódin		87
D	The Game of *Hnefatafl*		88
E	The Riddle of the Sow		90
F	Fródmar		91

APPENDIX A
SUPPLEMENTARY TEXTS
I
The beginning of the saga according to the U-redaction
Hervarar þáttr inn gamli finnsk svá skrifaðr
sem hér eptirfylgir[a]

Svá finnsk ritat í fornum bókum, at Jǫtunheimar[1] váru kallaðir norðr um Gandvík,[2] en Ymisland[3] fyrir sunnan í millum Hálogalands. En áðr Tyrkjar ok Asíamenn kómu í Norðrlǫnd byggðu norðrhálfurnar risar ok sumt hálfrisar; gerðisk þá mikit sambland þjóðanna; risar fengu sér kvenna ór Mannheimum, en sumir giptu þangat dœtr sínar. Guðmundr[b4] hét hǫfðingi í Jǫtunheimum; bœr hans hét á Grund, en heraðit Glasisvellir.[c4] Hann var ríkr maðr ok vitr,[d] ok varð svá gamall ok allir hans menn, at þeir lifðu marga mannsaldra. Því trúðu heiðnir menn, at í hans ríki mundi Ódáinsakr,[4] sá staðr, er af hverjum manni, er þar kømr, hverfr sótt ok elli, ok má engi deyja. Eptir dauða Guðmundar blótuðu menn hann[e] ok kǫlluðu hann goð sitt.[f] Guðmundr konungr átti son þann, er Hǫfundr hét; hann var bæði forspár ok spakr at viti; hann var settr dómandi yfir ǫll þau lǫnd, er honum lágu í nánd; hann dœmði aldri rangan dóm; enginn þorði né þurfti dóm at rjúfa.

Maðr hét Arngrímr[g]; hann var risi ok bergbúi; hann nam ór Ymislandi Ámu[h] Ymisdóttur ok gekk at eiga hana. Sonr þeira hét Hergrímr, er kallaðr var[i] hálftrǫll; hann var stundum með bergrisum en stundum með mǫnnum; hann[k] hafði afl sem jǫtnar; hann var allfjǫlkunnigr ok berserkr mikill. Hann nam ór Jǫtunheimum Ǫgn álfasprengi ok gekk at eiga hana; þau áttu þann son, er Grímr[l] hét.

Starkaðr áludrengr[5] bjó þá[m] við Álufossa[n6]; hann var kominn af þursum

[a] Title thus 203; Hér byrjask Hervarar saga U
[b] Guðmundr UH, Goðmundr 203 throughout
[c] Glasis- H, Glæsis- U, 203   [d] ok vitr om. 203   [e] hans 203
[f] Eptir . . . sitt 203, H, om. U   [g] Arngrímr U, 203, Hergrímr H
[h] Ámu UH, Arno 203   [i] var om. 203   [k] hann om. 203   [l] Gunnarr 203
[m] Starkaðr . . . þá U, hana hafði fyrr Starkaðr aludiús, bjó þá etc. 203
(áludrengr elsewhere 203)   [n] Álupolla U

[1] With the rationalisation of mythical cosmography, Jötunheimar, the land of the giants, was placed in the extreme north of Scandinavia (Lapland). (Cf. article on *Jötunheimar* in Hoops, *Reallexikon*.)

[2] Gandvík, i.e. the White Sea ('Bay of Sorcery'). The *H*-text places Jötunheimar 'in Finnmark.'

APPENDIX A
SUPPLEMENTARY TEXTS
I
The beginning of the saga according to the U-redaction
The old tale of Hervör is set down in writing
as follows here

It is found written in ancient books that to the north beyond Gandvík[2] it was called Jötunheimar,[1] and Ymisland[3] to the south between there and Hálogaland. But before the Turks and the men of Asia came to the Northlands giants dwelt in the northern regions, and some were half-giants; there was a great mingling of races in those days, for the giants got themselves wives out of Mannheimar, and some married their daughters to men from that country. Gudmund[4] was the name of a lord in Jötunheimar; his dwelling-place was at Grund, in the region of Glasisvellir.[4] He was a mighty man, and wise, and so old were he and his people that their lives lasted through many generations of men. For this reason heathen men believed that in his realm must lie the Land of the Undying,[4] that region where sickness and old age depart from every man who enters it, and where no-one can die. After the death of Gudmund men made sacrifice to him and called him their god. King Gudmund had a son named Höfund; he had the power of foreseeing, and he was wise in understanding. He was set as judge over all the neighbouring lands; his decision was never unjust, and no man either dared or had cause to thrust his judgment aside.

There was a man named Arngrím, a giant, who dwelt in the mountain-rocks; out of Ymisland he carried off Áma Ymir's daughter, and made her his wife. Their son's name was Hergrím, who was called Halftroll; at times he dwelt among the mountain-giants, but at other times among men. His strength was that of the giants, and he had deep knowledge of magic arts; he was a great berserk. Out of Jötunheimar he carried off Ögn Álfasprengi and married her; they had a son called Grím.

Starkad Áludreng[5] at that time dwelt at Álufossar[6]; he was descended

---

[3] On Ymir, the first being created out of Chaos, and from whom the giant race was descended, see especially *SnE*. 12 ff.
[4] On Gudmund, Glasisvellir, and *Ódáinsakr* see Appendix B
[5] Starkad Áludreng appears also in *Gautreks Saga* ch. 3, and something of the same information is given there, though Stórvirk is there made his son, not his father. [6] Perhaps Ulefos in Lower Telemark (Bugge, *NS* 351)

ok hann var þeim líkr at afli ok eðli; hann hafði átta hendr. Stórvirkr hét faðir hans. Ǫgn álfasprengi var festarmær Starkaðar, en Hergrímr tók hana^a frá honum, þá Starkaðr var farinn norðr yfir Élivága.¹ En er hann kom aptr, skoraði hann á Hergrím til hólmgǫngu² ok til konunnar. Þeir bǫrðusk við inn efsta fors at Eiði; Starkaðr vá með fjórum sverðum senn ok fekk sigr; þar fell Hergrímr. Ǫgn sá á hólmgǫngu þeira, en er Hergrímr var fallinn, lagði Ǫgn sik með sverði í gegnum ok vildi ekki giptask Starkaði.^b Starkaðr tók nú fé þat allt undir sik, er Hergrímr hafði átt, ok hafði með sér ok svá son hans Grím; óx hann upp með Starkaði. Grímr var bæði mikill ok sterkr, er honum óx aldr.

Álfr hét konungr, er réð fyrir Álfheimum; Álfhildr³ hét dóttir hans. Álfheimar hétu þá milli Gautelfar ok Raumelfar.^{c4} Eitt haust var gǫrt dísablót⁵ mikit hjá Álfi konungi, ok gekk Álfhildr at blótinu; hon var hverri konu fegri, ok allt folk í Álfheimum var fríðara at sjá en annat folk því samtíða. En um nóttina, er hon rauð hǫrginn, nam Starkaðr áludrengr Álfhildi í burt ok hafði hana heim með sér. Álfr konungr hét þá á Þór at leita eptir Álfhildi, ok síðan drap Þórr Starkað⁶ ok lét Álfhidi fara heim til fǫður síns ok með henni Grím son Hergríms.

Ok þá er Grímr var tólf vetra,⁷ fór hann í hernað ok varð inn mesti hermaðr. Hann fekk Bauggerðar^d dóttur Álfhildar ok Starkaðar^e áludrengs. Grímr fekk sér bústað í ey þeiri á Hálogalandi,^f er Bólm^g hét, ok var^h síðan kallaðr Eygrímr bólmr. Sonr þeira hét Arngrímr berserkr, er síðan bjó í Bólm^j ok var inn ágætasti hermaðr.

Þessu^k samtíða kómu austan Asíamenn ok Tyrkjar ok byggðu Norðrlǫnd. Óðinn formaðr þeira⁸ átti marga sonu; urðu þeir allir miklir menn ok ríkir. Einn hans sonr hét Sigrlami; honum fekk Óðinn þat ríki, sem nú er kallat Garðaríki; gerðisk hann þar hǫfðingi mikill yfir því ríki; hann var

---

^a hann 203   ^b Starkard 203
^c Runnelfar 203 *later corr.* to Raum-
^d Bauggerðar *U*, 203, Baugeiðar *H*
^e Starkaðs 203, *elsewhere* Starkaðar
^f á Hálogalandi 203, *H, om. U* (see p. 3, note 2)
^g Bólm 203, *H*, Bólmr *U*
^h var *om*. 203   ^j Bólmi 203   ^k þess 203

¹ Élivágar (usually explained to mean 'the stormy waves') were the great rivers from whose thawing ice the primeval giant Ymir was made (*Vafþrúðnismál* 31; *SnE*. 12).
² See the Glossary s.v. *hólmganga*
³ An Álfhild of Álfheim appears in many sources. See H. Ellekilde, 'Om... Álfhildsagnet i Hervararsaga,' *Acta Phil. Scand.* VIII (1933) 191 f.
⁴ i.e. the region north-west of Lake Vänern, between the rivers now called Göta-älv and Glomma.
⁵ On the Dísir see p. 26, note 2. There is evidence to show that there were definite cults connected with the supernatural women; from some

from giants, and he resembled them in his nature and in his strength; he was eight-armed. His father's name was Stórvirk. Ögn Álfasprengi had been the betrothed of Starkad, but Hergrím took her from him when Starkad had gone north over Élivágar.[1] When Starkad came back he challenged Hergrím to single combat[2] for the woman. They fought by the uppermost waterfall at Eidi; Starkad attacked with four swords at once, and won the victory; Hergrím fell there. Ögn looked on at their combat, and when Hergrím fell she ran herself through with a sword and would not be married to Starkad. Starkad took possession of all the wealth that Hergrím owned and carried it off with him, together with his son Grím; and Grím grew up with Starkad. He was big and strong when he grew older.

There was a king named Álfr, who ruled over Álfheimar; he had a daughter named Álfhild.[3] In those days the region between the Gautelf and the Raumelf was called Álfheimar.[4] One autumn a great sacrifice to the Dísir[5] was held at the house of King Álf, and Álfhild conducted the rites; she was more beautiful than any other woman, and all the people in Álfheimar were fairer to look on than any others in those days. But during the night, when Álfhild reddened the altar with blood, Starkad Áludreng carried her off, and took her home with him. King Álf called upon Thór to seek for Álfhild; and afterwards Thór slew Starkad[6] and allowed Álfhild to return home to her father, together with Grím the son of Hergrím.

When Grím was twelve years old[7] he went out on a foray, and became the greatest warrior. He married Bauggerd the daughter of Álfhild and Starkad Áludreng. Grím made his abode on that island in Hálogaland called Bólm, and thereafter he was known as Eygrím Bólm. Their son was called Arngrím the berserk, who afterwards dwelt in Bólm and was the most far-famed of warriors.

It was about this time that the men of Asia and the Turks came out of the east and settled in the Northlands. Ódin their leader[8] had many sons, all great men and mighty. One of his sons was called Sigrlami; to him Ódin gave over the realm which is now called Gardaríki, and Sigrlami became a

---

passages it seems clear that the guardian spirits were thought of as being dead members of the same family, and thus a connection is possible with the ancient English *Modra Nect* mentioned by Bede (*De Temporibus* ch. 15). *Dísablót* is more than once said to have been held in the autumn or early winter, as here. (See de Vries, *Altgerm. Religion.* II 375 ff.)

[6] This story was known to Saxo (ed. Holder 183, trans. Elton 224 f.), who says that the god Thór tore off four of the six hands of Starcatherus, son of Storuerkus, who was thus 'chastened to a better appearance.'

[7] i.e. the age of majority

[8] In a similar way, Snorri in the prologue to the Prose Edda elaborately euhemerised the heathen gods, and brought Ódin to the Northlands from Troy in *Tyrkland*; Saxo (ed. Holder 80) made the chief seat of the gods Byzantium.

manna fríðastr sýnum. Sigrlami átti Heiði dóttur Gylfa; þau áttu son saman; sá hét Svafrlami. Sigrlami fell í orrostu, er hann barðisk við jǫtun Þjaza.[1]

Nú sem Svafrlami spurði fall fǫður síns, tók hann undir sik ríki þat allt til forráða, sem faðir hans hafði átt; hann varð ríkr maðr. Þat barsk at einn tíma, at Svafrlami konungr reið á veðiar ok sótti hjǫrt einn lengi ok náði eigi á ǫllum degi, fyrr en at sólarfalli. Han var þá riðinn svá langt í skóginn, at hann vissi varla, hvat heim var. Hann sá einn stein mikinn um sólarsetr ok þar hjá dverga tvá. Konungr vígði þá útan steins með málajárni[a]; hann brá sverði yfir þá. Þeir biðja þá fjǫrlausnar. Svafrlami spyrr þá at nafni. Annarr nefndisk Durinn,[b] en annarr Dvalinn.[2] Svafrlami veit at þeir váru allra dverga hagastir; hann leggr þá fyrir þá, at þeir geri honum sverð sem best kunna þeir; þar skulu hjǫlt af gulli ok svá meðalkafli,[3] búa skulu þeir umgerð ok fetla af gulli. Hann segir, at sverð þat[c] skal aldri bila ok aldri við ryði taka, ok bíti jafnt járn ok[d] steina sem klæði, ok fylgi sigr í orrostum ok einvígjum hverjum er berr; þetta váru fjǫrlausnir þeira. Á stefnudegi kom Svafrlami til steinsins; fengu dvergar honum þá sverð sitt, ok var þat it fríðasta. En er Dvalinn stóð í steinsdurum, þá mælti hann, 'Sverð þitt, Svafrlami, verði manns bani hvárt sinn er brugðit er, ok með því sé unnin þrjú níðingsverk in mestu; þat verði ok þinn bani.'

Þá hǫggr Svafrlami sverðinu til dvergsins, ok fal eggteinana í steininum, en dvergrinn hljóp í steininn. Svafrlami átti þetta sverð ok kallaði Tyrfing; bar hann þat í orrostum ok einvígjum; hann felldi jǫtun Þjaza í einvígi; hann tók þá dóttur hans, er hét Fríðr. Þau áttu dóttur, er Eyfura hét, kvenna vænst ok vitrust.

Nú er þar til at taka, er Arngrímr berserkr er í víking ok réð þá fyrir liði miklu. Hann herjaði á ríki Svafrlama ok átti við hann orrostu ok áttusk við hǫggva viðskipti sjálfir; hjó Svafrlami hlut af skildi Arngríms ok nam sverðit í jǫrðu staðar; þá sveiflaði Arngrímr sverðinu á hǫnd Svafrlama, svá af tók; tók þá Arngrímr Tyrfing ok vá með ok felldi Svafrlama með honum. Síðan tók Arngrímr herfang mikit ok Eyfuru dóttur Svafrlama ok hafði í burt með sér. Arngrímr fór þá heim í Bólm ok gerði brúðlaup til Eyfuru.

[a] -járni *added later 203*
[b] Dyrinn *U*, Dulinn *H*
[c] þat *om. U, 203*
[d] sem *203*

[1] Much is told of a giant called Thjazi in the Prose and Poetic Edda (see especially *SnE*. 80 f.), but his end is there quite different: in the plumage of an eagle he flew over Ásgard and was killed by the Æsir, and Óðin set his eyes in heaven as two stars.

[2] The dwarf Dvalin appears in the *Waking of Angantýr* (verse 26/8 and note), but Durin appears only here in the saga; the name is found also in the *Vǫlospá* (10).

APPENDIX A

great lord over those lands. He was the most beautiful of men to look on. Sigrlami was married to Heid the daughter of Gylfi, and they had a son, who was named Svafrlami. Sigrlami fell in battle, fighting against the giant Thjazi.[1]

When Svafrlami heard of the downfall of his father he brought under his sway all the realm that he had held, and he became mighty. It chanced one day that King Svafrlami rode out hunting, and far on into the day he pursued a stag, without ever overtaking it before the time of sunset. By then he had ridden so deep into the forest that he scarcely knew which way to turn for home. At sunset he saw a great stone, and beside it two dwarfs. The king drew his graven sword over them, and with that sign held them outside the stone. They begged him to spare their lives, and Svafrlami asked them what their names were. One said he was called Durin, and the other, Dvalin.[2] Svafrlami knew that these were the most skilful of all dwarfs, and he laid this charge upon them, that they should make a sword for him, the best their skill could devise; its hilts were to be of gold and its grip also,[3] and they were to make its scabbard and baldrick of gold. He said that this sword must never fail and never rust, must bite into iron and stone as if into cloth, and that victory must always come to him who carried it in battles and single combats; this was the price of their lives. On the appointed day Svafrlami returned to the stone, and the dwarfs delivered over to him the sword; it was very beautiful. But when Dvalin stood in the doors of the stone he said, 'May your sword, Svafrlami, be the death of a man every time it is drawn, and with it may three of the most hateful deeds be done; may it also bring you your death!'

Then Svafrlami struck at the dwarf with the sword, and the ridges of the blade were hidden in the stone; but the dwarf leapt back into it. Svafrlami kept the sword and called it Tyrfing; he bore it in battles and in single combats, and with it he slew the giant Thjazi; he took Thjazi's daughter Fríd, and they had a daughter named Eyfura, most beautiful and most wise among women.

Now it must be told that Arngrím the berserk went out raiding, and he had command of a great company. He harried the kingdom of Svafrlami and fought with him, and they had a close fight together; Svafrlami struck off a part of Arngrím's shield, and the sword plunged into the earth. Then Arngrím swung his sword against Svafrlami's hand and struck it off; and he took Tyrfing himself and fought with it, and with it he slew Svafrlami. Then Arngrím took great plunder, and carried off with him Eyfura, Svafrlami's daughter; he went home to Bólm and wedded Eyfura.

---

[3] In Norse the 'hilts' (*hjǫlt*, plural) were the guard and the pommel; the handle was called *meðal-kafli*, 'middle-piece.'

II

The verses of the dialogue before the Battle on Sámsey as found in Ǫrvar-Odds Saga

The text taken as the basis is the vellum A.M. 344*a* (*M*) of the later fourteenth century. The fifteenth-century vellums A.M. 343 (*A*) and A.M. 471 (*B*) do not contain verses 5 and 6.

The more important divergences from *M* in *A* and *B* are included in the textual notes, but readings rejected from *M* which are of no importance are ignored, where there is manuscript authority for the reading adopted in the text. A full variant-apparatus is given in R. C. Boer's edition, Leiden 1888.

(Hjálmar:)

(1) Hervarðr, Hjǫvarðr,
Hrani, Angantýr,
Bildr ok Bófi,[a]
Barri ok Tóki,[b]
Tindr ok Tyrfingr,
tveir Haddingjar,
þeir í Bólm austr
bornir váru
Arngríms synir
ok Eyfuru.

(1) Hervard, Hjörvard,
Hrani, Angantýr,
Bild and Bófi,
Barri and Tóki,
Tind and Tyrfing
and the two Haddings:
eastwards in Bólm
their birthplace was,
sons of Arngrím
and Eyfura.

(2) Þá frá ek manna
meinúðgasta,
ógjarnasta
gott at vinna;
þeir berserkir
bǫls of fylldir
tvau skip hruðu
tryggra manna.

(2) I have heard of those men
as the most malign,
most unready
for righteous deeds;
that berserk band,
all black-hearted,
two ships emptied
of their trusty crews.

(Arrow-Odd:)

(3) Menn sé ek ganga
frá Munarvágum,
gunnar gjarna
í grám serkjum;
þeir hafa reiðir
rómu háða,
eru okkur skip
auð á strǫndu.

(3) Men I see moving
from Munarvág,
in their grey byrnies
for battle eager;
they have raging
raised up warfare,
and our ships are lying
on the shore empty.

[a] Bagi *AB*   [b] Tóki *AB*, Taki *M*

APPENDIX A

(4) Þá var mér ótti
einu sinni,
er þeir grenjandi
gengu af ǫskum
ok emjandi
í ey stigu;
þá frá ek fyrða
fláráðasta
ok ótrauðasta
illt at vinna.

(4) Fear beset me
for a single moment,
as they left the longships
loudly bellowing,
crying terribly
climbed the island;
I have heard of those men
as the most untrue,
the keenest of all
to compass evil.

(Hjálmar:)

(5) Hliðum vit fyrir
hjaldrviðum aldri,
þótt okkr
atalt[a] þykki;
vit skulum í aptan
Óðin gista,
tveir fóstbrœðr,
en þeir tólf lifa.[b]

(5) Retreat we never
from such trees of war,
although to us
aweful it seems;
we shall be this evening
under Óðin's roof,
two sworn brothers,
but the twelve shall live.

(Arrow-Odd:)

(6) En ek því[c] einu
orði hnekta:
þeir skulu í aptan
Óðin gista,
tólf berserkir,
en vit tveir lifa.

(6) That I rejected
with this only:
They shall be this evening
under Óðin's roof,
the twelve berserks;
we two shall live!

(Angantýr:)

(7) It eruð halir
harðir komnir
ór hlynviði;
fallnir eru ykkrir
fǫrunautar.[d]

(7) You men of war
from the maple-wood
are come boldly;
killed are all now
that came with you.

---

[a] atalt *em. Bugge,* at hallt *M*
[b] tveir ... lifa *added by seventeenth-century hand*
[c] því at *M*
[d] *after* fǫrunautar *AB add*: (ok *A*) farið í hǫll Viðris (Viðrir, *a name of Óðin*)

APPENDIX A

(Arrow-Odd:)

(8) Hér eru rekkar
    reiðir komnir,
    tírarlausir,*a*
    fara tólf saman;
    einn skal við einn
    eiga orrostu,*b*
    hvatra drengja,
    nema hugr bili.

(8) Here are captains
    come in anger,
    twelve go together,
    inglorious men;
    singly shall they fight
    and stand in battle,
    the strong heroes,
    if their spirit fail not!

Some fragments of this poem are preserved in *Heiðreks Saga*: the first half of verse 4; the second half of verse 5; verse 6; and verse 8 (though here *Heiðreks Saga* gives the two halves in separate verses); while the *U*-text has (in an extremely corrupt form) lines corresponding to the first half of verse 5 above. These are missing in *R*, though there is a trace of them in the prose ('Let us never flee away from our enemies'). Analysis of these verses in the MSS of the two sagas is very revealing of the way in which a poem could, with progressive weakening and corruption, slowly fall to bits.

Although the *Qrvar-Odds Saga* text is fuller, in individual verses it is no less badly damaged. No attempt is made here to rearrange neatly these ruins of a poem and produce an 'original version'; it would serve no purpose. There is a thorough-going attempt in R. C. Boer's critical edition of *Qrvar-Odds Saga* (Leiden 1888), which was rightly dismissed by Heusler as arbitrary and unfounded; since quite 'arbitrary' insertions, expansions, and rearrangements have obviously been made, it is hard to see that any critic's eye, however sharp, could undo the knot.

It is not even possible to say with certainty what sort of poem this once was; it has been thought that the verses descend from a *narrative* poem on the Battle of Sámsey, and it is certainly true that verses 1, 2, and 4 above do not at all give the impression of having always been used for the purpose to which the saga-writers have put them.

The name-verse (1) is clearly not at home in its present place in *Qrvar-Odds Saga*. The whole of the prose passage in which it occurs is very unsatisfactory, and looks as though it had been constructed around odds and ends of verse that were not always fully understood. It is more than likely that verse 1 was an isolated 'catalogue-strophe' that was taken up into this saga and put rather awkwardly into the mouth of Hjálmar[1]; in *Heiðreks*

---

a *after* tírarlausir *A adds* af tréskipum traustir drengir (*cf.* verse 2/1–2 *in RU*)

b orrostu heyja *AB, U*

[1] cf. verse 75 of the *Battle of the Goths and the Huns*, which obviously once existed independently of that poem.

Saga it was differently used, and resolved into prose. The *R*-text knows the names of only six of the berserk sons of Arngrím, whereas *H* and *U* give twelve; but the extra six are *Sæmingr, Brámi, Barri, Reifnir, Tindr* and *Búi*. The list reappears in part in the Eddaic poem *Hyndluljóð* (23), and this agrees with *H* and *U* except in giving *Tyrfingr* for *Sæmingr*; and Saxo has a version of it (ed. Holder 166), where the extra six are again quite different from other sources, except in the name *Tiruingar*. It is possible that Tyrfing the berserk owed his existence to the sword itself having got into the name-list; but the matter is unimportant, since none of the younger sons of Arngrím seem to have had more than a shadowy existence in legend, whatever their names were.

Some of these names appear again in the lists of the heroes who fought at the Battle of Brávöll (see the conclusion of *Heiðreks Saga*); and the author of the *Waking of Angantýr* uses the first two lines of the catalogue-strophe (verses 24 and 26).

III

Verses of Hjálmar's Death-Song found only in Ǫrvar-Odds Saga

The text and textual notes are here on the same basis as in the previous section of this Appendix.

(i) Fregna eigi þat
á fold konur,
at ek fyr hǫggum
hlífask léta^a;
hlær eigi at því
at ek hliða gerða,
snót svinnhuguð
Sigtúnum í.

(i) Ladies in that land
shall learn never
that from blows sheltering
I shrank backward;
she shall not taunt me
that I took to my heels
she the swift-minded
in Sigtúna.

(ii) Hvarf ek frá ungri
Ingibjǫrgu —
skjótt réð um þat —
á skapadœgri;
sá mun fljóði
fastnæmr tregi,
er vit síðan
sjámsk aldrigi.^b

(ii) From Ingibjörg
the young I parted
on the day foredoomed —
it was done quickly;
it will give her
grief hard-grasping
that on one another
we shall never now look.

(iii) Ber þú til sýnis —
sá er minn vili —
Hjálmars^c brynju
í hǫll konungs;
hugr mun gangask
hilmis dóttur,
er hon hǫggna sér
hlíf fyr brjósti.

(iii) To her sight bear you —
so I desire it —
Hjálmar's hauberk
in the hall of the king;
changed will her heart be,
chieftain's daughter,
when the blows she sees
on my breast's armour.

(iv) Sá ek hvar sitja
Sigtúnum á
fljóð, þau er lǫttu
farar mik þaðan;
gleðr eigi Hjálmar
í hǫll konungs
ǫl né rekkar
um aldr^d síðan.

(iv) I see them seated
in Sigtúna,
ladies reluctant
to let me depart;
but never again
shall gladden Hjálmar
cup or comrade
in the court of the king.

^a láta *M*, gerða *AB*
^b er vit ... aldrigi *M*; at hon síðan mik sér aldrigi *AB*
^c hjálm ok *AB*   ^d aldri *AB*

Not only is the *Ǫrvar-Odds Saga* version of this poem longer, but the order of the verses in the two sagas is totally different; there is a slight difference in the order between *R* and *U* also (*H* does not contain the poem, and merely refers the reader to the other saga). There is one place (verse 8) where the longer version is most curiously divergent from the shorter (see below), and another less important divergence (verse 9) where *U* agrees with *Ǫrvar-Odds Saga* against *R* (see the textual notes to these passages in the main text).

To say which version is nearer the original seems to be impossible. Most critics have believed that the shorter version is the older, but some have been equally positive that the other one is. As for the original order of the verses, there have been almost as many suggested rearrangements as there have been critics.

I give here a résumé of the argument of the poem in the order of the longer version, numbering the verses by their equivalents in *Heiðreks Saga*, and indicating the extra verses by Roman numerals.

5. Someone speaks to Hjálmar, and declares that he is mortally wounded.
   The death-song of Hjálmar
6. I am terribly wounded; Angantýr's sword has pierced me.
(i) The women at home shall never hear that I flinched.
11. I left the songs of women and joyfully went east with Sóti.
9. I left the princess on Agnafit, and she told me that I would not return.
(ii) I turned away from her; her grief will be great that we shall not meet again.
(iii) Take my torn armour into the king's hall; the princess will be moved when she sees it.
7. I owned five farms, but I was not contented; and now I must lie dead on Sámsey.
10. Take this ring to Ingibjörg; her grief will be great that we shall not meet again.
(iv) I see the women in Sigtúnir who warned me from the journey; I shall never again be glad in the king's hall.
8. The jarls drink ale in the king's hall at Uppsala (*but*: My father's men drink in his house, *Heiðreks Saga*); ale overcomes them, but wounds overcome me.
12. The carrion birds fly from the south; this is the last meal I shall set for them.

It seems quite clear that in the longer version verse 7 is in the wrong place, for it intrudes into Hjálmar's dying commission to his companion; otherwise this ordering seems not to contain any real infelicity. In the *R*-

APPENDIX A

text verse 11 is pretty plainly in the wrong place: in sense it would go much better with verse 9, which also begins in the same way—it is in this point that *U*'s order differs from that of *R*, placing verse 11 after verse 9. Apart from this, the sequence of the shorter version is not obviously wrong; the sequence of thought is different. It is not strange that it should be impossible to decide this question, for these verses are each essentially self-contained.

What is very strange is that whereas the longer version speaks in verse 8 of jarls in the Swedish king's hall, the shorter refers to 'housecarls' in the house of Hjálmar's father. It is notable that in the extra verses of the *Ǫrvar-Odds Saga* text the king appears several times: in verse iii Ingibjörg is *hilmis dóttir*, and Hjálmar tells his companion to take his armour into the king's hall, while in verse iv he laments that he will never again drink ale there. Where Ingibjörg is called *hilmis dóttir* in verse 9 in the *Ǫrvar-Odds Saga* version, there is a different reading in *R*.[1]

It is hard to be sure what has happened here. The editors of *Eddica Minora* held that the maker of the shorter version had deliberately excluded or remodelled all these references to the king; but why should he have done so? The alteration (if it is one) of the king of Sweden into Hjálmar's father is a move away from the story of *Heiðreks Saga*; it produces less coherence, not more. It is possible that in a very old form of the legend of Hjálmar, now represented only by his 'death-song' in *Heiðreks Saga*, the hero had no connection with the Swedish king, which only came to be made later; the alteration to verse 8, and the extra verses, would then depend on this later development in the story.

---

[1] Here *U* agrees with *Ǫrvar-Odds Saga* against *R*, as also many times elsewhere (see the textual notes). *U* also mentions (in the prose) the name *Sigtúnir* (a place lying between Stockholm and Uppsala), which is absent from *R*. *U*'s agreements with the other saga were brought about, I think, by direct knowledge of it (at some stage, perhaps early on, in the *HU* tradition).

IV

Verses of Hervör's dialogue with the Herdsman not found in R

The *HU* redaction has seven verses here, against four and half in *R*. Of the extra ones, verse ii below is certainly a part of the original poem; i and iii are narrative in content, and some have held that they are later than the dialogue-verses. In the following citations the text of *H* is followed; that of *U* is essentially the same, but badly corrupt.

(i) The first half of verse 18:

Hitt hefir mær ung	A maiden at sunset
í Munarvági	in Munarvág
við sólarsetr	fell in with a herdsman
segg at hjǫrðu.	his flock minding.

The close similarity of the prose wording in *R* to these four lines may suggest that they are a part of the original poem.

(ii) After verse 20 the *HU*-redaction includes another verse:

Men bjóðum þér	For your word's guerdon
máls at gjǫldum;	I'll give you a necklace;
muna drengja vin	hard will it be to hinder
dælt at letja;	the heroes' comrade;
fær engi mér	none can give me
svá fríðar hnossir,	such gay adornments
fagra bauga,	or rings glittering
at ek fara eigi.	that go I will not.

That this verse is genuine is demonstrated by *R*'s arrangement of the two subsequent verses in order to obtain a regular interchange between the speakers; verses 21 and 22 are in reverse order in *H* and *U*. That the *HU* arrangement is right is seen from the fact that in this version the herdsman's words 'fires are moving' precedes, as it should, Hervör's 'We'll faint not nor fear at such fire's crackling.'

It is plain that this verse had already fallen out of *R*'s exemplar, and from this it is clear that there stood one copy (at least) between *R* and the ultimate written source of all extant manuscripts of the saga.

The maker of the *H*-version took the first part of this verse to be the herdsman's and only the latter half Hervör's, which is absurd. Some early editors divided the verse between the two speakers in the opposite way, which is not unreasonable; but since otherwise each whole verse is given to one speaker only, the whole of this one should no doubt be given to Hervör.

APPENDIX A

(iii) The *HU*-redaction knows one other verse of this poem:

Var þá féhirðir	Fast then to the forest
fljótr til skógar	fled the herdsman,
mjǫk frá máli	from the words of this woman
meyjar þessar;	away hurrying;
en harðsnúinn	but the hard-knit heart
hugr í brjósti	in Hervör's breast
um sakar slíkar	swelled up mightily
svellr Hervǫru.	the more for that.

The right place for this narrative verse is at the end of the dialogue, which is where *U* has it, giving the unquestionably correct ordering of the poem thus (the verse numbers are those of the main text): i plus 18; 19; 20; ii; 22; 21; iii. *U* however puts iii into the mouth of the herdsman and alters the wording, though it is obviously really narrative, not speech; while *H* displaces it to a position after verse ii.

V

Verses of The Waking of Angantýr not found in R

The *HU*-redaction gives two verses of this poem between verses 33 and 34. In verse i the text given here is based on *U*; the form in *H* is rather different (see below). In verse ii I give the *H*-text; the divergences in *U* are insignificant.

(i) Ek vígi^a svá
    virða dauða
    at ér^b þolið
    aldri kyrrir,^c
    nema þú, Angantýr,
    selir mér Tyrfing,^d
    hlífum hættan,
    Hjálmars bana!

(i) Spells I set on you
    O slain warriors,
    to give you for ever
    easeless resting,
    unless, Angantýr,
    you yield Tyrfing,
    peril to bucklers,
    bane of Hjálmar!

(ii) Kveðkat ek þik, mær ung,
     mǫnnum líka,
     er þú um hauga
     hvarfar á nóttum,
     grǫfnum geiri
     ok með Gota málmi,
     hjálmi ok með brynju
     fyrir hallar dyrr.

(ii) Unlike mortals,
     maiden, I call you,
     roaming in darkness
     around the barrows,
     with the ore of the Goths
     and graven lance,
     with helm and hauberk
     by the hall's doorway.

That these two verses are left out in *R*, being part of the original poem, is clear from the beginning of verse 34: 'A human indeed I was held to be' has no point unless preceded by 'Unlike mortals, maiden, I call you.'

The last two lines of verse i above reappear in *R* at the end of verse 34, at which point there are two lines in *HU* which have no counterpart in *R*:

Verse i in HU	*Verse i in R*
hlífum hættan,	lacking
Hjálmars bana	

Verse 34 in HU	*Verse 34 in R*
dverga smíði,	hlífum hættan,
dugira þér at leyna	Hjálmars bana

^a vígi *H*, of ingi *U*   ^b þér *U*   ^c aldri kyrrir liggja *U*
^d *for lines 3–6 H has*: at þér skuluð / allir liggja / dauðir með draugum / í dys fúnir (fynir *H*). / Sel mér, Angantýr, / út ór haugi, *etc.* ('*that you shall all lie dead among ghosts, rotting in the barrow. Give me, Angantýr, out of the mound,*' *etc.*)

APPENDIX A

If verse i had not been lost from *R* it would there conclude no doubt with *dverga smíði*, etc. ('dwarfs' handiwork—to hide it avails not'). This is probably the right arrangement, first because *þann* in verse 34/6 has no noun to agree with, *smíði* being neuter, and secondly because the first words of verse 35 are *Liggr mér undir herðum / Hjálmars bani*, which evidently connect with the last line of verse 34, *Hjálmars bana*, with an interlocking which is seen elsewhere in this poem (cf. verses 35–6).

It cannot be said what the original form of verse i was. Corruption seems plain in *H*'s extra long line, with its repeated *dauðir*.

It may be noted here that between verses 41 and 42 *U* has a verse not included in *H*, which is composed of the first five lines of verse 36, then the line *úlfa grennir* ('feeder(?) of wolves'), and finally the last two lines of verse 40.

VI

Riddles peculiar to the H-text

(H 7)[1]
Hverr byggir há fjǫll?
Hverr fellr í djúpa dali?
Hverr andalauss lifir?
Hverr æva þegir?[2]
Heiðrekr konungr,
hyggðu at gátu!

'Góð er gáta þín, Gestumblindi, getit er þeirar; hrafn byggir jafnan á hám fjǫllum, en dǫgg fellr jafnan í djúpa dali, fiskr lifir andalauss, en þjótandi fors þegir aldri.'

(H 10)
Hvat er þat undra,
er ek úti sá
fyrir dǫglings[a] durum;
hvítir fljúgendr
hellu ljósta,
en svartir í sand grafask?
Heiðrekr koningr,
hyggðu at gátu!

'Góð er gáta þín, Gestumblindi, getit er þeirar; smækkask[b] nú gáturnar,[3] en þat er hagl ok regn, því at hagli lýstr á stræti, en regndropar søkkva[c] í sand ok sœkja í jǫrð.'

(H 11)
Hvat er þat undra,
er ek úti sá
fyrir dǫglings durum[d];
svartan gǫlt ek sá
í sauri vaða,
ok reis honum eigi burst á baki?
Heiðrekr konungr,
hyggðu at gátu!

---

[a] *In this phrase H always* dǫglings, *RU* Dellings (*cf. verses 48 ff. and note*)
[b] *thus 597,* smættask *281 with same sense*
[c] *thus 597,* regndropar søkkvask *281*
[d] Hvat er . . . durum *om. H*

[1] Throughout this section *H* refers to the two *Hauksbók*-copies, *281* and *597*, in agreement (see Introduction p. xxix). Errors of no significance in one or other of the two MSS have been ignored. These riddles are here numbered according to their place in *H*'s complete riddle-series.

APPENDIX A

VI

Riddles peculiar to the H-text

(H 7)[1]
>What lives on high fells?
>What falls in deep dales?
>What lives without breath?
>What is never silent?[2]
>This riddle ponder,
>O prince Heidrek!

'Your riddle is good, Gestumblindi,' said the king; 'I have guessed it. The raven lives ever on the high fells, the dew falls ever in the deep dales, the fish lives without breath, and the rushing waterfall is never silent.'

(H 10)
>What strange marvel
>did I see without,
>before the great one's gate;
>as silver fliers
>on the stone beating,
>but as dark ones sinking in the sand?
>This riddle ponder,
>O prince Heidrek!

'Your riddle is good, Gestumblindi,' said the king; 'I have guessed it. Your riddles grow trifling.[3] That is hail and rain, for hail beats upon the street, but raindrops sink into the sand and penetrate the earth.'

(H 11)
>What strange marvel
>did I see without,
>before the great one's gate;
>a dark-hued boar
>in the dirt wading,
>but on his back no bristles rose?
>This riddle ponder,
>O prince Heidrek!

---

[2] This verse is of the form called *Greppa-minni* (cf. *SnE.* 233), and is closely parallelled by two verses of Jarl Rögnvald's poem *Háttalykill* (*Skj.* A I 521), in which the first four lines of each are unrelated questions, and the last four the answers to them. The solution to this riddle is the only one that looks as though it were once in verse.

[3] But he is almost certainly wrong, nonetheless. The answer ought to be simply 'Hail'—'as white fliers they strike the rock (and rebound), but as black (having melted) they bury themselves in sand.'

'Góð er gáta þín, Gestumblindi, getit er þeirar; þat er tordýfill, ok er nú mart til tínt, er tordýflar eru ríkra manna spurningar.'

(H 13) Hvat er þat undra,
er ek úti sá
fyrir døglings durum;
ofarliga[a] flýgr,
arnhljóð[b1] gellr,
harðar eru hjálmum greipr?[c2]
Heiðrekr konungr,
hyggðu at gátu!

'Góð er gáta þín, Gestumblindi, getit er þeirar; ǫr er þat,' segir konungr.

(H 15) Hvat er þat undra,
er ek úti sá
fyrir døglings durum[d];
lýðum lýsir,
en loga[e3] gleypir,
ok keppask um þat vargar ávalt?
Heiðrekr konungr,
hyggðu at gátu!

'Góð er gáta þín, Gestumblindi, getit er þeirar; þat er sól; hon lýsir lǫnd ǫll ok skínn yfir alla menn, en Skalli ok Hatti heita vargar, þat eru úlfar, en annarr þeira ferr fyrir, en annarr eptir sólu.'[4]

(H 30) Hest sá ek standa,
hýddi[5] meri,
dúði dyndil,
drap hlaun und kvið;
ór skal draga
ok gjǫpta at góða stund.[f]

[a] ofarliga *em. Grundtvig*, óvarliga ('*unwarily*') H
[b] arnhljóð *em. Bugge*, armlod H
[c] hjálmum greipr *em. Edd. Min*, hillm H
[d] Hvat er ... durum: Hvat er þat er H
[e] loga *em. Grundtvig*, logi H
[f] ór ... stund *entirely corrupt; suggested reconstructions in Edd. Min and by Kock NN* § *3284*

[1] *arnhljóð* is not in fact a recorded word, but cf. *varghljóð* 'wolf-cry' in *Helg. Hund.* I 41.
[2] Among many conjectural restorations, this emendation at least suggests the sort of thing wanted: since the preceding two lines (as emended) could very well refer to a real eagle, the sixth should contain something to restrict the description to an arrow.

APPENDIX A

'Your riddle is good, Gestumblindi,' said the king; 'I have guessed it. That is the dung-beetle; but when great men ask questions about dung-beetles, they have talked too long.'

(H 13)
>What strange marvel
>did I see without,
>before the great one's gate;
>on high it skims,
>screams eagle-voiced,[1]
>and hard on the helm is its clutch?[2]
>This riddle ponder,
>O prince Heidrek!

'Your riddle is good, Gestumblindi,' said the king; 'I have guessed it. That is an arrow.'

(H 15)
>What strange marvel
>did I see without,
>before the great one's gate;
>the giver of light,
>but engulfer of flame,[3]
>for which wolves unceasing strive?
>This riddle ponder,
>O prince Heidrek!

'Your riddle is good, Gestumblindi,' said the king; 'I have guessed it. That is the sun; it lightens all lands and shines upon all men; but the wolves are called Skalli and Hatti—those wolves, of which one goes before the sun, and the other follows after.'[4]

(H 30)
>I saw a stallion
>bestride[5] a mare,
>with buttock under belly
>and bobbing tail;
>. . . . .
>. . . . .

---

[3] Grundtvig's emendation gives good sense and a paradox characteristic of the style: it gives light to men, but it swallows flame. The same idea is used in riddle H 33 below.

[4] The two wolves appear as Skoll and Hati in *Grimnismál* 39 and in *SnE.* 18. Skoll pursues the sun and Hati, offspring of Fenrir the great wolf, pursues the moon (but in *Vafþrúðnismál* 46–7 it is Fenrir himself who seizes the sun out of the sky).

[5] The verb *hýða*, pret. *hýddi*, means to 'take the hide off, flay, flog' (cf. English 'hiding'); but see Fritzner, *Ordbog*, s.v. *hýða*.

Heiðrekr konungr,
hyggðu at gátu!

Þá svarar konungr, 'Þessa gátu skulu ráða hirðmenn mínir.' Þeir gátu margs til ok eigi fagrs mjǫk. Þá mælti konungr, sem hann sá at þeir gerðu ekki at, 'Hest þann kallar þú línvef, en skeið meri hans, en upp ok ofan skal hrista vefinn.'[1]

(H 33)
Meyjar ek sá
moldu líkar,
váru þeim at beðjum bjǫrg,
svartar ok sámar[a]
í sólviðri,
en þess at fegri, er færa of sér.
Heiðrekr konungr,
hyggðu at gátu!

'Góð er gáta þín, Gestumblindi, getit er þeirar; þat eru glœðr fǫlnaðar á arni.'

[a] svartur ok sámur H

[1] This solution is obviously wrong: the 'mare' is the web on the loom,

APPENDIX A

> This riddle ponder,
> O prince Heidrek!

Then the king said, 'The men of my court shall solve this one.' They made many guesses, but none very good, and when the king saw that they could make nothing of it he said, 'What you call a "stallion" is a piece of linen, and his "mare" is the weaver's slay; up and down the web is shaken.'[1]

(*H* 33)
> Ladies I looked on
> in likeness of dust,
> on bed of stone they slept;
> black they are and swarthy
> in sunny weather,
> but the lighter the less one can see.
> This riddle ponder,
> O prince Heidrek!

'Your riddle is good, Gestumblindi,' said the king; 'I have guessed it. Those are embers grown pale upon the hearth.'

---

which is alternately raised up and pressed down by the rod or slay.

VII

Verses of The Battle of the Goths and the Huns not found in R

The following verses from *U* correspond to the prose passage in *R* between verses 80 and 81.

Heill kom þú Hlǫðr,	Hlöd, you are welcome,
Heiðreks arfi,^a	Heidrek's offspring,
bróðir minn,	my own brother:
gakk á bekk sitja;	on the bench seat you;
drekkum Heiðreks	let us drink the good
hollar veigar	draughts of Heidrek,
fǫður okkrum	drink to our father
fyrstum manna,	the first of men
vín eða mjǫð	of wine or of mead
hvárt þér vildara^b þykkir.	as the wish takes you.
Hlǫðr kvað:	Hlöd said:
Til annars vér	For something else
hingat fórum	have we sped hither
en ǫl at drekka;	than for ale-drinking;
þigg ek ei,^c þjóðann,	king, I care not
þínar veigar,	your cup to take
nema ek hálft hafi	if I have not the half
allt þat Heiðrekr átti	of Heidrek's riches
(etc., as verse 81)	(etc., as verse 81)

Some critics (Bugge, Heusler) have regarded this as a seventeenth-century composition from the transmitted prose (this prose itself being based on lost verses); Helgason on the other hand believes it to be 'certainly original.'

It does not seem necessary to dismiss the first of these verses at least as wholly the production of a later time. In a poem like this individual verses may have undergone through generations a continuous process of decay and regrafting, so that a distinction between 'old' and 'late' verses may be misleading if pressed.

^a arfi *em. Skj. (cf. verse 79/2),* feduz *U*
^b valdara *U*
^c þigg ek ei *em. foll. suggestion of Helgason,* þiggja ef *U*

APPENDIX B
GUDMUND OF GLASISVELLIR

Neither Gudmund nor his dwelling are mentioned in the Prose or Poetic Edda, but Saxo has much to tell of him in his eighth book.[1] Saxo's account concerns the journey of Thorkillus and his companions to seek the realm of Geruthus (*Geirrøðr*), a perilous attempt, of which

> those who tried it declared that it was needful to sail over the Ocean that goes round the lands, to leave the sun and stars behind, to journey down into chaos, and at last to pass into a land where no light was and where darkness reigned eternally.

Eventually they came *in ulteriorem Byarmiam*, and there in this grim region they met Guthmundus, a man of extraordinary size, the brother of Geruthus. Guthmundus invited them to be his guests. They came to a river spanned by a bridge of gold, but Guthmundus forbade them to cross over by it, 'telling them that by this channel nature had divided the world of men from the world of monsters, and that no mortal track might go further.'[2]

Throughout their sojourn with Guthmundus, Thorkillus was perpetually warning his companions against accepting the hospitality that was offered them: they must abstain from the food that was set before them, they must not speak to the inhabitants, they must not be tempted by the women whom Guthmundus offered them. Those of them who neglected Thorkillus' warnings on this last matter went mad; but the rest Guthmundus finally transported across the river.

They came to a 'gloomy, neglected town, looking more like a cloud exhaling vapour,' a dark fortress with the heads of dead warriors impaled on the battlements, and savage dogs guarding the entrances. The conception of the halls of Geruthus is a grim one, and it has power even in Saxo's swollen language: a picture of great riches amid hideous decay, almost as it were a great burial-mound, with gems and horns and golden vessels on a floor of snakes and dung, beneath a roof of spearheads, and everywhere a vile oppressive stench. 'Bloodless, phantasmal monsters' armed with clubs were yelling, others played a gruesome game with a goat's skin which they tossed back and forth. At last they came upon Geruthus himself, an old man seated upon the high seat with his body pierced through, and beside him

---

[1] ed. Holder 286 ff.; trans. Elton 344 ff.
[2] cf. the crossing of the *Gjallarbrú*, which was roofed with gold, by Hermód in his ride to seek Balder, *SnE*. 66.

three women with their backs broken. As they turned to depart they were overcome by the temptation to lay hands on the treasures they found there, and at that the whole place rose against them; from the battle that followed only a few escaped alive. These returned to Guthmundus' land, and (all save one) succeeded in resisting his blandishments and attempts to make them linger there.

Many features of this strange story reappear elsewhere: thus, the journey made by Thór to the dwelling of Geirröd the giant, during which Thór had to ford the river Vimur, 'greatest of all rivers,' (*SnE.* 105 ff.), has close connections with Saxo's story of Thorkillus.[1]

In *Þorsteins þáttr Bœjarmagns*[2] Gudmund of Glasisvellir himself makes the journey to Geirröd's kingdom, accompanied by the hero, Thorstein. As in Saxo, Gudmund and his men are of giant size (in *Heiðreks Saga* he was king or lord in Jötunheimar). The geography is similar to Saxo's account in that Gudmund's realm is adjacent to Geirröd's, but divided from it by a river, but in almost all other respects there is little to connect them; Gudmund, so far from being Geirröd's brother, is his reluctant tributary, and he appears rather as benevolent than as a cunning enchanter. According to *Þorsteins þáttr* Gudmund's father was *Ulfheðinn trausti*, but was 'called Gudmund like all others who dwell in Glasisvellir'; Gudmund's son was Heidrek Wolfskin, who ruled over *Geirrøðargarðar* after Geirröd's death. The place-name *Grundir* (*Grund* in *Heiðreks Saga*) also appears in this work.

It is only possible to combine the accounts of *Þorsteins þáttr* and *Heiðreks Saga* of the geography of these legendary legions if one believes that the latter account refers to the situation *after* the destruction of Geirröd and the taking of his kingdom by Gudmund; but it is easier to believe that traditions had become dim and confused by the time that these accounts were composed, and the relations of the legendary localities were differently interpreted by different writers. One must not think in terms of a great mythological atlas of the northern world, with legendary lines of latitude and longitude.

Gudmund of Glasisvellir, as he appears in *Helga þáttr Þórissonar*[3] bears a much greater likeness to the Guthmundus of Saxo.

The name Glasisvellir is usually connected with *Glasislundr*, the dwelling of King Hjörvard in the Eddaic poem *Helgakviða Hjǫrvarðssonar* (1), and with the grove (*lundr*) called *Glasir*, with leaves of red gold, which stood before the door of Valhöll (*SnE.* 122). *Glasir, Glasis-* is then connected with the group of words signifying 'amber' or 'glass' (Norse *gler*, O.E. *glær, glæs*, etc.), and *Glasisvellir* rendered as 'the Glittering Plains.'

---

[1] The pierced body of Geruthus and the broken backs of the women were due to Thór's visit.
[2] *Fornmanna Sǫgur* III 175 ff.
[3] Ibid., 135 ff.

Further reference may be made to Bugge, 'Iduns Æbler,' *Arkiv* V 13 ff.; Bugge, *Studier* 483 f.; Herrmann 587 ff.; and to the very interesting essay by R. Much, 'Balder,' *Z.f.d.Alt.* LXI (1924) 99 ff.

As to the name *Ódáinsakr*: Saxo (ed. Holder 105) tells of a certain Fiallerus being driven into exile to a place called *Undensakre* 'which is unknown to our peoples.' There was a place in Iceland called *Ódáinsakr*, reputed to be so called because certain herbs grew there which were a protection against death (Olavius, *Oeconomisk Rejse igjennem . . . Island*, 1780, II 288); and a corrupt form of the name is recorded from Norway (O. Rygh, *Norske Gaardnavne* III 43). Finally, Ódáinsakr appears as the 'heathen' name of the earthly paradise in the East ('but Christians call it the Land of Living Men or Paradise') in *Eiríks Saga Víðfǫrla*,[1] without reference to Gudmund of Glasisvellir.

[1] *Flateyjarbók* I 29 ff.

APPENDIX C
THE REFERENCES TO ÓDIN

The expression which is used in verses 2 and 3, 'to be Odin's guest,' implies 'to die in battle'; it is found more than once elsewhere. Those killed in battle passed into Ódin's presence in Valhöll, the Hall of the Slain, and he himself was called *Valfǫðr*, the Father of the Slain. In the tenth-century poem *Eiríksmál* Ódin speaks with the fallen princes in Valhöll of the coming of Eirík Bloodaxe to take his place there; and in the Eddaic poem *Grímnismál* (8) it is said:

> Gladsheim the fifth is
> where golden-bright
> Valhöll spreading stands;
> there does Ódin
> on every day
> choose out the champions slain.

The remark that Angantýr and Hjálmar 'showed each other the way to Valhöll' can be understood in connection with the later statement that Heidrek gave the slain of King Harald's army to Ódin, and with verse 100, where Gizur says, 'May Ódin let the dart fly as I prescribe it!'

There are many passages in saga-literature similar to these, in which an enemy or enemy army is in some way dedicated to Ódin on the battlefield; more than once a javelin is said to have been shot over the enemy host. Thus in *Eyrbyggja Saga* ch. 44 Steinthór cast a spear over Snorri's men *at fornum sið til heilla sér*, 'to bring himself luck, according to the ancient custom'; and in *Styrbjarnar þáttr* (*Flateyjarbók* II 72) Eirík, after dedicating himself in Ódin's temple to die after ten years if he should be victorious over Styrbjörn, met a tall man wearing a long hood, who put a cane in his hand and told him to shoot it over Styrbjörn's men, saying as he did so, *Óðinn á yðr alla* ('Ódin has you all!')

The javelin is constantly associated with Ódin; his own weapon was called Gungnir (*SnE*. 72, etc.), with a javelin he was himself marked before death (*Ynglinga Saga* ch. 9), and Sigmund's sword was broken on Ódin's spear (*Vǫlsunga Saga* ch. 11).

Passages from Norse and other literatures that bear on this subject are gathered together and discussed by H. M. Chadwick, *The Cult of Othin*, 1899.

APPENDIX D

THE GAME OF 'HNEFATAFL'

The name of the game is found in MSS constantly varying between the forms *hnefatafl*, *hneftafl*, and *hnettafl*, besides forms without initial *h*, and in late MSS *hnottafl*—a form which gave rise to the notion that the game was played with nuts.

There are a great many passages in the sagas where *hnefatafl* or other board-games are referred to, but none gives a clear account, and most offer only a passing reference. An article by F. Lewis in *Transactions of the Honourable Society of Cymmrodorion*, 1941, 185 ff., casts however a good deal of light on the matter; he is primarily concerned with the elucidation of the Welsh *Tawlbwrdd* (a game derived apparently from Scandinavia, and the name from Norse *taflborð*), but clearly *hnefatafl* was essentially the same game.[1]

These games belong to the type that have been called 'hunt-games,' in which one piece attempts to escape from the enemy, either with the help of defenders or without; but if with defenders, then these are outnumbered two to one by the attackers. They are thus altogether different in conception from 'battle-games' (chess, draughts), where there is an equal number of pieces on each side; for in the hunt-games the player wielding the attacking pieces will—given equal skill in both players—win, which no doubt accounts for their decay in esteem. The hunt-games are nonetheless games of skill and not of chance, and the statement, made time and time again, that *hnefatafl* was played with dice must be rejected.[2] It was played on a board of undifferentiated squares (either odd or even in number), with the *hnefi* on the central square (or central intersection) at the beginning of the game; the king's men were grouped around him at the start, and the attackers (probably) in four groups at the margins of the board. The latter attempt to pen him in so that he cannot move, while he, with the help of his men, tries to reach the edge. Pieces are taken when hemmed in between two others on the same line; but the possibilities with regard to the king's moves are unclear.

A board was discovered at Vimose in Sweden on which there seem to

[1] Another version is the *Alea Evangelii* or 'Game of the Gospel' (J. Armitage Robinson, *The Times of St Dunstan*, 1923, 69 ff., 171 ff., and frontispiece), and similar again in theme is the widespread popular game of 'Fox and Geese' (Norse *refskák*).

[2] In the solution to verse 59 both *R* and *H* refer to the *húnn* (die) in *hnefatafl*. Either this is a mistake, or the name came to be applied to quite distinct board-games.

have been 324 squares (18 by 18), as in the *Alea Evangelii,* and another from the Viking period was dug up in West Meath, where there are 49 holes arranged 7 by 7, with the central hole specially distinguished; here the pieces must have been pegged to their places.

Finally it may be mentioned that in Scandinavia, as also in Wales, the sets were often very costly, possessing sometimes an importance over and above their function; thus in the North boards and men were used to adorn temples (*Sturlaugs Saga starfsama* ch. 18,[1] of the golden set in the temple of Thór). Pieces of silver and of walrus-ivory are recorded (*Gull-Þóris Saga* ch. 14,[2] *Króka-Refs Saga* ch. 3[3]); cf. also the golden *toflur* of the gods in *Vǫlospá* 61. Among grave-goods have been found pieces of amber, bone, and glass; among the pieces there is sometimes one that is marked out from the remainder in one way or another.

[1] *F.A.S.* III (1830) 627
[2] ed. Kr. Kålund (*S.T.U.A.G.N.L.* XXVI, 1898)
[3] ed. P. Pálsson (*S.T.U.A.G.N.L.* X, 1883)

APPENDIX E

THE RIDDLE OF THE SOW WITH AN UNBORN LITTER

This enigma (verse 69) has a curious history. There is a legend told in the ancient poem *Melampodia*, ascribed to Hesiod, of a contest between Mopsus and Kalchas the seer.[1] Mopsus asked Kalchas how many young there were in a sow that was just about to give birth, and when it would do so. When Kalchas did not answer, he said himself that there were ten, among which was one male, and that it would give birth to them on the next day. When it turned out as Mopsus said, Kalchas died of mortification.

This is obviously a piece of divination, not a riddle at all. The Norse form represents a stage halfway between divination and riddle, so to say; it occurs in a riddle-contest and has the outward form of a riddle, but it has not yet sloughed off the particular, once-occurring event which must accompany the divination and confirm its accuracy. Regarded as a riddle it is insoluble; there are insufficient limiting factors.

In England the development can be followed a stage further. Aldhelm's verse, *De Scrofa Praegnante* (Aldhelm vi 10; *Opera* ed. Giles 266), is unquestionably a riddle; the individual accompanying event has now disappeared, and only the particularising of the actual number of young remains to hint at its history.

Bibliographical information on this subject is given by F. Tupper, *The Riddles of the Exeter Book*, 1910, 155.

[1] K. Ohlert, *Rätsel und Gesellschaftsspiele der alten Griechen*, 1886, 36 ff.

APPENDIX F
FRÓDMAR

In verse 13/1-4 (as emended) *hon* 'she' must be Hervör's mother; but who is Fródmar? It is odd, too, that Hervör should only here get to know who her father was; but as her ignorance is only shown by the remark of the slave ('the jarl forbids every man to speak to you of your parentage'), this might be possibly due to a misunderstanding of the verses, which do not necessarily presuppose it. The notion that Fródmar was the name of the swineherd ('I cannot boast of our noble line—even though my mother did win Fródmar's favour,' spoken in irony), as has been suggested, is not very credible.

The adoption of *U*'s reading *hefði fengit*, making Hervör say, 'even though I won Fródmar's favour,' does not seem to help. The curious statement in *R* (p. 30) that the foster-father of Hervör the second was called Fródmar may have some bearing on the puzzle, but it is hard to see what: *H* and *U* have Ormar here, as one would expect, since he is her foster-father in the *Battle of the Goths and the Huns*. Again, the dream that Hervör speaks of in verse 17 is referred to nowhere else.

The most likely explanation of these discrepancies is a shortening, conscious or unconscious, in the base-MS from which all the extant texts descend. Most critics have found these verses wanting[1]; but even if they are thought to be a late composition on the basis of a prose saga-text, the two obscure references in them must refer to something, and therefore that text does not now exist.

[1] 'Die äusserst platten Strophen,' *Edd. Min.* lxxvii; 'halt, tame, and spiritless,' *C.P.B.* I 495.

GLOSSARY OF TECHNICAL TERMS*

Alþingi Great Assembly. About A.D. 930 the *goðar* of Iceland combined to form the Great Assembly, which met annually in June at Thingvellir. The details of its composition and organisation in this period are obscure. When the Constitution was revised, *c.* A.D. 963, Iceland was divided into geographical Quarters (*Fjórðungar*), North, South, East and West, and the Assembly was composed of thirty-nine *goðar*, nine representing each Quarter, except the Northern one, which was represented by twelve. The twelve *goðar* from the Northern Quarter were not, however, able to exercise greater influence on the decisions of the Assembly than the nine representing each of the other Quarters.

The Great Assembly was divided into the Legislature (*Lǫgrétta*) and the Judicial Courts, both of which were controlled by the *goðar*. The Judicial Courts numbered four, one to try cases pertaining to each Quarter, and were called Quarter Courts (*Fjórðungsdómar*). About the year 1005, a Court of Appeal (*Fimmtardómr*) was instituted.

All householders whose capital wealth was above a certain standard were obliged to attend the Great Assembly in the following of the *goði* to whom they owed allegiance, or else pay a tax (*þingfararkaup*) to the *goði*.

Provision was made for lesser assemblies, the *várþing* in spring and the *leið* in autumn, at local meeting places (*þingstǫð*), of which there were three in each Quarter, except in the Northern one, where there were four. Three *goðar* presided at each local assembly. (See Aage Gregersen, *L'Islande. Son statut à travers les âges*, 1937.)

Berserkr a man capable of fits of frenzied rage, or running amok. Berserks were said to fight without corselets, raging like wolves with the strength of bears, and might be regarded almost as shape-changers, who acquired the strength and ferocity of beasts. During pagan times, berserks were highly prized as warriors, but under Christian law those who 'went berserk' were liable to heavy penalties. The word *berserkr*, 'bear-shirted,' implies perhaps that berserks sometimes disguised themselves as bears. The berserk-fury is described in *Ynglingas.*, ch. 6.

Drápa a sequence of strophes in scaldic form generally composed in praise of a king or great prince. The *drápa* is normally and properly embellished with a refrain (*stef*), which usually recurs at regular intervals in the central section of the poem (cf. the construction of *Hǫfuðlausn* in *Egilss.*, ch. 60). The *flokkr* was a sequence of strophes without refrain and commonly shorter than the *drápa*. Because of its more intricate form the *drápa* was thought to be more suitable as homage to a king, but lesser princes must be content with a *flokkr*, as in *Gunnlaugs Saga*. The poet Þórarinn loftunga is said to have incurred King Knút's wrath by composing a *flokkr* in his honour (a *dræplingr*, as the king called it). He saved himself by revising it and introducing a refrain, thus turning it into a

* This Glossary contains terms commonly employed in the Sagas and will be expanded as further volumes in this series are published.

drápa (cf. Óláfss. helga, ch. 172, in *Hkr.* II). (See J. de Vries, *Altnordische Literaturgeschichte*, 1941-2, I 87 ff.)

Festarkona a woman formally betrothed before witnesses in accordance with the provision of the law. The term *heitkona* is not found in the laws, but seems to have been used for a bride promised without legal formalities. (See K. Maurer, *Vorlesungen über altnordische Rechtsgeschichte*, 1907-10, II 517-18.)

Fylgia a personification of the essential nature or power of an individual or family. It often appeared in the form of an animal whose nature corresponded to the name or character of the individual it represented. The family wraiths (*ættaryfylgjur*) were protective spirits who were often seen in female form. (cf. J. de Vries, *Altgermanische Religionsgeschichte*, 1935-7, II 351-5; G. Turville-Petre, 'Liggja fylgjur þínar til Íslands' *Saga-Book of the Viking Society* XII (1937-45), 119-26.)

Glíma a form of wrestling still popular in Iceland. The combatants take a grip in each other's belt and attempt to make a throw by the use of various tricks, chiefly by rapid foot movements. (See Björn Bjarnason, *Nordboernes legemlige Uddannelse i Oldtiden*, 1905, 102 ff.)

Goði literally 'the godly one,' priest, and the title assumed by the chieftains of Iceland, whose office, called *goðorð*, combined secular with religious authority. At the beginning each *goði* was sovereign ruler over his followers (*þingmenn*).

The *goðorð* in Iceland probably numbered thirty-six when the settlement was first completed; their number was increased to thirty-nine c. A.D. 963 and to forty-eight on the institution of the Court of Appeal, c. A.D. 1005 (see *Alþingi*).

After the Conversion to Christianity (A.D. 1000) the *goðar* maintained their titles and secular authority, presiding at local assemblies, acting as legislators and appointing judges at the Great Assembly. The office of *goðorð* could be bought, sold, divided and even lent.

Hólmganga duel, literally 'island-going,' since duels were traditionally fought on islands, although a piece of ground, measured and marked out, was often substituted. Each principal might have a second, who protected him with a shield (*halda skildi fyrir e-n*). Blows were exchanged in turn, the challenged party striking first. A wounded dueller could escape further injury by payment of a stipulated sum, usually three marks of silver.

According to the sagas, the duel was a legal form of redress. Its abolition probably resulted from the institution of the Court of Appeal (see *Alþingi*), which greatly reduced the chance of legal deadlock. (See Gwyn Jones, 'Some characteristics of the Icelandic "hólmganga",' *Journal of English and Germanic Philology* XXXII (1933), 203-24; Eiríkr Magnússon, *The Saga Library* VI, 1905, 349 ff.)

GLOSSARY OF TECHNICAL TERMS

Jarl the original meaning was 'man of noble birth, warrior,' as opposed to the common people, *karlar* (cf. the Old English pair *eorl* : *ceorl*). As a title *jarl* was applied to hereditary Norse and Danish chieftains, many no doubt being in fact sovereign lords in earlier times; but with the reduction of all the petty chiefs to the status of liegemen under the king the word changed in meaning correspondingly. As a result the English word *eorl* was also affected in sense, whence ultimately Modern English 'earl.'

Lǫgberg the eminence at Thingvellir, the site of the Great Assembly, where the Law-Speaker had his seat and where all important announcements were made, whether by him or by other speakers.

Lǫgsǫgumaðr Law-Speaker, the highest officer of the Icelandic Commonwealth and President of the Great Assembly (see *Alþingi*). He was elected by the *goðar* for a term of three years and could be re-elected for further terms. As his title implies, it was part of the Law Speaker's duty to recite the laws at the Great Assembly, one-third of the code each year, covering the whole code in his three years of office.

The term *Lǫgmaðr* (Lawman) was at first applied in Iceland to anyone learned in law. In Norway, on the other hand, *Lǫgmaðr* was the title of the President of an assembly. After Norwegian law was introduced in Iceland (A.D. 1271-3), the title *Lǫgmaðr* replaced that of *Lǫgsǫgumaðr*, in accordance with Norwegian practice.

Mǫrk approximately half a pound in weight. It contained eight *aurar*, each *eyrir* weighing just under an ounce. Homespun cloth (*vaðmál*) formed, with silver, the chief staple of exchange and in the early period was Iceland's chief export. About A.D. 1000, one *eyrir* of refined silver was worth approximately twenty-four yards of *vaðmál*; unrefined silver had half the value of the refined. (See Þorkell Jóhannesson, *Die Stellung der freien Arbeiter in Island*, 1933, 37-42.)

Skáli originally small house, hut, hence apartment, room (cf. *eldaskáli*, kitchen), hall (cf. *drykkjuskáli*, drinking hall). *Skáli* came later to be used especially for 'sleeping room' (also called *svefnskáli*). A raised floor or dais (*set*), which ran along the greater part of each side wall, was used as a sleeping place for the household. The chief persons of the family often slept in a separate bed-closet (*lokrekkja*), which could be closed by a door or sliding panel. The *lokrekkja* was commonly placed at the inner end of the dais (*innar af seti*), between it and the gable-end. (See Valtýr Guðmundsson, *Privatboligen på Island*, 1889, 206 ff.)

Stofa principal room of the house, where the inmates would dine and occupy themselves by day. Along each of the side walls ran a boarded dais (*pallr, langpallr*), while a cross-dais (*þverpallr*) often filled the gable-end. In early times the fire burned on the low earthen floor, which extended down the middle of the *stofa* between the raised flooring on each side. This raised floor sometimes rose in steps, which served as seats; sometimes, however, benches were placed upon it.

The central section of the dais on one side was called the (*œðra*) *ǫndvegi*, '(upper) high seat,' and was occupied by the master of the house and his closest associates. The corresponding section on the opposite side was called the *óœðra* or *annat ǫndvegi*, 'lower' or 'second high seat,' and was commonly occupied by the chief guests. The cross-dais was often reserved for women. (See Valtýr Guðmundsson, *Privatboligen på Island*, 1889, 171 ff.)

INDEX

1 PERSONAL NAMES

Álfhildr Álfsdóttir 67
Álfhildr Ívarsdóttir 59
Álfr, king in Álfheimar 67
Alrekr inn frœkni, Alrek the Valiant 46
Áma Ymisdóttir 66
Angantýr (I) Arngrímsson 3–8, 10, 11, 14–20, 22, 69, 70, 78
Angantýr (II) Hǫfundarson 21, 22
Angantýr (III) Heiðreksson, king of the Goths 24, 26, 27, 45–9, 51–60
Arngrímr, the giant (*called* Hergrímr *in H*) 66
Arngrímr, the viking 3–5, 14, 19, 67–9
Ása Haraldsdóttir 60
Ástriðr Njálsdóttir 62

Baldr, the god Balder 44
Barri Arngrímsson 69
Bauggerðr Starkaðardóttir (Baugeiðr *in H*) 67
Bildr Arngrímsson 69
Bjarmarr jarl (Bjartmarr *in HU*) 4, 10, 20, 21
Bjǫrn at Haugi, Björn of the Barrow 61
Bjǫrn Eiríksson 61
Bjǫrn Járnsíða, Björn Ironside 60, 61
Blót-Sveinn, *see* Sveinn
Bófi Arngrímsson 69
Bragi skáld 61

Dellingr 34, 35, 43
Durin, the dwarf (Dulinn *in H*) 68
Dvalinn, the dwarf 15, 68

Eiríkr Bjarnarson 60, 61
Eiríkr inn sigrsæli, Eirík the Victorious 61
Eiríkr Refilsson 60, 61
Eiríkr Ǫnundarson 61
Eyfura, wife of Arngrím 2, 3, 14, 68, 69
Eygrímr bólmr, *see* Grímr

Eymundr Óláfsson 62
Eysteinn inn illráði, Eystein the Wicked 60

Finnr inn skjálgi, Finn the Squinter 62
Fríðr Þjazadóttir 68
Fróðmarr (*in verse 13*) 10
Fróðmarr, jarl in England 30

Gestumblindi 32–44, 80–2
Gizurr Grýtingaliði 21, 50, 54–6
Gizurr, king of the Gautar 46
Grímr Hergrímsson 66, 67
Grýtingaliði, *see* Gizurr Grýtingaliði
Guðmundr, king in Glasisvellir 20, 66
Gylfi 68

Haddingjar tveir Arngrímssynir, the two Haddings 3, 69
Hákon, king of the Swedes 62
Hálfdan snjalli, Hálfdan the Valiant 59
Hallsteinn Steinkelsson 63
Haraldr harðráði Sigurðarson 62, 63
Haraldr hilditǫnn, Harald War-tooth 59, 60
Haraldr inn granrauði, Harald the Red-bearded 60
Haraldr inn hárfagri, Harald the Fair-haired 61
Haraldr, king of Reidgotaland 23–6
Heiðr Gylfadóttir 68
Heiðrekr inn vitri Hǫfundarson, Heidrek the Wise 17, 21–50, 53, 55, 80–3
Heiðrekr úlfhamr, Heidrek Wolfskin 59
Helga Haraldsdóttir 24
Hergrímr hálftrǫll 66, 67
Hervarðr Arngrímsson 3, 7, 14, 69
Hervarðr, name of Hervör (I) 12, 20
Hervǫr (I) Angantýsdóttir 10, 11, 13–22, 77

97

INDEX

Hervǫr (II) Heiðreksdóttir 30, 52, 53
Hildr Heiðreskdóttir 59
Hjálmarr inn hugumstóri, Hjálmar the Great-hearted 4–8, 10, 17, 19, 69, 70, 73, 78
Hjǫrvarðr Arngrímsson 3, 4, 7, 12, 14, 69
Hlér, god of the sea 40
Hlǫðr Heiðreksson 26, 46–8, 51, 52, 56–8, 60, 83
Hrani Arngrímsson 3, 7, 14, 69
Humli, king of the Huns 26, 46, 47, 51, 52, 56, 57
Humlungr, i.e. Hlǫðr 49
Hvítserkr Ragnarsson 60
Hǫfundr Guðmundarson 20–2, 25, 26, 66

Ingi Hallsteinsson 63
Ingi Steinkelsson 62, 63
Ingibjǫrg Ingjaldsdóttir 9, 73
Ingigerðr Haraldsdóttir 63
Ingjaldr inn illráði, Ingjald the Wicked 59
Ingjaldr, king of the Swedes (called Yngvi in HU) 3
Ívarr inn beinlausi, Ívar the Boneless 60
Ívarr inn víðfaðmi, Ívar the Wide-grasping 59, 60

Kjárr, king of the Valir 46

Mær, wife of Ingi Steinkelsson 62

Njáll Finnsson 62

Oddr, see Ǫrvar-Oddr
Óðinn, the god Odin 6, 26, 32, 44, 56, 67, 70
Óláfr Bjarnarson 61
Óláfr inn helgi, Óláf the Saint 62
Óláfr skautkonungr or Óláfr sœnski, Óláf Cloak-king or Óláf the Swede 61
Ormarr, foster-father of Hervör (II) 52, 53

Philippus Hallsteinsson 63

Ragnarr Loðbrók, Ragnar Hairy-breeches 60
Randvér Valdarsson 59, 60
Refill Bjarnarson 60, 61
Rǫgnvaldr inn gamli, Rögnvald the Old 62

Sifka Humladóttir (called Sváfa in U) 26, 28–30
Sigríðr in stórráða, Sigríd the Ambitious 61
Sigrlami, king of Gardar 2, 3, 14, 67, 68
Sigurðr hringr, Sigurd Ring 60
Sigurðr Ragnarsson 60
Sigurðr Sýr, Sigurd Sow 63
Sóti, companion of Hjálmar 9
Starkaðr áludrengr 66, 67
Steinkell Rǫgnvaldsson 62, 63
Stórvirkr, father of Starkad 67
Styrbjǫrn inn sterki, Styrbjörn the Strong 61
Sváfa Bjarmarsdóttir (called Tófa in H) 4, 14
Svafrlami Sigrlamason 68
Sveinn or Blót-Sveinn, Svein the Sacrificer 62, 63

Tindr Arngrímsson 69
Tóki Arngrímsson 69
Tyrfingr Arngrímsson 69

Valdarr, king of the Danes, (i) 46; (ii) 59

Ymir, the giant 66

Þjazi, the giant 68
Þjófr, follower of Svein the Sacrificer 63
Þórr, the god Thór 67

Ægir, god of the sea 41

Ǫgn álfasprengi 66, 67
Ǫnundr Óláfsson 62
Ǫnundr uppsali, Önund of Uppsala 61
Ǫrvar-Oddr or Oddr inn víðfǫrli, Arrow-Odd or Odd the Far-traveller 5, 6, 7, 10, 69–71

INDEX

2 PLACE NAMES

Agnafit 9
Álfheimar 67
Álufossar 66
Árheimar 46, 47, 53, 56
Austrríki, the Eastern kingdom 60

Bólm 3, 67-9
Brávǫllr 60

Danaríki, kingdom of the Danes 59, 60
Danaveldi, kingdom of the Danes 59, 60
Danmǫrk, Denmark 59, 60
Danparstaðir, the banks of the Dnieper 46, 49
Dúnheiðr, the Danube Heath 55-7, 60

Eiði 67
Eistland, land of the Esths 59
Élivágar 67
England 30, 59, 62

Fýrisvellir 61

Gandvík 66
Garðar (*in* Garðakonungr) 28-30
Garðaríki 2, 3, 28, 59, 67
Gautelfr 67
Gautland 59 (Eystra Gautland, Eastern Gautland 60, 63; Vestra Gautland, Western Gautland 63)
Glasisvellir 20, 66
Gotaland, land of the Goths 52
Gotþjóð, land of the Goths 49, 50, 53
Grafá (Gripá, Gropá *in* U, Greipá *in* 203) 45
Grund 21, 66

Hálogaland 62, 66, 67

Harvaða fjǫll, Harvad-fells 45
at Haugi (Haugr, the Barrow) 61
Húnaland, land of the Huns 26, 46, 51, 52

Jassarfjǫll, Hills of Ash 55, 56
Jǫtunheimar 66

Kúrland 59

Mannheimar 66
Munarvágr 5, 12, 14, 76
Myrkviðr, Mirkwood 49, 52, 53

Norðumbraland, Northumbria 59
Norðrlǫnd, the Northlands 66, 67
Nóregr, Norway 18, 60, 61

Ódáinsakr, Land of the Undying 66

Raumelfr 67
Reiðgotaland 23, 25, 26, 59
á Ræningi 59

Sámsey 4, 8, 10-12, 20
Saxland, land of the Saxons 26, 27, 59
Sigtúnir 73
Smáland 63
Stiklastaðir 62
Svíaríki, kingdom of the Swedes 6, 60-2
Svíaveldi, kingdom of the Swedes 59, 60
Svíþjóð, Sweden 7, 61-3

Uppsalir, Uppsala 3, 9, 10, 61, 62

Valhǫll 6, 7

Ymisland 66

3 OTHER NAMES

Andaðr, name of a piece in a game 37
Asíamenn, men of Asia 66, 67
Danir, Danes 39, 46

Gautar 46
Gotar, Goths 46, 47, 53, 55, 57
Hatti, the wolf 81
Húnar, Huns 46, 51-7

Ítrekr, name of a piece in a game 37
Saxar (*in* Saxakonungr), Saxons 26
Sleipnir, the horse of Óðin 44
Skalli, the wolf 81
Svíar, Swedes 61–3

Tyrfingr, the sword 2, 3, 5, 6, 15, 16, 18–20, 22, 24, 29, 44–6, 48, 49, 57, 68, 78
Tyrkjar, Turks 66, 67
Valir 46

4 NAMES GIVEN IN THE HU-VERSION TO PERSONS UNNAMED IN R

Barri Arngrímsson (3)
Brámi Arngrímsson (3)
Búi Arngrímsson (3)
Haki (*in U only*), king of the Saxons (26, 27)
Hálfdan, son of Harald of Reidgotaland (24, 25)
Herborg (*in U only*), wife of the king of Gardar (29, 30)

Hergerðr, daughter of the king of Gardar (30)
Herlaugr, son of the king of Gardar (28, 29)
Hrollaugr, king of Gardar (28–30)
Ólǫf (*in U only*), daughter of the king of the Saxons (26, 27)
Reifnir Arngrímsson (3)
Sæmingr Arngrímsson (3)
Tindr Arngrímsson (3)

POSTSCRIPT

THE BATTLE OF THE GOTHS AND THE HUNS

This earlier essay which pre-dated the writing of *The Saga of King Heidrek the Wise* appeared in *Saga-Book, Vol. XIV,* 1953–57, published by the Viking Society for Northern Research, University College London.

THE BATTLE OF THE GOTHS AND THE HUNS

By CHRISTOPHER TOLKIEN

THE conclusion of the *Hervarar Saga*[1] is contrived from a poem, or rather the ruins of a poem, now commonly called in English "The Battle of the Goths and the Huns", in which is told in moving though much-damaged verse, interspersed with prose-links, how *Hlǫðr*, the bastard son of King *Heiðrekr* of Reiðgotaland by a mistress named *Sifka*, whom he had taken from the people of the Huns, set in movement a monstrous war against his half-brother *Angantýr* for the recovery of his portion of the Gothic inheritance.

It is enough to mention that this poem is commonly referred to as one of the oldest, if not the very oldest, pieces of heroic poetry in the Norse language to suggest its very great intrinsic value and interest. Evidence that some parts at least of it are very ancient is to be seen in its metrical form, in certain uses of words (in which an earlier, "pre-Norse" layer of language has been discerned), and in the substance of the poem itself.

But I propose to restrict myself to that aspect of the poem which has in fact received the most attention and excited the most curiosity, namely: if elements of "The Battle of the Goths and the Huns" do indeed descend from so remote a past, do they derive from any actual event under the sun, recorded in any book that may still be read to-day? The question is indeed one of great interest, and many writers have sought an answer to it.

According to the prose of the saga, King Heiðrekr had been slain by certain slaves of his, who, being nobly born, fretted against their captivity; and Angantýr

[1] The standard edition is *Heiðreks Saga, udgivet for Samfund til Udgivelse af Gammel Nordisk Litteratur ved Jón Helgason, København 1924.*

his son vowed that he would never seat himself in the high seat of his father until he had avenged him. He came upon the slayers one evening as he walked down to the sea by the river called *Grafá*; they were fishing from a boat, and he watched one of them cut off the head of a fish with his father's sword, *Tyrfingr*. The man then uttered a verse of four lines, preserved in the saga, in which he said that the pike he had slain by Grafá's mouth had paid thus for the death of King Heiðrekr *und Harvaða-fjǫllum*, "beneath the Harvath-Mountains". This name is of the greatest importance; for there cannot, I think, be any doubt at all that they are the Carpathians, and that the Norse form *harvað-* represents the same name after the operation of the Germanic consonant-shift, whereby original **karpat-* was regularly transformed into **Xarfaþ-* in Germanic. This is certainly a clue, and provides a fixed point in the geography; but it narrows down the field only to a mountain-range of vast extent, which in any case occurs in a part of the saga dealing with events that occurred long before the action of "The Battle of the Goths and the Huns". It is, nonetheless, highly significant; for I do not doubt that this remarkable half-strophe is a fragment of a lost poem (concerned, perhaps, with the death of Heiðrekr), of which maybe all other specific traces had been lost even at the time of the composition of the saga. The name *Harvaða-fjǫll* is otherwise unknown in Germanic, and such a survival is hardly conceivable except in poetry.

When Hlǫðr, the bastard brother, learnt of the downfall of his father, and learnt too that Angantýr had been taken as king over all the dominion that their father had held, he resolved to go to Angantýr to claim his inheritance. Now Angantýr held his court, according to the prose, at a place called *Árheimar*, in the region of *Danparstaðir*.[2]

---

[2] This is the way the best text (the vellum 2845 (" R ") of the Royal Library in Copenhagen) puts it; the 17th-century paper manuscript (" U ") belonging to Uppsala University has it the other way round, with *Danparstaðir* a place in *Árheimar*.

Most writers have either abandoned *Árheimar* as so far unexplained, or else have regarded it as a purely fanciful invention; while the element *Danpar-* has been related to Jordanes' form *Danaper* for the river Dnieper, and to the elusive figure *Danpr* who appears in *Rígsþula*, in *Ynglinga Saga*, and in Arngrímur Jónsson's reproduction of the lost *Skjǫldunga Saga*.³

When Hlǫðr arrived in Arheimar, he said to his brother:

> I'll have the half-part
> of Heiðrek's riches,
> of cow and of calf
> and creaking handmill,
> tools and weapons,
> treasure undivided,
> thrall and handmaid
> and their children.

He demanded too " the renowned forest that is named *Myrkviðr*", " the holy grave that stands *á Gotþjóðu*", and " the fair stone that stands *á stǫðum Danpar*". To this Angantýr replied:

> The bright buckler
> shall break, kinsman,
> men unnumbered
> in the grass lying,
> ere I grant the half
> to thee, Humlung,
> or ever Tyrfing
> in twain sunder!

He then made Hlǫðr a handsome offer in recompense, but the taunts of the aged *Gizurr Grýtingaliði*, the fosterfather of King Heiðrekr, sent him home in a great rage; and in the spring a vast army was gathered by Hlǫðr and his grandfather *Humli* the Hun-king, so vast that afterwards the land of the Huns was utterly despoiled of all its fighting-men. This huge force moved through *Myrkviðr*, which, as we have seen, was included by Hlǫðr in his demands upon Angantýr, and which,

³ *Rígsþula* 49; *Ynglinga Saga* cap. 17; *Bibl. Arnam.* IX, 1950, p. 336.

according to the saga-prose, divided the land of the Huns from the land of the Goths;

> "and when they came out of the forest they were in a land of broad populous tracts and level plains."

In these plains there stood a frontier fortress defended by *Hervǫr*, Angantýr's sister, and her fosterfather *Ormarr*.

> "One morning at sunrise Hervǫr stood on a watch-tower above the fortress-gate, and saw a great cloud of dust rising southwards towards the forest, which for a long time hid the sun. Presently she saw a glittering beneath the dust-cloud, as though she were gazing on a mass of gold, bright shields overlaid with gold, gilded helms and white corslets; and then she saw that it was the army of the Huns, and a mighty host."

After the defeat and death of Hervǫr, Ormarr rode day and night back to Árheimar. He told the king of these things; and Angantýr, looking round at his small company, replied:

> Full many we were
> at the mead-drinking;
> when more are needed
> the number is smaller.

But the aged Gizurr Grýtingaliði leapt upon his horse as if he were a young man, and asked the king where he should challenge the Huns to battle; and Angantýr replied that he was to challenge them *at Dylgju, ok á Dúnheiði ok á þeim ǫllum Jassarfjǫllum*:

> There often Goths
> have given battle,
> renown gaining
> in noble victories!

When Gizurr actually utters the challenge to the Hunnish host afterwards, he says, not "*on* all the Jassar-fells" in the words of King Angantýr, but "*under*" them (*undir Jassarfjǫllum*).

The great battle was fought out on *Dúnheiðr*, according to the prose, and lasted for many days, and all the time men thronged in to join Angantýr. After colossal carnage, so that:

"the rivers were choked and rose from their beds, and the valleys were filled with dead men and horses"

Angantýr slew Hlǫðr with the sword Tyrfingr. Finding his half-brother's corpse, he spoke the verses with which the Hervarar Saga proper comes to an end:

> Treasures uncounted,
> kinsman, I offered thee,
> wealth and cattle
> well to content thee!
> But for war's rewarding
> thou hast won neither
> new boundaries
> nor bright armrings.
>
> A curse was on us, brother,
> thy bane have I wrought thee!
> 'Twill be never forgotten;
> the Norns' doom is evil.

The various attempts that have been made to identify the names of the battlefield will emerge when I come to review the attempts to identify the battle itself. But first there is one vital piece of evidence to be mentioned, which lies in certain lines of the Old English poem *Widsith* (ll. 119 ff.), reading:

(. . *sohte ic* . . .)
Heaþoric ond Sifecan   Hliþe ond Incgenþeow (line 116)

followed two lines later by:

Wulfhere sohte ic ond Wyrmhere: ful oft þær wig ne alæg,
þonne Hræda here   heardum sweordum
ymb Wistlawudu   wergan sceoldon
ealdne eþelstol   Ætlan leodum.

This may be rendered:

"Wulfhere I sought and Wyrmhere; seldom was warfare stilled, when the host of the Hrædas [i.e. Goths] in the Vistula forest had to defend with their hard swords their ancient dwelling-place from the people of Attila."

The fivefold coincidence that must here be supposed, if *Heaþoric, Sifeca, Hliþe, Incgenþeow* and *Wyrmhere* do not correspond to *Heiðrekr, Sifka, Hlǫðr, Angantýr* and *Ormarr*, has led some scholars to assume (despite the lack of precise phonetic agreement in all cases) a fivefold correspondence; but not all.

It is now time to turn to the consideration of what this event on *Dúnheiðr* may have been.

The first full-dress " identification " was produced by C. C. Rafn in 1850, in the introductory notice to the edition of the saga in *Antiquités Russes*.[4] Rafn thought that the Battle of the Goths and the Huns was a legendary transformation of the battle between the Gothic king Ostrogotha and the Gepid king Fastida at the place called *Galtis*, past which flowed the river *Aucha*, which Jordanes describes in the seventeenth chapter of his history, a finding which Rafn based on various rather dubious similarities, among them the fact that the dispute in either case was over the possession of land.

In 1887 appeared Richard Heinzel's massive study of the saga as a whole.[5] In this work he took up a suggestion made by P. E. Müller fifty years before, and identified the Battle of the Goths and the Huns with the great battle of the year 451, the *bellum atrox, multiplex, immane, pertinax* of Jordanes, fought out on the Mauriac or Catalaunian Plains and commonly called the Battle of Châlons-sur-Marne, in which Attila, together with the Ostrogoths, the Gepids under Ardaric, and all the other nations subject to the Huns, with their " ruck of kings " (*turba regum*), as Jordanes calls them, met the Visigoths and the Romans under Aetius the Patrician, together with the Alans under their king Sangiban, and their other allies.

Heinzel's theory, however, is extremely complex, and I have not space to go into all his equations and parallels, which compel admiration but not belief. Hlǫðr derives his name from the Frank *Chlodio*, who was defeated by Aetius in 428, while Angantýr derives in

[4] *Antiquités Russes*, Vol. I, Copenhagen 1850; pp. 115 ff.
[5] *Über die Hervararsaga*. In *Sitzungsberichte der Kaiserlichen Akademie der Wissenschaften CXIV Band*, Vienna 1887; pp. 417-519.

part from Aetius. At the same time, an element in Hlǫðr's make-up or legendary constitution is the figure of *Litorius*, the Roman general and rival of Aetius, who laid siege to the Visigothic capital of Toulouse with the aid of Hunnish auxiliaries in 439, but was defeated and put to death by the Visigoths. The element of brotherhood in the Hlǫðr-Angantýr complex is provided by two Frankish princes, disputing over the Frankish throne at the time of Attila's drive into the west, one of whom turned for help to Attila and the other to Aetius. The origin of Gizurr Grýtingaliði is found partly in the Vandal king Geiseric, who early in 450, it is said, was instigating Attila to attack the Visigoths, partly in Saint Anianus, Bishop of Orleans, who organised the defence of that city against the Huns, and who by spitting from the walls precipitated a three days' fall of rain, which held up the operations of the besiegers, and partly also in a certain prophetic anchorite, who informed Attila on the eve of the battle of 451 that this time he would come to grief.

To explain the place-names of the Norse poem, which no one has thought of seeking in Gaul, Heinzel was obliged to postulate a subsequent easterly movement of the tradition of 451 and accretions to it among the Varangians at a much later period. Taking *Dúnheiðr* to contain *Dúna*, the Norse name of the Danube, and connecting *Danparstaðir* with the Dnieper, he further found the " fair stone " of Hlǫðr's demands to Angantýr in the renowned cave-monastery at Kiev, dating from the eleventh century, while the " holy grave " mentioned in the preceding line of the poem is no doubt the grave of Saint Antonius, the founder of the monastery.

Two years later, in 1889, Rudolf Much developed a new theory,[6] in which he related the two battles of the *Hervarar Saga*, that in which the " Amazonian " Hervǫr was slain, and the great battle on *Dúnheiðr*, to two battles recorded by Paul the Deacon between the *Vulgares* (i.e. Bulgars) and the Langobards. In the first of these battles

[6] *Askibourgion Oros* in *Zeitschrift für deutsches Altertum* 33 (1889), pp. 1-13.

Agelmundus King of the Langobards was killed, and his daughter carried off a prisoner. The daughter relates to Angantýr's sister Hervǫr, while Agelmundus is the Agelmund who appears in *Widsith* immediately after the mention of Incgenþeow and Hliþe. In the second battle the Langobards under their new king Lamissio were victorious; and this is the Battle of the Goths and the Huns. Much was also prepared to allow influence of traditions from the battle of 451.

What is most significant in Much's discussion, however, is his placing of the events. He held that the *Jassarfjǫll* of the Norse poem is the mountain-chain in Silesia now called the *Gesenke* — that is (roughly speaking) the continuation of the line of the Carpathians to the west, beyond the chief pass out of the Danube region. Both *Gesenke* and the first element of the Norse name have, he thought, the same origin: they are recastings of the Slavic name *Jesenik, Jasenik*, itself a derivative of *jesen, jasen* " ash (tree)", and meaning " Ash-Mountain". This will then be equivalent to the *Askibourgion Oros* of Ptolemy the Geographer; and the name *Dúnheiðr* Much explained from the tribal name *Lougioi Didounioi*, a people referred to by Ptolemy as dwelling to the north of the *Askibourgion Oros*. Arguing that the Langobards must have been at this time dwelling north of the Carpathians, Much supposed that the Huns came upon them through the gap in the mountains east of the Gesenke, and that the battle of which Paul the Deacon tells must have taken place to the north of the range, that is, in the modern territory of Cracow.

During the next half-century many eminent scholars wrote at greater or lesser length on the problem. For some time Heinzel's "Catalaunian theory" held the field, and was regarded very much as a proved fact. Thus we find Andreas Heusler, Eugen Mogk and Finnur Jónsson accepting it without apparent question.[7]

---

[7] Jónsson in *Lit. Hist.* II, p. 839; Mogk in *Altnord. Literaturgesch.* in *Paul's Grundriss*, 2. Aufl., pp. 837-9; Heusler in *Eddica Minora* (1903), introduction to *Das Lied von der Hunnenschlacht*.

Later, in the writings of Gudmund Schütte and Gustav Neckel,[8] a lip-service, so to say, is paid to the "Catalaunian Dogma", while the real underlying basis of the tradition is sought in quite different times and places; Neckel raising again the negotiations and subsequent fighting between Ostrogotha and Fastida, and Schütte looking to events *after* the death of Attila, to the later wars of the Huns against the Gepids, Ostrogoths and other subject peoples, and seeing in the name Heiðrekr or Heaþoric transformations of the name of Ardaric, the famous Gepid king, once the confidant of Attila, who led and inspired the revolt of the subject tribes against Attila's sons. Schütte adopted Much's localisations, and so sought for the Battle of the Goths and the Huns where Much had sought for it, approximately in the region of the head-waters of the Oder and the Vistula; for both these writers Widsith's *ymb Wistlawudu* was of course of prime importance.

With the discussions of R. C. Boer and Henrik Schück[9] a clean break was made with both Heinzel and Attila. The credit for taking the plunge is usually given to Schück, who did indeed the same thing as Boer and equally resolutely, but seven years later. The "Catalaunian Theory" found its last exponent in Gudmund Schütte, who was still defending it in 1933.[10]

However, the debate continued vigorously between those who sought the underlying event at the western end of the Carpathians (that is, in modern Czechoslovakia and southern Poland), and those who looked rather to a region lying beyond their furthest eastern foothills; between those who looked to events after Attila's death, and those who looked to events before it.

Thus Schück provided the most positive localisations

---

[8] G. Schütte, *Anganty-Kvadets Geografi* in *Arkiv for nord. filologi* 21 (1905), pp. 30-44. G. Neckel, *Beiträge zur Eddaforschung*, Dortmund 1908, pp. 256 ff.

[9] R. C. Boer, *Om Hervararsaga* in *Aarbøger for nord. oldkyndighed og hist.*, 1911, pp. 1-80. H. Schück, *Studier i Hervararsagan, Uppsala Universitäts Årsskrift*, 1918.

[10] *Acta Phil. Scand.* 1933, pp. 254 ff.

of persons and places. Believing, with Boer, that the Gotho-Hunnic war and the battle between brothers were originally quite distinct legends, he found the historical prototype for the strife of the brothers in the fighting between the Amalung *Winitharius* and the Hun King *Balamber* allied to the Goth *Gesimund*, after the death of Ermanaric; but the origin of the Gotho-Hunnic war in the victory of the Ostrogoths under Walamir over the Huns after the death of Attila. For Schück, the place-names point clearly to southern Russia.

Boer on the other hand was extremely sceptical, and placed no trust in any of the place-name identifications at all except *Dúnheiðr*, which he associated with the Russian river Dvina, and so looked for the battlefield in the neighbourhood of the Valdai Hills, northwest of Moscow, where the Volga, Dnieper and Dvina rise from the central plateau in relatively close proximity.

Otto von Friesen in 1920 and Arwid Johannson in 1932[11] both looked to the western end of the Carpathians; von Friesen's Huns moving north from the middle Danube by much the same route as the Huns of Much and Schütte had taken, and falling upon the " Nest-Goths " — i.e., the *Hreiðgotar* — of the Vistula valley. These were Goths who had never migrated into the south-east, but had remained, according to von Friesen's etymology of the name, in the " Nest "; their kingdom, with its centre in East Prussia but at times extending up the Vistula valley to the western Carpathians, and once united with the great empire of Ermanaric, survived, according to von Friesen, the onset of the Huns in the fourth century; and in the years following the overthrow of the southern parts of that empire the more northerly " Nest-Gothic " realm had to defend itself against the concentration of Hunnish power in Hungary. To these battles the Norse poem, and Widsith, refer.

For Johannson, however, as for Schück, the mis-en-

[11] O. von Friesen, *Rökstenen*, Stockholm 1920. A. Johannson, *piaurikr miR Hraiþkutum* in *Acta Phil. Scand.* 1932, pp. 97-149.

scène is the period of the wars between the Pannonian
Ostrogoths and the Huns under the sons of Attila. His
Huns followed the same route as those of Much, Schütte,
and von Friesen, but in the reverse direction; they came
round on the northern flanks of the Carpathians, passed
down the March valley, crossed the Danube, and invaded
Pannonia. But where Schück had taken *Dúnheiðr*
fairly vaguely as " the Danube plain", " the lower course
of the Danube", Johannson identified it specifically with
the *Marchfeld*, east of Vienna, at the confluence of the
Danube and the March. Moreover, under the name
Dylgja the March is probably concealed. An obvious
difficulty here is that the words of *Widsith*, *ymb
Wistlawudu*, must refer to a more northerly region.

In 1934 Hermann Schneider[12] concluded in favour
of the fourth century and the Gothic kingdom on the
Black Sea; in 1941 Jan de Vries[13] asserted that the poem
deals with an episode after the death of Attila.

Ironically enough, a remark of Schneider's, to the
effect that we must not think that we know much about a
deeply obscure period from the meagre informations of a
Jordanes, provided the starting-point for a completely
new theory, the latest contribution (I believe) to the
subject, providing the most precise historical foundation,
not only for the poem, but for most of the *Hervarar
Saga* too, which is treated as virtually an entity of equal
antiquity throughout. In 1946 N. Lukman[14] set out
to examine the whole matter afresh, starting from the
assumption that the history of Jordanes had so far
figured much too largely in the investigation of the Battle
of the Goths and the Huns, to the exclusion of other
earlier and better sources of information, chief among
them the History of Ammianus Marcellinus.

I cannot possibly do justice here to Lukman's complex
theory; but I must attempt to convey an idea of it. The

[12] *Germanische Heldensage*, II. 2, pp. 96 ff.
[13] *Altnordische Literatur-Geschichte* I, pp. 36 ff.
[14] *Goterne i Heidreks Saga: En Tradition om Athanaric?* in *Aarbøger for nord. oldk. og hist.* 1946.

source of the Norse poem is now found primarily in the events of the year 386, when a vast swarm of Goths, of the race of the Greutungi, appeared on the Danube; their leader was an Ostrogoth named Odotheus, but it is not clear to what extent the swarm was made up of other peoples besides. Since we are explicitly told that among the barbarians were men either too old or too young to fight, this was clearly not a descent upon the Empire by an army bent upon plunder, but a tribal migration; what set it in motion is unkown. The migrants on the northern bank of the great river asked permission to cross; the permission was refused, and the Roman army of the Danube frontier, under Promotus, prepared to resist their crossing. Spies were sent by Promotus to Odotheus offering to sell the Roman army for a price; but by accepting their offer Odotheus fell into a trap. Crossing the Danube by night in their innumerable boats, thinking to fall on the Romans unawares, the Goths were crushed by the great Roman ships which bore down upon them. The Danube was choked, it is said, with the wreckage and the corpses.

Odotheus, according to Lukman, is Hlǫðr. Odotheus demanded, in effect, the same treatment from the Empire as had been accorded to the Visigoths under Alavivus and Fritigern earlier; Hlǫðr demanded an equal share in the Gothic inheritance. The activity of Gizurr in the saga corresponds (Lukman seems to imply) to that of the false spies sent out by Promotus, though later in the demonstration we learn that he is also Gesimund, leader of the Ostrogoths. Ormarr is a reflection of a certain chieftain *Arimerios*, who dwelt north of the Danube at this time but whose fate is unknown. Heiðrekr is Athanaric, ruler of the Visigoths; and Humli contains the name of the Amal kings, and should really therefore be a ruler of the Goths, not the Huns. The two Gothic lords *Alatheus* and *Safrax*, who crossed the Danube in Rome's despite in 377, two years after Ermanaric's death and a year before Adrianople, taking with them the young Amalung prince *Wideric*, also appear in Lukman's reconstruction: Alatheus is Hlǫðr once more, *Humlungr* of the poem (in Angantýr's address to his half-brother) refers to the child Wideric, and Safrax is Sifka of the saga, the mistress of King Heiðrekr and the mother of Hlǫðr. The evil end that overtook Sifka in the saga is due to confusion with the story of Saint Sabas the martyr, one of the victims of Athanaric's persecution of the Christians. Finally, the appearance of the Emperor Theodosius at the scene of the battle in the Danube, and his generous terms to the survivors, is echoed in Angantýr's words over his half-brother's body, when he repeated in regret his unavailing offer. I do not propose to follow Lukman further, into his identification of Haraldr of Reiðgotaland (who plays a part elsewhere in the *Hervarar Saga*) with Ermanaric, and so forth.

From this mass of speculation and discussion some of what has been said can I think be rejected out of hand with the greatest confidence. In the first place, I think that those scholars who have said that the " Catalaunian " hypothesis must be abandoned are unquestionably right; and moreover, it must be unconditionally abandoned; that is to say, once that hypothesis has been rejected from its position as the kernel of the whole tradition, there can be no sufficient grounds for retaining it at all. I would base this rejection primarily on this consideration, among others. Such similarity as there is between Heinzel's construction and the situation in the poem is most visible, or least invisible, when we consider the dispute of the two princes over the Frankish throne. Here certainly there are two brothers, one of whom turns for help in his claim to the Hun King. But in the first place, they were not Goths. And in the second place, their situation was in all other respects wholly different. Both princes were quite subordinate characters in the great event, their quarrel caught up into a vast struggle that extended far beyond the borders of their own kingdom. And if their names and nationalities were sucked in and absorbed by the far larger figures of Aetius and Attila, it is strange indeed that their quarrel, enormously enlarged, should survive, together with their relationship, and be made into the circumstance whereby the lords of East and West, now likewise become brothers, were brought into collision. This consideration brings us to the most formidable objection of all: we are asked to believe that Humli has replaced Attila. If the Norse tradition really descended from that battle on the Mauriac plain, it would be simply incredible that Attila, *the* Hun par excellence of Germanic legend, should have been dispossessed of his rightful position as leader of the Huns in a battle in which he was, in historical fact, present. Whatever battle or battles may underlie the final portion of the Hervarar Saga, we may be sure that the Huns were not then commanded by Attila. (The words of *Widsith, Ætlan leode*, do not I think necessarily mean more than " Huns ").

Heinzel was of course well aware of this difficulty, and attempted to guard against it. It was a poetic necessity, he said, that the Hun King conquered in so colossal a battle should not remain alive; but it was nevertheless generally known that Attila did not as a fact die on the Mauriac plain. " Man brauchte also einen anderen Hunnen-könig", he wrote, somewhat ingenuously. The weakness of this argument merely serves to underline the objection.

Moreover, I think that all theories based on an unevidenced assertion of " mixture of tradition " should be rejected. By this recipe some of the primary features of the Norse poem are simply explained away; but when seeking for an historical basis for an ancient poem which concerns a great war between Goths and Huns, one may reasonably be unimpressed by a solution that offers a battle between quite other peoples, and enquire at once whether there is any cogent evidence, any really pointed resemblance, to support it. Thus, Much tells us that the Langobards have been replaced in the course of time by the more famous Goths. If there were a name in common between the two accounts; or one single feature in common not of a vague and general nature; his proposal might stand some chance of acceptance. But there is none.

The same is true of Lukman's historical river-battle between Roman troops and a migratory swarm of Ostrogoths and their allies. Lukman indeed outdoes Heinzel in perverse ingenuity. I do not think that it should need to be said, that to pick about in old histories, looking for names that begin with the same letter or contain one or two of the same consonants as those in one's text, will attain nothing. If heroic legend really evolved in this way, with the most chance and casual accretions and distortions — so that Safrax the Ostrogothic lord was "fused" with Sabas the martyr, and then (keeping nothing save a violent death connected with a river and the initial consonant of the name) developed into a Hunnish concubine — then, with our fragmentary materials, the chances against our hitting upon the correct combinations are so monumental that we may as well give up the game at once; or, at least, admit that it is only a game. And since the game has virtually no rules, I cannot be breaking any if I propose the theory that Angantýr is a legendary transformation of Constantine the Great. Hlǫðr is then Licinius, the Eastern Emperor, and the Battle of the Goths and the Huns descends ultimately, no doubt, from the battle of Chrysopolis on the Bosphorus in 323, whereby Constantine made himself sole ruler of East and West, after twenty-five thousand men had been slaughtered. Here is the "South-Eastern colouring" plain to see; and what makes the theory particularly attractive is that Constantine and Licinius were *brothers*-in-law. Lukman quite failed to produce any brothers. Admittedly, Licinius was not killed; but we have been instructed by Heinzel in the handiness of " Poetic Necessity". Heiðrekr is of course Diocletian; it may even be possible to work in the Council of Nicea.

Fundamental to this discussion are the lines of Widsith. It must be admitted at once that when in an ancient Norse poem Angantýr, Hlǫðr and Ormarr are involved in a battle between Goths and Huns, it would be an astonishing coincidence that an Anglo-Saxon poem should mention Incgenþeow and Hliþe, followed after a very brief interval by Wyrmhere and a reference to battles between Goths and Huns, and have nothing to do with the former composition. But the fighting referred to in *Widsith* took place *ymb Wistlawudu*. We are therefore faced with a dilemma: either the Norse poem refers to fighting in the same region (in which case the localisations favoured by Much, Schütte, von Friesen and Johannson have some prospect of acceptance), or it does not; and if it does not, then either we must rule out any connexion with *Widsith* and reconcile ourselves to a coincidence of a very curious kind — or *Widsith* has, so to say, got the facts wrong.

In favour of the view that the Norse poem does *not* refer to fighting in the Vistula valley is the major consideration of the name *Danparstaðir*. It is clear that the Vistula-region theories can find no place for this name; yet of all the names in the poem it is one of the only ones that can be localised with something like certainty.[15] This name is also known from a verse of *Atlakviða*,(5), where Knefrǫðr, bearing the errand of Atli, tells Gunnarr that Atli will give him, among other things,

> stórar meiðmar   ok staði Danpar,
> hrís þat it mæra   er meðr Myrkvið kalla.

[15] The name *Harvaðafjǫll* is yet more certain, and *Dúnheiðr* seems likely to mean the plain of the Danube, yet the Carpathians and the Danube are of vast extent, and it is only the connexion of them with the Dnieper that gives any sort of limited localization.

The latter of these two lines is almost identical with one in the Battle of the Goths and the Huns. But whether or not this verse of *Atlakviða* has been consciously imitated from the other poem, as has been commonly supposed, I do not think that *staði Danpar* in *Atlakviða* sheds any light on the original significance of the name; while the genealogical cardhouses gravely erected by some scholars in an endeavour to make the verse in *Rigsþula* about *Danr* and *Danpr* square with what Snorri says on the subject in the *Ynglinga Saga* and with what Arngrímur Jónsson says in his abstract of the lost *Skjǫldunga Saga* only go to show the hopelessness of trying to construct definite "trees" from such manifestly contradictory material.

That *Danparstaðir* contains the Gothic name of the river Dnieper, which appears in Jordanes as *Danaper*, was suggested long ago, first I believe by P. A. Munch, and this I think is unquestionably right. I do not think that the elusive character *Danpr* need be taken into account in a search into the remote origins, for I believe he owed his name and his very existence simply and solely to the name *Danparstaðir*, which was itself known in all probability from the Battle of the Goths and the Huns. I am strongly inclined to think that the original significance of the phrase, *á stǫðum Danpar*, was "on the banks of the Dnieper", taking *stǫðum* to be the dative plural of O.N. *stǫð*, fem. "landing-place", corresponding to a Gothic dative plural *staþam*, a word whose existence is vouched for by the dative singular *staþa*, occurring twice in Wulfila and signifying "bank" or "shore", cognate with Old English *stæþ*.

As to the "holy grave" and "the fair stone that stands beside the Dnieper", I have already mentioned Heinzel's identifications of these things with the cave-monastery of Kiev and the tomb of its founder. Beyond the fact that Kiev is on the Dnieper I do not see any circumstance in favour of Heinzel's view. I think it is far more probable that by the "holy grave" is to be understood a burial-place where rested a Gothic king, or kings.

The "stone" beside the Dnieper seems likely to have been a high stone in the chief place of the Goths, upon which stepped the king to whom homage was to be done, that he might be seen by all the people. That such was an ancient custom is beyond question. Thus the Chronicle of the Kings of Lejre, descending probably from the latter half of the twelfth century, tells that the Jutes led Dan to the stone which was called *Danaerygh*, and set him upon it, giving him the title of king. Olrik has shewn reason to believe that the Danaerygh lay in Viborg in Jutland, and that there also was the mound in which Dan was buried, and in which he sat upright and saddled on a horse within the tomb. It is not incredible that the "stone" of Hlǫðr's demand was (so to say) the "Lia Fail of the Black Sea Goths", and that the "grave" was the burial place of their kings, in or near the same place. It would be fruitless to search for its name; but it is remarkable enough — if this opinion is correct — that the memory of such things, and the name of the river by which they lay, should have survived in the North for a thousand years.

On this view, *Dúnheiðr* must contain *Dúna*, the Danube; while *Dylgja*[16] seems not improbably to be explained simply as the noun *dylgja* "enmity", or, in the context "battle"; in which case Angantýr must say, not

Kendu at Dylgju   ok á Dúnheiði

but rather

Kendu dylgju   á Dúnheiði.

As to *Árheimar*, is it perhaps conceivable that it is an invention on the lines of *ár-dagar*, "days of old" (Old English *gear-dagas*), and meaning "the ancient abode", used of a Gothic king's court in South-Eastern Europe when the original name had been forgotten?

[16] Assuming that *Dylgja* is correct; another reading is *Dyngja*.

If then this fundamental decision is made, the questions remain: what are we to think of the evidence of *Widsith*? And further: can we pin the legend to any particular event?

We have no choice but to suppose that the author of *Widsith* had heard tell of a Gothic people dwelling in the Vistula valley, and indeed von Friesen has shewn that the assumption of such a people is tenable. There, *ymb Wistlawudu*, there was fighting against the Huns, so the author of the Old English poem had heard. If we wish to connect the two traditions, then we must (on the fundamental assumption I am here making) suppose that the English tradition has transferred the legendary echoes of ancient battles in Southern Russia to a region closer at hand; if we are prepared to abandon the connexion, then we can admit that the reference in *Widsith* is quite possibly to historical battles between Goths and Huns in the Vistula valley; but they have no connexion with the Hun-battle of the saga. In that case, we must suppose that the mention of Hliþe and Incgenþeow together with the fighting *ymb Wistlawudu* is pure coincidence; it is after all true that their names are not mentioned in direct connexion with the wars against the Huns. This is not to say that Hliþe and Incgenþeow do not correspond to Hlǫðr and Angantýr; but simply that the Hun-battles do not correspond. — But is this credible?

On the whole, I am driven to conclude that ultimately both the Norse and the English reflect the same events, and that the latter has undergone a change as regards the setting of them. One may perhaps feel a certain reluctance to accept a view of the matter which proposes that a very corrupt and imperfectly-transmitted Norse poem, preserved in a late saga, is " right", while an English poem of the antiquity of *Widsith* is " wrong". One might well argue, indeed, that the *Widsith*-tradition has misplaced the *theatre* of war, but preserved a truer picture of the events themselves; that the situation implied in the Anglo-Saxon words:

þær ful oft wig ne alæg

— with its suggestion of repeated battles in a defensive war, as the heroes withdrew in the forests — has more the stamp of truth than the earth-shaking battle and colossal carnage of the Norse tradition. This may well be so; but I do not think that it necessarily conflicts with what has been suggested above about the clues which point to a much more easterly, and older, theatre of war.

We are led, then, to the Gothic kingdoms on the Northern shores of the Black Sea, and to the years after the first appearances of the Huns and their Alan subjects moving west across the South Russian plains. I do not see any cogent reason for following those who have turned rather to the following century, and the events after the death of Attila.[17] Now it goes without saying that such records as are preserved from the former period have been combed and combed again with the object of finding a situation which fits with or without forcing the data of the ancient poem set into the *Hervarar Saga*; and that one has no hope of discovering some new parallel, hitherto passed over unnoticed, unless it be some parallel that is in reality no parallel at all.

I believe that some sort of an "historical basis" did exist, in that period and in that region, and that it is to be looked for in the area roughly defined by "Lower Dnieper — Dniester — Eastern Carpathians — Danube mouths". Conceivably, if the historians of the Empire

[17] One of the arguments used in this connexion seems especially misleading. Schütte, for instance, urged that the fact that the Huns, according to the Norse poem, could not raise more than a beggarly 50,000 men, and that with boys of twelve years old, suggests that the smaller Hunnic armies of the years after Attila's death are referred to, not the great host of 451. (On the numbers of the Hunnish armies see E. A. Thompson, *A History of Attila and the Huns*, Oxford 1947, pp. 46 ff.). But the author of the saga obviously took a very different view. For him, the detail about the twelve year old boys was a sign, not only that the Huns assembled their entire war-strength, but also that their army was of the most colossal size imaginable. The supposition that the writer was correct in his figures but wrong in his interpretation of them is utterly improbable.

had been able, or had wished, to cast their net wider, we might have found in their writings some reference to a battle between Goths and Huns which fitted the data we possess. Certainly no scholar who has turned his attention to that age and that region has succeeded in making an identification remotely plausible. But it is clear that vast obscure upheavals were taking place during those dark years among the nations dwelling to the north-east of the Danube mouths, about which we know next to nothing; for these disturbances meant little enough to the Empire, until thousands upon thousands of fleeing Germanic tribesmen were clamouring for admittance on its northern frontiers. And thus the supposition that, had we more voluminous records of that time, we might find a reference to a Gotho-Hunnic war brought about in the main in the way the Norse poem describes, is not demonstrably false.

Yet is it probable? Behind the ruinous poem as it exists in manuscripts of the *Hervarar Saga* today there lie centuries upon centuries of transmission, of alteration and refashioning. Would it not be contrary to all experience and precedent if we *could* turn up the right passage in Jordanes, Olympiodorus, or Ammianus Marcellinus, writing a millenium before, for a cross-check? This might indeed seem to be an argument in favour of those forced " historical bases " I have dismissed. But, in dismissing them, my point was primarily that it is not useful to pile up these elaborate identifications unless they are, indeed, *extremely* plausible. Otherwise we enter a region of speculation where from the nature of the case there can be no possible form of testing or proof; a world of unarguable assertions.

Thus it may well be that crumbling verse-memories of the first Hunnic attacks upon the Goths, with some remote names preserved in the amber of a traditional poetry, is all that is really there, so far as the " History of the Black Sea Goths " is concerned. Certainly, if

we suppose that the names *Tyrfingr* and *Grýtingaliði*
contain the ancient Gothic tribal nomenclature of
Tervingi and *Greutungi*, the Visigoths and the Ostrogoths;
and suppose too that Humli the Hun-king of the saga
contains the Amal name, and that Hlǫðr, who in the
saga is half-Hun, half-Goth and is referred to as *Humlungr*,
is also the reflection of an Amalung prince, then we
cannot possibly think that the "plot" of the Norse
poem is "historical". Rather we should have to conceive
of an inheritance-feud between a West Goth (Angantýr)
and an Ostrogoth. But then of course not all these
identifications are of equal value; though the equations
Tyrfingr/Tervingi and *Grýtingaliði/Greutungi* seem highly
likely, with the corollary that *Tyrfingr* was not originally
the name of a sword in this poem at all.

One thing at least is clear: the search for a definite,
historical underlying event should be called off. And
once the attempt to fix upon such an event has been
given up, the question whether the contending brothers
were there from the start, as historical persons, or whether
they represent an early intrusion of legend — though
certainly a very early intrusion — becomes unanswerable.
One may compare the case of the death of Ermanaric,
and the long debate as to whether Jordanes knew more
about the matter than Ammianus, or whether Jordanes'
account is a legendary amplification of a later time.

In this paper I have attempted in brief compass
firstly to give an impression of a discussion that has lasted
for the better part of a century, and is scattered in many
books and periodicals in many languages, and secondly
to see what has emerged from it. If the facts are few,
the possible speculations they give rise to are not; and it
is inevitable that in attempting to set out the essentials
clearly I should have done very much less than justice
to the detailed arguments with which particular theories
have been defended. Moreover, it has been necessary
to leave quite out of consideration various allied questions,

such as for example that of the relationship between Saxo's story of the war between Frotho and the Huns,[18] which is undoubtedly connected with the present poem; but it seems quite clear that Saxo's account will not in fact cast any light on the ancient origins.

---

[18] Ed. Holder pp. 154 ff.; trans. Elton pp. 190 ff.

ALSO AVAILABLE

J. R. R. TOLKIEN
EDITED BY CHRISTOPHER TOLKIEN

BEOWULF
A TRANSLATION AND COMMENTARY
together with SELLIC SPELL

The translation of *Beowulf* by J. R. R. Tolkien was an early work, very distinctive in its mode, completed in 1926: he returned to it later to make hasty corrections, but seems never to have considered its publication. This edition includes an illuminating commentary on the text of the poem by the translator himself, in the written form of a series of lectures given at Oxford in the 1930s, from which a substantial selection has been made.

From his creative attention to detail in these lectures there arises a sense of the immediacy and clarity of his vision. It is as if he entered into the imagined past: standing beside Beowulf and his men shaking out their mail shirts as they beached their ship on the coast of Denmark, listening to the rising anger of Beowulf at the taunting of Unferth, or looking up in amazement at Grendel's terrible hand set under the roof of Heorot.

But the commentary in this book includes also much from those lectures in which, while always anchored in the text, he expressed his wider perceptions. He looks closely at the dragon that would slay Beowulf 'snuffling in baffled rage and injured greed when he discovers the theft of the cup'; but he rebuts the notion that this is 'a mere treasure story', 'just another dragon tale'. He turns to the lines that tell of the burying of the golden things long ago, and observes that it is 'the feeling for the treasure itself, this sad history' that raises it to another level. 'The whole thing is sombre, tragic, sinister, curiously real. The "treasure" is not just some lucky wealth that will enable the finder to have a good time, or marry the princess. It is laden with history, leading back into the dark heathen ages beyond the memory of song, but not beyond the reach of imagination.'

Sellic Spell, a 'marvellous tale', is a story written by Tolkien suggesting what might have been the form and style of an Old English folk tale of Beowulf, in which there was no association with the 'historical legends' of the Northern Kingdoms.

ALSO AVAILABLE

J. R. R. TOLKIEN
EDITED BY CHRISTOPHER TOLKIEN

THE LEGEND OF SIGURD AND GUDRÚN

Many years ago, J. R. R. Tolkien composed his own version, now published for the first time, of the great legend of Northern antiquity, in two closely related poems to which he gave the titles *The New Lay of the Völsungs* and *The New Lay of Gudrún*.

In the *Lay of the Völsungs* is told the ancestry of the great hero Sigurd, the slayer of Fáfnir most celebrated of dragons, whose treasure he took for his own; of his awakening of the Valkyrie Brynhild who slept surrounded by a wall of fire, and of their betrothal; and of his coming to the court of the great princes who were named the Niflungs (or Nibelungs), with whom he entered into blood-brotherhood. In that court there sprang great love but also great hate, brought about by the power of the enchantress, mother of the Niflungs, skilled in the arts of magic, of shape-changing and potions of forgetfulness.

In scenes of dramatic intensity, of confusion of identity, thwarted passion, jealousy and bitter strife, the tragedy of Sigurd and Brynhild, of Gunnar the Niflung and Gudrún his sister, mounts to its end in the murder of Sigurd at the hands of his blood-brothers, the suicide of Brynhild, and the despair of Gudrún. In the *Lay of Gudrún* her fate after the death of Sigurd is told, her marriage against her will to the mighty Atli, ruler of the Huns (the Attila of history), his murder of her brothers the Niflung lords, and her hideous revenge.

Deriving his version primarily from his close study of the ancient poetry of Norway and Iceland known as the Poetic Edda (and where no old poetry exists, from the later prose work the *Volsünga Saga*), J. R. R. Tolkien employed a verse-form of short stanzas whose lines embody in English the exacting alliterative rhythms and the concentrated energy of the poems of the Edda.

ALSO AVAILABLE

J. R. R. TOLKIEN
EDITED BY CHRISTOPHER TOLKIEN

THE FALL OF ARTHUR

The Fall of Arthur, the only venture by J. R. R. Tolkien into the legends of Arthur King of Britain, may well have been regarded as his finest and most skilful achievement in the use of the Old English alliterative metre, in which he brought to his transforming perceptions of the old narratives a pervasive sense of the grave and fateful nature of all that is told: of Arthur's expedition overseas into distant heathen lands, of Guinevere's flight from Camelot, of the great sea-battle on Arthur's return to Britain, in the portrait of the traitor Mordred, in the tormented doubts of Lancelot in his French castle.

Unhappily, *The Fall of Arthur* was one of several long narrative poems that he abandoned in that period. In this case he evidently began it in the earlier nineteen-thirties, and it was sufficiently advanced for him to send it to a very perceptive friend who read it with great enthusiasm at the end of 1934 and urgently pressed him 'You simply must finish it!' But in vain: he abandoned it, at some date unknown, though there is some evidence that it may have been in 1937, the year of the publication of *The Hobbit* and the first stirrings of *The Lord of the Rings*. Years later, in a letter of 1955, he said that 'he hoped to finish a long poem on *The Fall of Arthur*'; but that day never came.

Associated with the text of the poem, however, are many manuscript pages: a great quantity of drafting and experimentation in verse, in which the strange evolution of the poem's structure is revealed, together with narrative synopses and very significant if tantalizing notes. In these latter can be discerned clear if mysterious associations of the Arthurian conclusion with *The Silmarillion*, and the bitter ending of the love of Lancelot and Guinevere, which was never written.

ALSO AVAILABLE

J. R. R. TOLKIEN
EDITED BY CHRISTOPHER TOLKIEN

SIR GAWAIN AND THE GREEN KNIGHT
with PEARL and SIR ORFEO

Throughout his life Professor J. R. R. Tolkien held alliterative poetry in particular affection, and over many years he endeavoured to perfect translations for the modern reader of those middle-English poems of which he was most fond. Left unpublished after Tolkien's death in 1973, these translations have been collected and compiled by his son and literary executor, Christopher Tolkien.

Sir Gawain and the Green Knight tells the story of Christmas at Camelot. King Arthur won't begin to feast until he has witnessed a marvel of chivalry when a mysterious knight, green from head to toe, rides in and brings the court's wait to an end. He offers an implausible challenge to the Round Table: he will allow any of the knights to strike him once, with a battle-axe no less, on the condition that he is allowed to return the blow a year hence. Arthur's brave favourite for the challenge is Sir Gawain.

Accompanying *Sir Gawain and the Green Knight* in this book are *Sir Orfeo*, a medieval version of the story of Orpheus and Eurydice, and *Pearl*, the moving tale of a man in a graveyard mourning his baby daughter, lost like a pearl that slipped through his fingers. Worn out by grief, he falls asleep and dreams of meeting her in a bejewelled fantasy world.

Originally published without commentary, J. R. R. Tolkien's vivid translations of these classic poems are enriched in this edition with the complete text of his acclaimed 1953 lecture on *Sir Gawain* and a glossary provided by Christopher Tolkien, as well as introductions derived from J. R. R. Tolkien's own notes.

ALSO AVAILABLE

J. R. R. TOLKIEN
EDITED BY ALAN BLISS

FINN AND HENGEST
THE FRAGMENT AND THE EPISODE

Professor J. R. R. Tolkien was a distinguished scholar in the field of Mediaeval English language and literature. In his academic work he displayed the unique combination of philological erudition and poetic imagination which characterizes his creative work; unfortunately much of the best of it was embodied in courses and lectures which he delivered in Oxford but never published. His most significant contribution to Anglo-Saxon studies is to be found in his lectures on Finn and Hengest (pronounced Hen-jist), two fifth-century heroes in northern Europe.

The story is told in two Old English poems, *Beowulf* and *The Fights at Finnesburg*, but told so obscurely and allusively that its interpretation had been a matter of controversy for over 100 years. As elucidated by Tolkien, the story is a classic tragedy of divided loyalties, of vengeance, blood and death; it has the added interest that the Hengest who plays the leading role in it was very probably the Hengest who led the first Germanic invasion of Britain, and that the events it describes immediately preceded that first invasion.

Tolkien's original and persuasive solution of the many problems raised by the story ranged widely through the early history and legend of the Germanic peoples. This book will be of interest not only to students of Old English and all those interested in the history of northern Europe and Anglo-Saxon England, but also admirers of *The Lord of the Rings* who will be fascinated to see how Tolkien handled a story which he did not invent.

It was Professor Tolkien's own wish that the preparation for publication of this work on Finn and Hengest should be undertaken by Alan Bliss, who studied under him from 1946 to 1948. From three separate sets of lecture-notes, ranging in date from before 1930 to after 1960, Professor Bliss has pieced together a coherent statement of Tolkien's views expressed entirely in his own words.

ALSO AVAILABLE

J. R. R. TOLKIEN
EDITED BY PETER GRYBAUSKAS

THE BATTLE OF MALDON
together with
THE HOMECOMING OF BEORHTNOTH

In 991 A.D., Vikings attacked an Anglo-Saxon defence force led by their duke, Beorhtnoth, resulting in brutal fighting along the banks of the river Blackwater, near Maldon in Essex. The attack is widely considered one of the defining conflicts of tenth-century England, and is immortalised in the poem, *The Battle of Maldon*.

Written shortly after the battle, the poem now survives only as a 325-line fragment, but its value to today is incalculable, not just as an heroic tale but in vividly expressing the lost language of our ancestors and celebrating ideals of loyalty and friendship.

J. R. R. Tolkien considered *The Battle of Maldon* 'the last surviving fragment of ancient English heroic minstrelsy'. It would inspire him to compose, during the 1930s, his own dramatic verse-dialogue, *The Homecoming of Beorhtnoth Beorhthelm's Son*, which imagines the aftermath of the great battle when two of Beorhtnoth's retainers come to retrieve their duke's body.

Leading Tolkien scholar, Peter Grybauskas, presents for the very first time J. R. R. Tolkien's own prose translation of *The Battle of Maldon* together with the definitive treatment of *The Homecoming of Beorhtnoth* and its accompanying essays; also included and never before published is Tolkien's bravura lecture, 'The Tradition of Versification in Old English', a wide-ranging essay on the nature of poetic tradition. Illuminated with insightful notes and commentary, he has produced a definitive critical edition of these works, and argues compellingly that, *Beowulf* excepted, *The Battle of Maldon* may well have been 'the Old English poem that most influenced Tolkien's fiction', most dramatically within the pages of *The Lord of the Rings*.